Lithia Park
A NOVEL

Ra Lynn Lonewalker

Prologue

*I*f you listen carefully, you can hear Lithia Park murmuring in an ancient voice that seems to hold all secrets. Often the voice comes as a cold vibration pulsating through the air, bringing a stronger chill with every word.

The delicate veil between realities in Lithia Park gently releases the observer from the cares of life and the boredom of a complicated, overly critical, self-centered, noisy society. In Lithia Park we pause, and our rushing about, our sorrows and anxieties fade into a long-awaited hush.

If you are lucky, you might see trailing lights and shadows normally invisible to the naked eye. The energy is strong here. It bends and distorts the illusion we call reality and opens doorways from the aether, allowing spirits to walk between this world and the next. Glittering, mysterious, and crafty, it is watchful of who enters the park.

The park tells its old stories in flashes of lights, shimmering white luminous forms, and ghostly figures that walk the park's paths and trails, then dissolve into thin air.

Can all this be true?

Some say that when all is quiet and most of us are sleeping, footprints of souls long departed line the paths lacing the park together. Others speak of spirits sliding between trees or hiding behind bushes and shrubs, waiting for a particular person to happen by. You may see the park as empty. You probably won't see the shadows tracking your footsteps, but if you listen carefully enough, you might hear someone call your name from the emptiness.

Do spirits have any significance, or are they just glimpses, random encounters that can't be rationally explained in everyday language?

Beyond the ghosts, beyond the park's casual appearance, lie the deeper mysteries. We must be patient and remain observant to spot the symbols hidden here and there. Those who are patient and attentive may notice the secret codes woven into the park—symbols and codes revealing that the park is dynamic, forever shifting with spiritual energy.

How to see the spirits that inhabit Lithia Park? How to see the hidden symbols and codes, the secrets of Lithia Park? How to hear the murmuring voices?

First, we must set foot in the park, make contact with the ground itself. We are invited to come in, to touch the trees, feel the grass, smell the flowers, and see the flowing water. In Lithia Park, we are permitted to find union with something greater, to feel the pulse in the ground beneath our feet. Standing in this park, we are closer to the soul of our planet. We are in a place that allows us to reach into other dimensions, a place where we can interact with the spirits.

Here we find the essence of Mother Earth, which places us in the universe and gives us the ability to tune in to the three octaves of awareness—the solar spiritual octave, the lunar dream octave, and the earthly physical octave. (Some people call these realms, but the word "octave" reminds us that the so-called realms are contiguous.) Thanks to the earth's own magic we can move from the earthly to the lunar and further up into the spirit octave or realm. And if we accept Mother Earth's powers, we can access our planet's true magic in places like Lithia Park.

Sacred space.

What is sacred space but that space honored by our consciousness? Yes, all space is sacred, yet when a particular space is defined as a *temenos*, it is a precinct of spiritual significance. Remarkable things happen here. Our consciousness and energy become more highly defined and connected to the whole. In sacred space, we find a focal point where the human being communicates with higher spirits. This is where we can mingle with those who have gone before us.

Sacred space has seven cardinal points that we must acknowledge before we can commune. These are Above, Below, East, South, West, North, and Within, the seventh point that lies within the individual. It is true that within every one of us there is a spiritual gateway that connects our awareness first to the planet and the land and then, ultimately, to the universe. This awareness is, alas, lost to most of us today. We don't know how to find our abilities that are connected to our spirit. We're too busy being human and doing what human beings do to make a living. We don't have time to notice our own energy.

But walk away from the rush of the corporeal, mundane world. Come to Lithia Park and find yourself here, where the spirits might touch you, where they might see you for who you really are. Hush! Close your eyes. Let the moment be. Dance with the shadows in this place where fear will find you, where your secret dreams are the music that guides you. As you dance encircled by the beauties of the haunting spirits, you may sense that you've changed. Whatever you dread, whatever you conceal, whatever you bring to the park that exists deep inside your mind, the park will commune with that "whatever." And from this experience you will realize that something exceptional is happening.

Whatever you adore, whatever you offer, whatever you believe you need to live will twist, warp, and change here in Lithia Park. Say goodbye to your pride, let your strength dissolve, and allow yourself to be vulnerable here. In the moment of apprehension as the shadows have gathered around you, know that the spirits see you. Know that it's your innocent *self* they want.

Here in this park that spins out of time, where the image of the divine is a tree, you very well might stumble onto real magic and meet the vast supernatural. Hidden here in the park, away from the bustle and noise of the modern city where the faces never seem to smile and where the masses isolate themselves behind doors, away from those crowded cities of confusing crossroads that always lead back to the drudgery of work... here is a place where magic is at work. Here is where spirits are alive and dancing.

Lithia Park

Chapter 1

*W*inter had come to Ashland, Oregon. The leaves had fallen from the trees, and the blue skies had turned gray. Ruby Birk chased Yukon, her dog, down the street. He slipped through a break in an old chain-link fence obscured by a weak-stemmed vine, one of those common vines found in southern Oregon that grow thick on fences.

Yukon was acting odd. He was usually mindful of Ruby and listened to her. He always followed her, never tried to lead. And he hardly ever ran off in pursuit of anything. But today he had suddenly taken off after nothing and ran like a bolt of lightning as if chasing something, though clearly there was nothing running in front of him. Ruby hadn't known the break in the fence existed, so she was surprised when Yukon disappeared.

Ruby was by no means fit to be running after her dog. Besides the fact that she wasn't at all athletic, her clothes were cumbersome, and her heavy black boots felt like dead weight that kept her rhythm to more of a fast walk than a run. As she ran, she felt an uncanny feeling somewhere between humiliation and uncertainty.

Was anyone watching?

She spotted the break in the fence and forced herself through it. Just behind the overgrown fence a hidden and obviously forgotten stone staircase descended to the Butler-Perozzi Fountain. Ruby had been to the park many times, but she had never before entered the park through the fence at the top of the staircase.

Something inside her stirred when she first discovered the fountain. It was fresh and strange for her. She would never have guessed that, once upon a time, the fountain was the jewel of the park, the crumbling stone steps she descended, the main entrance.

She came to the peaceful park nearly every day, and almost always with Yukon in tow, as he enjoyed it as much as she. The park was near her home, giving her an easy escape from the world she felt unrelated to. She considered her instability in the "real world" as a direct cause for her dissatisfaction with the state of her current life. She couldn't trust her world, and so lived life through a pattern of isolation.

Yet, despite her loneliness, she trusted her solitude.

Today, however, thanks to Yukon running off into the cold winter mist, Lithia Park was an unscheduled stop. *At least it's empty!* Ruby told herself. She wanted to be alone here. Whatever Yukon was up to, she didn't mind because being alone gave her an opportunity to be free, to be here with nature. *Maybe that's what her dog was doing, too,* she thought. Enjoying the freedom to run without his leash. People often got annoyed seeing a dog running wild. Ruby was conscious of this and usually kept him on his leash. But today? Today was an exception.

The peace the park gave her seemed to open her mind to her celestial-self, the unseen but necessary element of her being that enjoyed the solitude. Her quiet side awakened here.

A breeze welcomed her. It was vibrant with the tingling purity of the winter's cold and laden with the wholesome, welcoming scent of pine, plus hints of frankincense, mastic, and other spices. But these scents made her feel... well... peculiar.

The absence of people meant all she could hear was the wind blowing dry leaves across the snow-covered ground. It had been an unusually cold season this year after four warm, dry winters. The Mount Ashland ski resort near the city hadn't even opened for ski season last year because of the west coast drought. This year, however, the snow was falling in late October, kept falling through November, and continued to fall now in early December, along with the temperature.

Shivering in her inadequate overcoat, Ruby looked around the park. One bright ray of sunshine had broken through the cloud cover, making the park look like an enchanted kingdom.

Ruby continued following Yukon, who was still running free in the park. Only Yukon really cared about her. If not for him, she would feel even more lost. He kept her grounded.

Lately, she had nothing to look forward to. Mounting debts, fear, and depression filled her life. There was never enough money. The weight of what she owed almost made her knees buckle, while demands for payment grew and grew.

Her old overcoat, which she had bought at a second-hand store for eight bucks, hung loosely on her shoulders. Under one arm she held her old, cracked, leather portfolio stuffed with her work—sketches, paintings, random drawings, and notes for art she might create in the future. Being an artist hadn't paid as well as she had naively expected. She maintained hope that her art would earn her a living, but her dreams of becoming a famous artist had vanished long ago.

Dreams.

Youthful dreams had faded as she grew older. She was now thirty-eight years old, middle-aged in her own mind, and the way time was moving it wouldn't be too long before she waned into old age. The thought of getting old scared her. She was certain that her dreams of painting in Florence, Paris, or Prague, or visiting the Mediterranean lands and walking hand-in-hand with a lover, had passed her by long ago.

She said the word *artist* aloud, and the sound of it brought the impression of isolated brilliance, a person with a hallowed aura, someone whose angelic hands massaged life into a masterpiece. When other people said *The Artist*, though, they usually meant an entertainer, an actor, a television celebrity, the lead singer in a band. That wasn't *her* kind of *artist*. The public declared that these modern-day so-called artists were the *true artists*, celebrities that lived on high, seated next to the angels that offered them mysterious gifts to distinguish them from ordinary humans. Ruby often wondered if her kind of *artist* was dead, and if so, for how long. A hundred years? More? She looked around the silent, empty park. *Is this*, she asked herself, *where my dreams come to die?*

Suddenly Yukon caught her attention. He was running around in the snow, sniffing and hiking his leg every once in a while to leave his mark. He was a mix of Malamute and gray wolf, with a fawn coat and a dark mask that held two different-colored eyes, one blue and one brown. His manner was playful and gentle, if a tad rambunctious. Ruby often joked that his different-colored eyes helped him understand the world better than any human could because, she claimed, the blue eye saw the spiritual world while the brown eye saw the physical one.

While her mind fumbled through her almost constant thoughts of art, debt, and her rotten life, she also realized that she was hungry and suffering, though not from the coldness of the winter, nor from the destitution she felt to her core almost every day. She hungered for mental sustenance, for something that would pull her out of the storms of her harsh psychological winter. She often imagined herself motionless, frozen, empty of both joy and inspiration. In such moods, she predicted that spring would never come. She feared that she would be stuck in a winter both literal and psychological for the rest of her life.

Even though she always told people she was an artist, she had yet to convince herself. Her greatest fear was that a critic (which, to an artist, is everyone) would call her a fake. It didn't take much for her to believe she was only going through the motions of being an artist. *After all*, she'd tell herself, *real artists know what they're doing. They're entitled to feel good about themselves and their work.* But not her. If only she were certain she was an artist, then she wouldn't hold her work in such low esteem. If only she were creative enough to paint something no one had seen before... If only she could paint something people would want to buy... If only her art could make a living for her... If only....

She gave Yukon the one long whistle that let him know that he was free to run around, then headed toward a second flight of fractured and weathered stone steps These steps stood directly in front of the fountain and led down to the park grounds. To her left, she noticed, someone had cleared away the snow to reveal a brass plaque. She paused to read it before going on. The plaque gave a brief history of the fountain and the park, which had been established in 1892, four hundred years after Christopher Columbus had arrived in the New World. The land had originally been designated as a city park; however, it only became noteworthy after John McLaren, who also designed the Golden Gate Park in San Francisco, designed Lithia Park in 1914. The fountain, sculpted by A. Frilli of Florence, Italy, had been added in 1916.

Reading the fountain's history struck a chord in Ruby. It made her curious about this fountain. She walked closer to examine and appreciate the skill that had gone into creating it. The wind dropped, and the great silence of the park surrounded her. The fountain, a true piece of art, stood as a testament to the men who had created it and the park in which it sat, men who were now long dead. But it did not reveal the secrets of their lives... their fears, debts, good fortune, courage, or weaknesses. It was, she thought, a statement set in marble, declaring that its designers' souls had existed not only for the park, or for Ashland, but for the whole world.

That's why artists create their work, isn't it, she thought. *To show the world.*

She walked around the fountain and gasped at the sight of recent vandalism on its west side. *Who would be so disrespectful?* Someone had bashed the decorative marble base with something heavy, like a sledgehammer, and broken off big chunks of it. And then there was the tag, a spray-painted urban glyph perhaps marking some wannabe crew's territory. Whatever the tag meant, it certainly didn't belong on this beautiful piece of art. *Disgraceful!*

Frowning, she continued walking around the fountain as a damp mist rose and swirled around her. A few dried leaves danced within the swirling air while she stood quiet and unafraid. As she watched the leaves, she saw the air outline a figure that developed into a flickering image of a man. The sight of the fuzzy figure made her eyes go wide. A strangled shriek tore through the air, startling her further until she recognized the scream as her own. The image vanished along with her cry, leaving her bewildered and staring at the area where the leaves still swirled.

She shook herself, feeling completely ridiculous. *Surely I imagined the whole thing.* Yukon had returned and sat grinning and panting apparently unconcerned by the commotion. Shaking her head, Ruby turned and went down the stairs and into the park.

A gust of wind blew at her, and within it she heard a voice.

Ruby? Ruby Birk!

The voice was simultaneously ghostly and soothing. Her heart slowed, and her whole body relaxed. She turned and looked back up the steps for the source of the call. The fountain suddenly looked different. There was something about it she couldn't quite identify. And that voice she'd heard... familiar, but so strange. In it she heard more than someone just calling her name. She heard—or felt—a connection. Yes, she had *felt* it. A connection to a place, to someone, to—

She had an impulse.

Feeling compelled to sketch the fountain, she turned and looked for the best place to sit and rough out a draft. An idea crept into her mind, slowly at first, but then it gained momentum. She walked down the hill a bit so she could see the fountain from a wider perspective. Sitting on a park bench, she opened her portfolio and pulled out a blank sheet of sketch paper and a charcoal pencil. She was ready to make her first stroke, but she felt a little light-headed, unable to orient herself to the reality around her. Her mind tripped over the ghostly image by the fountain and the voice she'd heard. She closed her eyes and shook her head, then straightened, opened her eyes again, and looked at the charcoal pencil in her hand. Her new idea was different from the kind of art she had been doing for many years. Her usual style was dark. She enjoyed drawing and painting graveyards, headstones, and mausoleums. But now she wanted to draw the park as it had looked in the beginning. A historical perspective piece. The beauty of the park and its fountain had inspired her to recreate John McLaren's park as it had been in his day.

Was life easier in 1914?

Ruby considered John McLaren. He must have had a robust constitution. She was certain he was different from her. Whereas she always doubted her ability to draw and paint, he must have been strong and confident. He had sculpted the land here into a beautiful piece of art, knowing it would satisfy the minds and souls of all who visited.

He must have been proud of his work. Prouder than me.

Ruby had little to show for the work she had done. Every day, she wondered if she was doing something anyone would ever care about. Every day, she lived under the spell of that powerful word, *DOUBT*. Being an artist of no reputation meant that every day she battled doubt just to get a drawing on paper or a painting on canvas. She had created many works of art, and she even believed that she had talent, but when it came to selling her work, she rarely succeeded.

In this day and age, it was money that seemed to be the measure of success. Pay was the validation of a person's craft.

Oh, how she wished she had faith, validation, and legitimacy—and the confidence of a successful artist.

She looked again at the fountain. *Did Mr. A. Frilli ever feel the doubt I feel?*

Life seems to get harder every day. I just don't belong to this world. Even though Edgar Allen Poe was a writer and she a painter, she often felt they shared the same path in life. She knew from studying his life and work in college that he too had struggled as a writer in his time. Although he was published, he was, like her, not well known and made very little money from his work. He had his own battles with depression. What she feared most was that her journey through life would be cut short as his had been. Edgar was said to have taken his own life at the age of forty because of his failures.

That's only three years older than I am. Will I live that long?

Often isolated, cold, empty, and fearing she was going mad, Ruby thought about her suicide. Yes, she called it her suicide. She had ownership of it. Sometimes she wanted to die, but she never had the courage to go through with it. But living... living was like sinking into black water, drowning forever. She had decided that if she became so broke that she had to live on the streets, that would be the time to end her life. If it came to that, would anyone even remember her?

Anyone who knew her would have said Ruby wasn't normal. She neither looked nor thought like other women her age. What made her so different? Ruby believed it was her soul. Her soul demanded she create art. Her soul that wouldn't allow her to be or become *normal*. Her soul had called her, had possessed her and persuaded her to take up the brush and paint on canvases she'd stretched with her own hands over the frames she'd made with scrap wood, using an old hammer and nails. Her soul demanded that she drag a charcoal pencil over paper, paper that she herself made from wood pulp that she got for free from a sawmill up the road.

Her soul, if it was aware of anything, knew she was an artist. Not merely "an artist," but an old-fashioned artist, the kind that makes her own supplies. Yes, her soul knew. Her mind, on the other hand, knew nothing of the kind. It argued with her soul. Her mind did all the doubting. Oftentimes, it was a struggle for her to understand which one—her soul or her mind—was in control. She understood that her mind had repeatedly out-reasoned her soul, had chained it up with links of logic, had imprisoned it in a prison of popular teachings. Indeed, it was her mind that took control when she created art. And it was her mind that forced her to calculate, gauge, and scrutinize every step of the process, almost to the point of overwhelming her soul altogether.

She gazed down at her hand, still holding the charcoal pencil, then gave a short whistle for Yukon to come closer so she could keep an eye on him. She could see him in the distance, jumping around, full of fun, as if someone were playing with him. There wasn't, as far as she could tell, but the dog was jumping higher and wagging his tail far more than he did when he was playing by himself. She whistled again, and he came and sat down next to her.

"Who are you playing with?" she asked him. After what happened earlier, she wasn't sure who or what might be in the park. "Are you seeing things, too? You're a goofy dog, and I'm goofy in the head!" He continued to wag his tail, and she could swear he was smiling.

With an effort, she pushed her logical thought process aside and laid her first stroke down, then swept the heel of her hand across the line to smudge it. She looked around. The park was still vacant, thanks to the freezing cold. Her logical mind took advantage of this by cursing at her for sitting outside on such a day, yet her soul felt a tingle, a spark. She blinked and tried to focus on drawing.

And that voice....

Stroke by stroke, she began to sketch the park as she imagined it had been a century ago when John

McLaren was creating it. She roughed out what she saw in her mind—a warm summer day, the great sycamore trees glowing green with warmth while they provided cool shade for anyone standing beneath them.

She drew almost mechanically at first. This was how she usually started a new project: disciplined, focused on technique rather than inspiration. But today... today something was... *different.* She was looking at a past era, so her imagination seemed to be more active than usual. She began feeling as if her hands were moving without her guidance. Her soulful mind had taken over, casting off technique and just creating without thinking about it. She relaxed into the flow of drawing. Then her hand did it. Her hand drew the thing she was always reluctant to draw. It wasn't much of a thing, just a bare outline, and yet there it was, plain and simple.

She'd drawn a person.

The figure stood at the top of the hill where, in time, the fountain would stand.

Years ago, in art school, she had tried to paint a portrait. She had been proud of her first real attempt at portraiture, had thought she was seeing her raw ability in it. Her instructor had been deeply critical, however, to the point that his so-called constructive criticism became twisted, hurtful words, leaving her with no confidence in her ability to draw or paint people.

"Your shadows are not nearly warm enough," he'd shouted. "What kind of idiot would make them so pale and gray! Your subjects' flesh tones are harsh and false. It would appear, Miss Birk, that you have no talent for portraits. Hold up your canvas for the class to see." He called out, "Attention, class! Please take the time to come and look at this portrait. This is exactly what you should *not* do. You should try to match the basis of color as you have it against your model's face and neck. Do you see what I mean? This is too weak, too off-putting." He stood taller, puffed out his chest and raised his voice. "Class, you must understand once and for all that weakness, either in conception or execution, is an unpardonable sin in oil."

From that day on, Ruby had resigned herself to never drawing the human form.

That had happened a dozen years ago, at least, and she was still angry with herself for never getting over the pain and embarrassment of that instructor's rant.

Now, as she looked down again at what her hand had drawn, she took a deep breath and held it. The figure was more a shadow than a detailed portrait, yet it seemed to her that the spell her art instructor had cast on her imagination had somehow just been shattered. She gave the drawing a nod and a satisfied smile, then tucked the paper into her portfolio, pocketed her charcoal pencil, and rubbed her hands together. Even though it was just past noon, she was freezing, and the cold was forcing her to get moving again. Feeling a little odd, she whistled for Yukon, who had wandered off again.

As she tried to comb her hair with her fingers, a gust of wind brought her that mysterious, spicy fragrance again, that wonderful scent she had smelled when she'd entered the park. Her imagination began to wander, eventually stumbling upon the mysterious voice again. The fragrance and the voice were both strangely familiar, but she still couldn't place how she knew them. She coaxed her mind to follow them and began chasing memories through a mental labyrinth. She'd been sketching as this was occurring, and thought, *If I keep this up, maybe I'll figure out why they feel so familiar.*

Suddenly, she felt a jolt charging through her body. She looked around.

It had quit snowing.

The voice spoke again. *Ruby.*

The park was empty.

Her heart racing, she hit a metaphorical pause button and stood perfectly still, facing forward. Strangely, she felt like she was being tickled, and began to giggle. Her left hand came up and pushed back her cherry-chocolate hair, which had fallen down and veiled her face. She didn't know why, but she felt giddy.

There is no one here. Am I losing my mind? Surely this isn't really happening! Maybe my sanity's waning from hunger. But is it my body, or my mind that hungers?

She heard the voice again.

Chapter 2

*T*he bell on the Kaleidoscope Gallery's door jingled loudly as Ruby walked in.

This building is perfect for a gallery, she thought. It was an artistic structure from the mid-1920s, a period when America embraced Art Deco as an inspirational change from the diverse and revivalist styles that preceded it. The historic two-story Knights of Pythias structure was richly embellished with hard-edged low-relief designs—largely geometric shapes, including swastikas, chevrons, and ziggurats. Archetypal decorations inspired by Native American artwork were also part of the Art Deco style.

Someone went to great pains to restore this place. Ruby's artist's eye could plainly see that great attention had been paid to restoring the little ornamental details, giving the gallery a comfortable air. The gallery's main floor was warm, with potted plants neatly placed between exhibits, adding both life and ambience to the room. Its quality approached that of an intimate museum dedicated to preserving the artwork of the famous as well as neighborhood artists. The elegant interior space was also furnished with several elaborate tables and chairs, as well as a long, beautiful counter. It was its old Ashland charm, mixed with the clean minimalism of a contemporary gallery, that helped it to revitalize the community. *This building*, Ruby thought, *is the perfect venue for an upscale gathering.*

The ringing bell caught the attention of the elegant woman sitting on a hand-carved chair at a hand-carved table in the middle of the gallery. Her long, beautiful, salt and pepper hair made her look about sixty.

"Hello," she said to Ruby. "Can I help you?"

Ruby laid her portfolio on the counter and opened it. Even before she spoke, she felt defeated. "Would you be in the market for a painting or a drawing?" she asked in a small voice.

The woman walked to the counter, leaned forward, and briefly studied Ruby's work. Then she looked up and gave a friendly smile. "We don't buy artwork here, dear. Normally you could put some of your work on consignment, but our gallery is quite full at the moment." She shook her head, which Ruby took to signify, *Girl, your art isn't nearly good enough for this gallery.*

Just as Ruby was starting to put her drawings back into her shabby leather portfolio, a man came out of the storeroom. He looked at Ruby, then at the woman. "Nora," he said, "is there something I can help with?"

"No, no... This young lady was asking if we wanted to purchase some of her artwork. I was telling her we don't buy artwork but consign it, and we hardly have any space left for a new artist at the moment."

"Now, Nora, are you sure you aren't being rude?" The man was wearing a black T-shirt with a yellow Batman symbol on the front and faded jeans with a potential hole developing near his left pocket. Ruby thought he might be an attractive forty.

"I am not!" Nora protested.

The man turned to Ruby. "My name is Dutch." He winked at Nora, then held out his hand to Ruby, who looked at it but didn't shake it. "Nora, here, is my older sister and partner," he added. "Would you mind if I took a look at what you have here?"

Ruby opened her portfolio again. She stood stiffly, feeling exposed, judged.

Dutch picked up her most recent painting. "Hmm," he said after a minute of examination. "A cemetery? And this... a tree that's grown around a headstone... Nice. Grim, but well-executed." He paused at the next painting. "This one of Mount Shasta is also nicely done." As he looked up at Ruby, he sensed that she was filled with distrust and frustration. "And what is your name?"

"Ruby," She pointed at the painting. "Just like it says in the corner of everything you've looked at. I sign my real name. It's not some made-up name."

"What's wrong?" he asked.

"Nothing." She began putting her work back into the portfolio.

"Whoa—no need to rush off! Let me see what else you have."

"I doubt I have anything the two of you want."

Dutch looked at her tattered, long, black wool coat, her blackish-red hair, her black nail polish, and her dark maroon eye shadow. Because he didn't know any Goth people, or what their statement was (if they were even making a statement), Ruby's appearance left him confused and unsure how to communicate with her. "Yeah," he said after a minute. "You're probably right. I'm sure if you were a true artist, you'd be proud to show your work."

His words struck deep into Ruby's soul. "Kiss my ass!" she snarled, turning away. "I don't need to take your shit."

But Dutch merely smiled. "Oh, so you *do* have some good art in that folder? Some art I might be interested in?"

Now she was feeling intimidated. She wasn't sure what to do. She began zipping up her portfolio, then stopped. "Fine, look." She shoved the portfolio at him. "Look at all of it."

"Thank you." He wasn't a bit angry. He took the portfolio and paged through it at a leisurely pace. He now saw through her appearance, and viewed a sad, cold, vulnerable woman. Behind her, through the large display window, he could see the snow was still falling.

"Why don't you have a seat, Ruby?" he said. "I don't know that I'll buy anything, but at least it's warm in here. Make yourself comfortable."

Nora came closer to Ruby and whispered, "It's okay. Please, have a seat"

With a look of stubborn disdain, Ruby climbed up on one of the bar stools by the counter. Lightly kicking the stool with her black leather boots, she looked out the window and saw a passerby petting Yukon, whom she had tied to a no-parking sign. Yukon, soaking up the attention from the stranger, was happy to wait for her. She wished she could be like him. He gave his trust freely. Ruby, however, didn't trust anyone without strong motivation.

Dutch studied her work, making little noises as he did. He held one piece out in front of him, propped it up on the counter, took a couple steps back, and looked at it from a distance. He then squatted down, tilted his head and looked up at it.

"Ruby," he finally said, "you know, it's not the extraordinary people that make extraordinary art, but the ordinary." He stood up and propped her painting of Mount Shasta against a miniature easel on the counter. He pointed at his T-shirt, "Can you imagine Batman painting The Birth of Venus? Or Nobel Peace Prize holder Jimmy Carter throwing a piece of Van Briggle pottery?"

Ruby didn't reply. She wasn't paying much attention to him.

But Dutch continued as if she had answered. "It's not our strengths, but our weaknesses, that carry us when we express ourselves, yet too often we misinterpret them as obstacles to our work."

"Yeah yeah... Whatever."

"Could you stop being so aloof? I'm a man of some experience, who has gained and lost many things, and from that I've learned to appreciate the little things... all the small details that make a person laugh, love, smile, frown, and cry." It was obvious that her negative attitude was finally beginning to irritate him. "When I look at your work, I see some serviceable skill, but absolutely no emotion. Why is that?"

"It's there," she said dully. "You're just looking in the wrong places."

"I'm sorry, but it just isn't there."

She glared right into his eyes, not flinching. She knew he was right, and she hated it. In fact, much of her work lacked emotion. When she painted, she focused on her craft, not on the sentiment of the subject. She feared all of her work had that flavor of ambiguity. She suddenly felt anxious.

Ruby was tired of being afraid.

Every day, for as far back as she could remember, she had felt smaller and less significant in the world around her. She had the sense that she had been at her best when she was born; every day since then, the better part of her was slipping away, as if aging robbed her of her sense of success, her sense of belonging.

Dutch tried again. "Perhaps you're too guarded. May I suggest that you learn to let go and allow your soul to flow through you to your brush and onto the canvas?"

"My soul? What is this, some New Age shop? I know this is Ashland, but if I wanted my fortune told, I'd go to someone a tad more convincing." He was staring at her. She couldn't seem to shake him. She tried again. "Drop the lecture, professor. If you don't like my work, that's fine. I'll just leave."

He looked away. "You've made some unique works here," he said. "Not many artists risk painting graves and cemeteries. Why have you?"

Ruby was acutely uncomfortable. She wanted to put a stop to the whole matter, but words escaped her. She feared saying anything without saying too much. "I love the symbolism," she said softly. "Cemetery art is still art, isn't it?"

"I suppose it is."

"The graveyard." Ruby pointed to elements of her paintings as she spoke, her voice still soft, but now with a touch of dignity. "I enjoy interpreting the symbols and artwork found there. Some are obvious designs—like this one, with the winged hourglass, a symbol for time flying by. And this headstone with an hourglass on its side, suggesting that time has stopped for the departed. There are more complex symbols, too, like this butterfly engraved in the headstone. To most people, it's just a butterfly, but it actually means the person lived a short life. And this one, a star. It means death couldn't overpower the light of the soul, which continues to shine."

Nora stepped closer to look at Ruby's work. "You know," she said, "making art can often feel dangerous. It's like a river that flows between what you're comfortable with and what you fear." Her tone lightened. "Ruby, what I like about your work is that your subject matter causes the viewer to experience this same feeling of danger."

"Thank you."

"Yes," Dutch added, "and with a little more passion, I think you'd really have something. This one with the arched gates and the fog settling on the cemetery is creepy, sure, but I want it to scare the shit out of me! Do you see what I'm getting at?"

She nodded reluctantly, but said nothing. Dutch wanted her to take his advice, but she believed that as an artist, she should be the expert, and therefore shouldn't need any advice. At the same time, though, she knew in her heart that she was lost in her distress, in need of assistance yet unable to take it. As he looked at her drawings of graveyards, she held back from telling him the most important significance of the graves, how they represented the isolated, empty, and aching feelings that clung to her.

"I like this one," he said. "The painting of Mount Shasta. We'll buy it."

Nora stepped forward. "We'll do *what*?"

"We'll buy this one," he repeated. "Yes, I love that mountain. There's something magical about it. Ruby did a good job of capturing the clouds and the angle of the sunlight." He turned back to Ruby. "Your depressing graveyards are cool, but they're not for me. I'll give you a hundred dollars for the Mount Shasta. However, if you say one negative thing, give one more off-putting display of attitude, then the deal is off. I want you to take the hundred dollars, say thank you, and give me a smile. I know you can smile."

Ruby slid off the stool. She looked unsettled, but gave him the smile. "Thank you, Dutch."

Dutch looked at his sister. "Well, pay her."

"I don't have a hundred dollars on me. You bought it, you pay her!"

Cracking a grin, he went into the back room and came back with five twenties, which he handed to Ruby.

Thinking quickly, Ruby said, "If you like Mount Shasta, I have a charcoal on canvas at home. I could bring it by for you to look at, if you like?"

"No, I'm afraid I'm only in the market for one, which I now have."

"All right. Well, have a nice day." She gathered up her things and started to leave, but turned back. "Dutch?"

"Yes?"

"Thank you so much. Really. This money will go a long way." She started to leave again, but paused, and turned again. "My mind tells me you didn't really want my painting."

"Well, your mind is telling you wrong. You did good work here, I liked it, so I bought it."

She glanced away from him for a moment, a smile slowly crossing her face, then looked back. Dutch was glad to see a genuine smile. She stuck out her hand, "I'm sorry I didn't shake your hand earlier. That was rude of me."

He took her hand and gently shook it. At the same time, he took the opportunity to do what she had done to him earlier: he looked her square in the eye. He opened his mouth to speak, but what came out surprised even him. "You are truly a lovely woman, Ruby Birk."

"And you, sir, have a very flattery way about you." She grinned and bashfully pulled her hand back, then walked toward the door. "Goodbye, Dutch. Nora."

He watched her leave the gallery, untie Yukon, and start walking down the street. He walked to the window, still watching her, when she stopped almost three doors away. She suddenly let out a squeal to celebrate having some money, jumping up and down, with Yukon bouncing by her in solidarity.

Dutch laughed. "That was the best hundred bucks I've spent in a long time."

"You're a sucker, you know that?" Nora said. "You'll be lucky if you get fifteen dollars for that."

"Sure, if I sold it, but look at her. She's starving, can't you tell? That money'll do a lot for her."

"Oh, I forgot! We're in the business of charity! Whatever was I thinking?"

He held up the painting and examined it again. "Besides," he said, "I'm not selling this. There's something about her... something special. Call me crazy, but I think she could be famous one day!"

...

Mrs. Bimby, a tall and acidic old lady, looked out between the slats of her venetian blinds. It was getting dark. The snow was picking up again. She watched the slight wind blowing debris around her yard, until her patience paid off and she saw Ruby and Yukon practically running toward the apartment she rented to them.

Mrs. Bimby made her way to the back door and opened it. "Ruby," she called, "do you have a moment?"

Ruby shrank at the sound of her landlady's voice. She drew in a deep breath and turned. "Yes, Mrs. Bimby?" She could see another woman standing behind Mrs. Bimby, a meddlesome neighbor who delighted in gossip.

"Ruby," Mrs. Bimby said as the nosy neighbor nodded, "You seem to be avoiding me. I can never seem to hear you coming or going." She nodded her head and turned to the neighbor and said, *sotto voce*, "She's almost like a sneaky little fox." The neighbor laughed.

Ruby heard this. "I don't sneak around, Mrs. Bimby! I've only been walking Yukon. You must just miss us when we come or go."

"Well, Ruby, I've been waiting to see you today, watching out my window so I could catch you and have a little talk."

"Oh? What about?"

"I think you know! The first of the month has come and gone without even a peep from you regarding your rent."

"Well, I—"

"Do you not want to live here? Is this apartment not up to your standards?"

Ruby pulled nervously at the fraying sleeve of her secondhand coat. "I do want to stay here," she said. "The apartment is perfect, it's just that I've been having some... economic problems."

Mrs. Bimby's face froze and her thin lips formed a rigid line. "Oh, how sad," she said sarcastically as the neighbor giggled. "How very sad indeed. So, I presume it's up to me to bear the burden of your 'economical problems'?"

"No, no," Ruby said. "I just need a bit more time. Nothing big, just a little more time, that's all."

"Time? Ruby, time is money! Do you wish to take advantage of an old woman?"

Hearing this, Ruby stuck her hand in her pocket and pulled out one of the twenty-dollar bills she'd received from Dutch. "Here," she said, handing it to her landlady. "This is all I have right now, but I'll get more! Can you settle for this for now?"

Goaded on by her visitor, Mrs. Bimby stepped out onto the snowy back stoop and nearly snatched the bill out of Ruby's hand. "For now?" she said. "This is all you have *for now*? This is nothing close to what you owe me!" She tucked the money into the pocket of her apron. "Something is better than nothing, though."

"I'm hoping to sell more paintings," Ruby said. "Then you'll get the rest."

"The rest? This is barely enough for the late fee! You owe me the full amount of your rent, and *soon*, young lady. I'm not running a poor house."

"You certainly know how to handle her," Ruby heard the neighbor say. "You've got her dead to rights!" The woman gave a loud laugh.

"At the very least," Mrs. Bimby said as she went back in, "it's entertaining when she owes me money. All she can do is take whatever I give her, or she's out!"

"Why is she always broke?" the neighbor asked. "She looks able."

"She's one of those artists." Mrs. Bimby's voice was filled with scorn. "She'd rather fiddle around with paint and brushes than get a job. Her pictures are nothing special, but she insists they're *art*." The back door slammed.

Ruby's fake smile faded, removed by her injured soul. She hoped Mrs. Bimby didn't know how broken she really was. She couldn't hide the pain she felt as she overheard the two women ridiculing her, judging her.

Shoulders slumped and struggling to hold back her tears, she found her key and walked ahead of Yukon up the stairs to her apartment.

I'm not living, she told herself. *I'm barely existing.*

She reached out to unlock her front door, when she noticed it was ajar. She warily pushed it all the way open. Yukon growled and ran in.

Chapter 3

Ruby's apartment sat high on Lantern Hill Drive. It had a vaulted ceiling of dark-stained wood, and large windows overlooking both the neighborhood and nearly the entire city. The windows also gave Ruby a wonderful view of the Sugarloaf and Table Mountains; a view, she always told herself, that was the main reason she continued renting from Mrs. Bimby. This was her inspirational home, her sanctuary, along with Lithia Park.

And someone was violating it.

The door's open... but is it a robbery? she wondered. *I've nothing of value.*

Her apartment was a typical artist's home, void of logical organization. Easels, palates, brushes, tubes of paint, and sketches were scattered all over, some on the secondhand couch, some on the old wooden table, a few on the pair of non-matching chairs, and even a couple poking out of the ratty recliner she'd found in a garage sale. Even though the recliner desperately needed some upholstering, it was still her favorite place to sit and relax.

Yukon had stopped growling once inside the apartment, and looked up at her as if to say, *There's nothing to be concerned about.* Searching around, Ruby spotted a heavy coat lying on a canvas she'd stretched yesterday, then the back of her infiltrator, who was looking at a painting on the easel.

She stepped forward. "Turner! How did you get in here?"

Without turning, he held up a key and waved it over his shoulder. "I still have a key."

"Jesus Christ! You just walked into my home uninvited?"

"Aw, c'mon, Ruby. You know I'm no stranger."

She was still angry. "I didn't see your car. Where did you park?"

"Around back." Ruby stood motionless as he began gliding around her apartment and examining her scattered works. "You act like I'm a thief," he said over his shoulder. "Breaking in here to steal something. I wouldn't take anything here, there's nothing worth stealing. I mean, just look at this abomination." He pointed at the easel and frowned.

Ruby was relieved it wasn't someone dangerous in her apartment, but she still didn't understand the purpose of this pest's visit.

"Same ol' Ruby," he said in an overly casual tone, "playing at painting, but making nothing worthwhile."

"Yup," she repeated, annoyed, "yup, same ol' Ruby."

Turner finally faced her. "Ruby, how are you doing?" He almost never showed signs of affection, but he now came closer and put his arm around her to draw her to his chest. Yukon pushed his nose up between them, working his body nervously forward in an attempt to block Turner, who looked down and said, "Yukon, get out of the way, you stupid mutt!"

It was Ruby who backed away, with Yukon at her side. "First you come into my home uninvited, then you criticize my art, and then you have the audacity to touch me, and insult my dog!" She took another step away from him. "I think you should leave. Now."

"Not so fast!" he said almost cheerfully. "You might want to see what I brought you, first."

She shook her head. "It's been over six months since I last saw you. So, tell me, what are you doing? Why are you here?" She squinted at him. "And what have you brought me?"

"It has been about six months, hasn't it?" He moved some papers so he could find a seat on the couch. "It's really good to see you, you know."

"And why is that?"

"Because seeing you always cheers me up?" He grinned.

"Bullshit! Nice try, but that's complete bullshit." She took off her coat and dropped it on the floor.

"Okay, okay," he said. "Come here, have a look at this. Look at some real art!" He laid a framed painting on one of the chairs, over two of her own works. "So... what do you think?"

As she looked at it, her eyes widened in astonishment. She was speechless.

"Well? Are you just blown away, or what?"

"Yeah..."

"I was at this estate auction," he said. "I was promised some very collectible work that I could add to my inventory, which was tempting enough, but when I saw this, I just had to buy it."

"I'm not sure what I'm looking at." Her hand covered her mouth. "What... I mean, how can this be?"

"Right? When I saw this I said to myself, 'I know Ruby, I know her work, and this couldn't be it.'"

"Why not?"

"Well, one: You don't paint or draw people; two: You've never been to Paris. And three, this is actually art."

She scowled at his insensitive words, but her scowl was quickly replaced by renewed shock as she examined the painting closer. She touched it lightly, recognizing it as her work, the brush strokes very much in her style, yet she had no recollection of painting it. "I'm... I'm speechless..."

"Oh, Ruby, it gets even stranger! Just take a look at this!" He turned the framed painting over, revealing an envelope taped to the back of the canvas. Turner opened the envelope and pulled out a very old photograph, the photo from which the painting had been done. He waved the photo at her. "See here?" he asked. "You're in this photo!"

She couldn't believe her eyes, but there she was, in the photo, standing with a group of strangers under the Arc de Triomphe. "Holy shit, you're right! That's me!"

"I know. Crazy-odd, right?" He chuckled and sat down as she examined the photo further. He gave her a minute to look, then spoke again. "You know, as an art dealer, I get to see things most people can only dream of seeing. Priceless pieces, kept in vaults. I could count on one hand how many people have seen them. Every day I'm thankful to be privy to things so rare. But even so, on the day I saw this painting... well, I knew I was looking at something truly amazing. An extraordinary piece of work."

She turned the painting over again and looked at the signature in the corner. *Ruby Birk, Paris, 1912.* "I... I... I don't understand. I don't remember ever painting anything like this. And the year... 1912... I wasn't even born yet! But... that's me! Or someone who looks just like me. How is this possible?"

"I assure you, this piece is genuine. It was painted in the early part of the twentieth century." Turner scratched his head. "I took this all the way back to San Francisco and had it authenticated." He gave a funny laugh. "Art is the journey, not the presentation, as I always say. If I didn't know you, I could look at this canvas, with all its intricate bits of this and that, and I would say the artist was there at that exact moment in time and painted a memorable moment to preserve it for the whole world to enjoy for lifetimes to come. However, I do know you, I know that you weren't in Paris in 1912, and I know that this can't have been a memorable moment because it couldn't have happened."

"That is the sobering truth, isn't it?" She looked away. "But I sure wish it'd been a memorable moment of mine."

"And would you wish for that handsome devil next to you to be part of that moment?"

She looked closer. "Why not? I don't have anyone now, I'm not against finding someone new, might as well be someone good-looking."

"Hey, what about me? You've got me, don't you?"

"Don't flatter yourself. Anyway, that boat sank three years ago. You know, when we divorced?" She looked away from the painting and directly at him. "Remember? You had a *free spirit.* You *couldn't be tied down.* You told me that, with all the travel you did, it was *impossible* for you to be alone every night."

"At least I was honest."

She shook her head. "I appreciated your honesty, but it hurt all the same."

"But I need—"

"Don't you dare sit here in my apartment and try to excuse what you did! I was nothing to you!"

"I need nothing," he said. "I'm free. I was and still am a man on his own journey."

"To hell with your *journey*! To think I spent eight miserable years with you before I finally took back *my* freedom! Thank heavens!" She shook her head again, as if to forget. "You got the house, the big-city lifestyle, the bigwigs in San Fran *and* NorCal, but me? I got squat. Not even any good memories."

His voice was suddenly tender. "Are things really so bad for you?"

She looked away.

"The brush isn't making much money these days, huh?"

She didn't look up. "Not much at all. It was my dream to live off my art, but maybe it's time to wake up, go out, and find a nine-to-five job in an office."

Turner's expression softened. "I'm sorry if you're mad at me. Even if you'd gotten more out of the arrangement, though, would the art you've been making have sold any better?"

Without speaking, she pulled her hair back with both hands and held the bundle with one hand while searching in her pocket for a rubber band with the other. Once she had her hair fastened, she went into the kitchen. "No, I'm not mad at you," she called back. "But you're right. I know my kind of art doesn't have a wide audience. Even so, I'm tired of starving. I'm sick and tired of not having rent money every month, not having enough to eat. Then there's the smaller things. I haven't been able to visit a salon for months, and my roots have suffered for it. I think I miss chocolate the most, though. I crave it, but there's just never enough money to buy any."

Turner followed her into the kitchen.

She was standing in the middle of the room. "Maybe... maybe it's time for me to grow up."

He went to her and embraced her again. "Things must really be bad if you're thinking of getting a job," he murmured as he gave her a light kiss on the cheek. "Ruby, you *are* a good artist. Maybe not the best, maybe you're not pioneering a new sort of art, but you're still a *good* artist, and an honest one. I've always admired your sincerity. Don't let the world change who you are. It wouldn't be the same without you being you."

She wriggled out of his arms. "I can get a real job and still be me." She filled a bowl with water for Yukon, who lapped some up, then went and jumped up on Ruby's bed. She went back to the living area and flung herself on the recliner.

Turner followed her again and stood looking down at her. "Can you?" he asked. "Having a job basically means giving up your soul to conform to society's standards. Corporations even have performance evaluation charts to measure your conformity." He sat on the arm of a nearby chair. "You would die in an environment like that."

"I'm slowly dying here!" She struggled to hide her frustration. "I'm still not sure what I'm going to do."

He stood up. "Well, I should head out. You can keep the painting. If I leave now, I should get home at a decent hour." A grin crossed his face. "Unless you'd like to give me a reason to stay?"

She pointed at the door. "Get out, asshole. I appreciate the painting, but you're dead wrong if you think that won you any favors!"

He smiled at her. "Aw, c'mon. You said yourself that you don't have anyone at the moment...."

She stood up and pointed at the door again. Hoping she would change her mind, he reached for her, but she dodged away.

"Go!"

Lowering his head, he turned and shuffled toward the door.

Ruby looked over at the painting for a moment. "Wait."

He turned. "I was hoping you'd change your mind."

"It's not that. I need to be serious for a minute. You said you bought that picture at an estate sale?"

"An auction."

"Where was the auction held?"

"Here in Ashland. Not too far from here, actually. The Jameson mansion. Do you know it?"

"Haven't even heard of it." She pointed at the painting. "I just can't imagine how that came to be."

"It's very strange," he agreed. "I just knew you should have it. Please don't ask what I paid for it, though. You'd be shocked."

"Especially since I didn't make a dime from it."

"I can help you out," he offered with a leer, "if you help me out."

"Get out! For real this time, get out!"

He didn't move. "You have a sweet soul, the soul of a sincere artist."

"Don't make me call the cops."

He made for the door again.

"Turner?"

"Yes?"

"The key. Give it to me. I don't like knowing you could just let yourself in here any time you feel like it."

He slowly twisted the key off his key ring and handed it to her, then walked out the door, leaving Ruby alone in her empty apartment. She felt a blanket of loneliness cover her. "Alone again," she whispered. *Alone.* She wondered if she should have let Turner spend the night. At least she wouldn't wake in the morning all alone. She shrugged, bolted the door, and dropped the key on the table.

She'd been diagnosed at the free clinic two weeks ago as clinically depressed. It wasn't helped by the season, which, though technically late fall in Oregon, felt like deep winter. Other people, who had money and a car, could retreat up to the Mount Ashland ski area, where the snow was new, and the sun was bright. People could be happy there. *The skiers, snowboarders, and families with their sleds,* she told herself, *surely didn't need antidepressants when they were there.*

But she wasn't, so she did. She couldn't see any happiness from where she stood. Unpaid bills, a pain-in-the-ass ex-husband, a nightmarish landlady, and the cold and snow were the only things in view. Her ex's appearance only reminded her just how lonely she was. She moved that mysterious painting onto an easel, then walked to the wall heater and sat down. As the coils became red, they began warming her, soothing her.

After enjoying the heat for a while, she rifled through her portfolio and found her sketch of Lithia Park. She decided to make room on the easel so she could pin up and refine her charcoal drawing. But when she tried to move the painting, it fell and hit the floor with a hard thud.

Something rattled. She picked the painting back up, carefully this time, and she heard the rattle again as she moved it. After some inspection, she discovered a tiny, hinged door on the back of the frame. Popping the little door open, she discovered a hollowed-out area with a wad of old newspaper in it. Curious, she pulled the paper out and smoothed it. Within the crumpled newspaper lay a beautiful necklace with amber topazes encased in rose gold bezels, and a double-locked clasp. It seemed to be in the Art Nouveau style of the late 19th century, but it felt somehow... older. Suspended from the golden chain was a comparatively simple-looking cross with a loop at the top. She took the necklace out of its wrapping and ran her fingers over the chain. When she came to the clasp, she snapped it open and, without thinking, put the necklace around her neck. It felt comfortable, and... familiar?

Her mind hummed. Her eyes went fuzzy, and suddenly she was in Lithia Park, but not as she knew it. Was this possible? Was it her imagination? She closed her eyes and pulled the necklace off. When she opened them again the familiar chaos of her apartment surrounded her. She laid the necklace on the table and eyed it suspiciously. Unable to resist, she ran her finger over the looped cross. *First the painting,* she thought, *and now this necklace... it's mystifying. Has stress finally pushed me over the deep end? This is all far too strange to be real!*

She turned to pin her drawing of the park to her easel. Creativity coursing through her, she picked up her charcoal and began the process of improving the rough sketch. Dutch's words echoed in her ear. *Perhaps you're too guarded. May I suggest that you learn to let go, and allow your soul to flow through you to your brush and onto the canvas?*

She took a deep breath and exhaled slowly, letting her mind relax and giving her soul room to breathe. Whatever was happening, it felt very much as though her soul were alive again and wanting to set to work creating.

She worked the whole night through. She wasn't sure if they were just fantasies, or if they were real visions of the past she was seeing and working with, but whatever they were, she was able to capture them quite nicely. She didn't finish until after the sun came up. When she stepped back to view her work, she suddenly became aware of just what she'd drawn. She couldn't explain it, but there was no mistaking it. The man on the hill, the same as she'd seen in her vision at the park... it was the same man as was in the old oil painting, standing next to her at the foot of the Arc de Triomphe, in a city she'd never set foot in.

Chapter 4

Ruby heard the same haunting voice that had called to her at the park early the next morning. It was asking her to "return." She responded by gathering up her drawing supplies and heading for the door. Pausing, she glanced down at the necklace, which still lay on the table. She grabbed it and stuffed it into her pocket, then called Yukon. They went back to the fountain at Lithia Park, and Ruby studied its features, its complexion, its form. She snapped the necklace around her neck and readied herself. As before, her mind clouded over, and the world began to distort and change. She felt something like a small earthquake under her.

She looked out beyond the park. She could just make out the top of Ashland's tallest building. As she watched, though, it started to fade away. Everything was shifting as the modern things dissolved, replaced by things which had existed in the past. An iridescent haze now surrounded the fountain. Soon all the familiar landmarks were warped or gone, while historic sights she'd only read about on plaques and in history books sprang once more into existence.

Time rewound right before her eyes.

All I need now is a white rabbit in a coat, she thought in spite of the situation.

Yukon, who had remained beside her during this commotion, nuzzled up against her. He lowered his tail, shifted his ears this way and that, and tilted his head, trying to maintain his equilibrium.

What Ruby was experiencing was powerful, yet enigmatic. She looked around at her new surroundings. *What year is it?* She knew she was in the past, but neither the park nor any mysterious voices offered her a clue to the date. Despite her temporal confusion, though, she had to admit slipping through time was rather exciting.

With all of the changes happening around her, it took her a moment to realize she was no longer chilly. On the contrary, looking up, she saw a clear summer sky. When the nausea she assumed any time traveler must feel their first time around started to subside, she walked down the second staircase, her eyes moving quickly, taking in the gorgeous flowers, the lush green trees, and the graceful summer birds in flight above her. She went to sit on her usual park bench, but it wasn't there. Not far from the staircase, though, she spotted another park bench. Was it her bench in its original place? She didn't know, but it was strange to see any bench in Lithia Park with clean, bright wood and free of graffiti and carvings left by attention-hungry children.

Her mind was awake with excitement. *This is all far too fantastic to pass up.* She sat down to gaze at Mr. A. Frilli's fountain again. Yukon seemed restless. "Go on, boy," she said to him. "Go play. I think I'll try to draw some more." She knew he understood every word she said.

As the big dog galloped away, looking as excited as she felt, she wondered if he knew they had passed through time. *There's no way to know.* She settled on the bench and pulled out a blank sheet of her hand-crafted paper. Holding the charcoal, she relaxed her mind. Soon she was ready. The world in front of her looked different from the everyday world she knew in her "real life," the world in which she was poor and depressed. But now she knew what was happening wasn't her imagination. This was much too real. She could actually touch the past. She felt herself sitting firmly on the park bench. The oak slats were hard, yet comfortable. Soon she heard the unmistakable sound of horses' hooves striking the surface of the road nearby and looked at the street to see a horse-drawn white buggy with U.S. Mail stenciled on its side. The postal worker held the reins in one hand and waved at

Ruby with the other. Intrigued, she waved back, and he smiled at her. She noticed he was wearing a tweed suit and a tie, not a uniform. She blinked her eyes, checking to see if they were working properly.

When she turned again, she saw that the fountain was not there. It was only an empty hill. She looked around again. She could clearly see that it was summer, not winter, and she was sure she was still in the city of Ashland, Oregon, and yet the view in front of her was when Lithia Park was being landscaped. She could see John McLaren and his workers with their picks and shovels. She had no idea what John McLaren looked like, yet her mind somehow knew that the man she saw was him. At the top of the hill, where the fountain would eventually stand, she saw another man. He was dressed in unusual clothes, compared to what the workmen were wearing. Now she could see that he was watching the men lay the foundation of the fountain.

He was the man from the painting.

Ruby's hand was working hard, diligently capturing the actions in front of her. Her hand was moving, drawing without commands from her mind. She was feeling like she didn't exactly have control of her own hand. It was sweeping out sketch marks, building a more detailed picture. Amazed, she watched as her hand danced across the paper. She had a sense of insistence that she must draw the images she saw before they vanished. Or before she shifted back to her own time and place. With some heavy effort, she pushed the thought of returning out of her mind.

Her hand was still moving quickly, leaving a distinct charcoal image, a good representation of an era long in the past. She watched as the lines, smudges, and negative spaces her hand was drawing became clearer.

Every once in a while, when she looked up to see what Yukon was doing, she noticed the comers and goers in the park taking a few minutes to pet him. No one complained that he was off leash, no one seemed bothered at all that he was running free. Somehow knowing her dog was safe, she returned her gaze to the drawing. She worked for the better part of two hours until she heard the call of an owl high up in an old cottonwood. She and Yukon both stopped what they were doing and looked at the massive bird. It was ghostly with distinct white plumage. Once the owl had Yukon and Ruby's attention, it spread its wings. The motion introduced a cold mist that swept across the park and rushed them back, quickly, painfully, to their "real" time in the present.

Cold, wet winter touched Ruby again, and she sank back into depression. The owl took wing and flew over her, circled once, and then flew away. Ruby's mind bounced from thought to thought about the miseries of her life in this time.

Defeated by consensual reality, she looked around. "Yukon!" she called. "Come on, let's go." But she couldn't see him in the mist, which was becoming ever denser. She whistled and soon heard the jingling of the tags on his collar. The picture she had drawn in that other time, that other park, was damp now. She tucked it into her portfolio.

"Hey, big boy. Are you ready to go home?"

Yukon jumped up and twisted in the air. He didn't seem to care where they went as long as they were going somewhere. If he understood any word in the English language, GO was the word.

Ruby buttoned her long coat and stood up to leave. With one last glance at the present-day park, she started for home. About a block from her apartment, she heard someone calling to her.

"Hey! Ruby girl!"

She looked around. This wasn't a call from the past. This call came from Zanique, a friend she had met the previous spring while she was drawing Mount Shasta. After their first meeting, they had quickly become close, at least as close as Ruby was willing to get to anyone.

"Hey, I was just on my way to your place," Zanique called as she pulled her yellow and black Hummer up beside Ruby and stopped. "I thought I'd come and get you for breakfast."

Ruby smiled. "Good morning, Zanique."

"Come on! My treat. Let's bounce over to the Morning Glory and get some pancakes." Zanique paused. "Unless you've already had breakfast?"

"No, I haven't, but I don't like taking advantage of you. I imagine you probably work too hard for your money to waste it feeding indigent artists."

Zanique shook her head. "If I ever let anyone take advantage of me, it'll be you, girlfriend. The first rule of maintaining life is breathing, the second is eating... you gotta eat, right?"

Ruby smiled in spite of herself. "Yeah, you're right about that."

Zanique opened her door and jumped out, then opened one of the cargo doors at the rear of the Hummer. She was just five feet tall, and to an onlooker seemed an improbable owner of such a large vehicle. When she motioned for Yukon to jump in, he was right there.

Ruby climbed up into the passenger seat. "Damn," she said, "this thing is huge! Why don't you get yourself an environmentally friendly car?"

"Easy. This one's paid off. And besides, it fits my lifestyle."

Ruby laughed. It felt good to laugh. It seemed to lessen her depression and take her mind off whatever had just happened to her in the park. If meeting Zanique this morning had any meaning, it was a healthy distraction. Ruby welcomed it. "And how would you describe your lifestyle?" she asked.

"Umm.... well, I'm not sure exactly... maybe adventurist? Alpinist? Cyberpunk? How would you describe me?"

"You or your lifestyle? I would describe you as, well, you're alluring, that's a given. So, I guess your lifestyle would be well-appointed."

"How do you mean that, 'alluring'?"

"Look at you! What I'd give to look half as good as you. You're so beautiful." Ruby pulled the door closed, and Yukon pressed his nose against the side window behind her. "Yes, I'd describe you as alluring... and you obviously have money. So wealthy, too. And from what I know about you, well, you like to play in the outdoors... so we can agree on Adventurer. Your lifestyle would be more adventurous than luxurious." She smiled. "That's how I see you, anyway."

Zanique reached across the well-upholstered engine tunnel and squeezed Ruby's hand. "You have a way with words, girl. Every word a compliment."

It was fairly early and, as they made their way to the Morning Glory Restaurant, they saw that many of the shops on Siskiyou Boulevard were just starting to open. The restaurant was bustling, and after a ten-minute wait, they were seated in a booth and given menus.

"I don't know about you," Zanique said, "but I'm starving."

Ruby nodded. "I haven't eaten a good meal in several days," she admitted. "There's no doubt about it, I sure could eat one now."

"You don't have to say a word. I could tell just by looking at you."

"Are you saying I'm looking sickly?"

Zanique held up her hands in defense, "I don't mean to offend you, girlfriend. I'm just saying you look like you've lost some weight. Most girls would take that as a compliment."

"I suppose."

"So what are you gonna have? And don't be bashful. It's my money to spend. You order anything and everything you want."

Ruby looked at the menu as if she were studying a map to paradise. "It all looks so good," she murmured. "Give me some suggestions. I never get to eat out like this. This is a real treat!"

"Well, I'm going to have the chorizo scramble and three buttermilk pancakes."

"Really? You can eat all that?" Ruby looked at her petite friend. Zanique was fit. She was a cross-country runner, a mountaineer, a snowshoe guide, and in the summer months, she was more... much more.

"No way!" Zanique replied. "But I want to taste all of it, so that's what I'm getting. Go on. Order whatever you want."

When the waiter came to take their order, he nodded to Zanique to order first. Ruby instantly became aware of how he took down Zanique's order slowly and with a careful eye, looking her over at the same time. Checking her out. Ruby expected that.

Men always took notice of Zanique. No one could tell by just looking at her that she wasn't what she appeared to be. But Ruby knew, and she giggled to herself. The guy finally asked her what she'd like to order.

"I'll have a veggie egg white omelet." She glanced at Zanique "Are you sure about that 'anything'?"

"Yes, I'm sure. Please get whatever you want."

"And the lemon ricotta french toast."

The waiter jotted it down on his pad and started off.

"Oh, hey." Zanique stopped him before he got too far away. "And please bring extra walnut butter and marionberry syrup."

"Sure thing," he replied. "And no extra charge to you."

"I'd bet you could get your whole meal free if you said the right thing to that guy," Ruby commented.

"Perhaps," Zanique said. "But I'm not that kind of person." After a short pause, she asked, "Have you had the walnut butter here?"

Ruby looked around the restaurant. "No. I'm not even sure I've ever been here before. Maybe once. A long time ago."

"Well, you are in for a treat," Zanique smiled. "That butter is the BOMB." She made a gesture of explosion with her hands.

"You know, Zanique, I don't get you."

"What do you mean? I'm a pretty simple person. Nothing too perplexing about me."

"Oh, yeah, you *are* perplexing. I just can't figure why you care about me, like, if I eat or not."

Zanique shrugged her shoulders. "I don't like to see people going hungry."

"But it's not like you're my—"

"Show me what you are working on," Zanique interrupted as she pointed at Ruby's portfolio.

Reluctantly, Ruby pulled the zipper and opened her old portfolio. "I've just got a few things in here," she said almost apologetically.

Zanique nodded. "I remember the second or third time I saw you. You were walking over by the graveyard. I thought you were homeless. And then I saw that you had this... uh, what do you call it? A portfolio? You reminded me of someone I used to go to school with."

"Oh?"

"Yep. She was always writing. You know... poetry. She never had the sense to stop and eat, either." She laughed. "Always writing."

"What happened to this person?"

The smile left Zanique's face, "Sad story. She passed away. Juvenile cancer."

"I'm sorry to hear that."

Zanique was silent for a minute, then, "I'm curious... why do you paint? You complain about your art not making you any money, and yet you continue to do it."

"Do you think I should quit and get a normal job?"

"No way! I was just wondering."

"I don't know. I guess it's a calling... like being called to become a priest or a nun." Ruby forced a laugh to cover how vulnerable she felt exposing the truth.

Reaching for the portfolio and pulling it closer to her, Zanique said, "I have a lot of respect for a person that's doing what they're called to do. Called by their spirit and not by dead presidents. Even if that artist is starving herself to death. Ruby, I respect your determination."

"Coming from you, that's quite a compliment. Thank you."

"I suppose it's logical," Zanique said as she paged through Ruby's work until she came to the damp drawing of Lithia Park in the past, "that there are people among us whose smallest and most familiar works of art are marked for distinction." She held up the drawing. "Wow, I love this sketch. I see the harmony of your work in it. It's so full and rich... the rhythm of your strokes... expressed with such idealism. With such natural skill."

Ruby hardly knew what to say. Finally, "I didn't know you had an appreciation for art." She tilted her head. "No one has ever commented on my work like that before. Thank you, Zanique."

Moving the portfolio, Zanique accidentally knocked it into her place setting. Her fork, knife, and spoon scattered across the floor and stopped at the feet of their waiter. He picked them up and went and got clean ones for her. Even though Zanique's eyes were still on Ruby's sketch, she noticed him and without a trace of self-consciousness accepted the new bundle and thanked him.

Her charm had already captured him. He looked like he had much he wanted to say to her, but he couldn't muster the words—or the courage—to speak them aloud. Embarrassed, he turned and went back to his station.

"He looks over thirty," Ruby commented. "And not a bad looking man."

"Are you suggesting something?"

Ruby smiled. "No. I'm just noticing the sparks as they fly by."

"Well, those sparks would soon turn to smoke if he knew."

Ruby smiled. At the same time, she wondered if it was difficult for Zanique to deal with her situation, being as dissimilar as a person could be. "If I were you," she said quietly, "I'd just be honest, and tell him... if it came to that."

"You are *not* me." But then Zanique had to smile. "I'll consider your advice, though. If it comes to that."

"What's the worst that can happen?"

"Rejection is a bitter pill to swallow. I know. I've swallowed many in my time."

"Yes, but every human who is more than a mere bundle of clothes finds you attractive. You should try. Just once. There are people out there that are accepting."

Zanique's smile turned rueful. "Evidently you never met my parents. Hell, *I've* never met my parents."

Ruby pressed her lips together, trying to keep herself from interrupting as Zanique continued.

"My parents literally left me on the doorstep of a church! I grew up in the foster system, and none of my guardians could deal with it. I wish I could have been what they wanted me to be... but you know Mother Nature. She can be a fickle bitch."

"You should embrace who you are," Ruby said in her most sincere voice. "After all, you're the best-looking woman I've ever seen, and if that's who you really are, then I support you completely."

"I embrace who I am. And I embrace both strengths. I just don't go around proclaiming it." She had to change the subject. "How about you? Do you have parents? And if so, do you get along with them?"

"Uh... well, yes, I do have parents. Living. And, no, we don't get along... exactly."

"How so?"

But before Ruby could go on, the waiter appeared with their food. He began setting plate after plate down until there was hardly any room left on the table. When he asked, "Can I bring you ladies anything else?" Ruby realized he had never once looked at her.

"No," Zanique told him, "you've done it all." She paused. "Oh, but stay close. You never know when a girl might need something."

The waiter smiled, lifted his serving tray, and walked away.

Ruby picked up her fork and resumed her story. "My parents are old-fashioned. Religious. They made it clear when I was young that I was a disappointment to them. I have a brother and a sister. My parents are satisfied with them. The four of them are a close family. They live in Seward, Nebraska. They didn't think I was 'normal' when I was a teenager, so they shipped me off to private school. I haven't been back to see them since."

Zanique nodded as she buttered her pancakes with walnut butter and poured marionberry syrup over them. Then she forked up a small piece of pancake and put it in her mouth. As she chewed, the look on her face became one of sure ecstasy. After she finally swallowed, she said, "Like I said before. I have a lot of respect for a person that does what she believes in. Girlfriend, you and I are what they call *throwaway children.* Our parents got rid of us. For whatever reason. Tossed out with the garbage. Well, I say, fuck 'em!" She took another quick bite. "You're a good person who is living life the right way.

You want to draw and paint... and you're doing it! Your parents missed out on what a wonderful person you've become. You and I may not be 'normal,' but who wants to fit in their way?"

Ruby was eating her lemon ricotta french toast and thinking it was just about the best thing she had ever eaten. She nodded her head.

"Most of the time," Zanique was speaking and chewing at the same time now, "a person thinks life is nothing more than just getting through it, day by day, as quickly, as easily, and as comfortably as they can. They go to work for a few hundred bucks. You know—a paycheck. And for what? Eating, sleeping, and dying?" Suddenly realizing she was talking with her mouth very full, she swallowed and took another bite. She chewed more slowly, minding her manners, even though she wanted to shovel the pancake in. "Then there are people like you," she said. "A person that's not thinking too much about money, food, or even sleep, for that matter. It gets a person like me to wondering if I'm not missing out on something." She pushed the almost empty plate of pancakes aside and pulled the plate of scrambled eggs and chorizo closer.

But she's wrong, Ruby said to herself. *I do think about those things. I worry all the time about money and food. And lost sleep.* She thought of death, her death, suicide, more often than she wanted to. She had to block out the thoughts of these things, in fact, so she wouldn't lose her sanity. Depressing and self-loathing thoughts sometimes crawled around in her head like rats producing babies at an absurd rate. They chewed and ate up the good in life just to remind her how much she was alone. One thing that Zanique had left out, though, was love, and Ruby longed to hear someone tell her, *I love you.*

She pushed her feelings down into the dark places again, that deep place where she kept them, and decided not to say anything at all about them. She just kept eating, taking bigger and bigger bites. After a minute or two, she looked up. "The combined flavors of the french toast and lemon and cream cheese are amazing! And that omelet was over the top, too." She couldn't even express her appreciation for having a real meal. "How can I even begin to thank you?"

"Sitting here with you," Zanique said, "I'm beginning to rethink my life. I'm wondering if there's more to it. Am I missing something? Should I be doing more?"

"But, Zanique, you live a very adventurous life! You've no reason to think you're missing anything. You're constantly challenging yourself, climbing another mountain, snowshoeing into the wild... why on earth would you think for even a minute that my life has more in it than yours?"

Zanique thought about it. "You're probably right," she finally said. "Yeah. But when I'm gone... dead and gone... no one will remember me. There's nothing of me that will be left behind that anyone will ever appreciate. But you? You have those beautiful pieces of art! Years from now... hundreds of years from now, people will gather in a gallery somewhere and admire the work of Ruby Birk."

"If you only knew." Ruby began. "My life is...."

The waiter was suddenly back. "Here's your check," he said. "I'd give you your breakfast for free, but my manager wouldn't like that very much." He was staring at Zanique again.

Without looking at the check, Zanique handed him a hundred-dollar bill. "Keep the change."

Ruby looked at the Ben Franklin before the waiter turned away and felt the burn of jealousy scorching her mind. *Zanique has money,* she thought, *and looks, and a guy is flirting with her. What do I have? Nothing. Zilch.* She kept her envy well camouflaged, however, because she valued her friendship with Zanique and didn't want the things she lacked in her so-called life to come between them. By now, Ruby wasn't even thinking about Lithia Park and her trip into the past. It had somehow flown out of her mind.

The waiter's eyes went wide when he saw the hundred-dollar bill. "Thank you! That's a huge tip!" He stood beside the table, uncertain what to do next, and then he suddenly asked, "Could I be so bold as to ask you for your number?"

Zanique neither smiled nor laughed. Instead, her expression turned serious, almost panicky, as she looked at Ruby. "This is always so awkward," she whispered.

"Awkward?" the waiter asked.

"If you knew me... truly knew me, you wouldn't do this."

There was silence. The waiter looked like he wanted to say something... but what could he say? And then he didn't care what he might seem like if he spoke. He only knew that he wanted to say it all to Zanique.

"I know a lot about dating," he began. "More than is respectable, I suspect." Pause. "Obviously, I haven't always come out on the winning side of it. But I've had some pretty full experiences in my life, and from those experiences, I can gauge the quality of my own emotions pretty accurately... and the attraction I have for you is unlike anything I have ever felt before."

"But you've only just seen me this morning," Zanique said in a quiet voice.

"That's not true. You come in here from time to time, and I notice you every time. But this is the first time I've worked up the nerve to talk to you." He pointed to another server. "Actually, I traded tables with him so I could talk to you." Longer pause. "Ask you on a date."

"What should I do?" Zanique was addressing not the waiter but Ruby, who shrugged her shoulders.

She looked up at the nervous waiter. "I believe I could work out some free time." She fiddled with Ruby's portfolio, "You name the time and place, and we'll meet you." She looked at Ruby again. "I never meet someone alone on a first date. Ruby, you don't mind coming along, do you?"

"There's nothing I like better than being a third wheel."

The waiter looked back and forth at the two women. "Okay," he finally said. "Uh, my name is Blake. Here's my number." He wrote his phone number on a blank page of his order pad and nervously handed it to her.

"I'm Zanique. And this is my friend, Ruby."

"Hi." For the first time, Ruby felt like he actually saw her.

"How about we meet at seven, Wednesday, at Zen Sushi? It's in Medford," he added.

"Ah... no," Zanique said. "I don't do sushi. How about seven on Wednesday at Callahan's? You know where the Mountain Lodge Restaurant is, right? They have steak, seafood... .seafood that's *cooked*. Will that work?"

"Sure. I'll be there." Blake looked at Ruby again. "Do you want me to bring a friend? We could make it a double."

"No, thank you," she said. "My life is complicated enough. I'm fine having dinner with the two of you."

He smiled. "It's settled then. Wednesday at seven."

"I'm sorry about that," Zanique said to Ruby after Blake had gone to wait on another table. "I'm so embarrassed."

"Don't worry about me. I'm fine." Ruby reached into her pocket and pulled out the rest of her money. "Please let me pay you for my food."

"No way! It's already bought and paid for." Zanique scooted out of the booth. "I've got some errands to run. You and Yukon can hang with me today if you want to. Unless there's some other place else you'd rather be?"

Ruby gave this a minute's thought. "Well, could you drop Yukon and me off downtown? I want to take my new drawings into a gallery and see if they'd be interested in them."

"No problem. But let's get together before our date on Wednesday."

Chapter 5

$\mathcal{W}$hen the bell above the door of the Kaleidoscope Gallery rang, Dutch was sitting quietly, lost in thought and gazing out his office window. He'd been sitting there for some time, not watching anything in particular. Hearing the bell, he got up from his high-backed desk chair and went out into the gallery. Though he caught himself smiling as soon as he saw Ruby standing there holding her portfolio, he immediately stifled the smile and told himself he was a professional and an adult, and he shouldn't be smitten like a teenager by a woman peddling her art.

At the same time, Ruby was watching Dutch coming toward her. With his thick, wavy, brown hair and his bright hazel eyes, he looked, she thought, like a model from the latest Territory Ahead catalog. At least he would if he didn't have those scars. Down the right side of his face ran a long, thin line, a shorter scar came off the corner of his mouth, and there was a third scar in his hairline. The scars made him look too rugged to be either a model or the proprietor of an art gallery. But aside from the scars, she thought, he had a handsome face with a straight nose and a mouth that looked soft. His body was manly, with broad shoulders, narrow hips, and a lot more muscle than Turner had ever thought of having. She wondered what it would be like to kiss him.

"Ruby Birk," Dutch said. "To what do I owe the honor of your visit?"

She smiled. "Hey, Dutch. I've been thinking about what you told me."

He looked out the showroom window and saw Yukon sitting on the sidewalk, waiting for her. "And what was it I told you?"

"That my work lacked emotion. Well, actually, you said a lot more than that, but the lack of emotion was the comment that stung the most."

"I'm sorry, Ruby. I—"

"No, no, please don't apologize. I needed to hear that. And face it. You're right. There isn't any emotion in my work. But I've been working on some new things. And... and I was wondering if maybe you'd critique them?"

The bell rang again, and they both turned.

Nora entered the gallery. "What are the two of you staring at?" she asked, taking off her gloves and coat. "Did I interrupt something?"

Dutch laughed. "No, you didn't interrupt anything. You just surprised us, is all. It was quiet and then," he pointed at the door, "the bell rang so loud."

Ruby became her usual shy self in Nora's presence.

"Ruby was asking me to critique some of her new work," Dutch went on. "Come on over here, and let's see what she's done."

Nora walked to Ruby first. "Hello, Ruby."

"Hi, Nora." Suddenly feeling confused and exposed again, she looked back at Dutch. "Uhh, maybe this wasn't such a good idea. I'm sure you guys are very busy. I don't want to waste your time."

"We have absolutely nothing to do at the moment," Nora said. "Please don't be afraid to show us what you're working on. We'd love to help you." She looked at her brother, who was nodding in agreement.

Taking a deep breath to steady herself, Ruby opened her portfolio and laid out her two new charcoal drawings of Lithia Park.

Dutch's eyes widened. "Now that's more like it! Good, *good*." He grabbed a countertop display easel and pinned up her completed drawing, then stood back and looked at it from different angles. "This is very good. The detail is so vibrant, it comes to life. I feel like I could reach out and touch the earth in this drawing."

Nora agreed. "I think you have something here," she said. "It looks familiar," she added, "but I'm not quite sure what I'm looking at."

"Well, it's an idea I had," Ruby said. "I thought I would do a series of works themed around the construction of Lithia Park. Back in the day, when the main entrance was where the fountain is. This first one is the groundwork. See?" She pointed at the top of the hill. "The fountain isn't there yet."

"Fountain?" Nora asked. "There's a fountain in the park?"

"Oh, yes, and it's beautiful."

Dutch picked up the other drawing and examined it. "This is very good, too. What photos are you referencing here?"

"I'm not. I'm just using my imagination." She smiled nervously. "The first one is the park in, oh, 1914. This one is 1916. "See? They're laying the foundation stones for the fountain."

"That's some imagination you have there. Just look at the detail!"

Nora looked from drawing to drawing. "And the man? He's in both drawings. Who is he?"

"I actually don't know," Ruby told her. "When I close my eyes to imagine the park back then, he's always there. In my vision. It's almost like he's haunting me." She did not mention the extraordinarily curious painting Turner had brought her, the one of herself in 1912 in Paris with this very same man.

"I love him!" Nora exclaimed. "He's so suave, with his vest and high collar and ... well, he's a man I'd like to run into."

Dutch grinned at his sister, then said, "Ruby, I think your idea's a good one. Finish the set, and I'll help you pitch them. We might be able to find a buyer that's into the historical perspective of the city. Of Lithia Park."

"You think so? That'd be wonderful... I could use the money. The way I see this series, each panel will build off the previous ones. If you can imagine...."

"You bet!" he said. "At the very least... if I can be so bold as to presume that you have new-found confidence?"

Fiddling with the curious necklace in her coat pocket, Ruby said, "Yes, things are definitely looking up for me at the moment."

"I think you've found your muse," he told her. "Would you let me buy you a cup of coffee?" He pointed out the window toward a fashionable coffee house across the street.

"I don't like coffee," she replied, "but a cup of hot chocolate would hit the spot. My body craves chocolate in any form, and hot chocolate is like mainlining it!" She laughed.

He turned to his sister. "You wanna come along?"

"No," she said with a grin, "you two go ahead without me. Ruby, before you go, may I request something of you?"

Ruby's eyes darted from Dutch to Nora, then back to Dutch. She was wondering what Nora might have in mind. For some reason, she didn't quite trust her. "Sure."

"Would you please bring your dog in? I'll watch him while you're gone. You can't take him in the coffee house, and I doubt with the cold we'll have many customers in here... and, besides, I love dogs and could use a little D. O. G. time."

Ruby gave her a wide smile. "Okay, but I warn you, Yukon's a big flirt. He loves the ladies."

"Great!"

...

Ruby was thrilled to have the beverage she often craved but could seldom afford. "Thank you, Dutch. You have no idea how much I appreciate this."

"Oh, I think I know exactly how much you appreciate it," he said. "I know a starving artist when I see one, and you're the epitome of a starving artist."

They were sitting at a table near the street-side window, through which they could see parts of the park. "So... Lithia Park, eh?" He took a sip of his coffee. "Why?"

"I love that park," she said. "No matter how horrible I feel, a walk through the park always makes me feel better."

"So, are you from Ashland?" he asked.

"No. I'm from the Midwest. Nebraska."

"Nebraska? I thought for sure you were from San Francisco.

"Nope, Seward, Nebraska."

He took another sip, but his coffee was still too hot and burned his tongue. "When did you move here?"

"Boy, you're the curious man today, aren't you? Be careful. I may just bore you to death."

"It's just a friendly conversation."

"Don't you have to go back to work?" She set her empty cup on the table.

"Nope! I'm the owner. I don't have to be anywhere I don't tell myself to be. Right now, I'm telling myself to be here with you." He looked down at the table, then back up at her. "How about another cup and you tell me more about yourself?"

"I'd like that." She smiled. "Another cup, that is." Actually, she was feeling a need to get something off of her chest. It was something Dutch had said the other day that was still bothering her. "Look, Dutch, I don't feel sorry for myself, like you said the other day. And I don't even think I'm as bitter as you seem to think I am. Life's been rough on me, and I'm a very cynical person because of that. But I suppose every artist has gone through difficult times, maybe more than I have. But that's what makes a good artist, right? They have to vent in some way, so they express themselves through their art. We can take a beating and survive only if we're convinced life is worth living and we have something to offer life in return." She paused as Dutch got the attention of the guy working behind the counter and signaled to him to refill her cup.

"But I'm faced with a very real problem," she continued when he looked at her again. "How do I live in a world where money is king? I don't want to conform! This capitalistic reality our world revolves about is something I strongly don't want to be part of. And because of that, well, without money I suffer."

Dutch nodded. "Ruby, I don't think you can compare someone else's hardship to your own. I can see you're in a difficult situation, and who can judge if yours is less than someone else's? Sure, other artists, musicians, authors, and so on went through hunger, poverty, and loneliness before their big breaks came. There are many examples."

The waiter handed Ruby's cup full of what she craved to Dutch, who set it down in front of her. The cup barely had time to hit the table before she scooped it up. It made him happy to see her enjoying something he could provide.

"Look," he continued, "I've known many artists from various disciplines, and I've come to understand that most who start out as an 'artist' end up quitting. But then there are those who are driven by some mysterious force. They're the ones that fate pushes. Everyone is subject to the common movement of human troubles. These troubles are common enough that we all survive them. But the artist? Well, they can be fatal. Often, a person has to choose between making art and getting a job. Like you said, money is king. The way to survive as a person and an artist is to become stubborn about your work. Defend it. Learn how *not* to quit."

"You must be reading my mind!" she exclaimed. "I've been thinking I should quit and get a career-type job. I'm so tired of not having any money... and I'm always afraid my work isn't good enough."

He scooted closer to her. "Listen carefully. Do you honestly believe that all the famous artists suffered only hunger, poverty, and loneliness? I say, and this is important, I say *they also suffered doubt.*"

Ruby nodded and listened carefully. She found herself trusting Dutch.

"Think about it," he continued. "I bet every person, past and present, working in a creative field doesn't know any more than you do. They doubted they had anything in them worth putting out to the public. You need to know that. You can undoubtedly survive any problem life wants to throw at you, as long as you believe. Have faith that you should survive... that there is some purpose for you and your art. But don't think for a minute that your relationship with doubt is exclusive. Every artist since the beginning of time has faced doubt."

She gave this some thought. "True," she admitted. "I'm ashamed to say this, but on second thought, well, I guess I have been feeling sorry for myself for a long time now. And when I came into your gallery... when you bought my painting of Mount Shasta, well, at first, your words hurt my feelings. But after I had time to think about what you said, I realized I need to make a change."

She had a bit of whipped cream on her upper lip that Dutch was watching as she spoke. He was trying to resist taking up a napkin and wiping it off.

She was still talking. "I'm so confused as to what to do. Rent is due, and I'm busted. Broke. I don't want to get a regular job. But my bills outweigh my bank account."

"Could I offer you…?"

She smiled a bashful smile and reached out and laid her forefinger over his lips. "Please don't offer me charity," she said. "Any assistance wouldn't be enough. It would only prolong the inevitable. I'm at a fork in the road. I need to choose which way to go."

He looked cross-eyed at her finger. Even the merest touch of the tip of her finger caused a stir within him. Slowly, she pulled her finger back and looked away. He licked his lips.

"Was it your family back in the Midwest… was it growing up there that inspired you to be an artist?"

She was staring off for a minute or two as he spoke, eyes focusing out the window at the park where freakish had happened, and then she slowly looked back at him. She wasn't annoyed with the question, she told herself. What annoyed her was that she didn't have a happier story to tell him. "Let's just say that my family and I aren't... well, we're not on the same page about anything. Let alone art. Besides, you've seen my art. There's nothing of the Midwest, family, or home in them, is there?"

As he smiled at her, she suddenly saw a mixture of adoration and endearment on his face. After a pause, he said, "Uh-oh. I'm afraid to ask. Not a happy childhood?"

"Not exactly." The recollection was more profound than she anticipated. "Forgive me if I'm not jumping at the chance to discuss my childhood, but I didn't really have one. I had what you might call an 'ultra-strict Christian upbringing.' I wasn't allowed to participate in the secular world—no music, no books or magazines, no art. Nothing that wasn't related to the church. Basically, we were only allowed to read the Bible."

Dutch leaned his elbows on the table and ran the fingers of one hand through his hair. The bright glow of the western sky lit up his rugged face. He hesitated a little, trying to figure out how to respectfully approach the heart of the matter. "Dark robed priests, sinners, strict rules," he said. "These are things I'm not familiar with."

"You should be grateful!" She went on almost anxiously. The subject needed to be voiced. "When I was thirteen, I was allowed to spend the summer with my aunt, uncle, and cousins in Chicago. That's where my eyes were opened to a whole new world. I was able to become a real person, an individual. It was that summer that I was exposed for the first time to art galleries, museums, and music."

"Well, I'm glad you got to enjoy yourself at some point in your young life," he said sincerely. "Plus, you were able to see and appreciate the arts. Who could find anything wrong with that?"

"Yes, well, when I returned home wearing new clothes, lipstick, pretty fingernail polish, and with pierced ears—well, you know that whole rebellious stage...." She paused and gave a little giggle. "You should've seen my mother's face! She hollered for my dad to come quick and look at me. They were both freaked out. They called the minister to come over for dinner so he could see what the devil had done to me. School was going to start the following week, and Reverend Krauss told my parents they had to do something drastic, do something *fast*, to save me from the evil that had befallen me."

Dutch's eyebrows went up. "Save you? Something drastic?"

"The next thing I knew, I was packed off to a private Christian Academy in Crestview, Florida. And that's when I knew my parents were done with me. They didn't write or phone or anything. No contact. Remember, I was only thirteen. I was convinced that something was seriously wrong with me for wanting more out of life.

"I spent six years of my life in ultra-conservative institutions. Four high school years and two at a Christian university. Trying to be the 'good girl' I thought they wanted me to be. Someone my family would love." She stopped. Her mouth tightened up.

Ruby began fiddling with her cup in a way that Dutch found remarkably interesting, caressing the edges lightly with delicate fingers. He could see she was searching her mind for the right words.

"I tried to be like them," she finally said. "I went around quoting Bible verses, advertising the words of God like they were something new, something hot off the press. But I was as stale as the pages of that old book. I tell you, I was really innocent, I knew where my panties were every night! But deep down, I couldn't swallow that conservative, submissive-little-woman shit they demanded of me."

Dutch lost it. He laughed loud enough for the whole coffee shop to hear. Conversations paused. Heads turned toward their table.

But sitting there, Ruby began trembling as the memories took her into the dark recesses of her mind where, hidden away from everyone, lay a terrible truth. Since leaving the university, she had done her best to bury these memories and all they represented. It was difficult and painful to recall her past, especially sitting there with such a nice man. She still saw her first sexual experience in a negative light. It had been the extreme experience that had driven her away from the university and all it stood for.

Yes, she had been innocent back then, shy, and with no desire to learn about sex. Even if she hadn't been aware of it, however, she always had an attractive light to her. She was a modern young woman with an innate rectitude that casual male observers noticed. She was different from the other girls on campus. When pushed into a corner, she was suspiciously liberal and cynical in her speech. And it was precisely her being different that had attracted her professor, Dr. Murick. She had a reputation for questioning the teachings and not conforming to them, either, so he understood fully that he could commit his trespasses and get away with them, perhaps even be justified for doing what he did.

She had never told anyone how Dr. Murick had taken her in his hands and forced her down. She remembered the cadence of his breathing, his drool that dribbled onto her skin, the feel of his weight on her, the unwanted penetration. She remembered how hard he'd slapped her when she began to cry. Her begging him to stop seemed only to fuel his excitement. This was the root of her darkness; the rat that scurried around in her head bringing depression, self-loathing, and the reoccurring thoughts of suicide.

Worse was how he had laughed at her while she gathered her clothes, saying all the while that she deserved it because she was a temptress. He projected the rape onto her as if it were her doing, as if it were her fault. The event... oh, the ugly event still bound her in great chains. It had shaped her future.

She had become an artist, and until recently she'd had that undeniable desire to paint graveyards and headstones. She longed to capture on canvas the idleness of death after life's struggles, the luxury of abandoning life when pain yields to decomposition, and fear dissolves into the past. To her, the grave wasn't something creepy. It meant rest, it meant peace and an escape from people like Dr. Murick, from a society that marked her as different.

She shook her head now and forced herself to let those memories go and focus on the present, on the kind man sitting across the table from her. "And I never went back home," she finished in a soft voice. "I haven't seen my family in over seventeen years."

There was a longer silence now. Ruby looked at the park across the street, at the leafless trees. Looking back at Dutch, she gave him a little smile.

As her proud eyes looked straight into his, Dutch tried to shield himself against her charm. He saw again that it was her difference from other people that made her fascinating, her difference that had caused him to take notice of her since the first day he met her.

"I'm sorry," she murmured. "I've been talking too much." She turned toward him again and gave him a long, considering look. "Can we stop talking about me?" she finally asked. "I'm tired of me! How about you tell me where you're from? Are you an artist? I'll bet you've been all over the world and painted everything from Stonehenge to naked women in Rio de Janeiro—"

"Whoa! Slow down! One thing at a time, please."

"Okay. Where are you from?" she asked.

"I'm from Crosby, North Dakota."

She had no idea where that was, but it didn't matter. "Did you grow up an artist? I've assumed you're an artist. Because of the gallery."

He shook his head. "Crosby's hockey country. I played hockey as soon as my feet could fit the skates. My dad wanted me to play a 'man's sport,' so I became a hockey player. Nora's the artist in our family, and it was through her that I began to have an eye for art. To appreciate art. Yes, when I was younger, I desperately wanted to dabble in art. Oils and brushes." He raised an eyebrow. "Because of Nora I knew many artists and admired all aspects of art, but any time I mentioned art at home, it disappointed my dad. Where I come from, there is one thing you don't do... you don't disappoint dear ol' dad."

She nodded. "That explains it."

For the first time, he looked as vulnerable as he felt. He shifted in his chair. "Explains what?"

Ruby looked down, hoping not to offend him. "The scars on your face."

"Yes, well… many years in the game will mess up your face. It's not a matter of *if*. It's a matter of *when*."

"It sounds like your dad had a good hold on you."

"He wasn't a mean man when I was growing up. He just wanted me to be tough and do something that went with being a *man*. I don't share his views. Anyway, I retired from hockey ten years ago… and that's when I made the big change to open a gallery with Nora and to try to become an artist."

There was an uncomfortable silence for a moment.

"So," she gave him a confused smile, "hockey, huh? Not much hockey around here."

"Not true," he shot back. "We have the Spartans in Medford."

"Medford has a hockey team?"

He finally let loose the grin he'd been holding back. "Not the NHL," he admitted. "They're a junior league, but I think they're more fun than the NHL. But that's just me."

"Were you a pro?"

"Yes. From 1992 to 1994. I played for the Toronto Maple Leafs, then the Colorado Avalanche… I went to the Stanley Cup with that team. Then I got traded to the New Jersey Devils, and we got to go to the Stanley Cup in 2000 and again in '03. I retired four years later. I had a lucky run being with those great teams. I guess I was in the right place at the right time."

"I know nothing about hockey. Who is Stanley?"

He threw his head back and gave out a bellowing laugh. "Someday I'll explain it all to you. If you agree to do this again."

In the deep places where she kept her secret pleasures, she was tingling with excitement. Dutch wanted to meet her again! *Damn, it's hard to take my eyes off him.* "I'd like that," she said aloud. "Another cup of hot chocolate and more conversation."

Chapter 6

Ruby had sat utterly motionless, her eyes wide open, examining the painting of the mysterious man standing beside her in Paris. She had sat there hour after hour through the night and into the early morning in dreamy silence that spoke volumes of her determination to solve this mystery.

I know this is madness, she kept telling herself. Feeling disoriented, she leaned closer to the painting. *This isn't possible. There is no way I was in Paris in 1912. I wasn't even born yet.* One part of her brain was afraid what the painting represented, but the other part of her felt comfortably drawn into the scene. This painting, this revelation in oil on canvas, had the power to lift her mood, and the happiness she gained by seeing him standing next to her was one of the purest emotions her life had ever granted her.

Lying on the floor and spread across her couch were sketches she'd made of the man. She'd been drawing him almost obsessively. On one scrap of paper was an outline of his brow, cheek, and chin. On the table lay a larger sketch of his broad shoulders, his neck, and his jaw. Next to this drawing were three or four more profiles; on the chair, a three-quarters view of his face; under the chair had fallen another page of his full face, handsome and smiling. Another drawing that had slipped down off the easel and floated under the table showed the mysterious man with another expression on his face. She had drawn him looking like an intolerable burden loomed over him. His eyes were sad, and if a drawing could speak, he might ask the future, *What is in store for me?*

In the light of the rising sun, Ruby saw a hint in the painting she hadn't seen before. She blinked her eyes in surprise. *One more thing to make my mind run wild.* It was nothing but a fine detail, easy to miss, but she saw it. It was a symbol, and in that symbol she thought of the life before her, the life of 1912 and this man. In both the photograph and the oil painting he and she wore golden wedding bands, symbols of committed love. That life in the past was far from the loneliness she felt in this lifetime.

She moved her legs and tried to stand up, but having sat there so long, her legs wouldn't cooperate. After some strong effort, she finally got to her feet, only to find that she was still unable to walk a straight line. She stumbled into the bathroom, ran a hot shower, and stepped in. It wasn't until she was out of the shower and drying herself that she looked in the mirror and noticed how she had been chewing on her bottom lip.

With a frown, she began to put herself together to meet the day. The undeniable compulsion to return to the park was upon her. She picked up the necklace, whistled for Yukon, and headed out the door.

The hint in the painting, the latest clue in this mystery was still in her mind as she set off for the park. *How strange life is*, she thought, *how strange that it offers happiness in such a strange fashion.* Reaching Lithia Park, she went straight to her bench, sat down, set her portfolio beside her, and laid the necklace around her neck. Then she sat back and waited for the ride.

Like silk curtains blowing in the wind, her mind began to flutter between then and now. She became more aware of the shifting of time as her inner mind let go of the here and now and embraced an unknown past. On one level, her conscious mind knew what was happening, for it was a rush that was too overwhelming to be considered a dream. At the same time, she admitted, it was something of a fantasy.

In her vision, the park was vibrating with energy, and at first it was hard for her to concentrate. But as the moments passed, her sight became clearer and the past came into focus. She heard a cry and turned to see the colossal white owl landing high in the tree across from her. For a moment, the owl stared at her as if it wanted to speak. The owl shifted and made itself comfortable on its perch. Then it lifted a wing as if waving to Ruby. Seeing this astonishing owl and realizing that she was in the past brought Ruby the odd sense that she was somehow returning to her place of origin.

Can this actually be?

Still in the past, Ruby picked up her charcoal and a clean sheet of paper and began to work. *Beautiful,* she said to herself. *It's beautiful.* Looking over at Yukon and watching him sniff the air, she knew that he, too, understood that they had traveled into the past. He was relaxed, and his playfulness reassured her that they were safe.

She gave him a low whistle, then started a fresh page, drawing lines and smudging them into images. The summer day warmed her and allowed her to sit comfortably, taking her time with her sketch. She hoped her mystery man would appear at the top of the hill again. This time, she had already decided, she would go to him, talk to him, touch him.

She inhaled deeply, waiting, anticipating his familiar fragrance. To her disappointment, she smelled only the fragrance of the flowers in the park. She looked around, but neither her mystery man nor John McLaren was there. *Oh, well,* she sighed, *at*

least the passers-by and the park itself are fulfilling.
Then, aloud, "Oh, I wish I could see you again! I want
to touch you, to speak to you, to understand who you
are... oh how I wish...."

Pushing her disappointment away and accepting
where she was and what she needed to do, she let
these desires go and centered herself. Her hand
continued working on the sketch, which would be one
more drawing in the series on Lithia Park. For how
long she had worked was anyone's guess, but she sat
working until she felt a tingle of cold touch her skin.

Winter?

As in a dream that gets invaded by a nightmare,
Ruby was painfully torn out of the past. It happened
so suddenly, she felt like she was being slammed
into by a moving vehicle. Everything was in motion.
Memories she didn't know she had were forced into
her mind at the speed of light, memories—and images
now—that sent a stream of emotions into her mind.
She closed her eyes and screamed, and everything
went black.

Then all was quiet.

She never knew how long she was unconscious,
but when she awoke, she felt a new tranquility settling
over her. She opened her eyes. She was alone in the
park, there was a sharp, cold breeze blowing over her.
Taking a moment to orient herself, she bundled up her
drawings and tucked them into her portfolio, wrapped

her scarf around her neck again, and whistled for Yukon. But he didn't come, and she couldn't see him. This was unlike him. He almost always stayed within sight. She whistled again. Again, no response. She began to panic.

"Yukon!" she cried aloud. Then she heard a faint noise under the bench she was sitting on. She bent down and looked. There he was, curled up beneath her in an attempt to stay warm. He raised his head looked at her as if to say, *Why are you yelling for me? I'm right here. Have been the whole time.*

She had to laugh. "Okay, come on, boy. Let's go home and get warm and get something to eat."

As they walked down the sidewalk, Ruby unhooked the mysterious necklace with her free hand, pulled it from around her neck, and dropped it in her pocket. She was trying to become accustomed to wearing it, but having it around her neck somehow made it difficult for her to walk normally because her eyes kept seeing things from another era. It required some effort on her part, in fact, to see what was around her here in the present. She tried to fight the disorienting sensation, which felt like motion sickness or dizziness, but it was no use. She couldn't wear the necklace and walk at the same time.

Besides that, she was shivering violently. How she wished she could afford a car. Oh, the freedom a car would give her. And it would have a heater in it!

As usual, Mrs. Bimby was peering out her window. Ruby and Yukon were halfway up the drive when Mrs. Bimby's back door opened.

"Ruby, is that you?"

"Yes, it is, Mrs. Bimby," she replied as cheerfully as she could.

"I'm an old woman. My eyesight ain't what it used to be."

Bull shit! Your eyesight is perfect, and you knew it was me coming up the drive. But okay, I'll play your game. Aloud, Ruby said, "You can't be too careful these days. But you're safe. It's only me."

"Yes, well... say, do you have my rent money yet?"

"Uh, no, not quite yet. But I did get twenty dollars for selling a sketch. Here, take it. I know I still you owe you for the entire rent. I promise I'll pay it soon." She handed over another twenty from the money Dutch had paid her. She was running out of money too fast and getting very worried about where she would ever come up with the rent.

"Twenty dollars," Mrs. Bimby grumbled. "Twenty dollars *here*, twenty dollars *there*. I don't recall your rental agreement stating that you can pay in increments long after the rent is due!"

"I'm truly sorry," Ruby said. "I'll get you the money."

Mrs. Bimby snatched the bill out of Ruby's hand. "I have an idea. Why don't you *get a job*? If you had a *job*, you wouldn't be in the same predicament every month." She turned, went in, and slammed the door behind her.

As she always did, Mrs. Bimby had just sucked up Ruby's good mood. Slumping in defeat, Ruby climbed the steps to her apartment. Each step seemed to take her deeper into depression as her feet felt heavier and heavier. Yukon was at the door long before she arrived and was pawing at it, an indication he was hungry.

Ruby inserted her key, turned the doorknob, and went in. Whenever she went shopping, she always made sure Yukon not only got food but got food that was good for him. He was more than a pet to her. He was her best friend, so she didn't skimp on his needs. Her care for him, however, left her with little money with which to feed herself. After scooping food into his dish, she opened a cabinet to see if it had anything she could eat tonight. It held minimal goods... a package of brown gravy mix, a can of stewed tomatoes, a partly-full bag of rice, and a quarter of a box of saltine crackers. With a sigh, she opened the stewed tomatoes put them in a pan and heated them. Then she added some saltines and ate her supper.

Even though it was tasteless and unsatisfying, she was thankful she had at least this much to eat. She was hungry tonight, and the unusual recipe filled her stomach.

After "dinner," she took off her dress and over-bust corset, then kicked off her shoes. After leaving Florida and the university, she had started wearing corsets and longer dresses. Her style wasn't contemporary; it was gothic, dark, antique. She found the old-fashioned clothing comfortable, especially the corset, which she felt was like body armor that would protect her from unwanted sexual advances. Also, considering how voluptuous she was, the corset seemed more functional. The corsets she had purchased when she had money were of high quality and worked well with her frame. And she never wasted her money on novelty corsets, the ones that were mainly for show and were very uncomfortable. She had discovered long ago that a good corset was more economical than a brassiere because corsets long outlasted bras.

Next, because she knew she wasn't going to have any visitors tonight, she pulled on one of her old cotton nightgowns. It was warm and comfy, and she often wore her nightgown to paint in at night when she couldn't sleep. She already had a feeling tonight would be a night of worry rather than a night of sleep.

The off-white flannel garment was marked with paint drips and splatters that made it ugly. Some spots were hard from dried paint, others were stains from wiping a brush after she cleaned it in paint thinner. No, this nightgown was certainly not something to receive guests in. She took comfort in her solitude and the freedom to wear whatever she liked. At least that's what she told herself.

Looking around the room, she wished, not for the first time, that she had television to take her mind off her meager existence. She'd had a TV once. A nice one left over from her divorce. But she'd had to sell it, along with many other possessions, to cover her August rent. For October's rent, she'd had to make the painful decision to sell the jewelry she'd inherited from her grandmother, the only person in her family who had ever seemed to love and support her. Even now, the thought of parting with her treasures almost made her cry.

She also hated herself for falling so far behind in her rent that she'd been forced to sell her grandmother's things. She was sure she had let her grandmother down. And now it was December, and she had nothing left to sell... other than her artwork. Which no one seemed to want.

Then she remembered: *Dutch said he thought my work on Lithia Park would sell. I'll go see him tomorrow and consign the two I have so far.* She didn't want to sell those drawings yet, as she really hoped to create the full series first, then sell the whole thing, perhaps to a collector. But she was used to doing things she didn't want to do. Being poor robbed her of the luxury of doing what she *liked* to do. She was surviving by doing things she *had* to do, like, she didn't want to eat stewed tomatoes out of a dented, discounted can for dinner. But what choice did she have?

Resentment surfaced again. She was keenly aware that other people had money and that they could afford things she couldn't. Like good food. A nice place to live. She especially resented those who were wasteful with their money. Day after day, she tasted bitter resentment when she encountered people who had more than she did and were conforming to the capitalistic ethic and being rewarded for said conformity.

Tomorrow I will conform, she often told herself. *Tomorrow I will go out and sell my soul to the devil so I can afford to live in this world and eat good food. I'll go find a job. I'll become normal and put all my artistic ways behind me.*

But she always choked on the thought, she always felt strangled by the unspoken words, and soon her feelings of fear and doubt began to rush toward anxiety. "But until tomorrow," she heard herself saying aloud, "until tomorrow, I'm an artist. Tonight, I will work at my craft."

First, she washed her dish and spoon and put them away. Then she pinned her sketch on her easel. Before she picked up the charcoal again, she put the necklace around her neck. And the past came into focus.

At the same time, the furnace came on. Although the heat seemed to relax her, the necklace was making her dizzy again. Within minutes, she found herself surrounded by the familiar scent of pine with a hint of frankincense, mastic, and the exotic spices she'd smelled before. She looked around at her apartment only to watch its walls seem to fade away. Her eyes went blurry, then there was darkness. She had the sensation of falling from a great height. It was oddly fascinating, she told herself, being in total darkness yet knowing she was falling down into the bottomless gulf of space, in absolute silence save for the strange hiss of her body rushing through the air. Then she landed gently and felt solid ground under her feet. Her sight gradually returned, and she found herself standing on a landing and looking up a flight of stairs at a tall door in an unknown house.

She heard someone calling her name. There was no doubt about it. This was the voice that had called out to her in the park. She was curious to the point of being mesmerized. She became more excited as all of her senses intensified.

Why?

"Yes, it's me," she said aloud as she climbed the stairs to the tall door, which was ajar. Her body was moving as if out of habit, climbing the stairs as though she had climbed those stairs a thousand times before. She did not hesitate when she reached the top. She opened the door and walked right in. She found herself standing in an elegant bedroom, facing a huge canopied bed and a fireplace with a warm fire burning in it. Then she saw the fur rug spread out on the floor in front of the hearth.

A hand reached out and fingers interlaced with hers. She looked down at her hand woven into a man's hand and saw the golden bands. Gently, cautiously she raised her head and turned. It was the man from the oil painting! The imaginary man she had sketched was standing right there! He had taken her hand!

The first thing she noticed about him was his eyes. His eyes would have been the first thing anyone noticed. The painting she had studied the night before had given her some slight hint of how astounding those eyes were, but actually seeing them, looking into those eyes was something no artist could capture. His eyes were breath-taking. The irises were hazel, yet, she had never seen the mixture of green, brown and amber hues in another human before. It was the depth and brilliance of his eyes that added to the man's magnetism.

She looked again. His smile was wide. Without a word, he led her out through the french doors to a balcony overlooking a courtyard. Light rain was falling, but in the west, the sky was clear. She could feel the cold of the drops as they touched her skin. In the courtyard below stood a beautiful orchard in full bloom. And there, up in the sky, streaking across the heavens from the east was a comet, its long tail shining behind it. Further away, she could see the shimmering lights of the Aurora Borealis. It was so beautiful, she gasped with pleasure.

"Halley has been with us for months," the man said. This was indeed his voice she had heard in the park. "And it keeps getting more spectacular."

"Halley's comet?" she asked.

"That's correct."

She looked around and took a deep breath, hoping to regain some kind of balance. Everything was so strange! She looked down at herself. Even her nightgown was dramatically different. Now it looked more like negligee that flowed with the curves of her body. It was made from a delicate, dark crimson silk.

She started to speak again, but he wrapped his arms around her and kissed her, a long passionate kiss. She inhaled his scent as his tongue touched hers. Being with him, having his arms around her offered her a feeling of security that she had never felt before in her life.

Who is this man?

He pulled away and looked into her eyes. "I have missed you so much," he said.

All she could do was blink her eyes. He was still there. "Do I know you?" she asked weakly, her voice hardly making a sound. "Where are we?" She was lost in the powerful undertow of his eyes. She had surrendered to his touch. It was a beautiful feeling to yield to his embrace.

He picked her up, and she wrapped her legs around his waist as he carried her back into the house and, still holding her, closed and latched the french doors. She wanted answers to her questions, but she was overcome by passion. He pressed his lips to hers again, kissing her more deeply this time. Her hands came up to the back of his head and she ran her fingers through his mahogany hair, then down the center of his back digging her nails in as she went. He groaned and started toward the bed, but their fervor became irresistible before he could lay her down. He leaned her against the wall beside the headboard. There were no words, and a part of Ruby was glad about that because she had no earthly idea what to say at such a moment. As he moved his lips down her neck, she grabbed the headboard. She was suddenly covered in goosebumps. She knew that a wildfire had been ignited in her and nothing could extinguish it. There was no turning back.

She felt the pillowy, old-fashioned mattress cradle her when he laid her down. Her nipples pushed against the silk of her nightgown. She pulled at the neck of the gown, and in that quick motion, her breasts were bare. He kissed the left one first, raising the nipple higher. Then he moved over the right breast.

His palm then came up and met her left breast and softly caressed it. He rolled over and took his place astride her. His hips began to grind against her. She released squeals of delight, then bit his earlobe.

She didn't know what was going on, but she didn't want to waste any time with questions. Whatever was happening, it felt right, it felt good, much too good to stop. She twisted her hips and felt him getting hard. She couldn't resist this man. She took his starched, collarless shirt in her hands and ripped it open. Buttons popped and bounced across the floor.

He gently turned her onto her knees and pressed against her while she braced her hands against the headboard. Reaching around her with both hands, he took hold of her breasts and lightly pinched her nipples. Her moan let him know instantly that she was accepting what he was doing. His hot breath was still on her neck as his hands dropped between her thighs, pulling up her silk gown until his fingers found their target. She felt a jolt of ecstasy when he touched her private place, his touch almost overwhelming. She was a loaded gun ready to go off. *Not yet,* she thought.

Letting go of the headboard, she pulled his head to her. She yearned for a kiss, another passionate kiss. *Where have you been all of my life?*

She pushed forcefully against him, and as he moved back, she knelt in front of him. His black trousers were formal and of high quality, but his belt buckle was old-fashioned, a style she didn't recognize. After a moment of fumbling at his waist, he reached for her, picking her up again and taking over to the thick, warm, fur rug before the fire. Gently he laid her down, then she watched him remove his clothes.

She looked up at his body. He was rugged in his nakedness, and the word that came into her mind was *lovely*. That soft word must be used, she thought, for *lovely* is pure and great. In her eyes, the man was loveliness incarnate. He seemed to radiate light.

He lay down next to her. Still wondering if he was real, she ran her hand across his face. *If Mother Nature ever created anything more attractive, she kept it to herself,* Ruby thought. She couldn't remember ever feeling more desire than she felt right now, right here with this man who was a stranger and yet not a stranger. She propped herself up on one elbow and leaned into him. Another passionate kiss. His lips felt familiar. Surely, she wasn't dreaming this sensual moment and every detail in it.

As she tasted the honey sweetness of his kiss, she was on fire with wanting him to go deeper and deeper into her soul. It was the inside of her that needed his touch. She had to let him reach in and touch her with the essence of a nourishing-force.

Where Ruby Birk came from, she had always been lonely. She had always felt that she'd lost all pleasure, lost everything she was fondest of... lived just this side of death. But now it was as if she were alive for the first time. But was she imagining all this?

In the past, others had touched the soft, sensitive places on her body. Other men, not many, but a few, had spent nights with her, other men had kissed her passionately. Her heart had bled with disappointment in these men as they took from her what they wanted and left her only soiled memories. But this man....

His hands were on the nape of her neck now, touching a hypersensitive spot. She was keenly aware of this particular sensitive place on her neck, but she had never told anyone about it. *How does he know exactly where to touch me?*

Her desire skyrocketed. She bit on her already sore bottom lip in anticipation of how far this fantasy might go. She felt the wetness between her thighs and groaned as she allowed herself to completely lose control. The sweet feeling of surrender was consuming her.

She looked up at him and wrapped her legs around his waist. "I want you inside me."

He gazed down at her, looking past her face and into profound places beyond the physical. "Ruby," he whispered, "I have missed you for so long. And to feel you with me now is extraordinary."

"Who are you?"

Without a word, he removed her nightdress and tossed it to the floor, then he glided into her. She soon forgot her question, dug her fingers into his back again, and almost immediately let out a long-suppressed wail. It was as if she had never been touched by anyone else. As he entered her, he erased her past... no professorial rapist, no ex-husband, no careless boyfriends, no moments of masturbation. There was only him. Only him.

But who is he? some part of her mind kept struggling to ask. *Who is he?*

Feeding her more of his manhood, he began thrusting in and out, increasing the rhythm. His face was contorted with rapture. Her arms were wrapped around him, holding him tight, and when she shifted her legs, he grabbed her ankles and pulled them higher. She pressed against him as he moved faster, thrusting harder and harder. She scratched his back and dug her nails into him so that he would bleed for her. The mixture of pain and pleasure seemed to drive him to greater heights of passion.

She, too, began to feel the pain of their fever. "Don't stop!" she cried, even though she was feeling tender. She wanted to live in this moment forever. He was making love to her in a way she had never thought possible. She plunged into a cascade of orgasms. One climax after another washed over her.

Her eyes wondered over him and came to a sudden halt when she noticed his eyes locking with hers as another orgasm rang through her. To her amazement this tall, erect man aroused her with pure delight, the kind of delight that is stronger than physical pleasure, the kind of delight that sweetens the soul with ecstasy. Captured in his gaze, she was living this moment with the depth of her soul, satisfied by the emotion of love.

Where is this deep sense of love coming from?

Wanting to taste him again, she pulled him into her so tightly he couldn't move his head. His hips were still in full rhythm as she began sucking wildly on his tongue. Nature compelled her to ride him toward another blissful explosion.

Are you in love? she asked herself. *Or are you being a slut? You don't know this man.*

Slut... Really?

She cast away the word and focused on his face, his movements, his organic smell. Yes, this was love, love from on high. His soul was making love to her soul. She rejected all obstacles and complications of this love.

More!

She wanted more. She also committed herself to give more. She wanted more of him. It was too good to end. She grabbed his buttocks, and then she braced herself against the floor. He powered on, faster, working toward something big.

"Yes, that's it!" She coaxed him on. "Harder. Holy shit, yes, oh baby, you've got me. GogogogoGO."

He groaned. Sweat was beading across his forehead. "Ruby!" he cried as they hit their final climax. He collapsed on her as they both struggled to catch their breath.

"I love you." She said it quietly first, then louder. "I love you. Oh. My. God. I love you—that was amazing!" She was panting so hard she could hardly speak. "I don't care if I'm dreaming or not. This was the most incredible—damn! No one has ever done me like this before... especially not a perfect stranger."

"I'm no stranger," he murmured, "and soon I'll come to take you home again."

"Take me home? What are you talking about?"

"Ruby, my love—"

"How do you know me?" A chill came over her. She had the sense that winter had arrived. Suddenly she was thinking of Lithia Park and the time from which she had traveled. Her logical mind commanded her to realize she didn't belong here. And the more her logical mind restrained her soul the more she felt hollow and lost.

He was still talking, but suddenly she couldn't hear him. She reached out to hold him, but he slipped through her arms and began to fade away.

"Don't go! Please don't go!"

She could see him reaching for her. His face was full of despair when she heard his last faint words.

"Ruby I love you...."

And he was gone. The whispering of his voice echoed around her, fading along with his scent.

"No! Don't go!" she screamed into the night. "Don't leave me!"

And in an instant she had the sensation of flight. She imagined herself as a butterfly soaring with the speed of rapture. The sky rushed past her with an unearthly shade of purple-blue as she rose into the air. The wind in her ear sounded like the whispering of angels. She leveled out and slowed down, eventually hovering, suspended, weightless in space. She was floating between up and down. She had lost all sense of balance, all sense of orientation—

—and then Ruby Birk was back to the freezing winter of Ashland, Oregon, back in the modern time, back in a world of weakness and misery. Her eyes scanned her apartment. She blinked several times to make sure she was in fact in her apartment. She felt a painful longing, the terrible ache of homesickness, a wistful longing for the essence of all that earth, all that nature, all that of love had to give.

What now?

She was changed in a way she couldn't describe. It was as if she had discovered a sacred truth and started on a journey home. This sacred truth seemed unknown to her five physical senses, but came instead from within, and how she knew this, she neither knew nor understood.

Who was that man?

Love? The love she felt was so strong and so comforting that she was grief-stricken to find herself alone and back in her apartment.

Love.

Love had teased her with happiness.

Love had abandoned her.

Love was cruel!

Chapter 7

*T*here are, as most women can attest, a number of stages in truly soulful weeping. Ruby passed through them all. First, she wept from the pain and heartbreak of her loss. Next, she wept from the isolation that loneliness brings, the desolation of being without a friend in the world. Then she wept the weeping that comes from the fall from heaven. Her long nightly hours drifted further and further from sleep as the pain her mind focused on became the pain of the unbearable ache of homesickness for a home and a man not of this reality. Her body throbbed. She wanted to be touched by the essence of all that art, all that nature, all that sacred places, all that her soul in the throes of love could offer. Anything but to feel her heart being drained out by the agony of longing. In the fullness of her womanhood, she lay on her bed weeping into her pillow, sad and afraid.

She tried to imagine the scent that always came with the unknown man, but all she could smell were the usual odors of her apartment, mainly paint and thinner. The magnitude of her ache made everything else irritating and trivial. It's false to think that suffering breeds self-pity. Very frequently, it breeds *something else*, and as Ruby searched for that *something else*, she cried herself into a state of exhaustion. It was this that brought her relief, and soon she was overcome by sleep.

The next morning, she awoke at daybreak in her own bed and wearing her ugly nightgown. She had no idea what had happened to her the night before. A fantasy? A dream? What she knew and was sure of was that she had made love with the man from the painting. She was certain of this because she was sore in all her sensitive places. But how had this love-making happened? Her mind was still fuzzy, and oh, how she wished she had awakened next to—if only she had a name for the man!

Her mind couldn't overcome the fact that none of the previous night's events could be real. It wasn't possible for him to be real. Perhaps Ruby could have admitted her heartbreak and sought out Zanique for help. But she didn't do that. She recalled the *something else*, and soon her frustration turned to thoughts of suicide, which now appeared to be not so much an act of a depressed mind as the finely tempered courage that prefers death to living in misery. The selfish desire for rest and departure held temptation, but the temptation could hardly be called self-centered, as she didn't want to harm anyone else. She only wanted to escape the pain. She was tempted to release her mortal life on the remote chance that she would save her true soul.

Stupid with weakness and an overwhelming feeling of inadequacy, she sat up in her bed. A passion of regret was consuming her, regret for all of her work that had only failed. The world had dashed her high hopes of artistic success. A love she assumed she would never have again, her love for a man who seemed to have been destroyed before she was even able to taste the joy of his existence had already vanished.

Ruby belonged to that order of people who are perpetually guilty of small awkward acts. She wasn't uncomfortable being social with people, but it seemed as if every move she made, every interaction she tried was awkward. And all that awkwardness stacked up inside her and became intense anxiety about life and the situations that life dumped on her. And now what was happening in her life was making her freak out with anxiety.

Yukon jumped up on the bed, wagging his tail and licking her face. "Good morning, big boy!" She hugged him. He lay down next to her and looked at her. "If it weren't for you," she said, "I'd wake up all by myself every morning. I'd hate to be that alone."

A soulful silence filled her little apartment. Yukon was able to bring her a calm moment during which she took inventory of her soul. She examined not her loneliness but her independence, her artistic aspirations, her Bohemian lifestyle and all that that antique term, sometimes called *la vie bohème*, stood for. She remembered her efforts to rise out of bitter poverty. As a Bohemian, she knew the fiery thoughts that held the creation of art to be above all other pursuits. Above almost anything else. She had chosen to reject the conventional lifestyle.

She also took inventory of the incomprehensible magical events that had come into her life. Much to her surprise, a cheerful thought bubbled up. And then—she couldn't hold it back—a smile came to her face, and then she let out a giggle at the crazy thought of it. She thought, *What if I had a blacklight and shined it over my bed... would my bedding look like a crime scene?*

She touched herself to make sure she wasn't imagining the pain. Her intimate areas were all swollen.

What the fuck? If it wasn't real, then why am I sore and swollen?

I dug my nails into his back, didn't I? She looked at her hand and saw the unmistakable bits of tissue and blood under her fingernails. Lying there with Yukon beside her, she fought against her logical mind and crashed against the world that told her this wasn't possible. She let go of logic and so-called consensual reality and fell into the enjoyment of the afterglow of lovemaking, even though she was still wondering about the man. He knew her... but how did he know her? Questions filled her head.

It took longer than she realized, but she was finally able to drag herself out of bed and slump off to the bathroom to get ready for the day. *I finally met someone I want to love me... and, poof!— he's a goddam ghost! Can a ghost make love? They must!* She stepped into the shower.

She had no ambition to meet the day. Her thoughts were now back at her unpaid bills and the lack of food in her apartment. She was hungry. As she brushed her teeth, she began trying desperately to fight off the depression that was creeping up on her again.

Last night, before Mr. Wonderful showed up, she said to herself, *I made a commitment to myself. Yes, I'll consign two of my charcoal drawings of the park. Then I suppose I'll ask Dutch if he knows anyone that might be hiring.*

The thought of doing something so much against her will made her want to throw up. Her soul was screaming at her not to go to work in an ordinary job. She could feel it kicking around inside her. *I don't blame it. Resigning from being an artist goes against everything I believe.*

She was so exhausted, it was as if she hadn't slept at all, but she forced herself to dress for the day and get to the door. She whistled to Yukon. "Let's go for a walk, boy."

Wagging his tail, he jumped to his feet instantly and bounced around in front of the door, making it difficult for her to open it.

Her mind was on the man from the painting. And now she began thinking about Lithia Park, too. *Why not go there first, before I do anything drastic?* she asked herself. Yukon ran down the stairs and was sniffing around the bushes beside the driveway when she remembered the necklace. "Yukon," she called, "wait there. I need to go back in for the necklace."

Her necklace was still lying on the table. She picked it up, then picked up the oil painting to take a closer look at the man she had made love with the night before. Whatever had happened last night, it left her confused, but also feeling loved.

Again she had to ask. *Love?*

Feeling mystified and still a bit giddy, she headed out into the cold air. She didn't care about the cold, as her long wool coat kept her quite warm. And now she wasn't particularly concerned about the weather, her depression, or even her financial situation. She only wanted to get back to Lithia Park. She wanted to fall through time again, see the past, and hopefully touch him one more time.

Him!

Who was this man?

She trembled at a sudden memory of looking into his eyes. She felt herself getting weak in the knees... and a curious sensation overcame her. She knew she had looked into the eyes of someone whose persona was so intriguing that it had once consumed her almost completely. She thought she recognized his soul in his eyes, his soul touching and loving her soul. She had always been an independent woman who was in charge of her life. But now....

It was, she realized, as if her body's trembling was its hope of shedding an odd feeling that fate was... she didn't know what fate was doing. But this man was now certainly indispensable to her. A happy necessity.

A male muse, perhaps? She felt alive now. Thoughts of this man were replacing thoughts of suicide. Art was coursing through her veins. Beyond her feelings for him, she also felt a strong need to create, to draw a new panel for her series.

In a less happy part of her mind, however, two thoughts of great concern were rising. First, when might she see him again? It wasn't like she could just call him or stop by his house whenever she wanted to see him. After all, he was a *ghost.* Second, she knew she had to accept commercial defeat and commit to finding a job. Dutch came into her mind then. *He might be able to sell my work.* She hoped so. She thought of Dutch with warm regard and fond affection. Her mind was laced with confusion as she considered his gallery. Yes, she assured herself, she could imagine her artwork being displayed there. She trusted Dutch and believed he would work hard to get her the most money for her work.

Money.

During the past several years, Ruby's mind had been filled with thoughts of how poor she was. If she lived in India, she kept telling herself, her poverty would be absolute. *The poor in India have no food or money. But I live in the United States. People can't see me suffering.* No, she wasn't without the means to survive, even though she did lack many necessities. What she really lacked was security. Her life was filled with uncertainties, like, how was she going to pay her rent? Her utility bills?

Not today, she told herself. *I will not let destitution bring me down today!*

With her portfolio under her arm and Yukon walking by her side, she carefully made her way around the side of Mrs. Bimby's house and to the street. She was surprised to see Zanique standing beside her Hummer at the curb.

"Girlfriend," Zanique called out as she opened the rear cargo door, "you need to get a mobile phone so I can get ahold of you. C'mon! Let's get some breakfast."

"No, not today," Ruby began, "I think I'm going to—"

"Come on, Yukon. Let's go."

As he barked and jumped up into the vehicle, Zanique laughed out loud. "The decision has been made," she said triumphantly. "You can't say no now. Your best friend is in and ready to go." She closed the cargo door, then climbed back into the driver's seat and fired up the Hummer. "I might just steal him from you one day. He seems to like me and my truck."

"Everything that is male likes you, Zanique. I guess I have no choice. Thanks a lot, Yukon." Ruby climbed up into the passenger seat and looked around. Neatly organized winter gear, like snowshoes, ice axes, ropes, and backpacks filled the car. "Where to this time?" she asked.

"I thought we'd try a different place," Zanique said. "Zee's Historic Inn. It's a bed and breakfast in Jacksonville."

"A person can't just walk into a B&B and order breakfast," Ruby said. "Breakfast is only for the guests... right?"

"Uh, this place will serve us anything we want. Whenever we want. Well, within reason. Trust me."

Ruby thought about this for a minute, then smiled. "Zee's? Don't tell me... you own it."

"Yep."

She pushed down her jealousy of Zanique's wealth. "I see you have your gear in back. Have you been out snowshoeing?"

"I guided some people on a moonlit trek through Lassen National Park last night. Have you ever been there?"

"Only in the summer. And I only drove through."

"Well, then, I've got to take you up snowshoeing under the full moon. Well, it doesn't have to be a full moon. With all the snow on the ground, a little bit of light goes a long way up there. It's a volcanic park full of hydrothermal areas. You know—mud pots and hot springs. But under the glow of the moon, yeah, it's exceptionally cool, in both senses of the word. I take care of everything. All you have to do is come along. As you can see, I have all the gear, too. You won't need a thing."

Ruby had to laugh "Take a good look at this hot mess of a person sitting here," she said. "Is there anything about me that screams 'I'm an outdoors person'? Anything at all? No," she said. "I'm not tough like you."

"Me? Tough? Nah. I just love nature and love to be surrounded by it all the time."

With that, Zanique drove to Jacksonville, a quaint town that sat among the magnificent madrones and pine trees that covered the foothills of the Siskiyou Mountains in southwestern Oregon's Rogue Valley.

The town had been founded and grown during the Gold Rush and in the 1850s had been Oregon's biggest city. Now it was a well-preserved historical town. Zee's B&B was an elegant Victorian bungalow built in 1858 that had been the mayor's mansion, a municipal building, and then a museum before she'd purchased it. Looking at the period building, Ruby was awestruck. It was exquisite.

When Zanique parked and let Yukon out, he ran around the yard, sniffing everything. "Come on, boy," she coaxed him. "This way." She turned to Ruby. "There's a fenced backyard. He can hang out there. He'll be fine while we eat."

Still feeling distracted and a bit sore from last night's sex, Ruby grinned and nodded. Even though she felt dreamy, she was able to look around at the beautifully groomed grounds. Whoever the man in the painting was, she knew she was in love with him and that knowledge made her smile.

They entered through the oversized back door. With ceilings eleven feet high, every door was tall. Ruby was stunned to see that the house was furnished and decorated for Christmas with period-correct items. It reminded her of the house with the balcony where she had made love last night. She took a deep breath and sighed again at the thought of him.

"This place must have cost you a fortune," she said to Zanique as they went into the sitting room.

She was trying valiantly to let the historic atmosphere divert her from constantly thinking about the man.

"It wasn't cheap," Zanique agreed. "But when I saw it, I just had to buy it. We opened for business seven years ago. Of course, when I bought it nine years ago, it was in desperate need of restoration."

"You restored this building? All the work?"

"Well, not me personally. I hired the work done. It took almost two years to complete, but the fun... the fun... that was in shopping for the furniture and all the ornamental things." She pointed at a lamp. "Like this antique oil lamp. I had it converted." She turned it on. "See? Power-efficient LED lights. Functional as well as period-correct."

Zanique gestured for Ruby to follow her through the building to the dining room, where she selected a table, pulled out a chair for Ruby, then took a seat herself. "It was like building the greatest dollhouse ever," she said, "and since I didn't get to build a dollhouse when I was a kid, you're damn right I was gonna do it now. I'm in my second childhood!"

Ruby was amazed. "How do you afford all of this? I mean... you just bought this place outright, then paid for the renovation? Surely being an adventure guide doesn't pay that well?"

Zanique looked away, "Money seems to find its way to me," she said in a vague tone.

Ruby ignored this. If only she were wealthy... "Where is everyone?" she asked. "I mean, the guests?"

"I'm not sure," Zanique said. "Breakfast is from 6:30 to 9:00. I called up and told them you, and I would be here around 9:30, so I'm guessing that everyone's out and about by now. Odessa will be here shortly to take our order. Jimmy's Eggs Benedict are off the hook!"

Sure enough, within a few minutes, Odessa, the morning hostess, came in. She hugged Zanique as soon as she saw her. "Zee, it's been ages since you've come by for breakfast. Where've you been keeping yourself?"

"You know me. Always running here and there. Always busy."

"Well, you shouldn't leave us unattended for too long. Who knows what we're capable of?"

Zanique smiled. "I'm sure you and Jimmy manage just fine without me hovering over you."

Odessa shook her head. "You really should come and stay over one night. Enjoy the house you brought to life. I'll bet you haven't stayed overnight in three or four years."

"That sounds about right." Zanique directed her attention to Ruby. "Odessa, this is my friend, Ruby Birk. She lives in Ashland, too."

Odessa shook her hand. "It's a pleasure to meet you, Ruby." Suddenly she remembered why she was there. "Oh! I'm being rude. I'll bet you're both starving. What would you like Jimmy to fix for you?"

Ruby had a ready answer. "Could I have a veggie omelet and some fruit?"

"Sure. No problem."

Zanique laughed. "You, always with your veggie omelet." She looked up at Odessa. "You know me. Eggs Benedict, hash browns, and some fruit sound good."

"What? No hotcakes?"

"Maybe one... no—two. Ruby needs a taste, too."

"Sure, I'll share." Ruby gave Odessa a smile. Odessa returned the smile, then left the dining room. Silence fell as Ruby looked past the doorway that led to the sitting room where an old-fashioned Christmas tree stood. "This house smells amazing," she finally said, pointing to a bowl piled high with oranges with cloves inserted into them.

"Odessa puts these around the house every year," Zanique explained. "They're called pomanders. I'm told that pomanders have been used as decorations since antiquity. I told Odessa she can do whatever she likes to the place, but the decorating should remain appropriate to the period of the house."

"She's done a great job. I mean, look at this place... everything just flows together."

"Thank you. I'm quite proud of this old house."

"As you should be." Ruby stood up, took off her coat, and hung it on the antique coat stand. Then she reached into the pocket. "You like old things?"

"Oh, very much."

"Will you take a look at this? Do you think it's an antique?"

Zanique took the necklace from Ruby and held it up. "Where'd you buy this? An antique store?"

"No. I didn't buy it. I found it hidden in the frame of an old painting." She watched Zanique examine the symbol that hung from the chain. "What is that?"

"It's an Egyptian symbol. Here, look." Zanique used her smartphone to find an image. "It's called an ankh... It's also called *the Breath of Life.*" She clicked on the first Google hit and read for a moment. "I don't want to torture you with all the details, but, basically, the ankh holds the secrets of life. With the magical ankh, you can unlock secrets to living and life. I'm guessing the ankh is a talisman, and wearing it brings you closer to the gods. According to the Internet, when you wear this, it signifies that you are a blessed child of Amun Ra."

Ruby looked at her friend. "Really? This plain-looking looped cross means all that?"

"Yes. And it's lovely!" Zanique laid the necklace on the table. "I like it, I mean, wow—look at the detail. The ankh and every link in the chain have hieroglyphs engraved on them. They're tiny, but they're there."

"I hadn't noticed," Ruby confessed.

"Oh, they're there, all right, and they're so sharp and crisp it looks to me like they were cut by a laser. Go on. Look closer."

As soon as Ruby began examining the links to see the tiny symbols, she began to feel strange again. She hadn't paid any attention the tiny details engraved in the chain before, but, sure enough, now she saw there were glyphs on the ankh and on each link, and every one was perfectly incised. All she could say was, "This is odd."

"I think your necklace must be very old," Zanique said. "And probably worth quite a bit of money."

"You do?" Remembering how earlier this morning she had been so concerned about her finances, she smiled at her potential good fortune.

"What is it?" Zanique asked.

"I have to be honest, even though I'm ashamed to tell you. I'm broke. I don't have any money to pay my rent this month. Or next month, for that matter. If I sold this, though, maybe I'd be able to take care of myself for a change." She bit at a ragged fingernail.

"Hey, you're getting all worked up. Don't do it. I can understand the stress of being poor. I was poor myself for a long time. There is nothing more frustrating in the world than a lack of money. Okay, relax, Ruby girl. I'll help you." Zanique thought for a minute. "I know dis guy," she said in her best movie Mafioso accent. Then she gave her friend a broad wink and picked up the newspaper page the necklace had been wrapped in.

Strange little compartment in a picture frame, Ruby thought as she smiled at Zanique.

Zanique looked up. "Hey—look at the date of this newspaper... it's dated 1910! And look at the condition. It's like... like it was just printed. This is crazy, you finding this necklace wrapped in this old newspaper." She spread the little page out in front of her and read aloud,

EARTH GOES UNHARMED THROUGH HALLEY'S TAIL

Astronomers hardly dare speculate what may be seen of Halley's Comet tomorrow evening when the full moon, which has so far obscured the comet's tail and luminous glow, has waned. If skies remain clear, viewers will be treated to a once-in-a-lifetime experience: the comet, brilliant meteors, and other celestial pyrotechnics such as the Aurora Borealis, which has accompanied the comet for the last two nights.

Ruby was frozen. The newspaper perfectly described her night spent with her mystery lover. She had seen the comet and the Aurora Borealis from his balcony. She felt a chill shoot up her spine.

Zanique set the newspaper back on the table. "Okay," she said, changing the subject, "now tell me about this painting of yours... the one with the hidden compartment in the frame."

"I don't know anything about it."

"You don't know? Are you kidding me? Is the painting some kind of secret?"

Just at that moment, Odessa appeared with their breakfast. "Here you go," she said as she set the plates of food on the table. "Jimmy put some special effort into fixing this. I hope you'll enjoy it."

Zanique smiled at her employee. "I'm sure we will, Odessa. Thank you."

"Yes, thank you," Ruby added.

Odessa politely excused herself and left them alone again. Zanique took a mouthful of pancake and tried to speak, but found it too difficult. She chewed, swallowed, and then said, "Tell me about the painting."

"Well, if you think all this is strange so far," Ruby said, "the painting is all the more bizarre."

"Are you kidding me? What? What's so strange about the painting?"

"My ex-husband, Turner... he bought the painting at an estate sale in Ashland. He's an art dealer, you see. He bought it and gave it to me because...."

"Go on... go on! Stop being so mysterious. Tell me!"

"Well, like I was saying, he bought the painting at an estate sale, and then he took it down to San

Francisco to have it authenticated. It was painted in the early twentieth century. In fact, the date's in the corner. It's dated 1912."

Zanique was almost beside herself. "And??"

"Well, the odd thing is... *I'm* the subject of the oil painting! It's like a self-portrait, and I signed it just like I do all of my work. As clear as day, there's my signature with the year, 1912. Right on the painting! I'm in Paris. Standing at the foot of the Arc de Triomphe." She blinked. "But I've never been to Paris. And I don't paint portraits!"

Zanique's mouth dropped open.

Ruby wasn't finished. "Oh, and to top it all off, there's an envelope taped to the back of the painting, and in that envelope is an old photograph of *me*. Of *me!* Apparently, I used the photo as a reference to paint the picture. But it's me in the photograph in Paris, and everyone in the background is dressed in early twentieth-century clothing."

"Unbelievable!"

"Yes. Unbelievable. Baffling!"

"No, I literally mean I don't believe you. I have to see the painting and the photograph. I mean, this is real *Twilight Zone*-type stuff." Zanique took another bite of her breakfast. "I don't know what to do next. Get the necklace appraised? Or go see your magical painting, complete with a photo and a hidden compartment?"

Ruby chewed for a minute, then said, "I'd like to get the necklace appraised and find out exactly how much it's worth." She held back telling her friend about the man in the painting and his making love to her. She thought that would be too complicated. Besides, that part was too personal. She still hadn't decided if he was just a fantasy or somehow... real.

Zanique began thumbing through her contacts on her smartphone. "Just let me put a call out and see if my guy is around," she said as she put the phone to her ear and waited for an answer. "Yes, Ezra? It's me. Zee. Say, I have a friend here that's stumbled onto an old necklace, and we want to find out more about it. I'm curious if you might know more about it, like, say, how much it might be worth. Lemme take some pictures of it." She motioned for Ruby to lay it out on the table, then snapped pictures of the ankh from several angles, then the chain, with close-ups of the hieroglyphs. "I'm sending photos to you now," she told Ezra. Then she disconnected and set the phone down.

There was a long pause. Zanique pushed her plate back as if to say she couldn't eat any more. Ruby stared at her. After a few minutes, Odessa came in and cleared away the dishes. "Is there anything else I can bring you?"

"No, thank you," Ruby said. "My breakfast was delicious. Please thank Jimmy for me."

"Oh, Jimmy'll be out in a few minutes. He has to finish cleaning up, but then he'll come and say hello."

"I can't wait to see Jimmy!" Zanique said enthusiastically. She was impatiently tapping her phone with her finger.

Several minutes later, the phone rang. It was Ezra.

"Did you get them yet?" she asked him. "I sent quite a few, so it may take a while.... Okay, I'll wait." She disconnected again and looked at Ruby and gave her a funny expression with crossed eyes and an odd sigh. After ten long minutes, her phone rang again. She listened for a minute, then said, "You called an expert and... yes, I see." She gave a quick look of concern at Ruby. "Are you sure... are you absolutely sure? Okay. You spoke to the expert; I'll take your word for it." Another pause. "But what should we do now?" After Ezra replied, she said, "Sure. We can bring it to you. When would be a good time? You'll be in town on Thursday?" She rolled her eyes. "Okay, thanks Ezra, we'll come to your house." She clicked off again.

"So," Ruby said, "what was that all about?"

"Well, according to Ezra, this isn't exactly a necklace."

"What? Then what is it?"

"He said he called an expert and sent him the pics, and the expert thinks this might be fake. The problem is, you have an ancient Egyptian ankh, an amulet with very old script incised in it. Ezra said that from what little his expert had read, it stated that this ankh comes from the land of the gods and is a vessel for forbidden knowledge... it's possible the language inscribed here predates the known ancient Egyptian language. He said if it's really authentic, then it's something very rare. An amulet."

"Amulet?"

"Yes, an amulet. You know, a talisman. According to Ezra, it's a magical object."

Ruby gave this new information some thought. "But can we sell it? Now that we know what it is?"

"No, not now. This item will take some time to find the right buyer."

"Great, just great. I need money *now*." She slammed her hand on the table. "I was hoping I could sell it *now*. So I can pay my rent. And buy some food." She could feel the uncomfortable, yet familiar, panic of poverty rising inside her. "I just need a break. You know?" She looked at Zanique. "I need to sell this now. I don't—well, I refuse to become a homeless person. I won't live on the streets. I won't—"

"Calm down, Ruby, it's okay. It'll be okay!"

"How do you know that? No! Evidently, my life's journey is destined to be a penniless one. I suppose I'm fated to suffer loneliness and a lack of money. I can't even afford to buy tampons. Do you know how shitty a person feels when they can't even afford to take care of their basic personal hygiene?"

Zanique nodded. "Yeah, I totally get it. I've been there. But listen! I'm going to help you fix this. Look, I know you won't take charity. So how about this? I love the necklace." She got out her checkbook. "I'm going to cut you a check for it, but I want you to hold on to it until we find out exactly what it is and how much it's worth. When you, and only you, have decided what you want to do with it, then you can either pay me back or give me the necklace. This check is just a deposit to help you out until you decide what to do." She signed the check and held it across the table. "Girlfriend, will you accept this?"

Ruby's hand shook as she reached for the check. Then her eyes went wide. "Ten thousand dollars?"

Zanique shrugged. "I'm sure it's worth more... much more! This money will hold you over until we can find a buyer. If we don't find a buyer soon, then I'll buy it from you at whatever the price might be after we have it appraised.

"I've never held a check written out to me for anything close to this amount." Ruby turned away to hide her tears. "But this check will do me no good."

"Why?"

"Once again, I'm too embarrassed to tell you, but, well... I don't even have a bank account anymore."

Zanique smiled. "Okey-dokey. First thing we do is go to a bank of your choosing and open an account so you can have access to these funds."

"Thank you. This will go an awful long way in paying my bills."

"I'm glad to do it."

"When do we go see your *guy*, uh, Ezra?"

"Ezra's out of the area right now, but he'll fly in just to see this necklace on Thursday. He has a house in Bandon. That's about a three-hour drive from here. We'll go together, and then we'll figure this whole thing out for you. Relax, girl! Everything's gonna be all right."

At this point, Jimmy the cook strolled into the dining room. "Hey, how was breakfast?" he called out. Zanique jumped up and ran to him, and he wrapped her in his meaty arms. Ruby was still wiping away her tears as Zanique got lost in the embrace of the oversized chef.

"Zee," he said, "it's so good to see you again. Why don't you come around anymore? Odessa and I sure miss having you visit."

"I know I should come more often. I miss the two of you, too. You're my family. Hey, I'll be here for the Christmas party, though. How's that sound?"

"You'd better be here," he said. "Odessa will never forgive you if you're not." He released Zanique and approached Ruby. "I'm Jimmy. It's nice to meet you."

"I'm Ruby, and it's very nice to meet you. And Odessa, too."

"Are you coming to the Christmas party?"

Ruby looked at Zanique, who was nodding wildly. "I suppose I am. But I don't even know when it is."

"Next Friday. Come early. We always have a grand ol' time. Zee here puts one on every year, but the poor girl is so busy, she doesn't always get to attend." He looked at his employer and smiled a wide smile, then gave out a big bellow of a laugh. "I'm glad you're going to be here this year. Oh, boy! It's gonna be a real bash." He shouted back toward the kitchen, "Did you hear that, Odessa? Zee's gonna be here for the Christmas party."

Odessa came into the room. "Stop yelling," she said. "You don't know if any of the guests are still in their rooms." She turned to Zanique. "Is it true you'll be here?"

As Zanique blushed and nodded, Ruby could suddenly see that Odessa and Jimmy were the closest things to parents her friend had. And she was absorbing the affection they were giving her.

Odessa steepled her hands under chin. "I'm so happy! And please stay the night. I always feel like it's safer if you leave in the morning rather than driving home in the dark... after all those celebratory drinks."

"You're right about that! Ruby and I will plan on spending the night."

"Umm, I'm not sure I can stay the night."

Zanique shook her head. "It'll be fine. Don't worry about it. I'm driving, and you're spending the night."

Odessa went over to the computer at the reception desk. "Should I reserve one room or two?" She looked at the screen again. "Wait, we have guests in all the rooms except the Bartlett Pear room." She looked at Zanique as if for permission, "Hmmm, I'm still waiting for the deposit of the Anjou room. I can hold that one for you, too. Will that do?"

"We can share a room." Zanique turned to Ruby. "The Bartlett Room is our deluxe room. It has a private bathroom. You'll love it."

"We're going to share a room?" Ruby whispered.

"It'll be fine," she replied. "We can move the daybed in... unless you're uncomfortable with that?"

"I don't know." She felt awkward. So much was happening.

"No worries," said Odessa. "I'll hold the Anjou Room for you. If that's okay with Zee."

"Odessa, I don't think the loss of one room for one night would put us into financial ruin. If no one takes the Anjou Room, reserve it for Ruby. Thanks."

And with that, Zanique and Ruby said their goodbyes and went in search of Yukon, who was happily lying in the snow chewing on a meaty bone Jimmy had given him.

Ruby loaded Yukon in the back of the Hummer, then climbed up into the passenger seat again.

"Life is always interesting when I'm with you," Zanique said. "That necklace of yours seems to be very special. I'm betting you'll get a mint for it."

"I suppose it's special," Ruby agreed. "But maybe that's just because it's so old."

"Ezra said it was special because of the magical words incised on it. He said the expert told him the words were a magical prayer to Isis, the *Mother of All Things*."

Ruby was speechless. *What the hell? What the hell is happening to me?*

Chapter 8

$\mathcal{I}$t was now Wednesday, and Ruby was a bit flustered. While she didn't want to be the third wheel on a date with Zanique and Blake, the waiter from the diner, she had promised Zanique she would go because it was their first date. Still, she was trying to think of an excuse, any excuse, to get out of going. Lying to Zanique with some made-up reason wouldn't do. After all, her friend had just bailed her out—big time—of a very bad situation. She thought for a minute, wondering what to do to make the date more comfortable for all three of them. Then she had an idea.

It had stopped snowing by the time she reached the Kaleidoscope Gallery. Melted snow sluiced off her wool coat when she and Yukon came through the door.

Hearing the bell on the door, Nora looked up. "Ruby! What a nice surprise." She came around the counter. "Yukon, I'll bet I have a treat for you in my desk drawer." As elegant as Nora was, she wasn't afraid to get down on the floor with Yukon and gave him a big hug and a kiss.

Ruby sat on the tall stool, smiling and watching Nora play with her dog.

"He really loves you," she said.

"Oh, he's a special dog!" Nora stood up and came back to Ruby. "Where's your portfolio?"

"Umm, it's... it's not that kind of a visit this time." She felt embarrassed. "Is Dutch around?"

"He sure is. He's in his office. You can go on back there if you like." Nora pointed at the door. "Yukon and I will be just fine out here."

"Thanks. I'll only be a moment." Ruby stood up and braced herself, trying to settle the butterflies that were rioting in her stomach. She paused outside Dutch's door.

"You don't need to knock," Nora told her. "Just go on in."

The door squeaked as it opened. Dutch was sitting at his desk. He looked up. "Ruby?"

"Hey, Dutch."

"Well, come on in! Here, have a seat." He jumped up and began picking up a stack of papers, sketches, and paintings on the only other chair in the room. "Here." He pointed at the chair and laid the stack on the floor next to his desk.

"You don't have to make a fuss," Ruby protested. "I'm fine." But seeing the chair was now cleared off, she sat down.

Dutch returned to his chair behind the desk. "So, what can I do you for?"

"Well, umm," her voice quivered as she spoke, "well... my friend Zanique is going on a date tonight. And, uh, she just met this guy and she doesn't feel exactly comfortable, and, uh... and...."

Dutch was trying to understand what she was getting at. "And?"

"And, uh... well, I recently got paid some money and thought, if you weren't doing anything tonight, maybe...."

Dutch smiled. Then he chuckled out loud. "Ruby, I'm not sure what you're trying to tell me. Your friend is going on a date, you have some money, and you're asking me if I'm not doing anything... I can assume a lot of things here, you know." He smiled again. "Can you be more specific?"

Ruby looked down at the floor. She had never asked a man on a date before. It was harder than she thought. She fought an urge to get up and run away. "Okay," she finally said, still not looking at him. "Okay, I was wondering if you would join me—*us*—tonight for dinner. It'll be with my friend Zanique and her date, Blake. It's a double date. I'm buying... it's on me... *if* you want to go?"

By now Dutch's face was red. He blinked and tried to find his tongue. "You're asking me on a date? Wow! What a surprise!"

"So, umm, if you don't want to... well, I understand."

"Are you kidding me? I'd love to! What time do I pick you up? Where do I pick you up?"

Ruby finally looked up. But she couldn't look directly at him yet, so she fixed her gaze on the calendar on the wall behind him. It was too late to take back her invitation, but now the reality of having him pick her up just seemed so... so uncomfortable. Her heart was pounding so hard she thought it was going to jump out of her chest. The sound of his raspy voice was sending chills down her spine. "Uh," she swallowed hard, "you don't need to pick me up." She was still looking at the calendar behind him. "How about if you just meet me— *us*—at the restaurant?"

A look of disappointment came over his face. "Hey, call me old school, but it's not much of date if I don't pick you up and drop you back home. It's the *gentlemanly* thing to do." He paused and studied her face. Which of them was more uncomfortable now? He couldn't guess. "But if it makes you more comfortable to meet there, well, yeah. Okay. What restaurant are we going to?"

Now that the date was set, she relaxed and exhaled, then looked at him for the first time since she had walked into his office. She didn't have a car and could ride with Zanique, even though riding with Dutch seemed like the better option. "Callahan's Mountain Lodge," she said. "I suppose you're right, though. How about I come back here to the gallery and we can go together in your car?"

Dutch looked around the office, anywhere but into her eyes, and caught himself smiling again. She had a way of making him smile. "That'd be just fine," he said. "However, if you come by here, I'd prefer to go home and change my clothes. Would you be uncomfortable sitting in my living room while I get ready?"

"No, that'll be fine." As her mouth continued talking, she wondered what she was getting herself into. "Reservations are for seven, so I'll be here at six... will that give you enough time?"

"That'll be plenty."

With another sigh, she stood up and walked toward the door. This had to be, she was telling herself, one of the worst ideas she had ever had. She was sure he had stayed behind his desk the whole time because he'd been using it as a shield. She thought one reason she loved dogs was because Yukon always wagged his tail when he saw her. She didn't have to guess if he liked her or not. But she couldn't even imagine what Dutch was thinking about her at this moment.

As if reading her mind, Dutch came around his desk and tapped her on the shoulder. She stopped and turned as he said, "You really surprised me. I never imagined you'd ask me out on a date. I feel honored! And I'm excited."

She smiled at him, then slipped through the door and back into the gallery, back to Yukon who was lying at Nora's feet, his tail thumping the floor. Dutch's gaze followed her.

Not a great way to accept her invitation, he thought. He wouldn't blame her if she had second thoughts about their first date. He shook his head. He couldn't have been colder toward her. Without a word, he watched her call Yukon and say something to Nora. And then she left. But the smile was still spread across his face. Damned if she wasn't adorable, just coming into his office like that to ask him out. For a shy woman, he thought, she was really brave.

...

It was six o'clock on the dot when he heard the bell above the door ring. He stepped around the counter as Ruby came in. She was wearing her long woolen coat, but her cherry-chocolate hair was pulled back and tied in a French braid and on her feet were black boots that disappeared under the fringe of her long, burgundy dress.

"I'm glad you came," Dutch said. "After all… earlier, uh, well, I wasn't the smoothest in accepting your invite."

Ruby giggled. She wasn't the kind of person that giggled, but it rippled out of her. "I wasn't put off," she said. "Besides, I really wanted to spend some time with you, and a date seemed like the appropriate way to get to know more about you."

He picked up his coat and opened the door for her. "I'm parked this way." He pointed up Main Street. "Uh, at least I think I am. I have to move my car every two hours due to the parking limit, so I get confused every day at quitting time as to the whereabouts of my car."

He laughed. "There are no designated parking places for business owners. That's the one thing I really dislike about this city—the police department. We essentially have no crime here, so they make up for it by giving parking tickets. I think the Ashland PD writes more parking tickets than any other town in the U.S."

She smiled. "If I didn't live here, I'd say you were exaggerating. But it's true." She nervously pulled at the frayed seam on her coat as they walked toward his car.

"Where's Yukon?"

"Oh, I left him home this time. We're always together, but tonight I thought it might be better if he stayed home rather than waiting in Zanique's car out in the cold."

He nodded as he found his car. "Ahhh, here we are. It's not fancy, but it's very utilitarian." He unlocked the passenger door of his white 1979 Land Rover Defender and opened it for her.

"This looks like something a person rides in on a safari."

He nodded. "I'm sure you've seen these on wildlife TV shows. They're great off-road. They're hard to get here in the States, though. Not many of these around here." He was proud of his Defender, but he could tell right off that she had no interest in cars or trucks, so he dropped the subject. He drove them to his house on Park Street.

"You live here... alone?" she asked.

"Yes, I live here... and, yes, alone."

"This place is big for one person."

As they walked up to his front door, the snow above the doorway that had melted earlier in the day suddenly broke free from the metal roofing and came sliding down. It landed squarely on Dutch's head and shoulders, knocking him to the ground.

"Dutch!" Ruby bent down and brushed the snow from his face. "Are you all right?"

"He looked up at her. "Well, except that I look ridiculous, I'm fine. And you're probably rethinking this whole date thing by now since you're alone with a clumsy fool."

Ruby giggled again and helped him up. "We're off to a good start, eh?"

"This is awkward." He shook his head, shaking off the snow like a dog shakes water off its back. "Well, at least that happened on the way in and not on the way out." He unlocked the front door, took off his wet coat, and they went in.

"You're not clumsy," she said. "It wasn't your fault. You couldn't have known that was going to happen. Not that much snow."

"But it did happen... Crap!"

As Ruby caught a glimpse of his chest through his wet shirt, an eager look came over her face. It wasn't just his wet shirt that was arousing her. It was the way he looked, so tough, his muscular physique, his facial scars glistening from the snow. And yet, at the same time, he seemed exposed. Vulnerable, like she had felt the first time he'd looked at her artwork. Passing through the door, they came together, and the nearness of him had a serious effect on her. A warm sense of desire rolled through her. She had to take a step backward to open up a bit of space between them. This was their first date, she reminded herself, but she found herself wanting him.

He seemed not to have noticed. "I'll be quick," he said. "It'll only take me a few minutes to shower and put on some dry clothes." He led her into his living room. "Here, have a seat, and here's the remote for the TV, you can just kick back and relax." He patted the couch, indicating a place for her to sit, and then he vanished up the stairs.

She fought against wanting to follow him up the stairs. *What is wrong with me?* She was far from naive, but at the same time, she wasn't the kind of woman who saw a man taking a shower as an opportunity. She favored a less complicated way of life. And yet... tonight she was seeing and hearing sexual suggestions where there weren't any. Dutch was making her crazy with the virility that just oozed out of him. Being soaked and disheveled from the falling snow made him sexier, in a messy kind of way.

Fifteen minutes later, he came back down the stairs, still wearing a silly grin on his face, the grin she always seemed to bring out of him. He was embarrassed by it. He thought he should have more control over it. "Well, I'm ready," he said. "Do you need anything before we go?"

She had to stare at him. It looked like he had taken note of what she was wearing, for the colors of his attire matched hers. His black shoes and slacks and the maroon button-up Brooks Brothers shirt went well with what she had on. *What man does that?* she asked herself. Even though their styles were different, they looked like they belonged together.

"You look good!" she managed to say.

"Thank you. I hate to admit it, but I haven't been on a date in a while. I'm extremely nervous."

She reached out with her hand and clutched his. "I'm nervous, too. It's good to be nervous together."

"I hope I don't sweat through my shirt."

Ruby giggled again. She wondered where the giggles kept coming from.

They walked out the door, and as he turned and locked it, he held her back for a moment. She thought he was going to kiss her.

"Let me go first," he said. "You know? The roof?" He pointed up. "I don't want you to get snow-bombed." He stepped out and looked up at the roof. "Well, I think most of the snow's fallen already, so you're good."

She stepped out and walked down to his vehicle. She couldn't help feeling disappointed that he hadn't taken the opportunity to kiss her.

Half an hour later, they arrived at Callahan's Mountain Lodge Restaurant, which sat in the Siskiyou Mountains just off the Pacific Crest Trail. If it had been daytime, the view would have been outstanding, but the darkness of the winter night gave it a different ambiance. As Dutch and Ruby stepped in through the front door, they could hear a band playing. Ruby immediately noticed the big fireplace that was crackling with life and warmth.

The hostess greeted them. "A table for two?"

"No. We have reservations for four. Under Birk... Ruby Birk."

"Yes, yes, I see it here." She picked up a grease pencil and drew a line through Ruby's name. "It looks like the other couple has arrived and are waiting for you." The hostess gestured for them to follow her. Just as Ruby had hoped, their table was near the fireplace.

"Ruby!" Zanique cried. "Here you are!"

"Dutch, this is my best friend, Zanique." Ruby looked around curiously. "Where's Blake?"

Zanique grinned and shook her head. "He's a no-show. I guess he couldn't handle this." She waved her hand in front of her, indicating her whole body.

Dutch shook her hand, then helped Ruby off with her coat and scarf.

Zanique was studying Dutch. "Ruby," she said, "I was surprised when you phoned and said you had a date for tonight... but, wow—where did you find this hunk of a man?"

"His name is Dutch, and he owns the Kaleidoscope Gallery in town. He's been giving me pointers on my work."

"I see. You've never mentioned him before."

Dutch, trying not to seem embarrassed, smiled at Zanique. "And," he asked, "how do you two know each other?"

"I met Ruby when I was coming off of a hike on Mount Shasta. She was down at the base sketching, and I was hot and sweaty and needed to rest, so I sat down and we started chatting. The next thing you know, here we are. The best of friends."

Ruby nodded. "Yeah, I was sketching out the beginning of what became the painting you bought from me," she told Dutch. "And the missing Blake," she glanced at the empty chair, "was our waiter the other morning. He asked Zanique out on a date, which was the whole reason for this...." She reached over and touched Zanique's hand. "I'm sorry he blew it off."

"No worries! I'm positive it saved me some heartache in the long run. He wasn't for me." Zanique turned her attention back to Dutch "I've never been in your gallery, but the storefront looks amazing. You must have some exquisite works of art in there."

He gave a modest smile. "We do have some great pieces."

"Speaking of great pieces of art," Zanique said to Ruby, "did you tell him about your special painting?"

Ruby glared at her. "Uh, no. It must have slipped my mind."

Dutch looked from one woman to the other. "What painting? Is it something I can help you with? Is it something you painted?"

Ruby shook her head. "I don't feel comfortable talking about it... because, well, the story has to do with my ex-husband." His eyes were solidly on her, however, so she felt obliged to continue. "To make a long story short, my ex is an art dealer. He was in town for an estate sale or something... I think he said it was at the Jameson Mansion. Anyway, he bought several pieces of art there. He singled out a particular one for me, an oil portrait painted in 1912. I think it's special, that's all."

Dutch's eyes widened. "I was there. It wasn't an estate sale, it was an auction, and there were some fine pieces. Most of them were more than anything I could afford. You should bring the painting by so I can get an appraisal for you."

"The Jameson Mansion," said Zanique. "Was it really nice?"

"Yes, it was," Dutch replied. "The place is too big for my taste, but it's beautiful. I especially liked the master bedroom. It has a balcony that overlooks the courtyard. And a nice fireplace. I like the thought of cool nights and having a fire in the bedroom." He paused. "It seemed really cozy." He picked up his menu.

Ruby had to smile at Dutch's description of the master bedroom, which sounded exactly like the room of her dream, the room in which she had made love to the man in the painting. Could it really be the same room? She tried to shake off the odd feeling that came over her. "Um," she said, "where exactly is the Jameson Mansion?"

Dutch put his menu down. "Not far from Lithia Park. It's on Nutley Street. You can't miss it; it's the largest house on the street. I guess it dates back to the late eighteen hundreds when it was the only house there. About seventy years ago, the property was subdivided into what is now a whole neighborhood."

Before anyone could say anything more about the mansion, the waitress arrived. After they'd given her their orders, Ruby looked at Zanique. "How about we visit the ladies' room?"

"Okay."

In the bathroom, Ruby turned to her friend. "Tell me, what happened to Blake?"

Zanique grinned. "I got to thinking about what you said that morning at breakfast, you know, about telling him who I really am. So then I called the restaurant and asked for him." She checked her look in the mirror. "When he came to the phone, I explained that I'm unique, a...."

"A hermaphrodite?"

"Umm, no one uses that word anymore. We usually say an intersexual person."

Ruby turned red from embarrassment. "Oh. Sorry!"

"It's okay; don't worry about it."

"And what did he say?"

"You can guess. He sputtered and stuttered around and then he finally asked what an intersexual is. When I explained that I was born with fully functional sex organs of both genders—well, what can I say? He got spooked."

"That dirtbag!"

"Oh, I'm not bothered; I expected it. I'm used to it." She grinned at Ruby. "But your man! He is *hot*! I'm jealous... and I'm so happy for you!"

"Thank you." Ruby looked down. "I'm surprised he agreed to come along. We aren't exactly cut from the same loaf of bread."

"Girl, you never give yourself the credit you deserve. Of course he agreed! Just look at you."

Ruby looked in the mirror. She didn't like what she saw. She swiped at her eyelashes with a mascara wand, then fluttered her eyelids, thinking she was about as attractive as she would ever be. She certainly didn't think for a moment that she was alluring, especially standing next to Zanique. Looking at both reflections, she was certain she was the ugly duckling in the room. "Well," she said when Zanique winked at her, "I guess we shouldn't keep him waiting."

As Dutch watched Ruby coming toward the table, a new grin spread across his face. Noticing it, she was desperately hoping he thought she was at least nice-looking. She also hoped he wasn't going to make a play for Zanique right in front of her.

Then three guys who were carrying snowshoes and backpacks and had obviously just come off the Pacific Crest Trail spotted Zanique.

"Yo! Zee!" one of them yelled without regard to the other guests in the restaurant. They ran up to their table, put their gear down, and took off their coats.

"Excuse me," Zanique said. She stood up and led the guys away. "What's up, guys?"

All three of them smiled at her. "We just had a gnarly day up on the PCT," one said.

"Spent a lot of energy," said the second, "so we came in here for some chow, drink, and sleep."

"We got a room for the night," said the third. "You wanna hang with us?"

"Thanks, guys, but I'm busy with my friends. Maybe next time."

She rejoined Ruby and Dutch, while the hikers picked up their gear and found their own table.

"Who were those guys?" Dutch asked.

"Just some guys I know from the trails around here."

"Zanique is an adventure guide," Ruby told him.

"You are? That's interesting. Is that your only job, then... guiding?"

She shook her head. "No, I do a variety of things. I'm also into charity work."

"Oh, yeah? Which charities?"

As Ruby sat listening to them chat, her mind began to take her to another place. She began thinking about Lithia Park, the painting, and the man in her dreams. She began to stare, dreamy-eyed, out the window and into the darkness.

"Non-profit work?" Dutch was asking Zanique.

"Uh, no. I wouldn't say that... it's kinda hard to describe what it is I do."

Ruby's mind was in the mansion that Dutch had described, in the master bedroom. She was certain the love-making in her dream had been real. *It had to be real*, the voice in her imagination told her.

Dutch and Zanique were still talking. "Do you work for the United Nations?" he asked, unaware that Ruby was staring off in the distance.

"I'm more of a consultant," Zanique told him. "I help organize people and build facilities, like shelters for battered women. Get food to hungry mouths, protection for the poor. Things like that."

"Impressive!"

For nearly five minutes Ruby sat motionless, staring off, her lips drawn up in a smile and a special bright sparkle in her eyes. She was dimly aware of the conversation going on at the table, but her mind was fully engaged with the man from the painting... the enchantment that had stirred her so many times. Tonight, however, she wanted to be with someone real, someone alive in the here and now. She wanted her mind to be engaged in thoughts of Dutch. In fact, she was beginning to feel concerned that this mysterious man was absorbing her. She feared that her future thoughts would begin and end with only him. He wasn't real, she had decided, yet there was undeniable love in her heart for him. She had to break out of this dream state.

"I didn't know all that about you," she suddenly chimed in.

Zanique shrugged her shoulders. "You know I don't like to talk shop."

"You like to keep us guessing," Ruby said.

"No. Work is so boring; I'd rather talk about things that are fun."

An hour and a half of conversation and eating passed, and the evening was wrapping up. The guys from the PCT were getting louder and, knowing they didn't need to drive anywhere, drinking hard liquor. Zanique was looking sleepy-eyed.

Ruby looked at her two friends. "The two of you have been really good to me," she said. "And as of late I've really needed a boost to my mood. So, thankfully," she winked at Zanique, "I have the money to do this, so

I'm buying your dinners tonight as a sign of gratitude. Thank you for being my friends." They both started to protest, but she stopped them. "I insist. And I will not hear a word from either of you. Just accept it. I'm buying."

"Well, on that note," said Zanique, "thank you, Ruby." She stood up and pulled her coat on, then turned to Dutch. "It was nice meeting you. I hope to see you again."

"The pleasure was mine. Take care."

"Yo, Zee!" one of the guys from the trail yelled across the restaurant again. "Have a good night!"

Zanique pulled Ruby close as they walked out the door. "I assume you want to keep this on the low-down," she whispered "though why, I have no idea. Anyway, I'll pick you up in the morning around 10:30. Then we'll drive over to see *my guy* about your necklace."

Dutch looked interested. "What are you girls planning?"

"Oh, nothing," Ruby said over her shoulder. "We're just planning a sort of girls' day out tomorrow. She was just asking me for a good time to pick me up."

Dutch shrugged and opened the passenger side door of his Defender for Ruby. At the same time, Zanique jumped up into her H1, brought the diesel engine to a roar, and sped off.

A bit later, Dutch pulled into Mrs. Bimby's driveway. "So." He looked around. "So this is where you live?"

She pointed past the house. "There's a studio above the garage. It's not much, but I like it."

Dutch got out of the Defender, walked around it, and opened the door for her. Then he took her hand and sucked in some cold air. As she climbed out, he realized he was holding his breath. He had no idea how to end this date.

Ruby looked down and swallowed. Nothing could have prepared her for this moment. "Goodnight, Dutch?" It came out sounding more like a question than a statement.

He heard the catch in her voice and wondered what he should do. On impulse, he took hold of her shoulders, pressed her back against the now closed door, and kissed her. It was supposed to be a brief kiss, but she pulled him in tight and deepened the kiss. His hands moved from her shoulders and down her arms, then to her waist. He liked the way she felt, the woman beneath her clothes. He enjoyed the way her body stiffened under his grasp.

As he hugged her tighter, she could feel the muscles in his back through his coat. The feel of him was feeding some of the places inside her that were hungry again. She wanted more. When he kissed the pulse point of her neck, she felt her heart come alive. She was throbbing all over. "Oh, yes!" His mouth moved back over hers, and she wilted against the door. When he finally pulled back, her fingers were still tight around his forearms, her mouth ready for another kiss. He held her at arm's length and they stared at each other, both of them feeling the sensation of the moment. Then his expression changed.

"What's wrong?" she asked.

"There's an old lady watching us from the window up there. I'm nervous enough without an audience."

"Oh, yuck! That's Mrs. Bimby, my landlord. She's pretty meddlesome. I was hoping she was in bed asleep."

"What should we do now?"

"Would you be disappointed if we called it a night?"

Dutch hung his head. "I would be very disappointed. But I respect your decision."

She giggled. "I'm disappointed, too." She leaned into him and lowered her voice. "Would you mind if I got Yukon and the three of us went to your place?"

His eyes narrowed and he swallowed hard. "I guess so. I mean—*yes!* Yes, please get Yukon and let's go!"

Chapter 9

*B*ecause Ruby didn't want Yukon to feel threatened or uncomfortable in any way, she and Dutch did their best to make him comfortable in Dutch's home. She had brought the dog's bed, food, and water bowl, and Dutch had already opened up a guest room for him. After exploring Dutch's house, the dog calmed down and went to his bed.

Taking that as a signal, Dutch took Ruby by the hand and led her to his bed.

"What makes you think I'm sleeping in here with you tonight?" Ruby asked.

"Uh, I'm sorry, I thought...."

She giggled. "I'm only teasing you." She was normally shy, but for some reason she felt adventurous and friendly tonight. Except for her erotic dream, she hadn't had *real* sex in a long time. Years! Could she, she was asking herself, consider being with the man in her dream *real*? Or was he just a fantasy? It had felt real. The day after, it had still felt real. And tonight, as she reflected on it, it still seemed real. However, her logical mind couldn't quite accept it as real. If the lovemaking she had shared with the man in the painting was real, then, she supposed, she had made love to a ghost. Now, with Dutch, she pushed that earlier, ghostly act of lovemaking out of her head and bit her bottom lip in anticipation of what was to come tonight.

"Is this the bathroom?" she asked.

"No, that's the master closet." He pointed. "The bathroom's over there."

"I'll be out in a minute."

Behind the closed door, she took off her boots and slipped off her dress to expose her vintage over-bust, red cherry-blossom corset with its black laces. Before leaving her apartment tonight, she'd added the matching panties and thigh-high stockings. Just for Dutch. Just in case. She hung her dress on a hook and came out.

Dutch was sitting on the bed, nervously waiting for her. When he saw her, he sat straight up. His attention suddenly fixed on the swell of her breasts above the corset. "Wow!" His stare dropped to her panties seductively huddled around her *mons veneris* in the curvature of her thighs.

Ruby stepped forward. "Being alone with a man is sort of new to me," she confessed. "I didn't want to come out naked, but I wasn't sure... is this okay?"

"It's fine!" Dutch swallowed hard again. "Just fine. Uhh, did you bring this... your corset... with you or were you wearing it under your dress all night?"

"This is what I always wear under my dress."

"You do? Oh, *you do!*"

"Do you like it?"

"Like it? It's threatening my sanity! I'm not sure you know what a physical effect you're having on me."

She reddened slightly and looked more closely at him. Then she smiled.

"Ruby Birk," he said, fully aware of his physical reaction, "you are jam-packed with surprises."

"Oh, I am." She came forward, straddled his legs, bent down, and kissed him square on the mouth. Then she kissed his neck and pulled on his muscular arms.

He wasn't sure how to react. "Are you teasing me again?"

"I can be a tease... if the situation calls for it." She was enjoying the power she was suddenly feeling. The excitement in the room was so strong she felt the hum of it sending flashes of heat through her. She giggled again.

"That innocent giggle," he whispered. "I'm afraid it's gotten us both in trouble."

She liked the way his raspy voice softened when he was excited. "Yep!" she said with a love nip on his ear. "We're in dangerous waters." She got off him and rolled the bedding down. "Are you going to stay in your clothes?"

He made no reply but only ran a slow hand down the length of her thigh as he searched her eyes. Seeing the expression on his face, she knew that the carnal drive was taking control over him. And, indeed, he pulled her down to the bed, hard, and she knew they were both ready. In seconds, his clothes were coming off. He was undoing his trousers; she was ripping off his shirt.

His hands trembled as he tried to unlace the front of the corset, but it was too much work. His hands went back to her waist. (She didn't share the secret of the corset: it had a zipper on the left side, and the laces were double knotted.) As he kissed her ravenously, he slid his hands under the sides of her panties and in a snap they were off and on the floor.

"Ruby," he managed to say, "I've gone past the point of no return. I can't resist you any longer. I'm going to do what I've wanted to do since I first saw you walking into my gallery."

She pulled away very slightly. "Maybe it's not too late," she murmured. "I could go now... before we do something we can't undo...."

His hands were working at her laces again. "I think it's way too late for that."

She reached down and gently stroked his manhood, her fingertips fluttering and tickling him. Nearly paralyzed by her touch, he went still.

"I don't think we should talk anymore," she whispered in his ear before she nibbled on it. "I think we should go with what our bodies are calling us to do."

Dutch took advantage of her suggestion. "Yeah." Without another word, he grabbed her wrists and held them with one strong hand above her head. Then he began moving slowly, using his strong body to exert pressure between her legs. Next, he began to breathe hot words into her ear, comments about her body, her manner, her erotic presence. She responded to the pressure and the words by arching her back and releasing a soft moan. She began to pant.

He gave up on the laces and entered her, and they cried out together. The feel of her around him was sweeter than he could have imagined. He was tingling from head to toe. His passion was getting ahead of him. He had to clench his teeth and slow down.

She wanted to cry out, but the cry got caught in her throat. It truly was past time for words. She was capable only of sounds, carnal, earthy sounds. She licked her lips, swollen now from his repeated kissing. She lifted her head enough to press a kiss on the top of his head.

He gained control and began moving more rhythmically, slow at first, but soon faster. She was moaning. She tried to speak.

"Dutch, you must go... go... go. Harder! Make it hurt!"

Dutch dug into a place in his mind he had never gone to before. He worked up the courage to throw romance aside and plowed into uncharted land, sailed into new waters. His natural tenderness slid to the side, making room for his animal appetite. He was a hungry man who needed sexual nourishment after the years of fasting. He focused all his sexual frustrations and thrust harder and harder. Soon the bed was rocking under them, banging against the wall as if to echo his hard work.

An untamed animal now herself, Ruby opened her legs wider, giving him full access. She could feel the whole of him going into her. She wanted to break free from his grasp, but she also craved his command over her. "Yes, Dutch... take me! Take me!" She bit his earlobe. "Harder."

He began to grunt. Where was he getting all the energy he was putting out? The bed rocked faster. "Ruby... are you close? I'm not going to stop until you come all over this bed."

"I'm there! Stop talking! Keep going!" Like a cheerleader, she began to chant. "Take me, Dutch! Take me! Take me! Take me!"

Rapture followed.

And in the other room, Yukon began to howl.

...

After her heart had slowed to its normal beat and the unmistakable weariness that follows sex had softened every muscle of her body, Ruby lay quietly in Dutch's arms and wondered why her body wasn't in the same state of euphoria that it had been in her dream with the man from the painting.

Her mind was confused.

When she'd made love in her dream, she'd felt love, true love, for the stranger. And tonight she knew she was attracted to Dutch, very attracted. In fact, she was ready to go again if he wanted to, but she also knew that true love was nowhere near them.

Fear struck her.

This was a moment, one moment, when she looked back and saw that fear, and it arose again when she looked into the future. She found herself caught in the middle of something unknown. She felt like she was looking at a half-finished piece of work. A half-done canvas was staring back at her, and she was afraid, afraid that she lacked the ability to finish it, afraid that if she did finish it, no one would appreciate it.

This moment, she thought, it was sexual imagination in control of her. In art school, one of her instructors used to say that when a person imagines their art, the first brush stroke, the first touch of the hand on the unmolded clay, that is when the artist is at his or her highest potential. But as the work takes shape and becomes something specific, the craft is worked, technique is applied, and then, inevitably, the imagination begins to fade.

Tonight, she was telling herself, their sex was those first few brushstrokes on fresh canvas. She was satisfied for now. But she was also afraid. Could the progress of their desires dwindle in possibility? As in art, when the execution ultimately reduces artistic options and the work moves toward completion... an ending? In effect, completion is the threat of creation because an end is coming.

She didn't want this to end. Not now. This wasn't love, but it was *something*, and she enjoyed the *something* they had just shared.

What does Dutch think about me? she wondered. *Because I fucked him, does he think I'm desperate and low in moral fiber?*

She couldn't envision Dutch's great strength yielding to the short-lived impulse of passion. On the whole, she was of a mind to admit that she liked Dutch better than any other man she knew. Her desires were the magnificent desires of the animal kind, and in spite of the calling of her body, she instinctively knew that between her and Dutch there was little room for the development of their souls.

Lying there, she was brought unexpectedly, and for the first time in her life, face to face with the truth that lies deeply hidden in human knowledge—that the richest experience in human awareness is when love is exchanged on the soul level. Making love to the stranger from the mysterious painting—that was when she had felt the soulful connection. It didn't matter to her whether it had been a dream or not. What mattered was the experience, the intensity of it.

With the stranger, it was *love*. She was certain about that. With Dutch, what they had was *goodness*. And goodness could lead to love. *Right?*

"Ruby, are you sleeping?" He interrupted her thoughts.

"No. I'm just thinking."

"Uh, I was wondering if you would stay with me for a few days… you and Yukon?"

"I'd love to," she whispered, "but I have some things I need to do."

He sighed in disappointment. He feared her leaving him in the morning, and that fear bothered him. He felt like he was losing control.

"But what I can do is… well, I'll leave Yukon's things here. We'll ride to the gallery with you in the morning, and I'll do what I have to do tomorrow during the day, and then I'll be back at the gallery before you close. And we can all come back here tomorrow night. Will that work for you?"

He hugged her. "Yes, that'll work just fine." Then he reached over and turned off the light and snuggled closer to her. For him, their lovemaking had been a symphony of wholeness. He was certain that their bodies and their minds were floating up somewhere between this existence and the nonexistent reality of fantasy. He was confused and ecstatic, and yet fearful—all at the same time. He was floating in the elation that carried his spirit up into heights close to heaven. But he was afraid to ask himself... what if he fell?

Love?

He tried to push the thought of love out of his head. It was nothing but an intrusion, something out of his emotional state, something more than his vulnerability. Being exposed, open to Ruby... that didn't bother him. What brought fear into him was having his loneliness filled, only to be threatened again by solitude.

Love was a premature emotion.

It also occurred to him that in Ruby's presence he felt himself a weaker man. There was something in Ruby—a quality that was neither brute strength nor overbearing personality—she exuded a kind of command that Dutch was now considering to be control... control of their future. He felt that the opportunity—the decision—for them to become a steady couple was up to *her*. He entertained the idea of a relationship with her, and that thought touched his heart. But if they continued to be lovers or if they broke it off—either way, it was her call. *Wasn't it?*

Ruby exercised no threat of leaving him behind, nor did she speak of a future with him. After all, this was just their first date. What could he expect? But knowing her this way, he was at the ready to make changes. Life changes. He was ready to change whatever he needed to change if it would make her happy. And these thoughts scared him. He imagined that her spirit was both beautiful and powerful. Should he yield to her power?

Was it true, Dutch now began to wonder, what his sister had once said with almost unspeakable cheerfulness: that what she admired most about Ruby was that she was nothing more than pure, simple, goodness manifest on earth?

Goodness.

He smiled. He now understood that the elation he was feeling was goodness. Ruby-goodness. Love might be close behind, but for now, there was nothing for him to fear. All he had to do was enjoy the experience. Neither he nor Ruby needed to be in control. Control would be the thing that might kill both the goodness and the love. He relaxed into the idea that they had equal power and that the future was bright. There was nothing to fear.

In goodness, sleep came for them both.

...

Ruby awoke in the morning to find Dutch wearing a long white bathrobe and standing beside the bed.

"Good morning!" he said. "I'm not sure if you're the kind of person that bathes in the morning or the evening, but I took the liberty of drawing you a bath."

Ruby sat up and stretched, then rubbed her eyes. "A bath sounds nice," she said. "My place only has a shower." Then she blinked and looked more closely at him. "I might fall back to sleep in the tub. Will you keep an eye on me?"

"Of course." Dutch turned and headed out the door.

"Wait."

He turned quickly. "What is it?"

"Can't a girl get a good-morning kiss?"

He slapped his forehead. "Duh! I'm sorry. I don't know where my mind is." He kissed her.

"Now that's better." She got out of bed nude and walked to the bathroom.

Dutch looked at the corset on the floor and scratched his head. It was alluring on her body, but damn it, if it hadn't frustrated the hell out of him in his many attempts to get it off her last night.

He also admired her as she walked away from him. "I let Yukon out," he said. "He's playing around the backyard. I was going to fix some breakfast. Would you like something? I was thinking eggs and toast."

"I'm starving." She was almost drooling at the thought of real food. The energy she's expended last night had taken its toll. "Two eggs and toast for me, please."

The bathtub, with big-clawed feet, seemed huge to her. It felt incredible as she slid into the hot water.

"I've put two towels on the counter for you." Dutch had followed her into the bathroom. "And soap and shampoo are... well, you'll figure it out." He turned and started out again. "Let me know if you need anything else. Or any help."

"Help?" She giggled again. "What kind of help would you give me in here?"

Thinking, *I could wash your back*, he backed out of the bathroom, scolding himself. It was an accident, but it sounded to him like his mouth had just suggested they have sex in the tub. "I'll be downstairs. Fixing breakfast."

Thirty-five minutes later, she came down and walked into the kitchen. "As good as new!" She was wearing the same clothes she had worn the night before. "Did I take too long? Are the eggs overdone?"

"No. I haven't even started them yet." He smiled at her. "I figured you'd like a fresh breakfast. I made coffee, though. Would you like a cup?"

"No, thanks. I don't care for any."

"Oh, shit—that's right, you don't like coffee." He looked at his cabinets. "I know." He turned and pulled out a small pan, filled it with milk, and put it on the stove. "Hot chocolate coming up!"

She sat down at the table and watched him working away in the kitchen. He wasn't so macho that he was uncomfortable in the domestic sphere. It was, she could see, actually the opposite. He was confident enough in his manhood that he easily took command in the kitchen and was creating a breakfast that she would have paid good money for. The smell of the bacon sizzling set her stomach growling.

"How do you like your eggs?" he asked. "Scrambled? Or dippies?"

She laughed. "What's dippies?"

"You don't know about dippies?" He put on an exaggerated expression of dismay, as if she were dumb. "I will have you know that dippies are the latest rage in Paris."

"They are? I'm sorry. I don't keep up with what's what in the world."

"Dippies are eggs over easy. You know," he gestured with one hand. "You pick up your toast and dip it into the heart of the yolk."

"Gee, I haven't had a runny egg yolk since I was kid. The thought of it makes me gag. But when you call them dippies, and describe them to me, I'm curious. I think I might like them. So two dippies for me, please."

"And how about Yukon... would he like some dippies?"

"Oh, good call. I don't normally have eggs to feed him, but since this is a special occasion, sure, fix him whatever you think would be good."

It occurred to her that sitting at the kitchen table... how nice it was to have someone to share small talk with, a handsome man who was working diligently to make her breakfast. He seemed to care about her well-being. It was another moment, a magical moment, a ritual he was weaving into their relationship, and the little ritual gave her comfort. It was the little things that were making this moment so special, like a fresh cup of hot chocolate to start her day. She recognized happiness, goodness, and she was thankful. Her winter depression was lifting. She could glimpse springtime, see that she would eventually enter spring. Her depression was softening, and she acknowledged that fact.

Dutch set the plate of dippies and toast and bacon in front of her. She wasn't sure if it was the hot chocolate or the pleasures of the kitchen that were warming her.

"What time do you need to be at the gallery?" she asked.

"I was thinking about leaving here in about twenty minutes or so. Would that be okay?"

She looked at the clock on the wall above the sink. "That'll work just fine. I'm supposed to meet up with Zanique at ten-thirty. If I get to the gallery by nine-thirty, then I have plenty of time to change clothes and sketch for a bit."

"What do the two of you have planned for the day?"

"Oh, we're just going out to Bandon to meet one of her friends." She dipped her toast into the egg, then brought it to her mouth. "He might be interested in some collectibles I have," she said, her mouth full.

"Collectibles?"

"Yes, well, it's more of a girls' day out than anything else. I've not been to the coast in some time, and Zanique thought it'd be fun." She didn't want to tell him about the painting or the necklace. She could feel herself already becoming protective of her privacy.

"You should have a good time," he said. "Bandon can be fun."

"Oh, you've been there?"

"Yep. Golf, you know. Do you golf?"

As she stood up, the chair tipped over and banged down to the floor. "Is there anything remotely close to resembling a golfer in this body?"

Looking at the Goth woman standing before him, he chuckled and thought how funny it would be to take her to a prominent golf course with her dressed the way she always did. Then he shrugged. "No, not really."

Ruby righted the chair and sat down again, then took the last bite of her dippie and chewed thoughtfully. Yukon came toward the table, and she watched Dutch feed him. She could see Yukon accepting Dutch, smiling at him. No one could ever tell her that dogs don't smile. Her dog smiled, no question about it. On the flip side, Yukon was smiling, but she wasn't. She was now aware of how different she and Dutch were from each other. What could their future possibly hold when they were so different?

"Maybe," he ventured, "maybe... if you want, I could teach how to play golf?"

Ruby wasn't sure if she was amused or offended by his offer. "Look," she said, more sharply than she intended, "let's just play this casual for now. I'm not the girl you want to show up with at a golf course. I'm not interested in learning how to play golf. If that's your thing, I'm cool with it. But I'm not... no, golf's not for me. With me, you get exactly what you see." She paused to wipe her lips on her napkin. "If you don't try to change me, we'll get along fine."

"Ruby, I'm not trying to change you. I was only inviting you. Offering to teach you."

"Thank you, but no, thank you."

Silence filled the room for a while. Both of them were in deep thought as the sense of emotional walls began to rise, strange, defensive barriers growing between them.

"I'm sorry," he finally said. "I didn't mean to offend."

"No, no, it's me that needs to be sorry." She stood up and fumbled noisily with her dishes and carried them to the sink. Then she picked up Yukon's clean plate and set it in the sink, too. "It's me," she without turning. "It's... all me."

He waited for her to continue, hoping that her sudden change in mood didn't imply reproach. *Was it in her glance,* he wondered, *a critical, disapproving expression?* She finally turned, and his eyes lingered for a moment on her sharpened expression, and he saw that there were three small creases between her eyebrows.

She lifted her head with the innocent tilt he had first seen in his gallery. "I feel foolish, ineffectual, and without an excuse," she said. "I'm sorry I got grumpy all of a sudden. I think I'm scared of... well, the thought of being so happy here with you frightens me. I'm not used to being so happy. For me, *happy* can be *scary*."

He went to her, kissed her, and held her face in his hands. "You scare me, too," he said, "but I think whatever this is you and I are experiencing, well, it's a thing of goodness."

His kiss felt reassuring, and she thought about whatever it was they were experiencing. She thought how easy it would be for her to believe this could happen every day if she chose it. And waking up to Dutch and breakfast every morning would be so easy to get used to.

Effortless intimacy. Goodness.

Chapter 10

*E*zra Arkin was obviously concerned with appearances. He knew his blue eyes and thick hair made him charming. But for some reason she couldn't quite identify, Ruby wondered if he was really a legitimate businessman.

He gave her a slight bow. "You like the suit?" he asked,

"Yes, it's very fine," she replied. "Armani?"

He frowned. "That could be considered an insult, but I'll let it slide. This, little lady, is an Ermenegildo Zegna. Nothing but the best for me!" He ran a hand over his hair to slick it back. "Without class, a man is nothing. Am I right... or am I right?"

Zanique was not impressed. "Sure, Ezra. You look tight, boy. I'll bet that suit set you back ten G's."

"More," he said with a smirk. "But who cares? It's only money."

Ruby shuddered. She was looking around the richly decorated living room in the custom home.

This home, the epitome of luxurious coastal living, complete with its private beach, all within a gated community, made her feel insignificant.

Zanique had told her that Ezra owned at least a dozen big houses around the country, and now she was trying to imagine what kind of life he must live. She couldn't comprehend a lifestyle that contained multiple houses and a private jet to fly to them whenever a person just wanted to change locations. Zanique had also told her that Ezra had flown in just last night specifically to see her necklace.

"Sooo," Ezra said, his tone way too casual, "you girls have something for me to look at?"

Ruby noticed that his eyes were focused on Zanique. He was obviously filled with desire for her. *That's why he dressed his best,* she realized, *and why he keeps slicking his hair back. He wants more than to look at my jewelry.* She hid her smile. *He wants to get with Zanique.* She stepped closer to her friend and handed her the item, then Zanique laid the necklace down on the Louis XV coffee table in front of the zebra-upholstered couch where Ezra was sitting. He took out a jeweler's loupe and began to examine it.

"Hey, Zee—where'd you steal this?"

She snorted. "I didn't steal it. It's legit."

As Ruby looked from Ezra to Zanique, her friend gave her a wink. She seemed to be winking a lot lately.

And, Ruby thought, every time she winked, it seemed to mean something sneaky. Ruby suddenly realized that she didn't really know very much about Zanique or her *guy*, as she referred to Ezra. He seemed to be uncomfortably shady. She began to worry about this situation. *What if my necklace is really valuable? Will Ezra pull out a gun and kill us both and take it for himself?*

Ezra had finished his appraisal. "Well, Zee, you do have the real deal here. This is old... *very old*. I used the pictures you sent me and asked around to several experts. They seem to think that this artifact," he chuckled, "yeah, it's so old, we can call it an artifact, anyhow, this *artifact* is at least five thousand years old, probably much older. And this necklace isn't solid gold."

"Crap!" said Ruby. "It isn't? So it's not worth much?"

"I didn't say that, little lady. I showed the pictures Zee sent me to people I know and... you know these tiny hieroglyphs here on the loop of the ankh and the ones on each link of the chain? They tell a story—"

"Wait." She didn't care about the age or the story. "So this necklace is rare... it's worth something?"

"The subject is even rare," Ezra said. "I have friends *in the know*, and through them I found *the expert*, and he informed me that it is a fact that the characters on this necklace predate the 'known' great

Egyptian ages. The necklace predates the Ziggurats of the Sumerians, too. We are talking the oldest known antiquity!"

Ruby looked skeptical. "Who was this expert?"

"Bernard Griffith is *the authority* on ancient scripts and languages. And, according to him, this is an example of the oldest writing in the world. He told me of a recent archeological discovery of some tablets on the Red Sea coast. The tablets were brought to the area from the Land of Punt. That's the land of the gods. These tablets are written in a script that preceded the known ancient Egyptian hieroglyphics. This same language is what is written on your necklace. The whole thing is strange because the technology to do this epigraphy on the chain and Ankh doesn't even exist today."

"Epigraphy?" Ruby asked.

"Hell, I didn't know what that meant either. But I've learned it means writing on something. On an enduring surface like metal or stone."

Zanique cleared her throat, "Am I hearing this right? This necklace had the oldest known written language on it, but it's got the most technical engraving on it?"

Ezra nodded. "That's right. Bernard says that these symbols are cut by an exacting kind of tool, something so precise that the equipment necessary to replicate them is centuries beyond us."

"But what does it say?" Ruby blurted out.

"Well, on the ankh there's a kind of incantation or prayer. Here, I put it in my tablet." He held his iPad up to show her. "Bernard did his best to translate it, but the old language is difficult. This is his best guess. It says, *From the land of the aromatic resins, from the land where the Gods reside, this blessing has found you. Go to the chosen place. Go with your beautiful form and prepare to travel beyond.*"

"Travel beyond?" As Ruby whispered the words aloud, a shiver ran down her spine.

"And that's just the ankh," Ezra said. "The chain has more—"

"So how old is this necklace?" Zanique interrupted.

"Like I said, far more than five thousand years old... well, that's a deduction from the writing on the tablets and now on this necklace. Bernard and the other experts are confused, though, because...."

Ruby picked up Ezra's jeweler's loupe and leaned in for a closer look at the old necklace.

"... and this is where it really gets weird," he was saying, "because the chain reads like an effing book. Notice that each link is octagonal, and what's etched on each side is in a different language... Egyptian, oracle bone script—that's ancient Chinese—and wait... it gets stranger. Olmec. The other languages are unknown.

"Olmec?" Ruby asked.

"The Olmecs, you know... ancient Mexico? The oldest people there?" Ezra looked down his prominent nose at her. Then he leaned toward Zanique and said, "Part of the inscription states that this ankh is made from extraterrestrial iron. It's gold plated."

"What is extraterrestrial iron?"

"Think about it... it's iron that came from a meteor or some other unworldly sources." He looked at Ruby again. "Little lady, you've got cosmic jewelry here! Genuinely cosmic. From *the cosmos*. And if that's true, then Bernard Griffith suspects that this particular ankh is the only one of its kind. Besides what's written on it, this must be one of the rarest necklaces ever to exist because of the material it's made of. According to the story on the chain here, this iron or metal has specific 'special' powers. The wearer of this necklace can do unusual things."

Two pairs of ears perked up. "What kinds of unusual things?" Zanique asked.

"Yeah," said Ruby, "what kinds of unusual things?"

Ezra gave an elaborate shrug. "Who knows? Put it on and find out."

Zanique turned to Ruby. "Have you experienced anything... er... *unusual* when you put it on?"

She wasn't about to tell anyone about her lovemaking while wearing the necklace. "Uh, no," she said after appearing to give the idea some consideration. "Nothing extraordinary. The only thing is, well, yes, I get motion sickness every time I put it on."

"I don't doubt that," Ezra said. "Look at this." He held the GPS app of his phone up to it, and the GPS went radical, jumping from position to position... loading map after map, but never settling on any one location. "Whatever this necklace is, it's gotta be for someone who knows how to use it. I'd be wary until I knew exactly what it was and how to use it."

At this point, Zanique decided it was time to get to the point. "So how much is it worth?"

"I have no idea."

"What? Come on, Ezra. Don't play dumb with me. How much?"

He waved his hands over the mysterious object on his coffee table. "I'm tellin' ya, Zee, there is nothin' to compare this to. As far as I'm concerned, this is exactly... priceless." He shrugged again. "Ladies, name your price and see if you can find a buyer. My friends say you could get an easy eight mil without blinking an eye. *If* it's real."

Ruby frowned. "*If* it's real?" she repeated.

"Well, you'd have to have this artifact tested by the scientific community. Authenticated. And if you start that, then you open a buncha doors to all kinds of problems. Like, where'd you get it. Is anything documented. If there's no documentation, if you can't prove a chain of custody, and since it's an ankh, an Egyptian symbol, then I imagine the Egyptian government could claim it was stolen, and, well, then that's a whole new can of worms. Ya know?"

Ruby nodded. "So I'm guessing this will be hard to sell," she said.

"Well," said Ezra, leaning back against the zebra hide, "selling is easy on the black market. And your friend," he nodded toward Zanique, "She's the best in the business. I'd make an easy bet you could get a quick two mil out there on the market. Right now." He laughed. "Ain't that right, Zee?" He looked back at Ruby. "And if she can't sell it, then no one can."

Ruby didn't know what to think. She turned to face Zanique. "You... you're in the black market?"

Now Zanique laughed. "It's not like working on Wall Street," she said. "we don't go around saying, *By the way, I work on the black market.* It's not like that at all. I know people that move merchandise, and sometimes it's not exactly legal."

Ruby leaned against the back of her chair and shook her head. "Jeez, I don't know, I'm just an artist, I don't know anything about moving merchandise on any kind of market. Just look at the sales of my artwork... not much moving there."

Zanique ignored her and turned to her *guy*. "Thank you, Ezra. How much do we owe you?"

"Slide me twenty large and I'm happy to keep my mouth shut."

Ruby's jaw fell open.

"Christ!" Zanique complained. "Man, you're killin' me here."

"Yo! I flew from Florida all the way out here to Bandon just to peek at your goods, so I don't think

I'm outta line. You got any idea what the cost of fuel for my jet is these days?"

Zanique shook her head. "Aw, man, quit your whining. You *live* out here, for Chrissake." She pulled out her smartphone and Ruby watched her fingers move over it. "Okay. Check your account. I just hit you for twenty. Are we good?"

He looked at his iPad and smiled. "Yeah, Babe, you're good. Nice doin' business with you."

"No problem," Zanique said. "Say, can I use your bathroom?"

"You don't hafta ask. You know where it is." Ezra pointed down a dark hall.

"Ezra's cool," Zanique muttered to Ruby, "so don't be scared... I'll be right back."

"No worries."

As Zanique left the room, Ezra motioned for Ruby to come sit on the couch with him. "Does all this make you nervous, little lady?"

Ruby sat at the other end of the couch. "I guess I didn't know Zanique as well as I thought. Can you tell me... is she really a... a criminal?"

He kept a straight face. "I suppose some might consider her a criminal, yeah, but I don't see it that way." He leaned back, and a big smile crossed his face. "You should hear the whole story before you go judgin' her. Are you capable of that? Hearin' the whole thing?"

She looked down the hall, then turned to Ezra and nodded.

"So," he began, "did she ever tell you how she grew up?"

"She said she grew up poor."

He grunted. "She grew up the hard way. In St. Louis. The way I heard it, her parents dumped her on a church doorstep, 'n' after that it was foster home after foster home after foster home, trouble 'n' more trouble. She was on the streets. By the time she turned thirteen, she was turning tricks on South Grand... you know. Surviving. Then she pulled herself up outta that hell."

"What did she do? Deal drugs"

"Ha! That's a laugh. You go straight for the stereotype. Drug dealer? Nah."

"Ezra, I have no idea what she's done or what a person in her shoes would do." She paused. "Is she a... a *violent* criminal?"

"Zanique? Oh, hell, no! She's a saint... entirely peaceful. Some would say she's a modern-day Robin Hood."

"I'm not sure I understand."

"You know—she pinches the rich and gives it to the poor. Well, after she pays herself a considerable service fee." He laughed again.

Ruby was sitting very still. "Okay. I'm listening."

"They call her the Deep-Net Hunter. And, well, to make a long story short, our girl has a special gift, and that gift allows her to navigate in and out of computer security systems *v-e-r-y* easily. She runs around the Net like you and I drive down the street. She spends most of her time researching and mining."

"Mining? For money?"

He shook his head. Was this girl really that naïve? Or was she just joking? He decided to play it straight. "She takes from the undeserving and gives to those that deserve it. Like you, I assume." He paused. "Do you have a bank account that she knows about?

"We set up a checking account yesterday."

Ezra laughed again. "Yep. There you go! That bank account she set up for you yesterday... that'll let her feed you some of the rewards she collects."

"But I don't want any dirty money."

"Oh, get real, little girl! Seriously? Have you ever seen a news story or read a financial article about some dumb-fuck CEO that has an annual salary, say, up past a billion, and then he's getting a year-end bonus of twelve mil? Oh, but wait—the folks that work for him? The real people building the company from the bottom up? While he's gettin' his bonuses, they're gettin' their salaries cut, gettin' their retirement cut, gettin' laid off. Wouldn't it make you feel good to know that someone like Zanique can reach into that greedy asshole's bank and take his twelve mil and distribute it amongst his employees? That's what she does. Discreetly. Undetectably. Anonymously. No ego at all. She doesn't take credit for anything."

"Really? She can do that?"

"I *know* she can. She's done it. Many times!" He sat up, reached over and lightly slapped Ruby's thigh. "Your girl's, like, a matchmaker. F'r instance, she did her research and found eight single mothers, women really strugglin', tryin' really hard to make ends meet. And what does our friend do? From her target list of rich companies, billionaire CEOs, oh, and my personal favorite target, the evangelists on TV that say they're usin' poor people's money to do God's work—God's work, my ass! Those hypocrite assholes are bigger thieves than she and I have ever been." He stopped abruptly, silently counted to ten, then went on. "Anyway, she found someone, I won't say who, and she just reached in and lifted eight mil off him. This dude runs an oil company, has over seven hundred mil in his portfolio, gets paid three mil a year, and then for a Christmas bonus he was getting another five mil. Like she said, *Why the hell should he get more fuckin' money? He's already rich.* So she turned him into a doer of good deeds and made some drops. One drop was a blanket drop, a monthly deposit, nothin' too big or noticeable, into each woman's checkin' account. Then a tange drop—that's a tangible, physical drop, where cash is delivered to the women with instructions on how to avoid the IRS."

"You almost make her sound like an angel."

"She is! But, girlie, that's not why she does it. And that's not all she does, either. Dig this! She's built a residential home in Salt Lake City for Alzheimer's patients."

"Wow."

"And this. One day she found out this particular gas company was frackin' in a neighborhood around a school. The water supply was gettin' poisoned, and they refused to clean up their mess. So what'd she do? She did some research and rerouted the company's accounts. She used their money to finance a private hazmat company to come in and clean up as much of the mess as they could. Then she paid another company to route new water into that area."

Ruby had to sit still and take all this in. "I knew she was a caring person," she said after a minute. "Generous. But I never knew to what extreme."

"Believe me, the corporate world is fully aware of her capabilities. They fear her. There isn't a millionaire that wants to draw her attention."

"How come I've never heard about... any of this? Is she on the FBI's most wanted list? I mean, surely this hasn't gone unnoticed."

"Are you kiddin' me? None of her victims are gonna publicly admit she found a way past their security. Their stockholders'd be frantic. There is no FBI. She's not on their radar. She gets away with it by blackmail and knowin' that every top company wants to keep the status quo. They're a secure investment."

He stopped and rubbed his chin. "Oh, yeah. I forgot to mention the women's shelter in L.A. that was built and financed with money from a CEO that abused both his wife and his mistress." He patted Ruby's knee. "You see, Zee found out this asshole was beatin' his wife. Sending her to the ER a couple times a month. He used his clout... and his money... to keep his ass outta the headlines. So Zee learns about this and she reaches out to his wife and helps her find a safe place. Then she turns around and takes twenty-five mil from the prick to build a new facility for battered women. Broke him down to less than a hundred thou in his checking account. But he couldn't complain! He had sources of income that were, let us say, off the books. Ya know?" He chuckled. "And these're just the things I know about. Zee's pretty tightlipped."

"Ezra," came a voice from the dark hallway, "are you telling my girlfriend ghost stories?" Zanique stepped forward. It was obvious that she'd been listening. She looked at Ruby. "I'm sorry you had to hear about my sinful ways."

Ruby could only gulp. "I like the idea of what you do," she said. "However... well, I'm not sure I understand enough about it to judge the right or wrong of it."

"There's not much right or wrong in what I do. What's wrong with this world is that a few people have all the wealth. The top one percent. People need me to find them and help them. The poor need me to find them and help them live better lives. The wealthy need me to find them and relieve them of their excess."

While she was speaking, Zanique put her coat on and gathered up her things.

Ruby felt out of place between Ezra and Zanique. She hardly ever sat down at a computer. She didn't own a cell phone. She didn't know any billionaire CEOs, and she had hardly any dealings with banks. How could she know anything about illegal activity?

"Well, Ezra," Zanique said in a breezy tone, "it's been fun. Hit me up next time you're in town." She took Ruby's hand. "Let's bounce, girlfriend."

Ezra stood up. "Hey, Zee, wait up. Would you wanna stay back and hang with me for a while? I'm not heading out right away. We could—"

"Are you kidding?" Zanique grabbed Ruby's shoulders and pulled her into her and slapped a massive kiss on her. As her tongue danced around in Ruby's mouth, Ruby's eyes went wide. Then Zanique let go of her and looked over her shoulder at Ezra. "Nah, Dawg, I've gotta get this momma home while she's hot... if you know what I mean." She pulled hard on Ruby's hand and led her out the door. They climbed into the Hummer.

Ruby pulled the passenger door closed. "Whoa! Hold up, Zanique—what the fuck was that?"

Zanique took a deep breath as she started the vehicle. "I'm sorry, Ruby. Ezra's wanted to get into my pants for years. I say no every time, but now he's getting more impatient. He's powerful, not a guy to mess with. One day he won't ask me anymore. He'll just take what he wants. Once he discovers my secret, though, well, he'll probably have me killed."

"He wouldn't kill you!"

"The hell he wouldn't! He's a proud, full-on, heterosexual man, and if he pulled my pants down and saw my peen sitting next to my cooch, he'd come totally unstuck! You bet he'd have me killed."

"So you kissed me...?"

"I figured if he thought I was a lesbian he'd leave me alone."

Ruby shook her head. "Then how about you give me a heads-up before you pull some shit like that again... I mean, damn, girl, I almost slapped you. No one just touches me without my permission. Got it?"

"Yeah. Totally got it." Zanique started down the street. "It was just a little kiss."

"Just a little kiss! I'm not a free ride at the amusement park."

"I'm sorry, Ruby, I really am. But didn't you like it? Even a little?"

Ruby turned away without speaking and looked out the window.

"Oh, come on." Zanique accelerated hard. "It wasn't that bad, was it?"

"I don't want to talk about it."

"Okay." They drove in silence for several minutes. Then, "Why was Ezra telling you all about my secret life, anyway? What did you ask him?"

"You used the words 'black market.' I just asked if you were a criminal... if you were a violent criminal. That's all."

Zanique looked sideways at Ruby. "I'm five foot, even, and soaking wet I weigh a hundred and two pounds. What makes you think I'm a violent criminal?"

Ruby shook her head. "I'm just dumb, I guess. The only things I know about criminals are what I see on TV. And I don't watch TV very often."

"TV? Ha! Well, I'm nothing that they could imagine on TV. I'm the most deceptive person who ever existed. You see me, and you think you know me. But I'm two very different people."

"That's for sure." Ruby finally turned to look at her friend. "Uhh, can you tell me about your childhood?"

"What, are you going to be my shrink now?"

"No. It's just that Ezra said you had a rough childhood. I know you were left on a church doorstep. I was wondering...."

"Look, the church didn't know what to do with me. I swear, after the first diaper change, when they saw my little junk next to my baby cunt, they must have thought I was the devil's spawn. They didn't want me. Then it was the foster care system. Which pretty much sucked. When nobody wants you, you know what? You go live on the streets. That's where I ended up. Way too young." She made for Highway 42, then resumed her story. "I was doing things I didn't want to do just to survive. I wanted to have a safe place to lay my head. Regular food to eat. Being poor sucks."

"It sure does."

"I was sick and tired of being poor, sick of everyone else having money and me struggling to feed myself. So I decided to find a way to get a lot of money and elevate myself out of the shit-hole I was living in."

"How did you learn to become this... this ... Deep-Net Hunter person?"

"I got an education! But I don't want to tell you any more than you need to know, so don't expect to hear how I did this or where I learned that," she said firmly. "Besides, I don't refer to myself as the Deep-Net Hunter. That's a handle someone else gave me. It's used by people who know me only by reputation."

"According to Ezra, you have a really good reputation. Impressive."

"Well," she was keeping her eyes on the road, "the most important thing you've learned today is that you don't have to pay back the ten thousand. I took that money from a pedophile. A Southern Baptist televangelist that was using his youth ministry to run his perversion and pay people off. Believe me, the money is better in your hands than his!"

Ruby looked meekly at Zanique. "I appreciate you helping me."

"And I *really* don't want to talk about money anymore."

As Zanique drove back to Ashland, neither she nor Ruby spoke much until she pulled into Mrs. Bimby's driveway and parked.

"So," she said as she shut off the Hummer's engine, "how about you show me this mysterious painting?"

"Umm, I suppose, but don't you have anything more pressing to do?" Ruby was reluctant. She really didn't want to share her man with anyone even if he was only in a painting.

"I've waited patiently. Please, may I see your painting?"

Ruby laughed a little nervously, "I don't mind, come on up."

"If you hadn't said yes, I was going to kiss you again." Zanique laughed and Ruby gave her a dirty look.

"Don't even try it."

Chapter 11

$\mathcal{A}$s Ruby and Zanique started up the stairs, they heard Mrs. Bimby's door open.

"Ruby, is that you?"

"Yes, Mrs. Bimby, it's me. How are you today?"

"Oh, I guess I'm alright for an old woman."

Ruby looked down at her landlady. "I don't think you're as old as you think you are."

Mrs. Bimby snorted. "Yes. Well, I'd be better if you had my rent money," she said.

"You know what? I do have the rent money. *All of it.* I even have a checkbook now. I opened a bank account. I could write you a check."

Mrs. Bimby looked almost awestruck. "You opened a checking account? You mean no more twenty-dollar bills every now and then? You can pay me in one lump sum? How did you accomplish this?"

"Uh, well, I sold some of my artwork." Ruby walked back down the steps, opened her bag, and pulled out a pen and her brand-new checkbook. Then she wrote a check for the rent she owed now and for next month's rent, too. She handed the check to Mrs. Bimby with a slight bow. "And from here on out," she said, "You won't have to ask me for it. I'll have the rent to you by the first of every month."

Mrs. Bimby held the check at arm's length and stared at it, then smiled. "This is good news," she said. "Very good news." She stepped forward and gave Ruby a hesitant but sincere hug. "I know I've harassed you a lot about the rent," she said, "but, honestly, I worried about you more. I knew you didn't have any money and could barely feed yourself, but I just never had the heart to ask you to move out. I was always hoping you would break down and go out and get a good, steady job."

"I didn't know you were worried," Ruby said. "Thank you for being so patient with me."

The old woman's face showed both concern and sympathy. "You know, when I was young I fell in love with an artist and his bohemian lifestyle. He was an incredible man, and I romanticized the way he lived. Besides being in love with him, I envied the likes of Leonor Fini, you know, the Argentine painter who was flamboyant, beautiful, and outspoken about women's rights. She was an artist that never apologized for attitude or artwork. Her paintings spotlighted strong women."

Ruby nodded as though she knew of the woman, but had no idea who she was.

"She was in the same league with Salvador Dali," Mrs. Bimby continued, "and Picasso and Max Ernst. You know?"

"I'm sorry, Mrs. Bimby," Ruby confessed, "but I'm not familiar with her. Though I have heard of Leonora Carrington."

"Well, it's not important. The only reason I bring it up is because I could plainly see that you're living the bohemian lifestyle, too. But more like the *end* of the lifestyle. And that worried me. In the beginning, bohemians are exciting and contradictory. They have the urge to be free, and they feast on their freedom and indulge their lack of responsibility. They have the urge to be wild. To always be in the moment. Then those moments grow into decades, and when the wildness fades, they have the urge to become serious and live in solitude. Then in the end, after not planning any security for the later years in life in the far too common event that they didn't become famous, they'd find themselves in a desperate state. They wasted their youth chasing dreams, but now suffered for the realities they'd passed by. Their so-called freedom evaporated, leaving them broken and alone." She paused and looked at Ruby, then at her petite friend, who, as far as she knew, might also be one of those bohemian artists. "I know the bohemian lifestyle all too well," she said, "and I will say that lifestyle usually has a very sad ending."

Mrs. Bimby's words struck deep into Ruby's soul, and she suddenly felt a connection between them that hadn't been there before. Ruby was now the awestruck one. Mrs. Bimby understood her more than she had ever guessed. She wanted to ask Mrs. Bimby if she'd ever been an artist.

But before Ruby could ask, Mrs. Bimby turned and started walking back to her house. She stopped and looked at Yukon, who was running around her yard and lifting his leg to mark his territory. "Ruby, I don't think I ever told you, but I care about Yukon a lot. Just knowing he's on the property makes me feel safer. And happier. Sometimes, you know, he comes and visits me." She smiled. "He pokes his head through my cat door and looks for me." She looked back at Ruby. "I care about both of you. Having you live up there in that apartment is like having family close by."

Ruby was so surprised, she could hardly speak. "Thank you, Mrs. Bimby!" she said after she and Zanique nodded at each other. "I'd like to think of you as family, too."

"Ruby, I'm so glad that your money troubles are over," Mrs. Bimby said. "Your money problems have been solved, and just before the holidays... what a nice thing that is."

Zanique had to laugh. "It is nice."

Ruby suddenly remembered her manners. "Oh, Mrs. Bimby, this is my good friend Zanique."

Zanique came down with her hand out. "I'm pleased to meet you."

"I know you," said Mrs. Bimby. "I've seen you waiting for Ruby, but you wouldn't drive your truck close to the house or into the driveway before today. I suppose Ruby told you I was a mean old lady?"

"No, not at all."

"Oh, you're a terrible liar." Mrs. Bimby chuckled. "But I don't blame her. I haven't been very nice to her. She had a right to hide her friends from me." She took Zanique's hand and shook it lightly. "It's a pleasure to meet you. You're so pretty. Are you an actress or a model?"

"Not me," Zanique said with a wink at Ruby. "I'm in the charity business."

That made Mrs. Bimby smile. "It's nice to meet you. I hope after today you will feel comfortable coming around to visit."

"The pleasure was all mine," Zanique said.

Mrs. Bimby waved and made her way slowly back into her house. When she was out of earshot, Ruby turned to Zanique and put her arms around her. "Thanks to you, I was able to pay my rent! That felt so good! A heavy burden has been lifted from me. Thank you again."

Zanique hugged her back. "I told you I'm happy to do it. I've known for a long time how desperate you were, but every time I offered you anything, you always turned me down. I'm glad you finally accepted some help."

Ruby whistled for Yukon, and they climbed the stairs to the apartment above the garage.

Zanique looked around Ruby's apartment. Was this, she asked herself, how artists live? Or just artists like Ruby? Art supplies lay scattered around, a rack of pulp paper was drying, blank canvases were stacked against one wall, and accidental drips and splashes of paint seemed to decorate the walls of the otherwise lackluster apartment. "So," she finally said, "this is where you keep yourself when you're not out drawing?"

"Yep. This is Home, Sweet Home."

"Well...." Zanique wasn't quite sure what to say. "It seems cozy enough."

Ruby laughed. "I imagine compared to your luxurious place, my apartment looks depressingly lackluster."

"Is that why you've never invited me over? You felt like my place was too fancy and yours was too gloomy? This place isn't depressing at all. As I said, it's cozy."

Ruby lifted the oil painting Turner had given her onto the easel. "This is the painting I told you about."

Zanique stood back and tilted her head and studied the painting thoroughly. Then she stepped forward for a closer look. "Holy shit! Girl, that's you, isn't it?" She looked again. "Whoa—this is some really freaky shit! Who's the handsome steampunk dude next to you?"

"Steampunk dude?"

"Yeah, or is it Goth? I mean, you're Goth, aren't you? He fits right in with your style."

"Uh, but I'm not Goth."

"Well, I doubt you'd call yourself an Emo, I mean Emo is mainly kids, right?"

Ruby shook her head emphatically. "I'm none of that. I'm just *me.*"

Zanique looked her up and down, then looked at the painting again, then looked around the room again. "Sure. But you can see how I get confused. Right? I mean, the vintage clothes, all the black and maroon, the pale face, the hair—"

"Yeah yeah yeah. I get it," Ruby said impatiently. "I've heard it all before. I'm pale. That's just who I am. And the black... well..."

"Hey, I'm not knocking you!" Zanique shot back, "I dig the look. In fact, I'm envious of it. I could never pull it off. I figure my real parents were... well, one was black, obviously, and the other was probably Asian, so with my skin tone, I could never pull off your look." She suddenly couldn't take her eyes off the painting. "But whatever you want to call him, he's gorgeous! I love the formal wear. I wish men would dress like that today."

"I keep wondering who he is."

Zanique turned back to Ruby. "Girl, if anyone should know who he is, it looks to me like that person should be you. Judging by this painting, the two of you are an item." She paused. "And the photograph?"

"Oh, yeah, it's right here." Ruby pulled the old photo out of the envelope on the back of the painting and handed it to her.

Zanique couldn't believe her eyes. "This is amazing! Mind-boggling! That's you sitting there with that guy... that handsome guy. You're so lucky! Whoever he is, he's obviously in love with you. Look at him. He has that face, you know, when you see two people in love, you just know they are by the expressions on their faces."

"Love?" Suddenly she could somehow see past Zanique and Yukon. She was overtaken by the feeling of how necessary this man was to her life. The love she felt for him was absolute. They had, she now realized, made love in the truest sense of the word. She knew it, but she still couldn't bring herself to tell anyone, not even her best friend.

Zanique looked up and turned in Ruby's direction. "I've been through a lot in my life," she said, "I've seen things, been places, you know, and I've learned a great deal in my life so far. Yet... looking at this painting, knowing all I know about the necklace, this painting, and now this photograph, well, I'd say that sometimes we have to simply believe what we can't comprehend. I mean, our universe is limitless, right? We can appreciate a limitless universe, we can accept it, and yet we really can't grasp it. Right?"

"I assume so."

"Well, if the universe is limitless and we move through it, since there is no end, maybe we'd end up back where we started. At our own beginning. What if we're looking at *your* beginning?"

"I'm not sure I get what you're saying. My *beginning*?"

Zanique grinned. "I'm not even sure what I'm saying... but what if this—" she gestured at the painting and the photo "—what if this was your previous life... and, as they say, life is a circle, so somehow you ended up starting this life here in Ashland. You said this painting was purchased here in Ashland. And you're in Ashland. Coincidence? I think not."

Ruby was shaking her head in confusion. "Maybe it's destiny, or maybe it's just dumb luck this all happened, but either way I just can't get over seeing... myself I guess, but like she is. The person in the photo and the painting looks, well, she looks enchanted, happy, even... happy with her man, happy with the comings and goings of daily life. Even her surroundings are happy! There isn't a hint of sadness or misfortune or even discontent anywhere around her!" She gave a rueful smile. "It's so unlike me."

"You're not happy?"

"Most of the time, no, I'm not. But since all of this has started happening," she waved at the painting, "and since I've been able to pay my bills, I can peek at happiness once in a while. It seems like it's something I could achieve now, whereas a week ago, happiness was nowhere to be found." She tucked the necklace back into the hidden compartment on the back of the frame. When Zanique gave her a quizzical look, she said, "No one would think to look there. It's the safest place I know of."

"It's a good hiding place," Zanique agreed. "But if you like, I can put it in the safe in my home."

"No, thanks. I need it here." She gave her friend a funny look. "I didn't want to tell you before, not while we were driving, but when I put on the necklace... well, I do get motion sickness. However, I also can see special places and things. With my own eyes. I think I can even see into the past. I'm not sure if it's 1912 I'm seeing, but it's definitely before our modern times. Maybe a century ago."

"I knew it!" Zanique gave Ruby a loving punch on the shoulder. "Now that's interesting," she added. "I'm curious. How does it feel, I mean other than motion sickness, how does it feel to see the past?"

Ruby shook her head. "I don't know how to describe it. It feels like there's something constantly asking me to believe in the impossible. And I do believe it! There is no fear when I'm back there in the past. I haven't always known where I've ended up, and the unknown usually scares the shit out of me, but something about being in that time puts me at ease. It's actually the coming back that I fear more. Every time I return, I feel empty again. Lonely."

Zanique looked at her sideways again. "Aha, I bet *he's* back there, isn't he... that debonair dude... you saw him in the flesh, didn't you?"

Ruby got up and fetched her portfolio, unzipped it, and pulled out some sketches. "See? Here on top of the hill? That's him. Then, in this drawing, that's him, too. And I'm not sure how I know it, but this guy here, this older guy, that's John McLaren, the designer of Lithia Park. When I have the necklace on, I see the world in that particular past, and I know more things about that time than I even get a chance to see while I'm there!"

"That is too wicked!" Zanique paused. "May I try it on? The necklace?"

"Sure. I'd like to know what you see. I'll be right here if you get lightheaded." Ruby took the necklace out of its hiding place and clasped it around her friend's neck.

Zanique sat quietly for a minute, calmed her breathing, and closed her eyes.

"Are you getting dizzy?" Ruby asked.

"No."

"Do you see anything?"

"Nope."

"Really?" Ruby sat back, disappointed. "I suppose now you don't believe me."

"I absolutely *do* believe you." Zanique opened her eyes and looked at Ruby. "I think this necklace only works on you, is all. After all, you're the one in the photo and the painting. All of this has to do with you. And only you."

Ruby considered this for a minute. "Maybe you're right."

As Zanique took off the necklace and handed it back to Ruby, she noticed a change coming over her. "What's wrong?"

"Nothing's wrong. Well... um... it's just that I've noticed something in the painting and photo that bothers me."

"What?"

"I think he's my husband!"

"Husband?"

"Look! Here in the photograph and on the painting. I'm wearing a wedding ring. And he's wearing a wedding ring, too!"

They sat staring at the painting as the winter leaves blew around outside her apartment. The swirling leaves danced with the falling snow in a ballet, the natural dance of the seasons that creates the enchanting energy of Lithia Park.

...

As promised, after Zanique left, Ruby and Yukon headed out to the Kaleidoscope to be there by six o'clock to meet Dutch. Out in the snow, Ruby looked up at the mountains, then up into the winter sky. During the day, it was an astonishing blue. Tonight, it looked like black satin spangled with diamonds. But, she told herself, this winter was unusual in that it was a wetter-than-normal year with colder-than-normal temperatures. And because of this, it seemed as though the clouds always hid the sky and the stars. The clouds arrived late every afternoon, descending from the mountains. Even when it wasn't snowing, the clouds seemed to lean on the city of Ashland, which sat hunkered down as if it were protected by the paws of the mountain. The city seemed to be enveloped by mountain and cloud as if it were neither part of nor quite attached to the earth.

She walked with a smile on her face. Had she been married to the man in the photograph? Did she have a husband in 1912? *Husband.* The word had a certain ring to it. She wasn't sure if it was wishful thinking, or something significant, but she felt like it could be possible. Maybe she was—or rather, had been—married. But how was that possible?

She looked up at the sky and, grateful for this evening's clarity, stopped for a moment to let Yukon sniff around. While waiting for him, she looked at the shops on Main Street and saw a group of people coming out of a parking lot, laughing and talking loudly, to the extent that Ruby felt they must be inebriated. She shuddered at the thought that they had just parked a car. *Driving drunk is bad enough, let alone on an icy night like tonight.*

But then her thoughts drifted back to him, the man in the picture. She could almost smell him. And suddenly, from out of nowhere, the wind twisted and pressed against her, seeming to be aiming its force specifically at her. She pulled her hood up and whistled to Yukon to keep moving. She started walking quickly. Within a minute, she was out of breath.

"Damn it... Goddammit!"

"And who are you damning tonight?"

She turned, not realizing she was already at the gallery. Dutch, who had been waiting for her, was holding the door open.

"You scared me. I had my hood up and didn't see you... was I really talking out loud? Oh, never mind. Hello, Dutch."

"I heard you loud and clear," he said.

She was gasping for breath. "I was cursing the cold... and my being... out of breath... It makes me feel old!"

"You're not old! And being out of breath has nothing to do with age. It has everything to do with the cold air." He locked the door behind them and pointed down the street. "My Defender's right over here. Let's get out of this cold weather."

They didn't speak as Dutch drove them back to his house. As if they had been together for years, Dutch simply asked, "So how was your day?"

She glanced at him, thinking how strange it was that anyone would care about her day. But, on the other hand, she liked being asked.

"I spent most of the day in the Hummer with Zanique," she began. "It was a nice drive over to Bandon." She turned in her seat allowing her body language to show that she appreciated his interest. "We had a nice girls' day out. I really enjoyed it. How was your day?" The words seemed just as strange coming out of her mouth. As far as she could remember, she had never once asked Turner how his day had been when they were married.

"Oh, you know," Dutch said. "The gallery. It can be a boring place sometimes, and in this weather... well, everything is so slow." He seemed fidgety, as though he were holding something back.

"What is it?" she asked him. "There's something you seem reluctant to say... Come on. Cough it up."

"Well, uh, it looks like we're going to have some company tonight."

Ruby searched his face, but found no clues. "Umm, okay. Who?"

He gave a nervous laugh. "Evidently, Nora and my parents are coming over."

"What?" Ruby pressed back hard against her seat. "Your mom and dad? *And* Nora? Nope, I can't, just drop me at home. I know a train wreck when I see one and that, that'd be a huge one."

"Come on. It's nothing, really. My family... well, they're impulsive. Some might say nutty. But whatever we are, we're close and we love one another. And tonight the Devils are playing the Blackhawks. It's gonna be a great game."

"Why didn't you tell me this morning? I know you're into hockey, and I don't want to change you, but, well, I just don't know about meeting your parents, watching a hockey game, and being in close proximity with Nora all at once. Nora is nice, but something about her just makes me uncomfortable." She could feel panic building in her.

Dutch nodded. "To be honest, this morning I was so happy waking up next to you I forgot about the game. And my parents coming over? They just invited themselves. I didn't know until about two hours ago. If you had a cell phone, you know, I would've phoned you."

"Dutch, I want to be with you, I really do, but not tonight. Please take me home."

Hearing her voice crack, he mentally cursed himself. He had put her in an uncomfortable situation, and now he felt as though he was asking too much of her. True, he had known her for only a short time, but his feelings were already running wild. He pulled his truck over to the side of the road.

"If that's what you want," he said, "I'll respect your wishes. But if there's any way you could find it in your heart to have dinner and visit... well, Nora thinks highly of you and Yukon. She's no threat. And my parents are quirky, but I think you might enjoy them." He leaned across the seat and chanced a kiss.

She let out a deep breath, unclenched her fists, and embraced him. She hadn't been spoiled by being a beautiful woman in this life. Men didn't generally take notice of her, and yet lately, with Dutch and her fantasy man... Well, she was enjoying the attention. His kiss relaxed her. The panic melted.

She touched his cheek. "Why did you kiss me?"

"I've wanted to all day long. I figured if you were going home now, I was going to kiss you now without any further delay. I didn't exactly want to do it when we got to your place with that old lady, you know. I knew she'd be watching, and that makes me uncomfortable."

She giggled. "Mrs. Bimby can make anyone uncomfortable. But she's really not so bad."

He stole another kiss. To Ruby, his kisses were like water to a thirsty wanderer in the desert. They tasted good and she wanted more. When he came in for another one, she yielded again.

"No!" she finally said. "Stop, stop. No more kissing. If I'm going to meet your parents, I don't want to look like I've been making out in the back seat." She ran a hand through her hair. "I'm a respectable woman, you know."

His eyes widened. "Yes, you are!" He looked at her, then at the road in front of them, then back at her. "So... you *are* coming to dinner?"

"Yes. So drive already, before I change my mind."

"More kissing later?"

"We'll see."

He laughed, stabbed the stick shift into gear, and pulled back onto the road.

"It might not be that funny after your family arrives," Ruby said in a faint voice. "I'm not a cultivated woman, not the kind of girl you bring home to dear ol' ma."

"Of course you are," Dutch said as he drove on.

Chapter 12

$\mathcal{B}$oth Ruby and Dutch could see how Yukon was watching them (especially Ruby) as they waited for Dutch's family to arrive. The dog could sense the stress and apprehension Ruby was giving off. His tail hung low, he was pacing the floor, and he wanted out several times. When they let him out, he patrolled the fence line as if he were looking for danger. Then he was back inside to check on Ruby, then back outside again. When a car pulled into the driveway, he stopped and watched. As soon as he saw Nora getting out of the car, his tail shot straight up and began wagging.

"Yukon, what are you doing here?" Nora asked as she opened the gate. He ran to her, and she knelt down in the snow and hugged him. When she finally stood up, she looked at the house and saw Ruby standing in the window with her brother. That's when she realized that Ruby was more than just a woman who stopped at the gallery for advice from time to time. Nora brushed the snow off her clothes and went to the door.

"I didn't know if I should knock or not," she said to her brother as she let herself in. "I'm not used to you having company." She gave a hesitant laugh.

"You know you never have to knock at my house," Dutch told her.

Ruby stepped forward. "Hey, Nora," she said with an embarrassed smile.

Nora walked forward and hugged Ruby. "I saw Yukon out back and figured you wouldn't be too far behind," she said. Then she turned back to Dutch. "Mom and Dad should be here any second. They were right behind me."

With a nod, Dutch went out to the driveway. Minutes later, Ruby heard a car pull in, then car doors slamming shut. She looked out the window and saw Dutch helping a big-boned woman with cropped blue and purple hair through the door. Ruby noticed right away that her nose was pierced and sported what looked like a tiny diamond stud. Behind them came a tall man with a flat-top haircut. He was looking down at the ground for sure footing. Once safely inside, he looked up. His eyes landed on Ruby.

"Who the hell are you?"

Nora took his arm. "Now, Dad, that's no way to speak to a guest of Dutch's. This is Ruby. She's an artist. We know her from the gallery."

"The gallery!" The old man frowned. "You talk about that place like it's a real business, instead of an enabler for layabouts to avoid getting a real job!"

Ignoring this judgment, Ruby held her hand out to shake his. "I'm Ruby. Like she said."

The purple-haired woman took her hand. "Nice to meet you, Ruby," she said with a sincere smile. "I'm Martha. And this old grump is my husband, Roger." Roger ignored them both and walked into the living room.

Ruby instantly liked Martha. She looked strong and personable. Had she been a weaker woman, Ruby thought, she probably would have been an alcoholic or found some other kind of crutch to lean on so she could put up with her cantankerous husband. But Ruby saw that she could clearly stand her ground.

Without a word, Roger began searching for the TV remote. As soon as he found it, he turned on the pre-game show and sat down in the middle of the couch. Ruby watched him for a minute, then looked at Dutch. Father and son were as dissimilar as two men could be. Roger's shirt was military pressed (she'd noticed the three distinct pleats down the back), his tie perfectly tied, his shoes polished. He was in his eighties, but his appearance made his age almost unimportant. The first impression anyone got from Roger, she decided, was that he had never evolved beyond the 1950s.

Ruby suddenly giggled to herself. Did Dutch ever press his shirts or wear a tie? She could see by the look on his face that he respected his father, but it was also obvious that they rarely agreed on any topic.

While Ruby was observing Roger, Martha put her arm around Dutch and told him that even though she felt put off by the fact he hadn't invited her over to help decorate it, his Christmas tree was beautiful, and his house was decorated nicely too.

Roger overheard the compliment. "A waste of time," he grunted, "putting up decorations for a few weeks then taking them down, storing them for a year, then doing it all over again. What a rigmarole." He seemed to be addressing the TV, not anyone in the room with him.

"Oh, hush," Martha told him. "If you don't have anything nice to say, then don't say anything at all."

Now he did turn away from the TV. "What?" he asked, the picture of innocence. "I wasn't complaining. I was only pointing out how this whole holiday season stuff is a waste of time. It's the truth. Not a complaint."

Martha turned to Ruby. "Don't listen to him. He's been this way for years and years. I'm not even sure why I've stayed married to him." She began to laugh, but Roger interrupted her.

"Dutch, when does the pizza get here? The game's gonna start soon, and I don't want to be interrupted."

Dutch merely smiled. "Nothing to worry about, Dad. It'll be delivered in about fifteen minutes. I'll pause the game when it gets here. You won't miss a thing."

"Pause the game? In my day, *real-time* was all we had. There was none of this pausing stuff. Pause the game? Hah! Can you pause life? Hell, no! You have to live every moment as it comes to you." He shook his head in disgust. "I don't understand you young people."

It was Nora's turn now. "Dad, you do realize that I'm fifty-six, don't you? Most people don't consider me young." She looked at Ruby. "To hear Dad talk, you'd think rock and roll started just yesterday, and we're still all afraid it might make us insane."

At this point in the family comedy, Dutch tapped Ruby's shoulder and led her into the kitchen. "Okay," he muttered, "maybe this—this whole family thing was a bad idea."

Ruby smiled. "I'm fine. It's fine."

He shook his head. "I didn't realize how dysfunctional my family was until just now. Having you here is making me self-conscious."

Just then, the doorbell rang, Yukon ran to the door, barking.

"The pizza guy is here," Martha called.

And Roger yelled, "Be quiet, will ya! I'm trying to hear what the announcers are saying!"

Nora spoke up. "I'll get the pizza. Everyone just relax. Yukon, it's okay, boy." Nora had a motherly way of putting order to the disorder.

While all this was going on in the living room, Dutch pulled Ruby into him and gave her a long kiss. "I wish they'd all just go away," he whispered when he came up for air. "I just want to be with you."

"I know it's kind of uncomfortable," she said, kissing his nose. "But it's okay. Really!"

"I'll make it up to you later. I swear."

"Stop. You don't have to make anything up to me. But we should go back into the living room." She stole another kiss. "The... er... entertainment will be over soon."

Dutch picked up the plates and carried them into the living room, where Nora had set the pizza box on the coffee table. Ruby helped Martha get the drinks. Then they all sat around the room eating pizza and watching the hockey game.

Somewhere in the first period, Roger looked away from the screen. "Son, I ran into Jerry the other day. You remember Jerry from the hardware store?" When Dutch nodded, he went on. "He said his daughter Sandy had gotten a divorce. You should give her a call before anyone else finds out she's single again. That is one fine looking woman, that Sandy. Son, you'd be a good—"

"Oh, that reminds me," Martha said. "I was playing bridge at Betty's and Jo dropped in. That Jo, she is so cute! The two of you made such a good couple. Why did you quit seeing her?"

Dutch could only shake his head. "Mom, you know exactly why we ended it. Jo got back together with her first husband. She might be, well, cute, but she was a bit unstable."

"Why, she made me laugh all the time!" Martha responded. "I don't think you tried hard enough to make that relationship last. You would've made a fine couple."

"Stop badgering the boy," Roger barked. "And be quiet. I'm trying to watch the game here."

Dutch looked over at Ruby and mouthed a single word: *Help.*

She just smiled. It was fun watching his parents make him squirm.

Suddenly Roger jumped up, pumped his fist, and yelled, "Attaboy!" The Devils had just scored. "That's showin' 'em! Right there in their own stadium, we score first." Ignoring Ruby completely, he looked at his son. "The first team to score usually wins the game, ain't that right, son?"

Dutch nodded and, with his mouth full, said, "Yep. That's right."

Nora just had to team up with the parents now. She couldn't resist goading her younger brother about his single state. "Dutch," she drawled, "whatever happened to that gorgeous girl? Holly? I thought the two of you made a beautiful couple."

His eyes narrowed, and he spoke through tightened lips. "You know very well. She moved to Seattle."

"Seattle?" Roger shouted. "You're better off without her. She's probably a Seahawks fan by now. We sure as hell can't have a Seahawks fan in this family!"

Ruby had to ask. "Are you serious?"

Roger looked at her as if seeing her for the first time. "Who the hell are you?"

Dutch stood up and planted himself beside Ruby. "Dad, this is Ruby. Nora tried to introduce you when you first walked in."

"I'm not a dumbass," the old man growled. "I know that's Ruby. I just want to know who she thinks she is, questioning me like that!"

"She doesn't understand your complex way of thinking," Nora said, "and justifying everything in the world by where or what your sports teams do or don't do." She set her plate on the coffee table. "I don't even understand. But I know enough from being around you that I have to be careful not to mention certain teams." She leaned toward Ruby. "You see, for hockey, Dad and Dutch are Jersey Devils fans. For football, Dad is a Green Bay Packers fan and Dutch is a 'closet,'" she made air quotes with her fingers, "Broncos fan. Denver Broncos, that is. And Dad is still pissed about a bad call a few years ago when Green Bay played Seattle. That's why Dutch can never have a relationship with a woman who is from or lives in Seattle. At least not until they redeem themselves."

"That's damn right," Roger said. "That was the year the refs were on strike, and the scab refs didn't know their head from a hole in the ground." He looked at Dutch. "And what the hell is this business about you being a Denver fan?"

"Dad, that's Nora just having her fun." He shot a look at his sister. "I'm with you. Go, Packers!"

Martha was poking around on the pizza, looking for a slice that had more pepperoni. "Yep. We're big-time Cheese Heads. We went to the Green Bay versus Chicago Bears game last year. It was damn cold, but we had so much fun."

Ruby was nibbling at her second slice of pizza and feeding Yukon the crust. She was also enjoying Dutch's interactions with his family, even though she knew in her gut that she would never fit in with them. She was not, for starters, a sports fan. Right now, in fact, she was feeling an urge to get up, gather Yukon and his things, and walk all the way back to her apartment. Listening to the loud hockey game blaring from the TV behind the family argument, she was, in fact, thinking how nice it would be to put on the necklace and retreat back in time to the man of her fantasy.

Voices were now being raised as Roger began yelling at the TV as if it were a person and could hear him and Martha was talking over him to Nora. Dutch looked squarely at Ruby. Their gazes locked, and Ruby felt her heart rate pick up. The idea of wearing the necklace and finding her fantasy man vanished from her mind. When Dutch looked at her that way, it was as if she could read his mind. His mouth was smiling, and his eyes were telling her he was surrendering his will, or at least yielding to the possibilities of... of a relationship? She acknowledged a new fact of her life: the affection between them. Her fantasy man would have to wait. She had to learn more about Dutch. She knew love wasn't quite the emotion she felt for him, but her passion for him couldn't be denied.

And then she began to wonder about the other women Dutch had been with, the women who had just been casually discussed over the pizza. Evidently, Dutch was a wanted man. He was handsome and, she knew, had charisma. But he didn't seem like a womanizer. She wasn't naive enough to think he didn't have a past, of course; after all, he was a middle-aged adult. Of course he had a past! Maybe he even had an ex-wife. But then it occurred to her, maybe she didn't really want to know his history. The man she was interested in was the Dutch of today, the man living (and being embarrassed by his family) in this moment. Knowing his story wouldn't make her feel anything deeper for him.

Knowing that his family was distracted by the hockey game, and that Ruby was distracted by his family, Dutch slipped away upstairs. He worked quickly so that no one would notice he was gone, then came back to the living room and calmly took his seat.

The evening ended with the Blackhawks outscoring the Devils, 3-2. Ruby felt awkward as the family left and she stayed. She knew that they knew she was staying the night with Dutch. And knowing that Nora knew somehow bothered her a lot.

With Dutch's family gone, the house was quiet. He put away the last remaining dishes and was tidying up in the kitchen while Ruby stayed where she was, on the couch with Yukon asleep at her feet. The only lights on now in the living room were the colorful lights of the Christmas tree. In that peaceful glow, she was suddenly immobilized by the sense that her life was spinning out of control. Her mind was confused between the emotion she felt for Dutch and the love she knew existed between her and the man in the painting.

She had been alone for so long. Everything she did, she did alone. She slept alone, worked alone, and ate alone. And now to fill her loneliness there were not one, but *two* men! The only previous relationship she could even almost compare to this was being married to Turner. That had been a roller-coaster ride for years, with him coming and going, leaving Ruby for other women, then coming back asking for her forgiveness, then leaving again. She had hated it. When he left her officially for the umpteenth and last time, she found herself suddenly lost, because when Turner left, so did all of her clientele and even her friends. No one seemed interested in her or her work anymore. She had come to realize that Turner was the social and sales person in the relationship, and without him she was quite alone. This revelation scared her. Any façade of control she had was lost with him.

But as far as she could tell, admitting her fear didn't account for much. What she needed was a resolution, and the only one that came to mind was to stay single, stay safe, and stay in control.

Could it be that the years of being single had worn her down to the point that she had allowed two men into her heart?

And if so, were these two men now a threat to what little control she'd managed to muster after all these years?

Should she take a chance on them? And then on which one? Or both?

"Well, that was a bit of a challenge," Dutch said as he came into the living room and walked around the couch. He came closer to her. "You look so serious... is everything all right?"

He had unbuttoned his shirt and it hung loosely over his well-worn jeans. His broad shoulders and semi-bare chest made her draw in a deep breath.

He'd broken her concentration in an unintentionally sexy way.

"I was just daydreaming," she said. "Your family is definitely quirky, but kinda fun, too. I told you I'm not close to my family. Seeing you with yours made me feel kind of jealous. Here it is, the holidays, and I always spend them alone. I wish I had a family to spend holidays with. You know, a family that I love and that loves me back?"

"I'll share mine with you," he said. "You can be a part of my family." As he sat down next to her, his body radiated comforting heat. She felt somehow included and could barely resist the urge to straddle him, submit to his masculinity and maybe draw a little from his strength and security.

"I'm okay with that," she said, "but only in small doses! I mean, I enjoyed tonight but...."

"But what?"

"All I'm asking is that we take it slow, slower than tonight. I wasn't ready to meet your family, but we got through it and everything is fine."

"Okay, I get it. I was afraid they scared you off."

"No, I don't scare that easily." Most of the time, she was unaware of what her body was doing. Her body simply went through its habitual programs: walking, breathing, doing all the day-to-day stuff. But being with Dutch, her attention was drawn to what was happening moment by moment. She was exploring this experience, getting her second taste of what it was like to be with Dutch. She let go of her preconceptions of what she should or shouldn't do and allowed this moment to take her into its current. She wanted to taste it all as she was carried along.

Without a word, he stood up and took her by the hand, then he led her up the stairs. He turned the doorknob and opened the door. She walked into the bedroom, now lit by the glow of half a dozen scented pillar candles. She could smell the vanilla wafting through the room.

As Dutch covered her eyes with a soft scarf, a faint nervous laugh escaped her lips, but without hesitation she allowed him to lead her further into the room. When she started to comment, he whispered, "Shhh. We've said enough tonight."

She fell back on her senses and focused on what she was feeling, touching, smelling, experiencing. He put the palm of his hand against her chest, then brought her hand to his bare chest. She admired the feel of both their hearts beating hard with excitement. To her surprise, Dutch led her not to the bed, but to the bathroom. Still not speaking, he slowly undressed her... until he got to her corset. "Uh... would you mind helping me this?"

She reached to her side and pulled the zipper down. If she hadn't been wearing the blindfold, she would have loved seeing the look on his face.

Admiring her body again, he helped her to the edge of the tub and guided her into the body-temperature water. She could smell lavender rising up with the steam. When he began to wash her back and shoulders, she moaned with joy. He worked his way over her chest, arms, thighs, and knees and on down to her feet, where the tickle reflex made her wiggle her toes.

He enjoyed her reaction, both the tickle and the low moans coming from her. Once he had massaged her body with the soapy sponge, he climbed into the tub with her, laying his legs over her thighs. She moved her hands and felt his skin with her fingertips. She bit her lip when she blindly touched his member and wrapped her hand around it. He gave out a groan of his own and moved her hand.

She heard him reaching for something on the vanity, then she felt his finger placing something sweet in her mouth. It was a piece of Belgian chocolate. He had bought a small tray of them especially for her, especially for tonight.

What she admired most about Dutch, she heard herself thinking, was that he listened to her. He had heard her when she'd told him how much she loved chocolate, and he had also listened to her when she'd told him she loved taking baths. Not only had he listened to her, but he had also incorporated her favorite things into their romance. She knew he respected her, too, and it felt wonderful to be respected by a man. Turner had never respected her. His lovemaking was clumsy and fulfilling only for him.

She took her time enjoying her chocolate, then swallowed and opened her mouth for another. By this time, the other chocolates were beginning to melt, so the next one he placed in her mouth was a bit messy and left a dark trail on her lips. He couldn't resist. He leaned forward and kissed the chocolate stains on her face. Water sloshed over the side of the tub and ran over the bathroom floor.

Now she pulled the blindfold off. Her eyes were wild with want and need. She pushed Dutch up to his feet. He stood there in the tub, and now she took a piece of chocolate and began to use the melting morsel to draw on his body. After she had a design she liked, she used her tongue to clean his skin. The tastes of the salt of his body and sweetness of the candy were driving her higher and higher.

He ran his fingers through her hair until her mouth claimed what she really desired, at which point he quickly braced himself against the wall. She pulled herself closer to him and took him deeper into her mouth. This act had been the furthest thing on her mind when she was downstairs and they were talking. In fact, she had never expected to perform this act on him. In the heat of the moment, it added to the exhilaration she was feeling.

She admired every inch of his well-sculpted body as she ran her hand across his chest, then down the length of his thigh. Her artist's fingers explored his anatomy. The biggest bone in his body, the upper thigh, was fused with a mass of lean, powerful muscles. It was obvious to her that he had a favorable relationship with his body and took good care of himself. All of his muscles, especially the ones that linked his torso to his legs, were powerful. Below his waist were heavy-duty structures that were ready for action. He had the build of a hockey player, she thought, the build of a man that could satisfy any woman.

This man who was looking at her on her knees with water trickling down her back and glazing over her backside was one of the most erotic sights she had ever seen. He obviously felt the same way as he stared down at the glint of her wet body in the candlelight, her full, feminine body moving with a pleasurable rhythm that pushed him further toward rapture. His body weakened under the spell of her mouth and began to gently convulse. Her eyes widened when his pearls of love came.

She leaned back slightly and blinked at him. When she swallowed, her face was flush, and her eyes were focused on him.

He thought she looked like a mischievous, naughty angel. Then, when her breath got caught into a series of hiccups, he thought she looked cute and unguarded, almost as if she had never done this before.

He stepped out of the tub, then pulled her out of the water, wrapped her in an oversized bath towel, and carried her into the bedroom, where he laid her on the bed. He lay down next to her, cuddling her close and stroking her hair away from her face.

They lay without speaking in a close embrace in the darkness. It was as if the silence was an essential part of their love-making.

She opened her eyes and discovered she was facing the window. Outside, the wind began to blow, tossing the crisp leaves around in a swirling motion. She watched them as if hypnotized. The night sky turned almost white as snow began to fall in the wind. Somewhere in the distance came a long forceful shriek, the warning signal of a distressed owl.

The call of the owl caused her to wonder. Lying there with Dutch beside her, his arms holding her tight, she began to wonder if he knew that there was a man between them.

He took her hand. She sensed that in his grip there was tension of some kind.

He finally broke the silence. "I want you so terribly."

"Want me? You have me."

Their hands wound themselves together, tighter and tighter, "I know," he said. "For tonight. But I want to know that you will be here tomorrow. And the day after that, and the day after that."

She choked in surprise.

"Did I say something wrong?"

She thought quickly, "No, my throat is a little irritated after, well, you know... the blowjob?"

It grew quiet again for a moment. The last thing he wanted to do was scare her off, but, on the other hand, he was feeling a strong need to express how he felt.

He tried again. "I really don't want a casual relationship with you. I'm of an age where the whole one-night-stand thing isn't fun for me anymore. My heart is really into you! I want to be able to tell people that we're in love. I want to shout it out so anyone, so everyone can hear. I want you to know that I'm in love with you."

She couldn't speak. She was overjoyed at his words, yet she felt some fear at them, too. In her mind, she had a husband, but that was in 1912. She didn't want to believe it, but it was a matter deeper than belief. Something in her soul knew it was true, and knew it was insurmountable. She wondered if this was what it was like to live a schizophrenic life, part of her completely in love with a man from the past, that part of her a wife to a husband, and yet another part of her soaring ecstatically with this man in the current time.

He was whispering to her again. "Would you agree to us having an exclusive relationship?"

His question hung in the air.

"Oh, Dutch," she finally said, "who we think we are and who we really are are often two completely different people, and it's impossible for us to see where one leaves off and the other begins. When I think about myself, I don't feel like I'm a stable woman. And I would hate myself if I hurt you. For your own protection, and I don't mean to deceive you, well, there is something that I have to learn, something I have to discover, something I have to understand before I can truly commit to anyone."

"*Something?*"

"I can't explain it to you. I can't explain it to myself, even."

"You and I might come from two different backgrounds," he said. "Our codes of behavior might not be the same. But please, don't let this... *something* influence what you feel about me." He paused, then quickly added, "I could help you sort this *something* out."

"I'm sorry," she had to say. "But you can't help me with this." She was still looking out the window dreamily, watching the snow and the leaves blowing in the wind.

"All I know," he said, "is that what you and I have is good. It's the best thing that has happened to me in a long, long time. I've fallen in love with you, and just the thought of it makes me happy. That's all that matters to me." He kissed her neck.

"Tomorrow I'm going somewhere with Zanique to try and sort it all out," she said. "I'm hoping I'll find the answers to my questions there."

"Is this *something* a man?" he asked.

She let his question go unanswered for the moment. *So Dutch does feel the man between us.*

With a deep sigh, he said, "It's a man?"

"Not exactly." Her damp body began to shiver as she pushed off the towel and climbed under the covers. "It's complicated, but it's not a man, it's more of a depression that I've been fighting."

"Depression?"

Ruby worked through her emotions, her daunting fear of discussing her depression with anyone. She felt she owed Dutch the truth, the whole truth. "Yes, if I'm honest," she said, "I've been depressed for years. I've never felt like I'm part of this world. I've never really fit into this society. I figured you might have guessed how lost I am from how I act and dress. For a long time, I've wanted to die. I thought of suicide a lot. I was thinking of suicide when I met you. If it weren't for Yukon, I doubt I would have even gotten the chance to meet you. I swear that wonderful animal is my spiritual guardian."

Dutch got under the covers with her and pulled her close to him again. "I had no idea," he said. "I mean, I could see that you were sad, and down on your luck, but I didn't realize it was so bad."

"But I did meet you," she said, "and I have strong feelings for you...."

"But?"

"Well, this is where it gets really complicated. About the same time I met you, while I was really depressed, my ex-husband showed up at my studio. He had brought me a painting...." And she told him the story of the painting and the photograph and the wedding bands. She even told him that she had seen this man in several visions. She left out how she and the man in the painting had made love a few days ago, which had paradoxically been in 1912. "So you can see why in just this short time I've had a lot to deal with. I went from being depressed to feeling wanted by you, to knowing I am—or was—a wife." She smiled into the darkness. "And my mind hasn't had time to catch up yet."

"Hold on," he said. "You don't really believe that this man back in 1912—that you're married to him? And even if you were married, that was over a hundred years ago... you're not his wife now."

"My logical mind tells me exactly that. But something in here, deep in here," she laid his hand over her heart, then laid her hand over his. "something in here isn't accepting that. Somehow, it feels like I'm being pulled back to that era, back to him."

"So what is happening tomorrow?"

"I don't know. Maybe nothing. Maybe something. But I have to try and figure this out. Thanks to you, I now know where the painting came from. Zanique is coming to take me to the Jameson Mansion tomorrow. I'm hoping I'll find out more about who this man is. Was. And my connection to him. I really want to know how it is that when I put the necklace on, I can see 1912. How can I experience things that happened before I was even born?"

"I don't know," he said slowly, trying to wrap his mind around her revelations. "Maybe the necklace has some kind of psychedelic property, and it's giving you dreams that feel real. There must be some explanation that doesn't involve the impossible."

"I know I'm asking you to believe the impossible, but I'm telling you it's the truth! Please, believe me!"

"I do believe you," he said. "It's just that what you're describing is not possible. I believe you are experiencing something that you are convinced is real. But there has to be a rational explanation." He was silent for a minute, then sort of grunted to himself. "I know this must be difficult for you. You're worried that I won't understand and you're worried that you might hurt me. I appreciate that. I shouldn't be so critical of what's been happening to you."

"Thank you, Dutch."

"Gee, we've both really laid our hearts out there tonight! I think it would be best if we just play this out day by day until it feels right for both of us." He combed through Ruby's hair with his fingertips, and a flash of the tenderness he felt for the woman he held in his arms left him almost breathless.

The owl called again. Ruby thought it sounded more cheerful now. As it flew off into the night, Ruby's eyes grew heavy. Behind closed eyes and in her sleep, time touched her like the wind that was gusting outside, blowing her back onto the path of the man in the painting, a path that led to warm summer days and a fire-lit bedroom at night. Life in the present could not intrude on the harmonic pattern of life in the past. He was there in her dream, this man without a name. He was indeed her husband, and in her dream it was 1912. There was no other time. She felt alive in her dream, more alive than she had ever felt awake. She belonged to the past, to the man, to history.

Dutch lay awake as Ruby slept. His imagination was running wild. Could he and Ruby share these few days and nights of love and then just let it go so she could be with another man? Sure, other people had done it. He'd done it himself when he was younger. But those were relationships that didn't matter anymore. They'd been purely carnal. But he couldn't just say, "All right, Ruby, let's be lovers a few times, and then you go your way and I'll go mine." Jealousy was present, but more than that he was afraid she would leave him, and he would live his life without her. The future was frightening. Could it be, though, that it was in the past where his rival existed? Could it be true that a man in 1912 was trying to take Ruby away from him? These thoughts bothered him more than he expected. There was *something* about what she'd said that seemed true.

He held her close while she slept, while she dreamed.

Chapter 13

The next morning, Dutch watched Ruby come down the stairs for breakfast. As she came into the kitchen, she squatted down and petted Yukon; only after that did she come to Dutch and kiss him. After a "good morning," she leaned against the kitchen island.

Dutch smiled contentedly. "Good morning," he said. "You look amazing in the morning." Then he remembered their conversation of the previous night. That made him frown a little.

Ruby started to walk toward the table, but then slowly turned and smiled. "Amazing?" she said. "I'm wearing the same clothes I wore last night."

Indeed, he told himself, she was wearing the same clothes. In the light of the morning sun, however, she looked different. No, he thought, she looked extraordinary. He thought anyone standing next to her would look drab and nondescript. "Yes," he said. "Amazing."

She wasn't sure what to say. Finally, "I've never been the pretty girl, the eye-catcher. So thank you for saying it, even if it isn't true." Even though she hadn't been a virgin back when she was in college, she had been without boyfriends. She had been single all through high school and all through college. Her weekends went by, her friends always had dates. She'd either been left behind or been the third wheel. After college, after she had moved and began attending the art institute, she'd met Turner, her first boyfriend. He'd even married her.

It occurred to her now that the sex she had with Dutch in his house was the kind of sex she'd always fantasized about in college when she was alone. She had spent night after night in her dorm room, masturbating herself to sleep as she envisioned a man like Dutch. The recollection, combined with her new feelings for Dutch, made her feel very confused now. Dutch was everything she'd hoped for in a man. She wished she could commit to him, but dreaming last night about her husband in 1912 and the love they shared... It all played with her mind. Must she choose between them? She was both bewildered and frustrated.

While Ruby was thinking these thoughts, Dutch was studying her. A faint, yet sharp thrill ran through him. He had nothing but respect for her, or at least that's what he told himself. Her cherry chocolate hair looked a little messy this morning, but he could tell she had made an attempt to control it with whatever product she'd found in his bathroom. It wasn't that her hair was unsightly; actually, he thought the messy look was cute. It was her face that touched his heart. It was beautiful, but not like fine china is beautiful. She had a face with a story. It was overflowing with life, and yet there's conflict. She's searching for something. *What is she searching for?* He didn't know. All he could see was the life.

"It's true," he said, "you look amazing this morning." He went to her and drew her to him and kissed her like a proper boyfriend would. He took one step back. "Some eggs and toast for breakfast?"

"Dippies, please."

"Oh, so you like my dippies?"

"Yes indeed! You've converted me from hard egg to runny yolk." She smiled and went to the window and looked at the new layer of fluffy, white snow on the ground.

He started the dippies. "The weather looks like it'll be nice today, aside from the cold."

He didn't see how still she had become at the window. He didn't see her interlaced fingers or the whiteness of her knuckles, the slight droop of her head. He only heard her voice as she said, "I suppose."

Her mind was heavy with thoughts of the choice she felt she had to make.

Dutch adjusted the burner. His face became serious as he thought his own thoughts. "Ruby," he said after a few minutes, "I hate to ask, but will you and Yukon come back here tonight? Or will the two of you go back to your home?"

Her reply was almost inaudible. "I think I need a couple of days back at my apartment. Besides, I'm committed to going to Zanique's Christmas party" She walked to the table. "But I'll be back after all that, I promise. Hopefully we can be alone. Would you mind if it's just you and me and Yukon? I want to talk, I want to tell you about what, if anything, Zanique and I learn at the Jameson Mansion."

Because Dutch wasn't expecting her to want to come back at all, he was enormously pleased by her reply. He came to her and took her in his arms again and kissed her lips with sudden passion. Her lips opened, and she wrapped her arms around him and held on to him as if this were the last time she would ever see him. And then, there in his strong arms, it came to her that she was being cruel to him. He was pure, honest, and profoundly honorable. He didn't deserve to be put on hold until she got her shit together. She began to feel the old self-hatred bubbling up again.

Dutch liked to think of himself as a realist. He accepted the inevitable, whatever it might be. If Ruby told him they could no longer be together, he would accept that, although it would be heart-breaking and he'd never understand. He wasn't sure how he would go on without her. He couldn't even imagine how a man from over a hundred years ago could be her husband. He attributed it to not having the sort of imaginative creativity Ruby possessed. Dutch lived in the small, tight home of his rational nature, but it was a small tight home that was clean and bright with honesty.

"I will make certain we are alone for that," he promised her.

Ruby stood in his arms and hated herself. She saw herself as unkind and sordid. She raised her head to look at him and suddenly said, "I'm not being fair to you! You are so good to me, so *very good* to me. Your goodness means everything to me. I'm sorry I've complicated what we have with my talk of a husband from a century ago who is really a stranger to me. I am truly sorry. I hope that when I return to you, I will be able to tell you it was all a big mistake. And we can continue..."

"Well, I hope what you find is what you want to find." He released her and turned to finish cooking the eggs.

...

Zanique's yellow Hummer approached the long, private drive that led to the Jameson Mansion on Nutley Street.

"This is where Dutch said the auction was," Ruby told her. "Do you think anyone is home?"

"A place like this has caretakers," Zanique said, stopping the vehicle. "Someone's always home." She got out. "Come on. Let's go see if they have any information about your painting."

Ruby jumped down and reluctantly followed Zanique to the large, ornate front door. She pushed the button for the doorbell, and they heard it chiming Beethoven's "Für Elise."

A slender, stately woman opened the door. "Can I help you?" she asked. She had a slight German accent.

"Yes," Zanique said. "My friend and I were hoping you could answer a few questions for us."

"This is not a museum," the woman said. "And we don't have tours or any bound historical books to offer. You will get more answers from the library. It's not far from here."

Zanique nodded. "Yes, ma'am. But, well, you see, my friend was given a painting that was purchased here last month at an auction. She was hoping to get more information. About the painting."

"Oh, yes, I remember the auction well. I allocated the inventory for it. Which painting was it?"

Ruby stepped forward. "It was the one of the couple in Paris at the foot of the Arc de Triomphe."

The woman looked closely at Ruby. "Have we met before?"

"No, I don't believe we have."

"You look familiar." She paused as she searched her memory. "Hmm, well, I guess you just have one of those faces that always seem familiar." She smiled. "It's cold out here, why don't you both come in, and I'll see what I can help you with... concerning this painting of yours."

The foyer was elegant and led to a large living room with oversized windows that looked out on the back of the property. They could see a vast courtyard and some domestic outbuildings not far from the main house.

"Are those apartments back there?" Ruby asked.

"Yes, they are. Back in the prime of this estate, though, the one to the left was a studio. The lady of the house was an artist. She did most of her work there."

Ruby's heart picked up as she imagined how nice it would be to have a big house where her studio was not also her bedroom, kitchen, and living room.

"I'm sorry," the woman was saying, "but I didn't get your names."

"Oh. My name is Ruby. And this my good friend, Zanique."

They all shook hands. "How nice to meet you both. My name is Helma, Helma Brost. I'm the estate manager." She motioned for them to have a seat. "I remember your painting very well. It was painted by the lady of the house," she paused and stared at Ruby. She looked a little confused, and then with a slight crack in her voice, she continued, "painted... out in the studio you just asked about. Her name was Ruby, too. Ruby Birk Jameson."

The same name as me? Hearing Helma say her full name made her feel light-headed. She grabbed on to Zanique's shoulder for balance, then asked, "And the man of the house?"

Helma pointed at a portrait hanging on the opposite wall. As they looked at it, Ruby's jaw dropped. It was the man she made love to just a few nights ago!

"This is Obadiah Jameson," Helma said. "He was a mystic, an archeologist, and a philanthropist. He found enough treasure on his expeditions to make himself a very wealthy man."

Ruby stood up and went closer to the portrait. She could plainly see her signature at the bottom, along with the year, 1916. The sound of his name was ringing through her like a bell. She recognized it. She knew his name on a soul level.

"Obadiah," she whispered, "Obadiah." She turned back to face Helma. "This is a beautiful portrait of him."

Helma studied Ruby cautiously. She recognized her not in life but from her image in paintings that dated back over a century ago. When she replied, her tone was slightly less friendly. "Yes, it is. But then, he was a beautiful specimen. He was handsome, without question, but he was also an eccentric. You can see it in his unusual dress for the era. He would fit right in today, dressed like that, but back then, well, he was, shall we say, peculiar."

Zanique was also looking more closely at the portrait. "I think he's hot!" she exclaimed.

Zanique's charisma broke the ice with Helma, and she gave a chuckle. "Me, too. Oftentimes, I catch myself looking at this painting and wondering if he could really be that good-looking, or if that's just how his lady saw him. Capturing a handsome man perfectly would've been fine, but I personally hope that the lady of the house, instead of painting his physical appearance alone, added some of what she saw under his skin, down in his soul." This little confession made her blush. "I guess I'm just a romantic at heart."

Ruby hadn't moved. "He's also one of the subjects in the painting I have at home," she said. "I find his image to be so interesting and mysterious. Besides being a mystic and archeologist, can you tell me anything else about him... anything personal?"

Helma cleared her throat. She wanted to say, *Don't you know?* even though logically, she knew this apparent doppelgänger shouldn't know much more than she did, but instead replied, "Obviously, I never knew him. I only know the stories I've been told about him. You see, he was a mysterious man. Evidently, he was very funny and out-going. He and his wife entertained often in this house. They had garden parties in the summer and holiday parties in the formal rooms during the fall and winter. They had a very happy life together. But then in 1926, tragedy struck." She seemed ready to say more, but stopped herself. Looking at Ruby aroused her curiosity. *Surely she's not the same Ruby. She couldn't be. But still...*

"Sadness? What happened?" Zanique beat Ruby to the question.

Helma took a breath, then looked down at the floor. "That was the year that Mrs. Jameson died. She was young—well, young by today's standards. Then, she'd be considered middle-aged. From what I understand, she was hit by an automobile while walking to Lithia Park, supposedly her favorite place to go when she wasn't with him. Tragic irony if that's true, killed on the way to her safe space. After her death, he was not the same man. He became very reclusive."

Ruby began to feel odd, very odd. It wasn't her imagination. She felt strange hearing about how her past self had died. Was it grief for her former self, or was it her love for this mysterious man? She still wasn't sure if time travel was real, but learning about how the past Ruby had died freaked her out. If she could go back in time, would it be only to be killed by a car? Would her life with Mr. Jameson again be cut short?

In her pocket, her hand toyed with the necklace. All of this information, combined with the peeps of whatever it was the necklace did, was fascinating and disorienting at the same time. She felt herself taking leave of this plane of existence, as if she had climbed to a great height.

This feeling... it was as though she was looking at reality from a great height, from a space and time far removed from the here and now. The only way she could describe it was, well, like she was crawling out to the extreme edge of one of Saturn's colorful rings and peeking out into infinite space, then narrowing her view down to look upon Earth. First, she just saw the bright blue orb, floating far below, then she looked further and saw her place in it, not where she was, but where—and when—she should be.

It was blissful, an extraordinary experience, but at the same time it was as if this experience was meant to be, supposed to be. More importantly, this experience belonged to her and her alone. It was her reality to crawl over, even though being at that height made her a bit dizzy. She now knew that if she went back in time armed with this information, she could avoid death and live a long and happy life in the time she belonged to.

She swallowed hard. "How sad."

"Yes, indeed," Helma agreed. "One would think that in death we are finally free from whatever binds us here on earth. But after living in this house, I believe now that love really has no earthly ties. It can chain the soul forever."

"Why do you say that?" Zanique asked.

"I've heard things, you know, voices coming from thin air, especially at night. I've heard him calling her name."

Zanique's eyes were wide, and she was shivering with excitement. "If I were here alone, late at night, and I heard a voice calling... I wouldn't give a damn if it was for his lost love or whatever. God, I'd shit myself while I was running out the front door!"

Helma laughed. "You might think that," she said gently. "But it's not a ghostly kind of call at all. It's very human. And very sad. I'm not afraid when I hear it. There is something so comforting about this house that I never feel alone or afraid." Her explanation lightened the mood. "Besides, from what I know about the Jamesons, they had a lovely marriage. They traveled quite a lot, as you can tell by the painting you have. That painting used to hang in the master bedroom. It came from their honeymoon in Paris. I imagine they admired it often."

"Could I see where it used to hang?" Ruby asked.

"Why not? I'm not in the habit of showing the house to anyone, but hardly anyone comes by wanting to see it." Helma smiled and gestured for them to follow her. Having Ruby in the house suddenly made her want to find the answer to this strange riddle.

"Did he—Obadiah—did he die in this house?" Zanique asked with a wink to Ruby.

"No, he didn't. The story goes that ten years after his wife's death, he went on an expedition, during which he vanished. No one on his expedition team knew what happened to him. Everyone made it back except him. This house was placed in a trust with specific detailed instructions that I follow to this day."

"What kind of instructions?"

"Well, like the auction last month. I had instructions about what pieces to sell on that specific date. No rhyme or reason that I could see, but it was what the instructions in the trust demanded."

As they climbed the majestic staircase to the second floor, Ruby reached out and grabbed Zanique's arm. She was feeling faint. Clutching the necklace in her coat pocket, she had a sudden recollection of knowing this manor intimately, of walking the floors, of climbing these very stairs, of walking into the master suite. When Helma opened the door, Ruby gasped. There before her was the room with the fireplace. She was looking at the very site where she had made love to Obadiah.

"Obadiah," she whispered.

There was a slight scent in the room, something only she could smell. It was the penetrating scent of Obadiah.

Helma gave her a questioning look, then pointed, "Over there, above the bed. That's where your painting hung for many decades."

Ruby was having trouble breathing. The shock of seeing the room, the overwhelming familiarity of the house, and its owner's name—it was all too much. Her mind was wondering why this was happening, but then it shifted to *how did this happen?* Then, *what does it all mean?* Ruby walked to the french doors and looked out. "During the holidays," she said, as if possessed, "they decorated the trees down there, and the house, too, of course."

Again, Helma looked at her oddly. "I wouldn't know about that," she said. "The south gardens are an outstanding part of the property, though, and I can easily imagine them being decorated for almost any occasion."

"Yes." Ruby stared down at the courtyard and felt her mind relaxing. "And the Millennium Gardens on the east side were especially symmetrical, with climbing vines that grew up the sandstone balustrades... oh, and the rose bushes back there made a lovely backdrop to any summer party."

Helma frowned. "Are you asking me or telling me?"

"Yeah," said Zanique, "it sounds like you've been here before. Like you attended their parties."

With hardly a pause, Ruby said, "And on the west side is the pear orchard, which runs to the end of the property, the border is made up of conifers and ponderosa pines. I can almost taste the pears now."

"What are you talking about?" Zanique asked.

"To the west," Helma said, "there aren't any pears or conifers or pine trees." She gave Ruby another strange look. "There is a fence, and beyond the fence are the neighbors. If you ate any pears from this property, that happened a long time ago." She squinted at Ruby, who was still standing at the french doors. The sun shone through, casting her in its intense radiance. "*Mein Gott!*" Helma cried out. "You... You're *her,* aren't you?"

Zanique looked at Ruby and then at Helma. "What do you mean she's *her?*"

"She's the woman in the painting! The painting that hung right there for years and years. I recognized you downstairs. I thought my eyes were playing tricks on me, but the more I looked at you, the more I knew you had to be her, but... but...." Helma walked toward Ruby, holding one index finger out as if she were about to touch something hot. She gingerly touched Ruby. "Are you a ghost?"

Ruby's hands began shaking and she went light-headed as their voices began echoing through her whole body. She had the feeling of loss of balance, of slipping, of clutching something. Of a shock zipping right through her, of a shatter breaking reality. Of moving figures, voices, laughter and love. Her eyes rolled up into her head. Outside, beyond the french doors, it started to snow. Inside, in this familiar bedroom, Ruby crumpled to the floor.

Zanique ran to her.

"Ruby Birk," a ghostly voice called.

Ruby was taken back to a distant spring afternoon, when the pear trees on the west side of the property were crowned with blossoms. As if summoned, she found herself walking among the pear trees. The sun was setting and the shadows were long. He came to her from behind, surprising her by wrapping his arms around her.

"Obadiah!" she cried out.

"Ruby!" He twirled her around in a dance move. "I knew you would come back to this house!" He twirled her again, "Soon we can be together. If you so choose." He pulled her into him and held her in his sheltering arms. "The winter equinox is when the veil will be thinnest and allow you to cross."

She inhaled him. His aroma was intoxicating. Her mind wanted to doubt what was happening, it wanted to disregard his every word. But her soul had no doubt that he was real, that she was hearing something important, something she needed to know. "The winter equinox?" she asked.

"Yes." He pulled from beneath his shirt a necklace exactly like hers that he was wearing. "Bring Yukon and your necklace to Lithia Park under the full moon on the winter solstice."

"I'm not sure when that is."

He gave a smile, "Midnight, December 21. That's when I'll come for you and bring you home."

"Are you my husband?"

"Indeed."

"And we live in Ashland, in this house?"

"Yes. Come back to me, and we will once again make our lives here in this house. And I will take you places... all the places your heart desires to see."

She felt a shudder of energy flow through her, as it always did when she fell through time. "Where will you take me?"

"Oh, my dear, don't you remember? I've promised to take you to Florence. Paris. Prague. Down to the Mediterranean Sea and to the Gates of Gibraltar."

"You did?" She felt the excitement of her dream travels rise within her.

"All you have to do is say you will meet me on the equinox."

"I don't understand any of this, but I believe you. I'll be there."

He wrapped her in his arms again and she felt like she was home. She had been homesick for so long, but it had always been a homesickness for a place she couldn't identify. Now, it finally clicked. It was here. This time, this place, this man... this was her home! "It's good to be home," she told him.

"'Tis good to have you home! And soon it won't be just for a visit."

"But how is this possible? I mean, I was born in 1979. But I see that you and I were married in 1912. How—"

"Shhhh, it would take too long to explain. Just know that your necklace is the key. When you have the key, you can come to me. You are able to visit me, but on the winter solstice, you can cross over for good. Bring your necklace and Yukon and meet me in Lithia Park on the winter solstice."

"I will. I will." Her voice faded, and she leaned into him. Then she slowly raised her head. "I want to be honest with you," she said. "In my time—in 2018—I'm with a man. His name is Dutch, he's a good man. I didn't realize I was married to you until recently. Do you still want me if I've been with another man?"

He was silent. She felt him tremble.

"Oh, Ruby," he said, "there is nothing to forgive. You have lived your life the best way you knew how. I know about Dutch and Turner. I don't own you. You are an individual who is free to make her own choices. This is one such choice, and I would understand if you chose instead to stay with the man you don't doubt is real, and I don't doubt would be as good to you as he could be."

"I choose you because I know in my soul that our love is the best love possible."

"How do you know that?" he asked.

"When you touch me, when you make love to me, I feel *love*, love that is indescribable. But it's good love! The best love I have experienced." Her heart was pounding with such power that she became short of breath. The heat of the setting sun now shone across her face. She knew only that it was comforting and peaceful to be here in the orchard with him, and with the uncertainty as to the actuality of this experience being far away in her mind. "But more, I feel the intense gravity to you. So much so that I concern myself with you more than I am concerned about myself. I think of you every moment of every day. And... and when I'm not with you, I fear the loneliness that almost certainly follows. That's why I know I'll choose you, and how I know I love you."

"I knew you would come back to me, but I'm so happy for it all the same."

She liked the sound of pride in his voice. "I don't know if I'm insane, or what," she began. She was smiling at him, first with her mouth, then with her eyes, and then it was as if the spring day had pushed away her winter forever. She could see that her fears and insecurities might evaporate one day soon. Happiness was truly obtainable with Obadiah.

He pushed her cherry-chocolate hair away from her face and kissed her. "I miss my best friend as much as I miss my wife."

She didn't move. Her muscles stiffened and held themselves tense, as if not to disturb the moment. Time went by as they stood holding each other, and then all at once an explosion seemed to burst in her heart, an explosion of agony. She knew she would be leaving him, leaving this time, going back to where she had come from. "I love you Obadiah," she managed to say before the moment ended. The words felt good coming out of her mouth; in fact, the sound of his name made her lips tingle. As she began to dissolve back to her modern life, she managed one more kiss.

"Obadiah... Obadiah," Ruby heard herself speaking. She didn't want to float away.

Seeing Ruby's eyes roll up into her head, seeing her body quiver and shake, Zanique thought Ruby was having a convulsion. She yelled at Ruby. "Ruby! Ruby!"

Excruciating pain slammed into Ruby's brain. She screamed, then opened her eyes. But she was unable to process the images around her. Her eyes could see, but her brain couldn't interpret what her eyes were seeing. *I'm lost! Where am I?* An avalanche of emotions ripped through her, and her mind could not process any of them. A glimpse of Obadiah's face, then peace flashed through her, but fear pushed it away. She enjoyed an overwhelming feeling of love, but it too was suddenly torn apart by terror. Her mind was overwhelmed by color, light, thought, emotion, memory, and heat.

I'm going insane! "I'm going insane!" she repeated out loud, putting her hands to her head. She screamed again, then fell limp.

"Ruby! Come on, Ruby!" Zanique was holding her head, rubbing her temples. "Come back to me."

The brightness dimmed, and eventually the room's ambient light came from the soothing sunshine through the antique glass windows. Ruby sensed herself drifting. Not falling, but gently floating down as if she were riding in a hot air balloon.

Her mind became quiet.

Rest.

Loneliness enveloped her. Tears flowed.

She desperately wanted to go back. The thought of emptiness caused more tears to fall. Ruby wanted Obadiah, she wanted him to hold her, she wanted her husband that loved her.

Her body was chilled when she opened her eyes. "Zanique. Wha—where?" For a few minutes, Ruby didn't move, then she began looking around to orient herself. Part of her mind was aware that she was back in the present mansion, but another part of her mind was still wobbly and held only one thought—to be back with him.

I have to concentrate. I have to relax. She looked around again. Then everything was quiet. Zanique was quiet. Helma was so quiet that she was unintentionally holding her breath. It was as though Ruby's screams had caused so much distress that nothing but concern lingered in the huge mansion.

She squinted, struggling to focus, but eventually Zanique's face came back into full view.

"What the hell just happened to me?"

"I don't know." Zanique rocked back on her heels. "You sure freaked me out, girlfriend. You looked like you were having some kind of seizure."

"A seizure?"

"You were jerking and mumbling, calling Obadiah, and your eyes... Jeezus Christ, your eyes rolled up into your head and all I could see were the whites. Goddammit, Ruby, don't you ever freak me out like that ever again!" Zanique gave Ruby's leg a slight shake. "Are you okay? Do I need to drive you to a hospital?"

Am I okay? She took a minute to check out her body. "Yes, I'm okay. I'm fine."

"Where'd you go? What'd you see? What happened to you?"

"I'm not exactly sure. I was there, back in 1912 with him. We were talking and then I got dizzy, and there were all these colors... and pain... sharp pain in my head. But I'm fine now." Yet the loneliness remained, and Ruby was fully aware of her heartache.

Obadiah? The winter solstice? Was he coming to take her home? She wanted him to be real, she wanted him in her life.

Could it all be true?

There were no answers.

Ruby rubbed her forehead. Her head ached, she felt sluggish, and her body was heavy. She pulled her hand out of her pocket and unclenched her fist, revealing the necklace.

"That necklace obviously did *something* to you," Zanique said. "Can you describe what you felt? What did you see?"

"I have an overwhelming feeling of nostalgia," Ruby said after a minute. "It's like I'm homesick. Homesick for a home I haven't been to before." She closed her eyes as if chasing down a thought. "I don't know, this is all so strange. I wish I knew what Obadiah, this necklace... and the painting at home all mean."

"I agree it's mighty strange," Zanique said, her voice entirely free of irony. "But I feel like there's gotta be a reason for all of this. Like, maybe someday this will all just click, and make sense."

"I sure hope so."

"What did you and Obadiah talk about?"

"He said he was going to bring me back to his time, back to this place, when it was... our home?" She began rubbing her head. "He promised to take me to Florence, too. And Paris. And Prague. And to the Gates of Gibraltar. All of the places I've wanted to visit."

Zanique and Helma looked at each other. "I'll be taking you to the hospital, girl," Zanique said.

As Ruby's mind began to clear, the faces and bodies of her friend and Helma became clearer. She smiled at them and blinked her eyes. "No, it's okay.

I'm so sorry, I've been having some odd spells lately."
She looked up at them. "I'm so embarrassed."

"Don't be," said Helma. "If I had a seizure and
visited with Obadiah Jameson, or saw an image of
myself in a painting that was over a hundred years
old, I'd be having spells, too."

Zanique took the necklace from Ruby's hand. "Let
me put this thing away before you go trippin' on us
again."

Ruby managed a smile. Then she had to ask
another question. "Helma, do you really believe it's
me in the painting?"

"You have a very close resemblance to the woman,"
Helma replied in a cautious tone, "but I doubt it's
actually you. I mean, she died... Ruby Birk Jameson
died a long time ago. As far as I can tell, you're no ghost."

Ruby studied Helma closely for a moment. "My full
name," she said, "is Ruby Birk, and my signature is
exactly like the signature on the portrait downstairs.
It's also the same as the one on the painting of me in
Paris back in 1912."

Helma took a step back. Her face was blank. She
glanced at Zanique, who nodded to confirm what
Ruby had said.

"I... I... I don't know what is happening to me,"
Ruby said, "but there is some connection here that is
outside my understanding." She looked at her friend.
"Zanique, I don't feel very good. Would you mind
driving me home now?"

Zanique shot her a look, "You mean the hospital... right?"

"No, I want to go home. I'm fine. Really! Just take me home."

They helped Ruby stand up, then Helma and Zanique each put an arm around her and walked her down the stairs. "Lean on us," they said. "We'll help you down." As they walked, they felt Ruby's body still trembling.

"You are welcome to come back anytime you need to," Helma told her. "I imagine you'll have many questions. I think this is the beginning of something...."

"The beginning of what?"

"I don't know. But I believe in love. True love. And if you *are* the woman in the painting, he's been calling for you for a long time. Maybe if you come here, you might connect to him. Somehow. Maybe love really does circumvent the restraints of time!"

In the Hummer, Zanique asked, "So, I'm taking you home?"

"Yes, for the last time, home, please. I don't feel good."

Zanique patted Yukon, who had his head over her shoulder from the back seat. "Hey, boy." Then she started up the Hummer and delivered them to Ruby's home above Mrs. Bimby's garage.

Chapter 14

The next evening, Ruby stayed home to work on a new painting, a portrait. The necklace bounced against her neck as she did a series of vigorous strokes. Her mind was hovering somewhere between cause and effect, between fear and joy. It had left the 21st-century world and ended up somewhere in the early 20th century. While her hands were working, her eyes were seeing that world, and her mind was occupied with Obadiah Jameson. He was sitting for his portrait, and it was shaping up nicely. He was her world of art now.

The wonderful, wholesome scent of pine, with its hint of frankincense, mastic, and other spices had hypnotized her. They were casting such a strong spell over her that she remembered nothing in her twenty-first-century world—not Helma, not Mrs. Bimby, not Zanique, not even Dutch. In her mind there was only Obadiah. It was as if the life she'd known, the depression, the loneliness, all of it was being dissolved by this strange new future filled with happiness.

Happiness?

Could it be possible?

"Obadiah. Obadiah." She had to say his name out loud. The sound of it seemed to banish her solitariness. Her episode at the Jameson Mansion seemed to have left her wanting more of the man. She had come home dazed and in an ethereal fog. She was struggling to think of what this could be, then it hit her.

Love.

She was lost in a strange love. The art of love. An utterly new kind of art. Art, love, life—everything was so very different now. Even if Obadiah were some kind of imaginative episode, some mental illusion, her reality was now a very different place.

Perhaps her visit to the Jameson Mansion had triggered something within her. Whatever it was, it was making Ruby impatient and restless.

A loud knocking broke the spell and jolted her back to the present. Yukon barked and ran to the door. She quickly removed the necklace and laid it on the table. Then she opened the door.

"Are you ready?" Zanique asked before Ruby could even say hello.

"Ready? Ready for what?"

Zanique gave her a disappointed look. "Well, let's see... today is Saturday the seventeenth. What's going on? Oh, yeah, my Christmas party!"

Under the spell of the necklace, Ruby had forgotten all about the Christmas party at the B&B. "Oh. Gee. That was tonight, wasn't it?"

"Yes, it *is* tonight. And please don't tell me you're not coming."

"No, no, I'm coming. Just give me a minute to fix myself up. I can't go anywhere looking like this."

Zanique smiled. "Sure, take your time. I'll just relax here with Yukon." She plopped herself down on the only place there was to sit, half a cushion on the couch. She had to push sketches aside to find even that much room.

"Really?" Ruby asked. "I can take my time?"

"Uh, no, you really can't. We're supposed to be there by seven. Jimmy's making dinner for everyone, and it'll be rude to be late. Come on, girl, jump to it! We gotta bounce!"

Thus encouraged, Ruby began rushing around and getting herself ready. On her way out the door, she called Yukon. "Come on, boy. You get to go, too." At the last minute, she grabbed the necklace and shoved it down into her pocket. She no longer felt comfortable being without it. It was a part of her now. They jumped into Zanique's Hummer, and she rushed for the highway.

Feeling a bit perturbed by running late, Zanique held back the negativity she was feeling and said, "How are you feeling since your episode at the Jameson Mansion?"

"I'm fine. It was strange, what happened yesterday, wasn't it?"

"Uh, strange, sure. If you want to call it that. I'd say fucking scary! But you can say strange." She gave Ruby a quick sideways look. "You didn't put the necklace on again, did you?"

"Oh, no. I'm not going to do that again until I'm in a controlled environment. I wouldn't just wear it to a dinner party."

Zanique smiled. "It's good you left it at home for tonight." As Ruby looked down at the floor, Zanique knew her friend had it with her.

"I always carry it with me," Ruby confessed. "It's as if the necklace is a part of me now."

"Sure, I get it. Just don't go having any convulsions tonight... please."

Ruby nodded.

It was seven thirty-four when they arrived at Zanique's B&B. They slipped Yukon into the fenced backyard to run free while they ate. Zanique had already planned to feed him plenty of leftovers after dinner. She had phoned ahead to let Odessa and Jimmy know they would be late. Though that made her feel a little better, she was still a touch annoyed by Ruby's forgetfulness.

Everyone else was already seated at the table. They shouted out the usual holiday greetings as Zanique and Ruby took their seats. A minute later, Odessa came into the dining room, hugged Ruby, and complimented her deep crimson evening gown. Then she went over and, like a mother, hugged and kissed Zanique.

"I'm so glad the two of you made it," she said. "I was getting worried."

Zanique shot a look at Ruby, "We're sorry," she told Odessa. "We hope we didn't put anyone out too much."

"No problem," Odessa told her. "Jimmy kept everything warm." The chef was standing at the buffet table, ready to carve a beautiful prime rib. "Please take your plates, everyone," Odessa said in her announcer's voice, "and head on over to the buffet."

One by one, the guests lined up to fill their plates as Odessa served the dinner salads and rolls. But Ruby found the chitchat boring. Her mind was still off in another era. She was wishing she could have stayed home and finished her painting. She'd rather be thinking about Obadiah than mixing with Zanique's friends.

A gentleman with gray hair and a white beard sitting directly across from Ruby got her attention. "Zanique tells me you're an artist," he said. "Have I seen any of your work?"

"Yes, I am an artist. But I doubt that you've seen any of my work." She was being respectful, but she really couldn't care less about table conversation. "And you, sir, what do you do? Professionally?"

"Me? I'm an author and historian."

"Might I have read any of your work?"

He smiled. "As you put it so eloquently, I doubt that you have read any of my work."

Everyone at the table was chatting with their immediate neighbors, and no one was paying any attention to Ruby and the author.

"Do you enjoy writing?" Ruby asked, feeling obliged to be polite and continue the dialogue.

He thought for a moment. "I'm not sure if you could say I *like* writing," he said thoughtfully. "I'm more *possessed* by it. I'm called to do it from a higher place. It's a spiritual calling, if you will." He paused. "If I had a choice, I'd be normal. You know, have a normal job with a reliable paycheck and health insurance and benefits."

Ruby had to smile at this. "Yes, I do know. I know all too well what it's like to be working in the arts, to be driven to do something most people don't recognize as 'real work.'" She suddenly remembered what Dutch's father had said. She gave the man a genuine smile. "I've been different all of my life. I've never really gotten used to it."

He gave a knowing smile. "Ahh, yes, the risks of being different. Certainly, we learn early on in life that others have the power to single us out... to bully the one that is different. For us to follow the path of our heart, all the while knowing what our chances of being successful are... well, that is a difficult road indeed. But as for me, I always believe that someone somewhere understands what I've written and in some way, it has helped them in their lives."

She nodded. This was turning into an interesting conversation. "Yes, I think being understood is a basic human need. And in art or writing, well, it's our way of reaching out to humanity. To communicate. To be understood. But we do so at the risk of 'normal' people thinking we're weird and crazy." As the man nodded, she said, "I admit it straight up. My work is evidence that I'm different, that I'm alone on so many levels. I'm not what people call normal. I do not want to be normal."

"It is my pleasure to talk with someone that understands my pain," the man said. Then he grinned at her. "Do you know the artist Edvard Munch and his piece *The Scream*?"

"Of course I do."

"I'm sure he was a very different person, too. There is little doubt that he had similar trials and tribulations to the ones you and I share. I've come to learn that his mother died when he was young. His father raised him. Unfortunately, his father was mentally ill and was in no shape to raise children. Edvard suffered a harsh and nontraditional childhood, and it was that abnormal childhood that made his work so successful. I'm guessing it would be nice to own *The Scream* and have it hanging somewhere in your house, but I doubt it would be nice to have

Edvard Munch hanging around in your house." He laughed out loud.

"Funny," she said. "I think Ben Shahn said something similar about Van Gogh."

"Indeed. The point is that being different doesn't mean you are doomed to be unsuccessful. If you were successful, you would still be you, and if you're like me, well, I will always be alone in the world. Success won't change that."

"I don't know that I will always be alone," she replied. "But I will always be different."

"I like that," he said. "Cheers to us for being different." He held up his glass of wine and clinked it to hers. Everyone at the table joined the toast, even though they had no idea what it was about.

The man went on, speaking more quietly. "Our work is honest work, if it is anything at all. No other occupation has to be as painfully honest as ours. Working in the arts is truthful work. We lay it out there for others to judge." Ruby noticed that he wasn't eating. He was totally engaged in their conversation, just holding his fork above his plate. "Our work vibrates in perfect synchronization," he added. "Why, it's magic!"

"Magic?" Ruby gave him a quizzical look. She noticed that she wasn't eating, either.

"Sure," he said. "We create magic when we work." He spoke calmly and rationally, as if anyone would understand. "What we do touches the invisible world of ethereal forms. It has constructive power to help us reach our goals. Works of art, works of magic—they're related in their infinite potential and distinctive limits. Good art relies on your strength of character and mental ability to focus so you can produce it. It is limited by fear, frustration, and depression. And it is through the magic we cast that we find harmony. You, Ruby, have the divine spark. I can tell. You can tell, too. It's the divine spark that calls you to take up the brush and dip it in the paint and spread it on the canvas."

Ruby had to blink. "Magic? Divine spark? You talk as if I'm a witch."

"A witch?" he repeated. "What is a witch but someone who can control the changes in her life?"

She had to think about that for a long minute. "I've never thought of what a witch is or isn't."

"Think of it now. Magic is nothing more than the methods and tools used to move or manipulate your given reality. Life is constantly changing, and a witch can manipulate the changes to meet her needs."

"I'm not sure I agree," she said. "I'm an *artist*, I paint the things I see, I live my life in the given reality. I don't manipulate anything."

"Is that true?" He raised an eyebrow. "When you paint, do you always paint the 'given reality'? Are there times when you paint a scene you see somewhere else? From a place that no one else in this consensual reality has seen?"

Ruby thought about this, too, then suddenly realized she had been painting Obadiah and Lithia Park. A different reality. She had been manipulating her reality. "Come to think of it," she finally admitted, "I have."

"I thought so. And has the reality you painted influenced your given reality?"

"Yes, it has."

"You see? You have created magic, my dear. Magic is what frees us. Fear is what imprisons us. If we are aware of our power, then we can walk into the unknown with confidence. The most important thing about the work we do is that *we can do it alone*. People like us have everything we need within ourselves. When we commit to using it, we see results."

Ruby began picking at her food, mostly to avoid saying anything. She was thinking about her travels through time, her time with Obadiah and how they had made love, real love.

Magic?

Even though this man sitting across from her was a stranger, he seemed to know her. He was talking about magic... and wasn't she living in a magical time of her life? "Magic," she began slowly, "is a power that we choose to use?"

"Yes, it is."

"Could it be that when we choose the act of lovemaking, could that be a source of our magic?"

"Oh, now that is powerful magic! During times of passion, you are at your highest self. If you are wrapped up in passion with someone else, the two of you are in your higher selves, and your physical consciousnesses become as one, a *very strong one*. Then the two of you can direct or focus your power toward an agreed-upon goal, and this will manipulate the reality of the objective in accordance with your will."

"Powerful? How powerful?"

"Limitlessly powerful. You could travel in time, channel the spirits, bend the future. Do almost anything you put your mind to. You used the term lovemaking... just knowing the difference between lovemaking and sex is adding power."

"It is?"

"Think about it, Ruby. You mentioned a very important and powerful ingredient; *Love*. Love is an especially magical property, but so is a talisman that connects us, or a specific place where we feel connected. Sacred love, sacred talismans, sacred spaces—they're all examples of properties that focus your inner, or you might say *soulful* magic. I'm sure you have a special place where you feel connected?"

Lithia Park. The ankh. Obadiah. Those were her sacred place, her sacred talisman, and her sacred lover. She knew this man spoke true. "Yes," she said. "I have a sacred place. And a talisman."

"Wonderful!"

"My talisman was given to me. I'm told it's very old. I don't know much about it." She laid her fork down. "Uh, could I show it to you? Maybe you might know something about it?"

"I would be delighted." His eyes became livelier and he sat up straighter.

She carefully handed the necklace across the table to him. He held it gently, but his face was almost expressionless.

"Now this is a strange thing, isn't it?"

"So, you know something about it?" she asked, almost in a whisper.

"Indeed. This has some powerful magic in it." He hesitated for a moment. "There are messages engraved upon these links." Closing his eyes, he held the necklace close to his forehead for a minute, then opened his eyes and examined each engraved link. "This one says, *Prepare yourself for your journey with this ankh.* And this one, *Stand on the consecrated ground and cast your spell with love...* the links then go on to say that when you are standing on the consecrated ground, and when the moon is in its correct phase, you will depart for your journey."

"The links say all that?" Ruby could feel a new warmth in this room filled with people chatting on many topics. "I'm amazed that you know what those symbols mean," she added, her voice still quiet. "I was under the impression that very few people knew these symbols."

"As I mentioned before, I'm also a historian. Your necklace says much more." He hesitated, then leaned in closer to Ruby, who was studying him with skeptical interest. "Let me be frank with you, Ruby. I'm not here by coincidence. My name is Bernard Griffith, I'm an associate of Ezra Arkin."

Ruby's eyes snapped wide-open as she instantly recalled that Ezra had told her and Zanique that Bernard Griffith was his expert. She chuckled nervously and took another look at the man. "I knew something was afoot," she finally said. "You... this whole...." Her face turned red and she attempted to get up from the table.

"Wait," he said. "Please stay and give me time to explain."

She reseated herself and leaned slightly forward. She also picked up her fork again, just in case anyone was looking at her.

"I'm sorry if I upset you," he said. "First, I *am* an author, and everything I said is true." He gave an apologetic wave. "I wasn't trying to deceive you. I just wanted a way to approach you. When Ezra sent me photos of this necklace, I didn't believe my eyes. I told him the truth; that this necklace is more than a necklace. It's powerful magic from before recorded time."

"Fine," she said in a flat voice. "But that doesn't explain why you're here at this party."

He wrapped his fingers around the ankh. "Like I said, this talisman is unbelievable. I had to meet you! I hoped I could ask your permission to see it. Ezra told me that Zanique had told him in passing that the two of you would be here at her B&B tonight. I immediately booked a room so I could introduce myself and ask you about this." He smiled. "but we started talking, and before I knew what was going on, you handed it to me! Again, I'm sorry if it seems like I manipulated the situation." His kind blue eyes were fixed on her face. "Amazing, isn't it?"

Ruby finally smiled. She picked up her glass of holiday punch, took a sip, and returned the glass to the table. "The ankh is amazing," she affirmed. "I might even go so far as to say it seems supernatural."

"Have you had any extraordinary experiences with this charm?" he asked.

"Yes, Bernard, I have. I seem to have been transported back in time. To a specific time and place. I can't explain it, but I've been there, and I've interacted with people from the past, and then I am returned to this time. From what I can tell, there is no rhyme or reason to what's happening. It just happens." She confided this in hopes that Bernard had knowledge of the ankh that would help her. She had taken a leap of faith. She trusted him.

"Well," he said, adjusting his reading glasses and holding the necklace closer to his eyes. "it's hard for me to explain what this ankh really is while we're sitting here at this table." He took his glasses off.

"First, I would have to explain that the way ancient people looked at life was completely different than we do today. For instance, they didn't worship the gods and goddesses as we think of worship. They looked at life as wholly spiritual, and the spiritual life was not only religious, but scientific technology based on celestial energy. The divine was constant and involved in everyday living. I imagine they were in a state of constant prayer, but not prayer like we do, selfish and pleading for gifts from God. No, they were in a more harmonic balance with the divine. It was respectful worship that flowed through daily life. It was of great importance for them to affirm the sacredness of the land. They knew that whatever they did to the earth they also did to themselves."

"How so?"

"Respect the earth, and you respect yourself. Disrespect the earth, and you disrespect yourself. If the land is sacred, then we are sacred. If the land is disposable, pollutable, expendable... what then are we?"

She was trying to follow his reasoning. "So how does my interaction with the earth have anything to do with this ankh?"

"Let me put it this way. Your true self and the land are as one. Relating to a specific area or environment, however small, brings you to a universal awareness, a divine awareness. Magic begins with your body. You become aware of your own physical location, your sacred space, the place you feel is hallowed ground. This sacred place, under certain circumstances, say, with this ankh, leads you into ethereal vision, into a transpersonal awareness. In the sacred space with your sacred mind... and assisted by your sacred talisman," he held up the ankh, "you channel a celestial relationship with the divine. But keep in mind it starts in a very small way. Awareness of the earth. And it grows into a truly compassionate, sensitive, and harmonious connection to our sacred planet." Bernard's expression changed. "Earlier you said that you have a sacred place that you hold above all other places."

"Yes, I do." But she hesitated to name Lithia Park.

"Good. That's very good."

She looked thoughtfully up and down the table, then looked back at her new friend. If he was indeed a friend. "I hadn't considered anything like... like what you're saying, before. It takes my mind, a sacred place, and this ankh so that I can see the past." She paused. "But wait—I've had visions and experiences in a few different places. Are all of them sacred spaces?"

He lifted a pitcher of holiday punch and refilled their glasses. "In a way," he said, "but some places are weaker than others, and so in those places your time in an experience is limited. But it's your ankh that makes it possible in those weak areas. Your ankh is like a powerful battery filled with divine power from the cosmos. This small device is powerful enough to allow you to move through time, even though the earth under your feet isn't divinely sanctified."

"Is it technology? Or magic?"

"Ah, you make a good point. For me, technology implies that the user aims at gaining knowledge of the world. Magic implies the user aims at gaining self-knowledge."

"So perhaps magic and technology are two sides of the same coin?" Ruby asked.

"You could look at it that way. Yes... yes, in fact, if you want, we can think of one side as being emotional and personal, whereas the flip side is rational and objective. And in our day and age, one side is mocked and misunderstood, whereas the other is thought of as complete and authoritative. And further, given the two sides, one must consider what is sandwiched in-between. The center. The center is where the nature of our world exists. The magician respects nature, befriends nature to do the good work for the planet. Science often looks at the earth's force, Mother Nature, as an object and exploits her resources without respect or permission. Do you see the difference?"

Ruby's eyes were now sparkling. "Yes, I can see the difference.

"Back to your ankh. Science says time travel is impossible. Yet you have experienced it yourself. No one told you about it or tried to convince you of it, yet you went specifically to a place and time, and then returned here, to a specific time. Meaning, this ankh seems to be programmed. Had it not been, you would've randomly traveled back in history and quite possibly never come back to us. You might have been lost in time in some haphazard moment. It is remarkable that you were there, that you lived in a past moment where you could fully interact with its inhabitants." He cleared his throat. "I'm sure you asked yourself why."

"Of course! I still do."

"This ankh is thousands of years old," he said, handing the necklace back to her, "and yet it was designed for only one person to use. No one else can be affected by it. Or affect it. This is truly yours, Ruby. It was made for one user, and can take you to many destinations if you learn how to direct it."

Ruby was silent. At this moment the magnitude of the situation struck her as it had not before. "Magic," she whispered. "Sacred places. Mother Nature. This sounds like we're making up a story."

Bernard spoke in low tones to keep their conversation between only them. "Of course it does. But there is more. It's celestial, or should I say, divine. Or maybe absolute power."

Her head was bowed, her face lost in the growing obscurity of his words.

"Imagine the tumblers of a lock," he said. "You need the combination for all of the tumblers to line up and open the lock. So we have you, the sacred body. We have a sacred place. We have the sacred talisman." He pointed at the necklace. "But what is lacking is the celestial piece. According to the necklace, the celestial piece is an alignment of some kind, I assume, a solar alignment."

She took a deep breath. *The winter solstice.* But she didn't say this out loud.

"Ruby, I envy you. It appears that you have been cast into a journey, a crossing beyond personal will and personal boundaries into the unknown."

"But it frightens me. I enjoy going back in time, but all the mystery around it scares me."

"Don't be afraid my dear. It's nothing but change. Change is eternal and absolute, and no amount of not believing in change will alter the law of change. Even if you had never come across this ankh, you are destined to change. So why not take charge of your change? Why not navigate the path of change to a course you would rather be on? Use this ankh and your consciousness, and you can reshape your life."

"Yes." Her lips formed the word, but it was soundless. Her eyes became fixed on the necklace, its engravings.

"You see," he said in a gentle voice, "what seems impossible is really quite possible."

She touched the necklace and could not speak. Her hands fell into her lap. Then in the silence, a beam of light began to blaze around her. She saw warm sunlight, quiet and calm, glittering on the trees of Lithia Park. *The sacred place*, she told herself. The earth's green grass was under her feet as she strolled through the park, moving from light into shadow, from shadow back into light. She could hear an owl calling from the distance. The park stood clearly in front of her, and when she looked to the right she could see a dirt road that ran straight until it reached a wooded area, then turned and went over the hill where she knew the Jameson Mansion sat.

She was acutely sensible of the dinner party, the other guests, everything around her. She fixed her attention on the road that led to the home where she presumed her husband lived. She looked back over her shoulder. There she could see the dinner party and Bernard talking to her, and yet her mind was empty of that realm. It moved with her soul, leaving only her body at the table. Obeying that strange hunger for experience, Ruby allowed herself to fall through time, plunging into a dimension of blissfulness that was as vivid as any other reality. She was about to go down the road to Obadiah when, without warning and against her will, there rose before her a face she knew and loved. She heard words.

"Hey, what are you two so engaged in?" Zanique awoke Ruby from her spell. She was holding a serving tray of stuffed mushroom caps.

Ruby shook her head to regain her equilibrium. "Uh, well," she laughed, "magic and the thought that I might be a witch," she said sotto voce.

Zanique put the tray on the table and gave this a minute's consideration. "I can see you working with magic, girlfriend, but a witch? I don't see that. You're too... you're more of an angel."

"Angel or witch," Bernard said. "Either is correct. At least in my opinion."

"How do you mean that?" Zanique asked him. "Aren't all witches bad? Evil?"

"No, not at all." He laughed. "There are good witches and bad witches. There are also good angels and bad angels. Good or bad, they can all work magic, but witches are here in the physical world, and angels live in the spirit world."

And now Ruby suddenly felt very uncomfortable. She wanted to leave. She took a deep breath. "Zanique," she said, "this is Bernard Griffith... he's Ezra's expert."

Zanique gave them both a funny look.

"Indeed I am," he told her. "Although I don't know Ezra very well, he did send me pictures of Ruby's necklace. I just had to see it for myself, so I booked a room here. I won't make a nuisance of myself by overstaying my welcome. I'm just passing through. I plan to finish the week snowshoeing on the magical Mount Shasta. Then perhaps a stay in a cabin at Stewart Springs. I leave here tomorrow."

"Nice!" Zanique exclaimed. "You like to snowshoe, too?"

"I'm an earth person," he said. "I have a good relationship with Mother Earth."

"That's a good way of putting it," Zanique said. "I suppose I have a good relationship with the earth, too. I feel most like myself in the outdoors, like, when I'm trudging through the snow."

"You snowshoe?"

"I do! I'm a guide. I have all the gear for just about anything adventurous outdoors."

"That's good!" he told her. "Out there on the mountain is where I feel my mind, body, and soul are balanced. At a point of equilibrium. Out there on the mountain and in the snow, I'm able to free my mind completely from this materialistic world, and that's when the stories I write come to me. Once I get down from the mountain, well, then I go back to writing my novel."

Zanique walked to his side of the table, dragged up an empty chair, sat down next to him, and began talking about snowshoeing in the mountains, something Ruby had no interest in. Now that Zanique had joined the conversation, the usual happened: the man's attention was captured by Zanique's beauty. The attraction could not be denied, and he seemed to have forgotten all about Ruby and her necklace.

She felt alone again. She finished her dinner, which was now cold, and gazed at the other people still at the table, some eating dessert, some listening to other people's conversations, some still talking to friends. Ruby felt out of place again. But she hung in there and tried to make herself look like she was enjoying the party, even though she was actually reliving the conversation about magic with the stranger across the table. Something began tingling inside her as she began to imagine how she might be able to alter her reality.

"Silent Night" was playing in the background as the dinner finally began winding down. Ruby mustered up the courage to excuse herself from the party, saying she had to go into the backyard to check on Yukon. After finding him quite content to be in the snow, she climbed the stairs to the Bartlett Pear Room. This was a large, ornate guest room with its own bath, complete with claw-footed tub. Odessa had made up a daybed that Zanique had already declared was her own to sleep on, freeing up the queen-sized bed for Ruby. She studied it. The bed appeared to be a whole lot more comfortable than the shabby bed she had back in her studio apartment. She rubbed her eyes. She was looking forward to getting a good night's sleep in that bed.

As Ruby was thinking about bedtime, Zanique remained downstairs, talking to Bernard and then to Odessa and Jimmy and finally to the last of the partygoers. Ruby had had as much celebration as she could tolerate. Now she was, so to speak, dog-tired. She decided a nice hot bath before crawling into bed would be the perfect ending to this night. As the old-fashioned deep tub filled, she looked out the window at the snow flurries falling out of the sky.

She always took pleasure in meeting Zanique's friends and witnessing Zanique's generosity toward others, a trait that made Ruby more conscious of how generous and wonderful her friend was. But Bernard, she thought, was strange with his babbling about magic and witches and realities. The word *magic* seemed to vibrate through her.

She used the small complimentary bottle of bubble bath. Climbing into the suds and hot water on such a frigid night made her feel ecstatic. She could sense her realty drifting away. She wanted to see Obadiah. She needed to feel his body against her. Her loneliness was burning her soul.

"Obadiah," she called.

She got out of the tub and retrieved her necklace and put the necklace around her neck. She was hoping to use the liberating bathwater to enhance her experience of touching the past. She was hoping that wearing the necklace would help her find him. Sure enough, the hot water combined with the power of the necklace elevated her senses. She seemed to intuitively understand how all this worked. Soon came the familiar disorienting effect. Her spirit, intellect, and emotions dissolved into the steamy vapor in the room.

Magic.

Imagination was in control, just like when she began to work on a blank canvas. Her creative potential was never higher than in the magical moment of her initial brush stroke. Her desire, the hot bath, her necklace—these were her first brush strokes, and her potential was indeed high.

Most places have their own peculiar smells. Tonight, as she closed her eyes, she let her mind relax completely. She began to smell the day-to-day odors of the B&B, the cooking and cleaning, the aromas that the guests brought into the house. There was also the distinct underlying essence of the house itself. She could smell the scented decorations Odessa set around the B&B: the old-fashioned talcum, the antique roses, the seasonal ornamental pomanders. The smell of oranges, cloves, and cinnamon was comforting and grounded her in the common reality. She instinctively knew that if she left this time, left this reality, she remained anchored by these smells. And now that a tether had been set for her, she didn't want to be tethered. At the same time, the tether seemed important. She was ready to let go. She focused on her breathing. Reality began to vibrate.

Chapter 15

*Z*anique was quite happy: the holiday dinner had been excellent and beautifully presented by Odessa and Jimmy. Her chef's special touch of hand-selected herbs and spices enhanced the flavors of the prime rib, lobster, and au gratin potatoes.

With dinner finished, she went to the back door and let Yukon into the mudroom, where she presented him with a plate of meat and shellfish.

"Merry Christmas, my furry friend," she said as she hugged and kissed him. When Yukon returned the kiss with a long lick on the side of her face, she giggled and patted him again, then watched him eat his holiday dinner. After he ate she played with him in the back yard and then made a bed for him in the mudroom. Getting him settled for the night, she said, "Good night, Yukon. I'll be down first thing in the morning to let you out." With that, she made her way upstairs. The house was becoming quieter with all the guests, including the mysterious Bernard, returning to their rooms. She wondered about him as she climbed the stairs.

Even before Zanique opened the door to the bedroom, Ruby, who was basking in a hot bath in the claw-footed tub, sensed her presence. But that was the last thing she identified within the present time, for suddenly she could smell something else—a scent that made the other, commonplace smells dissipate. The scent of frankincense and mastic filled the bathroom. The signature smell of Obadiah.

She opened her eyes. He was standing beside the tub, looking down at her. Their eyes locked. His image was intoxicating to her, but seeing him standing there in physical form was something altogether different. His eyes were amazing, the irises the greenest of greens, like perfect emeralds set in porcelain white orbs. The effect of his gaze was chilling. It wasn't his expression, but more the brilliance and depth of his eyes that spoke to her. Love was their message.

"Could you hand me that towel?" she calmly asked him.

"Of course," Zanique replied as she came into the bathroom. She looked down at Ruby. "But it's right there, girlfriend. Only an arm's length away. Why do you need me to hand it to you?"

Zanique was standing in the bathroom, but Ruby couldn't see her. All she saw was Obadiah, and it was Obadiah who handed her the towel. Like Aphrodite arising from the waves, she stood up out of the water and accepted the towel. Stepping from the tub, she lightly dried herself, then stood naked in front of him.

"Don't worry. I took care of Yukon. He's got a nice bed in the mudroom." Seeing the odd look on Ruby's face, she hesitated, but then asked, "Did you enjoy the party?"

Ruby gave Obadiah a devilish grin. "It's so strange, this thing we have."

Zanique looked more closely at her friend, but failed to notice the ankh through the steam. "What *thing* do we have?"

"I'm not sure," Ruby said in her dreamy voice, "but I know I love you." She reached out and touched Obadiah, then wrapped her arms around his neck and kissed him. "I want you to make love to me!" She took his hand and led him toward the big bed. Her damp body glistened in the lamplight. She lay on the bed and wrapped her legs around his waist to pull him closer to her. "Oh, God! I have wanted you for so long." She began pulling his clothes off and tossing them on the floor.

It was Zanique who was being disrobed by her passionate friend. "Whoa," she said, not resisting, "I never knew you felt this way about me."

A pile of clothes now lay next to the bed, and Ruby had her legs spread open. Obadiah responded. She could see how hard he was. He slowed things down by lightly touching her skin, then kissing her on the neck. But she didn't want to go slow. She knew what she wanted, and so she pushed his head down to the source of her sexuality. She arched her back.

Zanique looked up from between Ruby's legs, "Um... are you sure you want me to do this?"

"Yes! Yes! I've never wanted anything more! Please... if you don't act fast, I'm going to explode." Ruby's voice filled the room.

Obadiah worked so skillfully that within seconds Ruby was digging her nails into his back again. Her spasms rippled the full length of her body. Her mind raced faster than the speed of light, carrying memories from a lifetime ago that came and went. This man, Obadiah, meant more than sex, more than making love, and yet when she saw him, all she wanted was to feel his skin against hers. She somehow knew there were questions she wanted to ask him, but questions were pushed back into the hidden corners of her mind. What was important, what she needed, was to feel him.

Then his tongue hit her g-spot. She felt her temperature spike, she was burning hot with desire. So hot, she thought, it might cook her soul alive! Her moans could be heard throughout the house.

Zanique paused. "Please, Ruby," she managed to say, "there are other guests in the house."

"I'm burning up," was all Ruby could say. "Don't talk! Not now, I'm so close!" She pushed Obadiah's head back down. The work of his tongue cast a splendid enchantment over her. His hands reached up and played with her tender breasts, enhancing the sensation. "There," she nearly shouted, "that's it, right there... RIGHT THERE!"

"Please quiet down," Zanique pleaded from between Ruby's legs, her hands nonetheless playing with renewed vigor with Ruby's surprisingly soft breasts. Zanique felt the helplessness of unfamiliarity, but also the feeling of her own desire. The powerful desire to execute an act of pleasure came over her at that moment, and she, too, could have shouted in a frenzy because her soul had reached the boundary between its angel and its devil. Ruby was pushing the top of her head, calling for her to do things she had never dreamed of doing to her friend. The excitement stormed through her, it threatened her security. There had always been boundaries in her life, but tonight a boundary was being stretched. Ruby was testing her limits.

Who is this woman? Zanique was asking herself. *I thought I knew her, I know nothing about her, she's a girl with remote secrets, and somehow she can take command over me.* At this moment Ruby was like the most treacherous waves in the ocean, the highest peak of the mountain range, the depth and the height that were too irresistible to pass up. Zanique had to make that dive, had to climb that challenging peak, no matter the cost.

Behind her innocent smile, Zanique thought, *lies something quiet, yet disturbing.* She began her task, working hard to satisfy Ruby. Zanique's heartbeat was in pursuit of Ruby's climax.

The shadows on the wall reflected something beautiful. But this kind of sex had a swiftness to it, Zanique thought, and the speed of it was thrilling her, driving her mind and body into a belly-aching yet thrilling place. Looking up from between Ruby's legs, she saw on Ruby's face a look of almost fear, her forehead furrowed, her eyes half-closed, expanded blue veins appearing ghostlike from under her pale skin, her jaw clenched. But then her eyes went wide and began staring down at her. Their hearts were racing faster and faster, until at last Ruby threw her head back and shouted with elation at her volcanic climax.

A long pause followed. The quiet moment was almost like nothing else existed in the world, like there were only two women who loved each other. Or at least that's what Zanique thought.

But then Ruby began to stir again. "I want you inside me. Make sweet love to me."

Obadiah climbed onto the bed. Nothing needed to be said, his passion and yearning were as strong as hers. His body was strong and fully muscular, and she could feel the weight of him on her. He tongue-kissed her, then rolled down to her hard nipples. The sucking aroused her further, but then he suddenly stopped. As he rested on top of her for a moment, they lay there, breathing hard and heavy, savoring the moment. As he stared into her eyes, she was overcome with the love that came from some mysterious place within. Suddenly tears of joy began to flow. The adoration she felt while being with him again was so overwhelming that she trembled under his weight.

She wrapped her arms around him. "I love you," she whispered.

"I love you, too," he replied.

"I... I... I... love you, too?" Zanique reluctantly replied.

And then Zanique panicked. Why was she taking on the male role in lovemaking? This was an act that went against her usual instincts. But she was willing to take the leap. Her life had always been full of risk, and she'd realized at an early age that if she didn't take risks, she might never move forward. It took courage to leave the relatively secure garden of her emotions and move out into the unfamiliar landscape where Ruby was taking her.

Zanique reached down for her penis. It was erect, hard as rock, and ready. As she entered Ruby, she felt like she was flying. She was soaring at a great speed, she was overwhelmed by an ecstasy that was propelling her mind and body into a feverish place. She was pressed hard into Ruby's body, the skin of her legs, hips, and stomach all hot. Zanique's hips drove her forward. The feel of Ruby under her was sweet and intimate. As she worked, her chest became tight. She realized she'd been holding her breath. As she suddenly gasped for air, the oxygen hit her blood, mixing with the adrenaline, and she, too, cried out, her scream filling the room with the sound of victory atop a wail of rebelliousness.

As Obadiah entered Ruby, she gripped his back and dug in. Every inch of him stimulated her, she gyrated against him. She became aware that she was smiling, and some part of her mind thought it must be a stupid-looking smile because she had no control over it. She was certain it was an idiot's grin of delight. She let the smile go and bit his shoulder, dug in deeper with her fingers, and bucked harder against him.

Zanique began to moan. She had never had anyone dig their fingernails into her back before. The pain of it was oddly liberating. She went with it, using the pressure of Ruby's fingers as a gauge as to how fast she should move.

Look at that smile! She must love me. Love? Could it really be love? Zanique was having trouble digesting the word. *Love* was a strong word, not one to be uttered or taken lightly. There had been few times in her life when anyone had told her they loved her, fewer times when those words were spoken with romantic intensity.

Obadiah moved slowly, deliberately, in and out, gently, but fully penetrating her... sexually, mentally, spiritually.

He is so sexy! some rational part of Ruby was thinking. *He's sophisticated and blessed with a streak of self-confidence. He knows he's in control. His confidence is more than just personal pride. He must hold a pride of the mind, a deep belief in his own ability. He has a conviction about him that shouts that he can take on anyone in the world. On any terms.*

But... but some part of her mind was looking for something to ground her in consensual reality, something of the "real world." *But is he real? Is this really happening?*

"Oh, yes!" Ruby screamed. "You've got me now, come on... take me!"

Obadiah began thrusting faster, more forcefully, and she responded by arching her back and crying out for more.

Being born with the organs of both sexes had never seemed to be of any real benefit to Zanique. Until tonight. Zanique had always assumed that the female side of her was dominant. She had been attracted only to men. But there was something very sensual about Ruby tonight... something she couldn't resist. She was shocked at how aroused she was and how hard her penis was. Of course, it had gotten hard before, but nothing had ever excited Zanique enough for it to get so completely stiff. *Tonight*, Zanique thought, *it's hard enough to scratch a diamond.*

It was strange, had been strange from the onset. Ruby had never made an advance before. Zanique considered their times together. Never once had Ruby even flirted with her, other than to say she thought Zanique was beautiful. And tonight, during the Christmas party, although Ruby had chatted about this and that, she had seemed to be a bit nervous about sharing a room. Zanique had reassured her that they had separate beds. *But what happened between dinner and her soak in the bathtub?* When Ruby came out of the bathtub, Ruby was unstoppable.

Zanique kissed Ruby again and, pulled by Ruby's contractions, increased her pelvic thrusts. Zanique's knees were trembling. She wanted to give the best performance of her life. She wanted to make love to Ruby. She was still shaken by Ruby's words: *I love you.* Even if she wanted to stop, how could she stop when her friend was begging her to make love to her? Zanique was a giving person, and tonight she was giving her all.

As the tempo picked up, Ruby began groaning. Her hands cupped Obadiah's face. "Yes, my Love, take me, do me... do me. You know the way, do it!" She moaned louder, and her body began to shake. He slid in and out in a quickening cadence, she raised her legs and rocked to his rhythm until they both hit the highest mountain peak.

There was a moment of breathless silence. Ruby was still savoring the rapture of Obadiah's lovemaking. The ardor of the last orgasm lingered, the ecstasy still shining in her eyes, and in the next moment she found herself yielding to another passionate kiss.

"I'm trying to decide whether I love you more when I'm here with you or when you are lost in time to me," she murmured.

"For me," he replied. "I love you infinitely more when we're together, and I'm in pain when we're apart."

Zanique was frozen, both by her words and by the fact that she couldn't move because Ruby's legs were wrapped around her lower body and her arms were tight around her neck.

"I suggest," Ruby said to Obadiah, "that you don't leave me unattended ever again so there is no pain between us. I have always wondered if happiness could be achievable only through love. Now I know. Happiness is achievable without love, but love takes happiness to a much higher level."

Ruby released Zanique, and she lifted off. As their eyes met, it seemed to Zanique that every other experience of making love that she'd ever had in her life was nothing but a shadow. Everything before now had been utterly devoid of this mysterious passion that Ruby ignited. Here in Ruby's face she saw the charm and wonder of lovemaking made luminous. Zanique's emotions quivered as she began to ask herself if this impulsive act was indeed love, and if so, would it last? Or would it perish in the coming days?

"Shall I tell you what it's like for me?" Obadiah asked in a voice that was like a song to Ruby's heart. "I've been without you, alone in a dark place like a plant that grows in a dark cave reaching toward the light and never finding it. Endlessly reaching for the light." He kissed her again. "And now I've come to the light!"

"So, I'm your light?" Ruby asked.

"You are my love, and love is the light."

Her hand reached up and gently caressed his face. "It's so strange, isn't it? Love, being in love, knowing love. If not for you, I wouldn't know it even existed on this level."

"Not true," Obadiah replied. "Love would have introduced itself to you through another...."

"Yes," said Zanique, "it is strange, how you keep speaking of love." She was being seized by one of those reactions that are possible only in periods of joyous yet confusing excitement. "How did I ever get tangled up in you?" she asked. She cradled Ruby in her arms and enjoyed the feel of her skin against hers. They lay motionless on the bed. She felt humbled as she looked at Ruby, who had closed her eyes. Zanique saw, or at least she hoped she saw, gratitude and relief on her friend's calm face.

Obadiah and Ruby lay motionless on the bed. He continued to hold Ruby in his arms and saw, or at least he hoped he saw, gratitude and relief on his wife's calm face.

Lying in the comfort of her husband's arms, Ruby wanted this quiet moment to last forever. But her dream of this man was infected with uncertainty, and now it was melting swiftly into an unspeakable realization that something about it wasn't... *wasn't real.* At the same time, however, it seemed to her that she did have a choice and that she could—*should*—choose the journey of love and joy in preference to the journey of grief. Rejecting Obadiah would cause her nothing but grief. The emotions he brought to her were like nothing she had ever imagined. They were healthier than her old dreams.

But she also felt an impulse to jump back into the uncertainty that she had temporarily left, to gain some time in which she could prepare for the happiness he assured her was hers and only hers. Her soul trembled as if from some barely noticeable shock of disillusionment, and she knew that Obadiah would fade away soon just as he had done every time since she had discovered him. She felt she was in a singularly vivid dream from which she would unwillingly wake much too soon. And then she would be back in her "real life." She would remember this dream as simply a function of her dual nature, of the Ruby Birk of today and the Ruby Birk in the pictures. It was as if even her emotions belonged less to her "real" existence and more to an unconscious projection of thought that manifested as Obadiah.

She knew that in his absence, her uncertainty would gain power and the impulse to reject him, to reject her time with him, would rise up once more in her logical mind. Once he was gone again, she would see him as a shadow that she desperately tried to give substance to, attempting to give permanence to the most impermanent.

The smell of him was beginning to fade away. She feared the inevitable, that he would soon fade away altogether. "Don't go," she whispered. "Please don't leave me. "Stay. Stay with me all night long, keep me close to you, keep me warm. Can you do that?"

"Of course I'll stay with you," Zanique whispered back.

In Ruby's eyes, Obadiah was right there beside her. But his commitment to stay with her all night was far less powerful than Zanique's, and then doubt crept into the room when he told her that he couldn't stay.

"I'm so afraid that I'm losing my mind," she told him. "Please reassure me that we will be together."

"I promise that I'll come for you." He caressed her cheek. "But think about it, my dear. You have free will, you get to choose. You can choose the life you want to live."

"But I don't have to think about it! I'm ready to be with you! Take me away... let's leave together tonight."

"No, not tonight," he said. "Not yet. We must wait. Besides, waiting will give you time to contemplate your decision."

She heaved a sigh. "Well, if you insist, I will think about it."

"If you decide you want to come with me," he said, "meet me in the park. Bring Yukon and the necklace. Come to me under the full moon on the winter solstice."

"I will be there," she promised, and he faded away as exhaustion took over her mind and body and she fell into sleep.

"Shhhh. Don't be afraid, Ruby. I'm right here and I'm gonna stay with you all night. Sleep now." Zanique snapped off the light.

...

In the dark of the night, Zanique lay quietly so as to not wake Ruby, who was curled up against her. Her eyes struggled to focus in the shadows. She was thinking about how warm she was, warmed by the exciting fires of discovery. Her mind wondered about the guests in their rooms. Surely they had overheard the activities in the Bartlett Pear Room. Those guests might have gasped when they heard Ruby cry out for more. And did they feel the warmth of her discovery?

She reached down between her legs and gently cupped her penis. *Curious thing, this penis,* she thought. *Since the beginning of time, it's been mostly men who've established the governments and religions of the world... men who all had one of these peculiar things.*

She released it, but then it was being pinched between her thighs, so she tugged at it, and moved it over. *It's amazing how powerful a penis is. It doesn't have to be hard and large, it can be flaccid and just hang there, but it's still a powerful tool.*

Should I have such a powerful tool?

I've never used it before like I did tonight. Not this way.

Her mind went back in time, back to when she was twelve years old. She was in sixth grade in Mr. O'Grady's class, and there came a moment one day when the world changed for her. Mr. O'Grady put two big posters up in the front of the class. One poster showed the anatomy of the male sex organs, the other showed the female organs. Mr. O'Grady told the class to always behave with the best and most mature behavior, and then he proceeded to discuss things like fallopian tubes, testicles, and genitals.

Thanks to another change in foster homes, Zanique had been new to the school, and her mind wasn't focused on Mr. O'Grady or what he was talking about. She was looking out the window and waiting for the bell to ring. She didn't realize it at the moment, but as she watched the clock, she was watching her childhood ticking away. After school, she walked home with her new friend, Fred. (Zanique was a tomboy and always played with boys.)

"I'm worried," Fred told her.

"Why? What about?"

"Mr. O'Grady said boys have 'genitals.' The S means more than one, right? But I have only one penis, not genitals. Do you think that's a bad thing?"

Zanique felt a rush of concern come over her. "I only have one, too," she said.

"But you're a girl. You don't have one or two or anything. You have a vagina. Mr. O'Grady said that girls only have a vagina. Weren't you listening?"

"Yeah. I heard him. I have one penis and one vagina."

She would never forget the look on Fred's face. "You're kidding! You don't... do you?"

"I do."

"Prove it!"

So they ran into the alley and stopped behind an old, green Buick where no one would see them. Safely hidden, she pulled her pants down for him to see. Fred got down on his knees and stared. He had no idea what on earth he was seeing. It was confusing. Whatever was going on down there, he was sure, it wasn't what Mr. O'Grady had showed them with his posters.

"See?" Zanique said. "I told you."

"Well," Fred finally said, "it looks to me like you have genitals with an S. I only have one and you have two." He looked sad. "There must be something wrong with me 'cause I only have one. I wish I never heard about genitals."

Tonight, while Ruby slept, Zanique shook her head sadly as she remembered that Fred had asked his parents about his poor, singular genital. When they explained that it was Zanique who was the strange one, he came to school the next day and told everyone about her. It didn't take long for her to be ostracized. Children can be cruel, and living in a childhood that was already filled with the rejections of one foster home after another, the cruelty of the children caused a lifetime of damage. Zanique hated the taste of this memory. She tried to push it away.

The power of a penis, she thought. Then her mind went to the famous book, *Men Are from Mars and Women Are from Venus*. It bothered her that from the moment a child is born, it is identified and quickly, instantly, exiled to Mars or Venus. Babies are isolated by their gender, complete with color-coordinated clothes: blue for him, pink for her. When Zanique was born, what color did they swaddle her in? Which planet did she belong to?

Neptune! she thought. *Because it's the planet of obscurity.* She would never easily show her mysteries. And with that pleasant thought, she lightly kissed Ruby's bare back and finally drifted off to sleep.

Chapter 16

"Complicated" did not even begin to describe the situation Ruby found herself in the next morning. She looked at the ankh she had removed sometime in the night and laid on the nightstand. There it still sat, carrying with it a whiff of ancient magic and divine love.

She was fully aware that Obadiah had come to her and they had made sweet love again. But she couldn't explain why she and Zanique were both occupying the same bed. And more... why were they both naked and in bed together? She scratched her head. *What the hell happened last night?*

Obadiah, Obadiah. Everything about him seemed pure and clean. His features were as elegant as Michelangelo's David, his raven hair so black that it gleamed blue, and his eyes so strong and beautiful she thought they could see forever. She also loved the way he carried himself with such confidence. And he was so refined. She had the impression that what

Obadiah wanted from love and life, he took. Or at least charmed it into coming to him.

If he is anything at all, she told herself, *he is a being of slow, throbbing, addictive, erotic energy. I'm obsessed with him. I need to understand his love with all of my senses. I need—*

Zanique woke up. Their eyes met. Then she smiled the cutest smile Ruby had ever seen on her face, sat up, and rubbed her eyes. The sun was peeking through the window and bathed her in its glorious, warm light.

Ruby couldn't take her eyes off her. "My God, you're beautiful!"

Zanique ran her hand through her hair. "Thanks," she said, "but I don't feel very beautiful right now." She tried to think of something clever to say, but her talent for repartee seemed to have run away this morning.

Ruby was still gazing at Zanique when a wave of unease washed over her. She took a deep breath. "So... what's next?" she asked. "Breakfast?"

Zanique raised an eyebrow. "Um... really? 'What's next' is your big question?" She turned slightly so Ruby could see the bite mark on her shoulder and the scratch marks down her back. Then she turned back to face her friend. "What the fuck, Ruby! I'm at a loss for words."

Ruby swallowed hard. "Did I do that?"

"You have a real Dr. Jekyll and Mr. Hyde thing going on, don't you? I mean you're all quiet and shy in public, but behind closed doors? Look the fuck out!

Ruby couldn't speak.

And Zanique wasn't finished. "You're dangerous, Ruby Birk! You seem to have a real predilection for surprise love-making. Are you an adrenaline junky? I only ask because that crazy shit you pulled on me last night rocked my world." She held up a trembling hand. "Look! I'm still shaking."

Ruby still couldn't speak.

Zanique looked pensive for a moment. "Girl, you took me to a whole new level last night. And I'm not sure it was just physical... or maybe mental?" She shook her head. "I'm not sure. Maybe soulful? The body, the mind, the soul... it doesn't matter, does it? You got me to turn my back on what I claim is safe ground when it comes to sex. I learned to, so to speak, embrace something new last night."

But I was with Obadiah, Ruby thought. *I left this reality for another time, but all the while I was feeling like I'd lost myself, the me in this time and place. And I couldn't turn back!*

"Ruby?" Zanique asked.

"Oh. Sorry. I was just concentrating on what you were saying. Look, I felt really disoriented last night. And I still do this morning. I'm not even sure what all happened last night."

For a moment, there was quiet between them.

An edgy quiet.

Then Zanique raised an eyebrow and smiled again as she leaned forward, wrapped both arms around Ruby's neck, and kissed her. "Thank you for a very special experience."

"You're... uhh... welcome?" It was more a question than a statement. Ruby had no idea what she was being thanked for. What had happened in this bed last night? She thought it was best to move cautiously.

"So," Zanique murmured, "last night you said you loved me. Is that true, or was it just something to say in the throes of passion?"

Ruby pulled away slightly and looked at Zanique again. She was beautiful, even first thing in the morning. Ruby wished she could look just half as good. She also really wished she could recall what had happened and why Zanique was in bed with her this morning. What had she said? What had either of them said?

"Well," Ruby felt herself blushing, "I guess love is a funny thing. And—" thinking fast "—and I'm afraid I didn't put much caution into what I said last night. I hope I didn't offend you, but, yes, I'm finding that every day I'm near you I love you more." This much was true. Ruby had found love for Zanique, and if she had spoken of love last night, then she certainly couldn't deny it this morning. She did love her friend... only it wasn't passionate, romantic love. It was sisterly love. And now, after what must have been a very sexual night, things were problematical.

Ruby had no idea what to say or do.

She inhaled sharply and looked away from Zanique. She wanted nothing more than to admit to what had actually happened last night—who she had actually been making love with—but she also knew how Zanique had been rejected over and over in her life. And she sure as hell didn't want to be one more person to hurt her that way. She thought maybe she would play along. She looked at Zanique again and took stock. Her friend's hair was a tangled mess, her cheeks were rosy, and her eyes were astonishing; something sparkled in them. Then her playful grin suddenly changed to a look of vulnerability topped by a *you-gave-me-the-best-night-of-my-life* expression.

Weird. Majorly weird.

Ruby was entirely confused. *How could I make love to Obadiah while somehow having sex with Zanique? That is so fucking weird!* She spoke aloud. "That smile on your face... shame on you! You hardly know me, and last night you put your mojo on me." She gave a fake laugh. "You corrupted me."

"Corrupted *you*? Really?" Zanique hopped up onto her knees and took Ruby by the shoulders. "God damn, woman, *you* tarnished *my* reputation! This whole house knows what we did last night. I'm sure they heard everything."

"Really? Do you think Odessa and Jimmy heard us?"

"Ya think? You were so loud I'm thinking people in Ashland heard you." Zanique stopped and gave Ruby another quick kiss, "But I don't care. Let 'em all think what they want to think. I loved every minute of it. It's gonna be a little uncomfortable at breakfast, but I'm sure we will manage."

Ruby spoke quietly, slowly, fearfully. "I'm sorry I was loud. I sure don't want to offend your guests. Or Odessa and Jimmy. I mean, well, this is your business and... and I should've been more respectful."

Zanique laughed. "Aw, don't worry about it. I'm the owner here, and I doubt it hurt the business too bad. I'm sure we'll be getting some colorful reviews for the next six months."

"Oh, God! I'm sorry!" Ruby buried her face in a pillow.

"Last night," Zanique said, "you cried when you said that you loved me. That meant so much to me! I've never heard those words said so lovingly before. And then, when you asked me to stay with you all night long? Well, I just melted.

"I... I... I honestly don't remember much. My mind was in another world."

"Do you want to know what it was like for me?"

"Uh, yeah, sure."

"It was like a stellar explosion. Supernova, baby. You got me to go supernova!"

Ruby lay still with her hands under her cheek, watching Zanique talk in her usual animated fashion. Indeed, she was loving her at this moment, but loving her at a distance and as a friend, not a lover. Zanique had been on her own journey, just as Ruby had been. But somehow their journeys had collided last night.

"I swear I touched heaven last...." Zanique stopped and looked down at Ruby. Her face contorted. "Oh. My. God. I'm in love with you, Ruby. But I... I don't want to be in love you! Or anyone."

Ruby's face softened, then froze in mute alarm. *Oh, shit* she said to herself. *What about poor Dutch? If he ever found out about what happened here, he'd be so hurt!* She didn't want to hurt anyone, and this scene with Zanique was turning into a major mess. She imagined Dutch asking her "How was the party?" and her responding, "It was great! Zanique and I banged hard last night." Just the thought of how he'd react to that made her cringe.

Zanique got off the bed. "I have suffered a broken heart so many times I don't think I dare do it again." She was still uneasy over last night's euphoria. "I mean what's the use of loving when nothing seems to come from it? Love has given me more pain than anything else in my life." Her face went pale. "Girlfriend, I'm afraid!"

Ruby met her friend's strong tenderness with an effort not to run away. She sat still, fearing that any movement she made, no matter how small, would lead to an eruption of panic. And then Zanique bent down and kissed her again. Ruby kept still, pushing down her alarm. But she must have blinked, or maybe she turned ever so slightly away. Whatever she did, it somehow communicated to Zanique that she was unhappy. She didn't respond to the kiss.

Touching her own lips, Zanique wondered if the magic was already gone. As she studied Ruby's face, an unclear yet sharp thrill ran through her. Nonetheless, she held her mind seriously in consideration of Ruby. "I'm sorry. I guess I shouldn't be kissing you so much."

As she had done in her brief "affair" with Dutch, Ruby hated herself for the sexually intimate complexity she had created. For an instant, and only an instant, she saw Sapphic love shining in Zanique's hazel eyes.

Love?

Zanique?

Could love actually live there between them?

But then she felt enormously troubled to see her friend standing there unable to control her vulnerability and pain. "I'm sorry Zanique, I do love you, but…." She stumbled searching for the right words. "You see, I'm no good. I'm not a good person at all, and I hate myself in my heart because of what I manipulated you to do last night. I let my affection for you cross the line." She reached for Zanique's hand, trying to hold back a haze of developing tears, "I'm a very confused person who is so very afraid she is losing her sanity. I didn't—don't mean to draw you deeper into me."

Zanique squinted at her and smiled ruefully. Ruby had just said she hated herself for jeopardizing their friendship. Zanique understood so many things with her silent perception, like love stirring unseen and unsuspecting in the depth of friendship. "Do not have any illusions about me, Ruby, I'm not a resigned woman by nature, nor am I a good woman. My mind contains uncharitable thoughts, and I get confused, too." Her voice shook as she went on. "I guess I never really knew you until last night. How is it possible that I was so blind, and so stupid, and so self-centered that I didn't see your attraction for me?"

Ruby laid back and looked up at the ceiling, pulling in a deep breath, holding it in for a moment, then releasing it as if the stress and panic she felt were exhaled with it.

At the same time, Zanique looked at Ruby, naked among the pillows and bedcovering—her elegant legs, rounded hips, perfect waist, heavy breasts with dark rosy nipples, thick and kissable lips. She wouldn't consider Ruby overweight, but she was zaftig, voluptuous, and there was a softness to her. Zanique saw her friend's luscious magnetism as a quality from a forgotten time, not from this age where gaunt is considered beautiful. There was a tension in Ruby's body this morning, and her face held an expression of anxiety. She had a focused look in her eyes that made Zanique wonder if she could see through the ceiling into another world.

Zanique broke the awkwardness of the moment. "I'm going to take a hot shower. After last night, I need to get clean." A grin broke across her face. "That was one wild night, girlfriend! Nothing like pushing life to the limit, living on the edge in order to feel alive, wouldn't you agree?"

Ruby nodded slowly. "Yes, turning your back on safety and embracing risk does seem to revive the soul. But you've always been the adventurous one. This whole adrenaline junky thing is new to me."

"Before last night I would agree with you, but... Ruby, you are so full of shit! You are definitely an adrenaline junky. And you're good at it." She laughed.

Ruby smiled back at Zanique "Can I join you?"

"What??"

"In the shower?" Ruby got off the bed. "Is it okay if we share the shower?"

"Umm... I suppose." Things seemed so crazy that Zanique was beginning to wonder if she were somehow in someone else's mind.

"Look," Ruby said, "I don't know if what we did last night was good or bad, all I know is we made love and not showering with you would be like eating the cake but passing on the ice-cream."

"You know what? Bernard was right. You are a little witch."

In the shower, Ruby realized that Obadiah was coming for her soon, and one day she would have to say good-bye to her dear friend. She held Zanique's face in her hands, an indecipherable expression on her face. "I will always love you, and no matter what, you will always be special to me."

But Zanique couldn't hold back any longer. "I'm sorry," she said. "I don't want to be in love with you. Honestly, I don't want to hurt you, Ruby... but could we... would you mind... oh, fuck, this is hard!" She closed her eyes and prayed for the right words to come to her. "Something inside me is telling me that what we did was special. Sure, we made love, but it was only this once. She turned away. "I don't see a future for us as lovers."

"Sure, Zanique. Anything you say." Ruby leaned forward and kissed her on the cheek. Her lips were wet and soft. "For us... thank you for last night. It was lovely." And oddly, now she felt empty and lonely. She felt a chill reaching into her heart. If she were honest, she didn't want to be in love with Zanique, either; the truth was that she was never in love with her like that. But there are so many emotions associated with love-making that Ruby was fooled into feeling the rejection from her was legitimate.

"Yes, what we had last night was beautiful," Zanique finally said. "But I can't see us carrying on a relationship... and I'm afraid if we tried, it would destroy our friendship. That last thing I ever want is to lose you as my friend."

Nothing but the shower water could be heard. Both women were at a loss as to what to say next.

Feeling uncomfortable, they both got out and toweled off, avoiding each other. But then Zanique began to giggle, and then it turned into laughter.

"Girlfriend, you were so loud last night!" Her laughter was uncontrollable. "You pushed my head down between your legs and screamed RIGHT THERE! Over and over again. Oh my god, you were so loud." She tried to catch her breath. "I was scared out of my wits! No one has ever begged me to fuck them like you did last night. I mean I have never taken on the male role before. You are bat-shit-crazy when it comes to sex... and loud... holy shit, this whole house knows we did the dirty deed hard."

Ruby failed to see the humor in their situation. "Dear God, I can't face anyone this morning! Was I really that loud last night?"

Zanique tilted her head to one side and repeated. "I keep sayin'... girl, you were roarin'!"

"I'm so embarrassed! Please, is there any way we can sneak out of here?"

"Because you love me," Zanique said in a dignified voice, "I will accommodate you. After you get yourself ready, I'll get us out of here without anyone seeing us. We will disappear in the wind." She chuckled. She didn't feel like seeing anyone else, either.

When they were dressed and ready to leave and she was sure breakfast for the guests was over, Zanique snuck downstairs and made sure no one was around, then went back up to their room and got Ruby. "Come on. Let's go. Odessa and Jimmy are in the kitchen cleaning up, so if we go now, we can slip out unnoticed." They crept down the stairs and through the door, gathered Yukon, and jumped into Zanique's Hummer and sped off.

After a few blocks, Zanique slowed the vehicle. "So, shall we go get something to eat?"

"No, I'm not hungry. Would you mind just dropping me off at my house?"

Now Zanique felt the burn of rejection in Ruby's words. "You bet I'll drop you off," she said stiffly. "I guess you want to be alone now after what we did?"

Ruby saw the indignant flash in her friend's eyes and heard the nervous quiver in her voice. "No, it's not that," she said. "I'm just still trying to figure things out, you know, Obadiah, my husband, me, the past. My wanting to spend time alone has nothing to do with you."

For a brief moment, Zanique didn't answer. Then she pulled to the curb and sat there in silence, staring at the road. Then she turned toward Ruby. "And I suppose now you will stop seeing me altogether."

"Hey, it was you that didn't want a future with me," Ruby protested. "You're the one who said, 'I don't see a future for us as lovers.' Of course, I still want to hang out with you. I just want to go home and chill out. Think about things… like Dutch, Obadiah. Everything's happening so fast. I just need time to think."

"Oh, so now we are going to blame *me* for this? Point out the things *I've* said, the things *I've* done." Zanique was aware that she was now jealous where jealousy shouldn't be. The men in Ruby's life were her competition. Ruby had touched hidden emotions in her, hidden behind very protected walls. No other woman had ever done that before; as a matter of fact, no person had ever done that before. She wanted to retreat, she wanted things to go back to normal between her and Ruby, and the knowledge of this made her feel crazy, and out of control. Yet it wasn't unhappiness she was feeling. She trembled as if from some almost imperceptible shock of disillusionment as she knew again the sense of romance, eroticism, and unreality… they'd all come from Ruby. Her heart fluttered like an imprisoned bird. "Okay, I'll take you home so you can get back to your men."

Her face, her voice, the gesture of her outstretched hand startled Ruby. "Zanique, please don't do this. I'm serious. I just want some time to think. Please understand me. I swear I'm not trying to ditch you." She paused. "We're still friends! I'd like to see you again soon… no later than tomorrow?"

Zanique smiled, and the strong planes of her face melted into lines of softness and laughter. She was bewitched. "Look at me," she said, "being all fussy. I get that way when I don't get enough sleep."

"I understand," Ruby said. "I really do."

"Oh, what about Yukon?"

"What about him?"

"Can I take him home with me? I don't want to be alone after last night."

Ruby's eyes lingered on her for a moment. Yukon was her most trusted friend. She needed him with her, but how could she refuse Zanique now, at a time when she was afraid to be alone? "For how long?"

"Just for lunch and a hike up a mountain trail. Please?"

"Are you going through a drive-thru for lunch? You can't take him into a restaurant, you know."

"Girlfriend, you don't know me very well. Climb in the back and look under that white tub with my snow pants, gaiters, and snowshoes in it."

Ruby clambered over the seat and into the cargo space and lifted the lid of the plastic tub. "You're kidding, right?" She held up a red vest that had *Service Dog* written in white letters on it. "Oh, no... no, you can't be serious. You don't need a service dog."

"What? Of course I'm serious. Here, look." Zanique opened her wallet with the other and showed Ruby a service dog I.D., an official badge with Yukon's picture on it. "I made this the other day," she said. "I figured it would come in handy... and today it's handy." She laughed.

"Okay, go ahead." Ruby looked at Yukon, who was staring at Zanique. "How can I say no when he's staring at you with love in his eyes? Why don't you keep him tonight and bring him 'round tomorrow?"

...

The afterglow of Ruby's night stayed with her all day. Even now, several hours later, she was still euphoric. Back in her apartment and sitting in her favorite chair, she found herself reliving her night with Obadiah, making love, hearing him say that he was coming for her soon. The ecstatic sense of relief she got from knowing she would be going "home" soon overwhelmed her. *What a mind-bending past few weeks I've had*, she thought. *A life-changing experience with the enigmatic Obadiah.*

She leaned back and closed her eyes, and immediately, without warning and against her will, there arose in her thoughts the seductive face of Dutch. She could feel his masculine magnetism. Then her thoughts jumped to the beautiful Zanique, and the insane night they had just spent together. These two new people in her love life had gravity, too. Why, then, did she desire Obadiah's love so much more?

Her introspection was disturbed by this question. All three of these people should not be loved and forgotten, or merely forgotten without being loved. They meant so much to her at this time, in this reality. Each one was special, caring, and tender to her. Her mind was a crush of thoughts and emotions. She was trying to think things out, but she had no hope of escaping from the endless merry-go-round of her thoughts about the varieties of love.

She needed to have a clear head.

She decided that the best way to get through the day was to get things in order. After all, she was departing for the past very soon. The winter solstice was less than three days away, her day of departure. The final goodbyes would be said soon.

By mid-afternoon, Ruby heard the familiar hooting of the neighborhood owl. She looked out the window and saw that it had stationed itself in the tree near her studio apartment.

"I knew you'd be coming to see me," she told the owl. She finished packing a small bag. "I'm glad you are here. You can come with me and help me explain all this to Dutch."

The owl, symbol and carrier of feminine magic and wisdom, answered with another hoot. Ruby studied the owl: it had a face, and she knew there was a soul behind it. This majestic bird seemed to possess all the mystery of enlightenment and shadow. She had begun to suspect that the owl was connected to Obadiah in some way, and seeing it perched outside her apartment now seemed to support her theory. Her mind was fastened on Obadiah and the intensity of life, the radiant energy of romance. Staring at the owl, she realized that she was now seeing the past without the aid of the necklace. The owl was able to channel her mind beyond the veil and back to her husband. She smiled at the bird.

Shaking her head as if to shake away a spell that had been cast upon her, Ruby returned her focus to her apartment. She got down to serious work, organizing it and putting things in order for her departure. When she was finished, she made her way to Mrs. Bimby's house.

"Mrs. Bimby," she said when her landlady opened her door, "I wanted to pay the rent for the next twelve-month period." She handed her a check written for the amount.

Looking baffled, Mrs. Bimby simply asked, "Why?"

"I'm going away for a while, I wanted to make sure you had the money."

Mrs. Bimby tilted her head without a smile. "Oh, you're leaving... for how long, dear?"

"A while, but, if it's okay with you, I'd like to leave a key with my friend, Dutch. I'm on my way to tell him I'm leaving, I'm sure he would like to make use of my studio while I'm gone. He's an artist, too. Plus, he'd keep an eye on things for me."

"Hold on. Ruby, you're making me nervous. Are you going to do something drastic?" The older woman didn't wait for an answer but instead shot out two more questions. "Why are you making such a move so fast? And when are you leaving?" She had witnessed firsthand Ruby's depression, and her fear now was Ruby was talking about a plan for suicide.

"Mrs. Bimby, there's no need for you to worry, I'm going somewhere very safe. I'll be leaving on the twenty-first."

Mrs. Bimby breathed a sigh of relief. She could plainly see that Ruby had a new glow about her. "That's the day after tomorrow!"

"I know."

"I suppose this Dutch can use your studio. If you trust him, then I can, too," Mrs. Bimby said. Then she paused and thought about things she'd observed over the last few weeks. "Does this have something to do with love? Being in love affects us women in very strange ways... it can alter our lives in so many ways. It's love, isn't it?"

"Love?" Even though she laughed, Ruby blushed. She couldn't deny it. "I can't hide anything from you, Mrs. Bimby. Yes, every move I make from this hour forward is all about love." For an instant, she met Mrs. Bimby's eyes with an earnestness that was almost equal to what was in her heart. The younger woman in her almost cried out for help from this older, wiser woman. But then the owl entered the conversation with a hoot that distracted her, and she realized that there would be a reward in her silence. In her next breath, in some way, there was confidence.

"He's a lucky man." Mrs. Bimby said.

"Who is?"

"The man you're chasing. The man that has asked you to leave Ashland with no return date."

"Yes, well, let's hope I'm not making a big mistake."

And there, between the two women, arose a profound emotion. "Love is the Breath of Life for Every Soul," said Mrs. Bimby, believing she was quoting some ancient wisdom she'd read someplace. "The mystery of the soul, universal life, spirit and matter, fiber and urge, vibration, the quiver of motivation—all those are nothing but the working of love." She reached out and touched Ruby's cheek. "Go on," she said, "seek out your happiness, and I hope it'll keep you away forever. You will fail if you leave here for pleasure, or the desire for money, or for social standing, but if you leave for true love, you will have many happier days."

Ruby's legs were wobbly under her when she left Mrs. Bimby's door, feeling like she'd just heard a prophecy. She was trying to think what to say to Dutch, how to explain all that had happened, and how their relationship would be over. She had to get to his house and wait for him to get off work. She had to see him. The owl flew above her, guiding her, protecting her. Ruby feared the last few hours she had left in this reality. She knew they would be difficult hours.

Chapter 17

$\mathcal{I}$t had been a cold day, and as evening came on, it got even colder. Ruby stood in Dutch's living room in the growing darkness, wondering what to say to Dutch when he got home. Without turning a light on, she wondered if she should even be there in his house. Not this way... not with her life stretching out in abnormal ways. Perhaps it would feel more comfortable if their relationship had been stronger, had some history behind it, a future ahead. But not the way it stood now, she realized, not with all of it behind them and nothing ahead. After all, Obadiah was coming for her and would be taking her home in less than thirty-one hours.

She walked around the living room before heading upstairs. The room, the whole house in fact, was essentially a man's house, furnished for comfort rather than for beauty, and she noticed in it a perhaps unconscious endeavor on his part to keep only large, useful furnishings. There were only two decorative ornaments in the room, both of which stood above the mantel. One was an exquisite bronze figure of a hockey player at the instant of making the winning goal. Above it hung the other decoration, a large work done in charcoal and pencil of two knucklehead Harley Davidsons racing down a dirt road with a B-17 Flying Fortress low overhead. In the lower right-hand corner was a signature that read *To Dutch, the best forward in the NHL. Your friend T. Fritz.* As this was likely the last she'd see of it, Ruby admired the masculine décor for longer than she expected, but then she made her way upstairs.

In the bedroom now, she snapped on a light. It was colder here than downstairs, so she pulled her dress closer to her as she sat on the bed. Her old-fashioned dress was chic enough, she felt, not to lose its bravura. It was cut very simply, with a full skirt, a tight bodice, and long sleeves and a high neckline for added warmth.

She was shivering slightly, but not so much she couldn't rub a little rouge gently into her cheeks, blending it up toward her eyes and into her hairline. She dug into her purse until she found her Keme Black eye shadow, then looked at her face in the mirror as though seeing it for the first time in a long while. She was never one who wanted to look at her reflection, not that hers was a dreadful face in any way, but, well, it wasn't particularly beautiful, either.

She did admire her eyes with their dark auburn brows and long lashes, an unexpected brunette accent against her fair complexion and cherry-chocolate hair.

She was nervously keeping busy, worried about how to tell Dutch what had happened at the Jameson Mansion, as well as at the Christmas party. And Obadiah. And how she knew for certain that he was coming for her. How could she tell Dutch goodbye?

As the darkness outside grew heavier, her nervous energy began to fade. She began to tremble. She was mentally exhausted as she asked herself for the umpteenth time, and perhaps for the last time, if it were possible that Obadiah was only part of her imagination. Or was he a ghost?

She heard the front door slam. It drove every thought from her mind, and she stood up and walked out of the room. When she looked down the stairwell, she saw Dutch standing in the hallway and adjusting the thermostat.

"Damn, it's cold out there!" He spoke as if addressing some invisible person.

Ruby was sure he didn't know she was in the house. "I know," she said as she began descending the stairs, "I've been shivering." She noted his faded jeans and thick woolen sweater, his body that was strong and younger looking than his face.

"Why did you sit here in the cold?" he asked, not even sounding surprised to see her. "You could've turned the heat up."

"I don't like to change the settings of other people's devices," she replied. "Not in their cars or in their homes."

He smiled. "Now that's just silly. There is no reason for you to be cold in my house. I turn the furnace down low when I'm not home. No wonder you were cold." He reached for her and drew her into him. "Let me warm you up."

They stood in silence, pressed against one another in the cold darkness. Then they started walking toward the living room, moving together in silent rhythm as if they had lived together for years. Dutch turned on the lights in the living room and Ruby went to the Christmas tree and plugged in the colorful holiday lights. Their silence, Ruby thought, was almost worse than words. It carried more than words ever could. It seemed to speak aloud all the things that she didn't yet wish to say. And Dutch, with his presence, there by her side again... he seemed to be pressing somehow against her decision.

Outside, in the cold and darkness, an owl landed high in one of the trees on Dutch's property.

He turned to her. "Where is Yukon?"

"Oh, he's with Zanique."

Dutch gazed at her, which made her feel more

nervous, but she worked to conceal it, showing only a fraction before hiding it completely. In the next instant, she smiled at him. He considered her smile to be one of her most memorable strengths. It was a smile that shone from her lips to her eyes.

"Well," he chanced the question, "what did you find out at the Jameson Mansion the other day?"

She took a deep breath. "Zanique and I got to the mansion. It was so beautiful, and we rang the bell...."

Her words entered his ears with a sweetness that made him love her even more. As her story unfolded, he knew it was indeed love that he was feeling, but it was a love only he felt. Her love, and he was sure that she did love him to some degree, wasn't the soul-mate kind of love he had hoped for. The tenderness that flooded his heart was that of a man in love with a woman, but in her story about her day at the mansion he heard an admission that her love, her soulful love wasn't for him. It was for another man, for that man's soul. It was the love of a wife devoted to her husband, a husband that loved her more dearly, more divinely than he ever could.

Now it was his turn to inhale deeply. The appeal she made to him tonight, sitting on his couch, helpless, was an appeal that was woven of the strongest fibers of the heart. It came from her immortal soul, which, she claimed, had ascended to a place higher than this earthly reality. There she had discovered that all her love belonged to this other man, one who seemed to be living in another time entirely.

Ruby cried out for Dutch to forgive her. She begged him to understand that she had no intention of hurting him, and she regretted any pain she had placed on his heart. The burning he felt inside told him to fight as hard for her as he had ever fought for anything, to fight with jealous vigor and defend the love he felt so strongly. But listening to her words and watching her body language, he felt on a deeper level that there was nothing upon the earth nor in the heavens that would be strong enough to contend against the power of her soulful bond to Obadiah. All of Dutch's yearnings and emotions shrank before Ruby's desire for Obadiah.

In great sorrow, but with a definite enchantment, she began to convince Dutch that his ambition, his love for her, was for naught in the presence of the connection that joined her to her husband.

He had to speak. "Listen to me, Ruby," he said in a voice whose quiet authority silenced her for a moment. "You don't have a problem on this earth that I'm not willing to share. Whether you like it or not, I'm a part of this. What you say about your love for your husband... Obadiah, I understand it. I get it! And if your husband lived here in Ashland, *right now*, out of complete respect for you, I would step aside. But that's not what we're talking about, is it? He doesn't live here now. He lived here over a hundred years ago. And for you to go back to him...." He paused because he didn't want to sound condescending or sarcastic. "Well, just how is that possible? How are you going back to him? I have to admit... it's a little hard to believe."

Ruby couldn't bring herself to tell him about the winter solstice, so she simply looked at him. Then, "Honestly, I'm not terribly sure of the mechanics myself. I just know that I'm going home. Like he told me."

"When?"

She still held back, kept the date a secret for fear he would somehow stop her from going to Lithia Park on the solstice. "I'm not sure."

"As far as I know, Ruby, no one has traveled through time. It's not possible!" He took her hand now, purely for the comfort of feeling her touch. The warmth of her hand calmed him. He was getting frustrated, and wasn't sure what to believe.

Although she left her hand in his, she looked out the window. "I know this all sounds crazy," she said in a soft voice, "and maybe I have gone insane. I fear that I'm being foolish. But I only know that my experiences with Obadiah feel very real to me." She looked into his eyes. "Dutch, I am afraid." She looked down at the floor. "I've never been afraid like this before...." Her voice trailed off. She put one hand over her mouth and pressed back against her fear.

"You're afraid?" he asked. "I mean, a moment ago you sounded so sure, so confident about this man—"

"I'm afraid," she repeated. "When I'm with Obadiah, I feel like that's where I belong. And... and my life up until I met you, well, it's been dreadful. I've been an outcast. I've been poor, I've barely survived. Sometimes I just wanted nothing more than to die. And now with you? With you, I get confused because I see that my life has gotten better. If not for you, I wouldn't be afraid, I wouldn't hesitate. I would know with undoubted certainty I belong to the past with Obadiah." She paused. "And yet, as time moves forward into the future, just like you do, I begin to doubt all of this. Of course, I've sat and considered how impossible it is to travel back to 1912." She smiled. "Sometimes I wonder if I've lost my mind! Am I imagining this whole thing? But you should've been there. Helma Brost, the caretaker of the Jameson Mansion... as soon as she saw me, she knew who I was! She even poked me with her finger to see if I was real. Yes, she thought I was a ghost. And those paintings of me? You must have seen them when you were at the mansion. Besides that, I have a painting and a photograph of me with Obadiah back at my apartment... evidence!" She was sounding panicky. She began fidgeting with her skirt. "Dutch, I love you, I really do, and I enjoy being with you... you must know how much all this pains me... to have to tell you about Obadiah... that he's coming for me. That I'm going home."

"Going home?" He frowned. "I don't understand. What exactly are you afraid of?"

"I'm afraid that by telling you this, I will lose you, and what if all of this is just my mind playing a cruel joke on me? I've been alone for what seems like my whole life. I don't want to be alone again! I don't want to lose you." She managed a small smile. "Who on earth knew that having two men love me would be so difficult?"

She giggled. After a minute, he smiled.

"I told you I'm a part of this," he said when she stopped giggling, "and whatever you have to face, I'll face it with you. Call me a dumbshit, but I love you enough that I'll stay by your side until he comes for you. And... and, well, if he doesn't come for you, then I promise I will be here for you! I won't judge you in any way. I will never say you were crazy." He made the cliché gesture with his index finger circling at his temple and smiled again. "And I'll hope that one day we can laugh about all this together."

She wrapped both her arms around his strong arm. "You mean I won't be alone?"

"I'll be right here with you."

"Oh, that's a comfort! Do you have any idea what it's like being this honest? It's hard god damn work!" She brushed a tear away.

Dutch took both of her hands in his. They came to rest on her lap. "For the short time I have known you, Ruby Birk, you have raised me up," he said gently. "You have brought higher feelings into my life." A strong need fell upon him. He needed for her to choose him over Obadiah. But he didn't want to manipulate her into it. He wanted her to make that decision on her own.

It seemed to him as though his whole life, all the worth and purpose of it, was bound up with this unusual woman. He pulled her to him, tightening his arms around her as a devotee might cling to his god. There was almost a superstitious element to his love, a feeling that, despite what he knew of the universe and its mechanics, because this story came from her, it was possible.

"I love you, Ruby," he repeated. "I can't help myself... hell, I don't want to help myself. Whatever happens, whether you go to Obadiah or if you stay with me, I will love you no matter what."

Her head was resting against his chest now, and she could feel his heart beating. She could also feel the strong throbbing of her own heart. She kept her voice very quiet and controlled as she spoke again. "I'm not a wicked woman. I swear!" She lifted her head, and her wet eyes flashed and deepened with her strong denial of what she'd been told... once upon a time. "I will forever be sorry that things happened the way they did between us. And I hope that each tomorrow will be kind to you."

She became quiet because now the enormity of the situation pressed harder on her shoulders. But then she asked, "Am I a destroyer of hearts? Have I come into your life as a defilement? Do I poison the air you breathe? Have I demolished your peaceful life?" She could not suppress the echoes of damnation hurled at her all those years ago. "Dutch, you are such a good and kind man; you don't deserve this."

"You are talking irrationally," he said. "It's my choice to love you, and I choose to love you very much, even knowing you will be either the greatest happiness of my life or the deepest misery. Whatever the result is, it's my choice. My life is richer having loved you."

She kissed Dutch for the sweet words he had just spoken, but then she heard the shriek of the owl outside. The sound pierced through Ruby's fear, lifting her mind beyond the shadows of doubt to the other side where the light and warmth of summer existed, where happiness and Obadiah's promise of a better life waited for her. She could hear Obadiah's voice in her mind. *I am coming for you.* She felt a rush of confidence, a taste of ecstasy that came from 1912.

Just a moment ago, she had felt her way growing dark; she'd been stumbling blindly, wondering what to believe. And now? Now her mind was focused on the coming full moon and the winter solstice... and what lay ahead. She was elevated from the ordinary of the mundane world up to the height of her ideal world. And she was indeed ignorant of the forces that were at work here. All she could think of was the power of *magic*.

"Obadiah said he's going to take me to Florence, Paris, Prague, down to the Mediterranean Sea to the Gates of Gibraltar." She spoke in a monotone, as if hypnotized, her voice low. The thought of Obadiah had caught up with her, and her emotions had grown stronger. "It'll be a great thing to get back to my time! Back to where I belong." In her mind, she was already seeing the world of 1912. "Everything moves slower back there, you know. Most people don't have telephones, and the automobile hasn't caught on much yet, either."

Dutch pulled away from her, but she didn't move. She sat still, her eyes fixed, mind trained on the unseen.

"Just think of it," she said. "I'm only beginning to live. Here I'm thirty-seven, and there I'm only twenty-eight." She paused as if to collect a thought and then seemed to change the subject. "Dutch, I want you to use my studio when I leave. Use it as a place of refuge, a place in which to create. I just know you will produce some incredible pieces. The rent has been paid for the next year. I've explained it all to Mrs. Bimby. She is expecting you. Also, there you will find my paintings. They are yours now. I leave them to you. I hope you can look at them with fond affection."

...

The owl cried again, calling to Ruby. The bird's yellow eyes reflected from the street lamps below. The ghostly messenger was coaxing Ruby to listen carefully to her inner voice. The glory of *going home* lay ahead. Life itself appeared as full, as valuable, as her desire. Hearing the owl's call, she felt a curious sensation of detachment, as if she was drifting away from her undesirable and peculiar place in this life. She rose to her feet.

"I'm sorry, Dutch. I have to go."

She had done what she came to do. She'd explained herself, begged for forgiveness from this good man. But now she knew what her true path was.

She got to her feet, gathered up her old wool coat, and walked to the door. "I hope your heart doesn't suffer from my leaving," she said. "My heart is in pain from losing you, Dutch, but my soul is strong, very strong. There is nothing left for my soul to learn here. If I remained with you here in this time, I know that the suffering... well, we both would suffer. I would always want to be with Obadiah. I would always need to be with him. And that would cause you more pain. I must be with him!"

Dutch had never seen her like this. Her face was blank, her eyes were not seeing him or anything around her. They were seeing what wasn't there, another time, another place.

She pulled the door open to the wind that was blowing outside. "Oh, listen to that wind coming down from the mountain. It sounds like spirits struggling to rise above the ordinary, to pull away from the weight of some tremendous gravity."

"What?"

"Good-bye, Dutch. I will always hold happy thoughts of you in a special part of my heart."

She walked out of his house. As she made her way down the dark street, the owl flew over her head, and that peculiar wind was at her back. The gust was rising and in it she could smell Obadiah's signature odor. It followed her as she walked away from Dutch.

That curious wind had also cast a spell over Dutch. He stood just inside his door as if placed there, molded to the threshold. He wanted to chase after her, to plead with her to stay, but he couldn't move, couldn't speak.

As she faded from sight, he thought, *Maybe it was selfish of me to think Ruby had brought joy to my life. Maybe it was wrong of me to plan to have her here with me for the rest of my life. Maybe I loved a woman whose life was too complex for any one man. Maybe I'll see her tomorrow and we can talk some more. Maybe Ruby just needs some time to herself.* He found himself able to move now. *Maybe I should get some sleep now.* Slowly, quietly, his heart broke in the most extraordinary way. A sensation of gratitude followed the breaking. He was thankful to have known Ruby for the time he'd had. He gathered up his memories of her as if he were picking flowers. The way her smile crossed her face as she giggled. Dreamily he closed his front door and made his way upstairs. The spell eased the pain of her absence, calmed him to the point where he had no desire to eat dinner or do any other thing. Mindlessly, he walked up the stairs and put himself to bed and fell quickly into a deep sleep.

Ruby.

Obadiah.

Ruby Birk Jameson

...

She was drawn unexpectedly and by an unknown force. She couldn't resist the urge to walk fast. She listened to the whispered urgings, the subliminal calling. There was undeniable advice coming from somewhere that made her restless and demanded that she act. The sweet sound of something greater than herself was chanting to her, leading her forward. Her feet glided effortlessly down the twisted paths of the unexpected, all the while with an attitude of gentle acceptance.

She understood the forces at work here. They were coming from somewhere within her, but also from a higher place. The soul. It wasn't her own feet that were pulling her. It was nothing like ordinary walking, for she was being pulled down the street by the beautiful and indistinct encouragement from the ever-knowledgeable soul within her, the soul that is ever profoundly aware of its purpose.

The ancient voice of Lithia Park called to Ruby as she walked.

Chapter 18

$\mathcal{A}$lthough the winter moon, ruled by Artemis, daughter of Zeus and Leto, was large and looked full to the naked eye, it was not quite full. It seemed to be resting just above the tops of the trees when Zanique and Yukon pulled into Ruby's driveway. Yukon leaped out of the Hummer, dashed past Zanique, and ran up the stairs to the apartment. The door was closed, so he waited at the landing for his friend. Each step Zanique took yanked at her heart, but her pride wouldn't let her succumb to her emotions. She knocked on the door.

"Hey, it's great to see you!" Ruby said as she opened the door. She immediately squatted down and hugged Yukon. "Hey, big boy, it's good to have you home!"

Zanique handed her a box. "Hey, Babe! I brought you a present."

"What is this?"

"It's a cell phone. Now you can call me whenever… No more hit and miss when we're trying to connect."

Ruby set the box on the table without opening it. "Thank you," she said, "but I don't need it."

"But...." Zanique stiffened at the rejection. "Oh, okay, never mind."

Ruby was immediately sorry that she'd been so dismissive. "It's sweet that you bought me a gift," she said, "but, honestly I don't need it." She gestured toward the couch, and Zanique sat down. Ruby knelt on the floor before her. "Remember when I told you that Obadiah was coming for me?" she asked. "Coming to take me home?"

"Yeah, I do."

"Well, he's coming for me soon. Tonight is our last time together."

Zanique rolled her eyes. Unlike Dutch, she didn't care if she seemed condescending. "Are you out of your fucking mind? Obadiah is dead! That girl sitting there in the painting—" she pointed at the framed painting "—she's dead, too. They both died a long time ago. Ruby, Obadiah isn't coming for you. I'm sorry to tell you this, but your home is here in this apartment. Get real, girl. Stop with this bullshit that you're going back in time."

Ruby smiled and tried not to sound impatient. "I know they're dead. Death comes to us all at some point." She smiled again. "He said he was coming for me and I promised I would go back with him." She touched her friend's knee. "Be happy for me."

Zanique could only look away and shake her head in frustration.

Ruby stood up. "What do you want from me?" she asked. "What do you want me to say?"

"I want you to look me in the eye again and say you love me," Zanique said. "Like you did the night we spent together. I want you to pick up that goddamn cell phone and tell me, 'Thank you, I'll call you every day and tell you that I love you.' That's what I want you to say."

Instead of reaching for Zanique's gift, Ruby walked over to the painting and stared at Obadiah. "You said, and I agreed, that we would be friends," she said without looking at Zanique. "Love, romantic love, was off the table…. Right?" When Zanique didn't reply, Ruby spoke again without looking at her. "I do love you, Zanique. As my best friend. I do. But he's my husband, and his love—no, *our* love is so far above any other love I've ever felt. I'm committed to him. We're in love because he's also my best friend, because I remember being this woman." She touched the image of herself in the painting. "This woman in a painting painted in 1912. I remember being happy then. With him. Can't you see that what is happening to me is greater than me? Greater than any of us? Yes, it's impossible. But *it is happening.*"

Zanique stood up. "No, it's *not* happening. You're letting your imagination run wild with you. Sure, you've had some freaky things happen when you wear the necklace, but come on! There is no way that Obadiah, who is dead, may I remind you, is going to walk through that door and take you back to the mansion, oh, and back to 1912, I might add... a hundred and six years ago!"

"We'll see."

Zanique's pride finally fractured, then crumbled. She began screaming at Ruby. "Do you know what you've done to me? Do you have *any* idea? I come over here with hopes that something special will happen between us. I brought you a cell phone in hopes that you would be excited because now you'd have a way of calling me. But, instead—what? You're telling me that, not only do you not want me, but you're leaving me for a man from over a hundred years ago! Well, that's a fine how-do-you-do!" Tears began to fill her eyes. Her voice dropped. "Ruby, I can't get you out of my mind. I didn't sleep at all last night, and when I did sleep, I kept dreaming of making love to you. What have you done to me... *what?*"

The shriek came from somewhere inside Zanique that she was unaware of, and it startled her as much as it startled Ruby when it came out. The outburst was harsh and beyond her normal voice. She didn't like the sound of that scream. She was afraid that if she spoke, her voice would reveal a woman whose heart has been captured, a defeated woman. She was afraid she'd sound like a wild animal. She wasn't out of control; the animal inside her only wanted to be touched, petted, fondled. But her pride was strong enough to keep that animal tethered and hidden.

Ruby finally turned and went to her friend. "I'm sorry," she whispered.

All Zanique could say was, "You don't have to go. You can stay with me. You can come live with me. We can make this thing work."

Ruby shook her head. "I can't."

Zanique ferociously wiped her tears away. "Okay, how about this? Is it asking too much for you to go back in time and divorce that good-looking son-of-a-bitch and then come back to me?"

Ruby had to laugh at the absurd suggestion. "Yes, that's asking too much."

"I knew you were going to say that." Zanique sat back down and adjusted herself. "I can't explain it," she said in a quieter, calmer voice. "But after spending the night with you, I feel like something is very different. Don't you feel it? I swear you put a spell on me. Something's changed and I feel... I... I just want to be with you for the rest of my life. You know? Total commitment?"

Ruby nodded, but moved away from her friend and closer to her easel. "I do feel that something has changed," she said. "But that change doesn't mean that I'm going to stay here. I'm going home... it's time for me to go home."

The words hung there, heavy, unpleasant, unwanted. Zanique wanted Ruby to commit to her, even if it were just a commitment of friendship, and Ruby didn't want to say the things that would hurt her friend's feelings. But her words had been said. They hung in the air, powerful and foreboding.

Yukon was now pacing nervously, going back and forth between the two women, nudging them with his nose in hopes of soothing the pain and anger that was filling the room. He could sense the stress, heartache, and frustration better than humans gave him credit for. As Ruby kissed him on the nose and hugged his neck again, he wagged his tail. He climbed up next to Zanique and licked her cheek, then began nuzzling her face, which tickled her and made her giggle.

"Yukon, stop that. It tickles!"

An owl swept into the crown of the tree outside Ruby's apartment, let out a cry, and looked in the window. Ruby sat back down on the floor, distracted by sudden memories, half-spoken conversations, out-of-focus images, and lingering odors. Memories from another century that blurred in and out of each other with no beginning, no end, no boundaries. Memories of an impossible past with Obadiah, his aroma lingering so sweetly, his voice low and captivating. Entranced in the impossibility of it all, Ruby sat staring off into space.

As Yukon jumped down from the couch and trotted off to his water bucket, Zanique righted herself, and it dawned on her how much she'd miss Yukon, too. He was her buddy. The thought of losing him too made her feel more abandoned than ever. She looked at Ruby for any reassurance, but Ruby was transfixed.

And it was Ruby's unemotional silence that bothered Zanique the most. *This isn't* ordinary *anguish,* she told herself. *It isn't* irrational *anguish, either. No, this is* exceptional *anguish that I'm feeling. A particular anguish that comes from the soul.* She couldn't describe it, nor could she name it, but there was something extraordinary that existed between her and Ruby. It was more than love, more than friendship, more than....

Ruby didn't have to speak; her body language was plain enough. Zanique was being pushed out of Ruby's life, no longer her intimate friend, no longer a part of Ruby's private life. She had been profoundly released, exhaled out, and sent away.

How could she turn off all of her feelings so quickly? Zanique wondered. She spoke again. "Do you want me to go?" She stood up but refused to look at Ruby. "I should just go."

Ruby blinked suddenly, refocused on the present, on the room, on her friend. Seeing Zanique, she mumbled, "Umm... no. You can stay."

"I can stay? I'd like it better if you said something like 'I want you to stay.'"

"I do want you to stay."

"Why're you doing this, girlfriend? You're hurting me!"

"I'm not trying to do anything to you." Ruby came closer to her, "You once told me you wanted me to be happy. That's why I'm going back home. I'm happy there."

"I want you to be happy," Zanique said, a sense of urgency in her tone, "but I thought I could be the one who brought you the happiness you needed. I never thought you'd up and leave me and take my heart with you."

"Of course, this... this situation saddens me, but please try to understand that I find it difficult being here in this world you and I share, in 2018. I'm at the end of my life here. My life with you, Dutch, and Ashland. This is the end of my life here, but it's the beginning of my life elsewhere. Back there with him. It hurts me knowing that I've caused you or Dutch any pain. I imagine that both of you think I'm being selfish. Maybe I am being selfish. I have no idea what memories you have of me, if you cherish them. Maybe you both think I'm the best thing that has happened to you, and because I'm leaving I'm taking away that feeling. But I'm sure you'll meet someone else who will replace me in your heart. You really will find happiness after I've gone."

"No." Zanique's voice was low and scratchy. "I said no! No, I won't find happiness after you go. And, no, I don't want you to go away."

"Oh, sweetie, there has to be an end to this story. You and I will both go on doing different things in different times, but this story—the one taking place here and now—has to come to an end. Surely you know that the end, that death, eventually comes to all things." Ruby felt herself in such a fretfully heightened state of sensitivity to everything that she had to stop and catch her breath. "I'm preparing to leave. Unceremoniously. Silently. Unnoticed from this time back to Obadiah. I want to leave this place peacefully. I don't want to hurt you, but it's time I go back to my husband. He's waiting for me."

Zanique was still skeptical. "How do you do that?"

"Do what?"

"You speak so convincingly, I start to believe you. You're actually convincing me that you're returning to Obadiah and back to the past... like, as if people do it every day. Ruby, listen to me! It's not possible! You will be here next week and the week after that and the week after that. You're not going anywhere." She bit down on her lip and put her hand over her mouth and swallowed the bitter taste of disappointment like some awful medicine.

"Please let this be good-bye," Ruby whispered, "and trust me that I'm leaving for a better place and time."

Zanique's arms were suddenly around Ruby, her lips pressed against Ruby's cheek. "Oh Ruby," she said, holding her tight, "this will be good-bye then?"

When Ruby spoke again, her voice was quiet and controlled. "My sweet Zanique, I'm sorry, I truly am."

"You know, I've never felt this way about anyone else, and I doubt I ever will again. It's so strange, this feeling I have about you. It's a kind of pronounced grandeur, a brilliance that words can't describe. I just wish you felt the same way about me. If only you'd choose me. To stay with me."

"Please don't do that." Ruby tried to back up a step, but Zanique's grip was too firm. "Please don't try to weaken me any further. I'm very weak right now. Zanique, you'll always be an enormous part of my life, but if I chose to stay here with you, if I said no to Obadiah," she pointed to the stack of paintings, "if I stayed here… well, I would go back to being miserable. Painting graves and cemeteries. This is good-bye. I promise you."

Zanique's kiss was gentle and long and searching. When she finally released Ruby, she didn't speak but only turned away, stood motionless for a minute, then walked to the door without looking back. Then she walked out of Ruby's apartment and closed the door behind her.

She walked down the stairs, feeling odd emotions, strange tuggings at her heart, and with each step, her heart broke more and more. She felt like she was walking to a funeral.

Death?

Was love dying tonight?

Down in the driveway, Zanique stood, shivering in the cold and watching big flakes of snow beginning to fall. The brightness of the moon allowed her to see the owl up in the tree and she wondered if Ruby really could leave this time and return to 1912.

"If she finds peace back there," Zanique said as she unlocked the yellow Hummer, "back there with the love of her life, even if it's only a dream that others can't see, then may she dream always."

...

The meteorologists would say in the days to come that a *spontaneous arctic blast* hit the Rogue Valley the night of the winter solstice. That was the night that Ruby and Yukon left her studio for the last time and walked to Lithia Park. The sky was clear all day and all night, and the full solstice moon was shining in all its glory when the arctic blast hit.

Walking into the park under the city lights, Ruby was shivering in the cold. An owl accompanied her, flying in circles twelve feet above her head. Then it landed in a pine tree as she came to the park bench, where she sat and waited for Obadiah to come. She looked up at the owl and admired its beauty. Yukon curled up at her feet and let the wind blow at his back.

The wind continued to blow as it had for the past few days. It was bitterly cold, and Ruby thought the wind was sharp enough to cut her like a long, cold, sharp knife. Yet inside the wind, she heard a comforting voice that enveloped her and reached into her.

The voice asked her if she were ready to come home?

"Yes." She spoke firmly. "Yes."

She felt the earth beneath her begin to vibrate, then saw the big buildings of the city around the park beginning to shimmer. The world around her was now in motion. Solid, immovable objects were quivering, and everything that had anchored her to 2018 began to evaporate. The solid, permanent city of Ashland, Oregon, dissolved into a blurry collage of color and texture. What was right had moved left, what was once up was now down.

Ruby felt her departure to her core. She was moving away from a world where she had always felt like a stranger. And that world was moving, too, changing, becoming something else above which she was detached and suspended. She was joyous to feel this transition, she welcomed it without a thought in her mind about what she had done in her present-now future life. With Yukon beside her, she drifted away from the cold. They glided up and away. She had the delightful sense of moving on to a place more comfortable.

Did I just fall up through the sky?

She was dizzy. She'd lost her bearings. The only thing she was certain of was the quickening frequency of the change that was happening around her. Up and away she went, slipping into the past. It tickled as she was pulled through a century of changes.

Ruby laughed.

...

It was sometime after two in the morning that Zanique was awakened by the sound of her own voice calling out. She'd been having a disturbing dream of Ruby so vague that she felt rattled. She was ashamed that Ruby was now the main character in her dreams. Alone in the dark, she pulled her quilt around her in defense against the sudden chill she felt. She caught her breath and replayed the details of the dream. Slowly, Ruby's hands were on her, her lips were on her neck.

"I love you," Ruby whispered in her ear.

"Babe, why don't you stay with me?"

"I must go, but please take this," And Ruby handed her the ankh necklace. "It's important that you have it now."

"Why is it important for me to have this?"

"Soon," Ruby said with a smile, "you'll have all of the answers to your questions, but first you must learn what questions to ask."

"I don't understand."

"I'm sorry. Obadiah is waiting." Ruby got up from the bed and walked toward Zanique's bedroom door. She looked back. "I have to go."

Zanique's heart was racing with something close to fear, then she got out of bed quietly, sneaking out of her bedroom with the intent of following Ruby back to Obadiah. When she got to her living room, she clearly saw Yukon standing there and happily wagging his tail.

"What are you doing here, boy? Shouldn't you be with Ruby?"

Yukon followed her when she went and opened the front door and stepped out into the cold. He stood by her side while she looked up and down the street. No Ruby in sight. A large owl flew over her head, and Yukon ran after it. She could see him going, going, going until he was out of sight.

Crazy dream.

Zanique reluctantly went back to bed and lay there, trying to make sense of Ruby and why she had become the most important person, thing, or perhaps everything, in her life. She felt nervous, as though she had lost complete control over her own being.

What had Ruby done to her?

...

The cold had crept in through the walls of his well-insulated house and gathered itself around him. Dutch, in bed and asleep, was struggling with a dream that had come uninvited. Ruby was walking just far enough ahead of him that she couldn't hear him calling her name. Yukon was walking beside her as they made their way into Lithia Park. Now Dutch began running, trying to catch up with her, but when he was at the park's entrance, he couldn't see them anymore. He didn't know which path he should follow. He chose left. As he walked, he began to notice that the park looked very different. The people in the park were different. He looked beyond the park. Ashland was different. He saw a horse-drawn flatbed wagon go by, and then an ancient automobile came clattering down the street. The people were dressed in clothes of a century earlier.

He made his way through the park, calling out for Ruby.

"I'm here, Dutch."

She came from behind him and put her arms around him.

He turned and looked at her. "I thought I had lost you."

"You have." She kissed his neck. "I'm gone now. I'm home. You've followed me home."

"I—I *what*?"

"Yes, it's 1912, and I live right over there." She pointed, and Dutch could see a small part of the Jameson Mansion. "I'm home."

"But what about us, Ruby? What about...."

"Shush, I'm home now with my husband. There is no more *us*. I'm sorry." She took his hand and they walked deeper into the park. It was warm; the sun was shining bright. It was summer.

"So, that's it, then?" he said. "You're home and I'm just a memory now?"

"Dutch, you have to go back. You don't belong here."

As Yukon came round and leaned against Dutch's leg, he reached down and patted him. He loved both of them. They were a package deal, no Ruby without Yukon and no Yukon without Ruby. She let his hand fall and began walking away. He felt lost and entirely alone.

"It's not so bad, Dutch," she called back to him. "If you look, you'll see a sign. A silver lining will reveal itself in times to come. You will have control over your heart again... in time."

She began to fade away, and the park was fading, too. Dutch closed his eyes and began willing his breath to slow. He was doing what he thought was the way back to her, slowing his breathing, relaxing his body, and trying to clear his mind of all emotions. He feared if he were too tense, he would cut the energy that connected him to her, to the past, to 1912. He felt weightlessness around him, but now he couldn't feel her energy anymore. The soft fragrant breeze of summer passed around him, then it faded, too.

He then fell into darkness.

From the darkness of his dream came the sound, a sound that filled the air around him. A moan. A prolonged, deteriorating moan like the flow of a river. His emotions allowed him to understand the sound for what it was. He was listening to the sound of his own mind, and it was grieving.

Something swept past his elbow in the blackness. A faint light began to grow. He heard a sigh that hardened into a whisper. "Dutch," Ruby whispered, "my friend will show you the way back."

Still in his dream, an owl had landed on a railing across from him. It perched there, staring at him with its big yellow eyes. The owl seemed to be connected to his emotions. It somehow cast a spell of encouragement around him. The dream ended.

His shivering made him lose his concentration on Ruby. The dream was fragile, precious, but the cold had taken it away. His heartbeat picked up, his breathing came back to normal, and his slackened muscles now tightened. He was nervous.

Chapter 19

$\mathcal{J}$ustine MacLane was utterly shaken when she told the police officer, "I thought I was looking at a mannequin sitting there on the park bench."

It was about midday on the day after the solstice when Justine had walked through Lithia Park and discovered Ruby and Yukon, both fatally frozen. She had immediately called the police, and now reluctantly looked at Ruby again while the officer took her statement, thinking to herself *She looks like she's alive, as if she might move, as if her eyes might blink at any moment. This woman, she looks so full of life that she can't be dead. She just shouldn't be dead!*

Ruby's body sat frozen to the park bench, her eyes still open as if gazing at the park. She was still wearing her secondhand-store wool coat and her well-worn leather portfolio was still tucked under her arm. Yukon's lifeless body lay at her feet.

Officer Williams, who was taking Justine's statement, was also troubled by the sight of Ruby.

What troubled him the most was that Ruby had a smile on her face. He scratched his head and asked himself, *What the hell was she doing out here in the middle of the night, anyway?*

The ambulance he summoned arrived, and the EMT's off-loaded a gurney and rolled it toward the bench. Fascinated neighbors of the park were now walking across the street and down the hill and gathering into a small crowd whispering about what must have happened. How had that body gotten there?

"Froze to death?" an EMT asked Williams. "Is that your assumption?"

Williams looked up from his notes and nodded. "That's what it appears."

The EMT's muscled Ruby's stiff body onto the gurney and covered her. Just then, a woman broke through the crowd and let out a cry. Williams, surveying the park one last time, looked at the woman.

"Excuse me, ma'am," he said, approaching her. "Do you know this woman and her dog?"

"I can't see the woman, but I assume that is Ruby and, this is Yukon." She reached down and ran her hand down his lifeless back. "I was a friend of hers."

Officer Williams had found Ruby's ID in the pocket of her coat, and now this woman had just confirmed that the dead woman was Ruby Birk. "I'm sorry for your loss," he said, putting a caring arm around her shoulders and walking her away from the ambulance and the bodies. "You don't want to remember them this way, you should go now."

She nodded her head. "Thank you, officer." She struggled to tell him more, that Ruby had been a talented artist, but she knew she needed to get to work and carry this terrible news of Ruby with her.

...

Dutch was working in his office at the Kaleidoscope, trying to shake off the dream he'd had the night before. It still felt so *real*. The content of the dream wasn't as troubling to him as the emotions it left him with. When he heard the bell above the door ring, he went to see who it was.

"Dutch!" Nora cried. "It's Ruby. They found her and Yukon."

Dutch grabbed her by the shoulders and looked her straight into her eyes. "What are you saying... who found Ruby? Where? What...."

"She's dead, Dutch!" As Nora fell into him, he felt the weight of her body against him. But it was nothing like the weight of the news she had just voiced. That, he thought, was so heavy it might be an elephant sitting on his chest. He couldn't breathe. He almost sank under the weight. It was the hardest news Dutch had ever received, terribly hard news, and he struggled to keep his self-control. Like any man who'd been taught all his life to be strong and not to break into sobs during hard times, he repressed his own feelings and held his sobbing sister. If it was true that Ruby was dead, he wanted to scream, too, he wanted to die, he wanted to go back a few days to when Ruby had sat in his living room with him. He almost decided he was in a movie. But, no, he told himself, this wasn't a movie. And people don't come back from being dead. Surely his sister had been mistaken.

"Are you sure about this?" he managed to say. "It was her?"

She nodded and took a deep breath to steady herself. "I was walking to work, and as I was passing Lithia Park I saw the ambulance and they were loading the gurney with someone laying on her side, frozen in a sitting position. They had the sheet pulled up over her so I couldn't see her, but then I saw Yukon...." Nora's voice cracked, and she began sobbing again. The thought of Yukon and Ruby, both dead, seemed somehow appropriate. And yet, their death was all the more heartbreaking. "Someone found her sitting on the park bench with Yukon at her feet. By the fountain. They froze to death!"

If Nora had more to say, Dutch didn't hear it. It didn't seem to him that he really understood with the whole of his brain anything his sister was saying. He wasn't able to take in the consequence of her words. He could feel nothing but a frightening sensation all over his body, as though his own life was ebbing out of every pore. Every nerve and fiber in him seemed to have gone slack, and an intense, throbbing ache grew in his chest. His eyes stopped seeing the world around him, his throat became unbearably tight. If Ruby were really gone, then everything was gone, and he was lost. He felt the cruelty of death robbing him of his love. His own future was slipping away. Finally, he was in so much physical pain and distress that it took away his voice.

His knees suddenly gave way, and he fell to the floor, taking Nora with him. He wasn't as strong as he'd always thought. Now he began wailing, hating God for taking Ruby.

Not even his sister was able to calm him, for she too was broken. She loved her brother deeply and knew that with this news, her brother's heart was now shattered.

"She's gone, Dutch. I'm so sorry."

They sobbed together.

...

Zanique was at the Morning Glory having brunch when she overheard two police officers in the booth adjacent to hers talking about the frozen bodies one of them had found in Lithia Park.

"It was really weird," one of the officers said. "The woman was just sitting there. She looked alive, but she was frozen solid. Her dog, too. A wolf breed with a thick coat—froze to death!" He shook his head in disbelief.

"Well, it was awful cold last night," the other officer said. "I don't doubt they froze. The news is calling it a spontaneous arctic blast. At one point, the temp was *minus* 44. And that was without the wind-chill factor!"

"Really? It got that cold last night?"

"It sure did. It's got to be the strangest weather event that ever happened in Ashland."

"It's all so strange," Officer Williams said. "The weather, the woman, the dog.... She was just sitting there with a leather folder under her arm and a smile on her face." He shook his head. "I'll never forget the way she looked sitting there. I tell you, man, she looked totally alive to me. She was literally and figuratively frozen in time. She was... she was... kind of enchanting, if that's even somethin' you can say about a corpse."

"Jeez, dude, you're creepin' me out," the other officer said, but then he quickly added, "I'm sorry you had to go on that call. I c'n see how that could mess with somebody's head."

At first, Zanique digested what she was hearing, but then she denied it, and then, after some thought, she couldn't resist turning to the booth where the cops were sitting. "Did you happen to get her name?" she asked. "The... the frozen woman? You've just described someone I know very well... was her name Ruby? Her dog's name was Yukon."

Officer Williams looked down at the floor. He knew he shouldn't have been talking about work in the diner, but his feelings and the effect of the scene needed to be vented somehow, and who better to tell than his friend and fellow cop? "Umm, I'm sorry, ma'am. I can't divulge that kind of information."

Zanique's hand began to quiver, her eyes welled up, and she pointed at him in a non-accusing way. "You don't have to say another word. I know it's her. She's dead. I had a dream last night, and I knew something was off this morning. And now I know why."

"Again, I'm sorry," Officer Williams said.

Zanique looked up at the ceiling, not knowing what to do with her emotions in a public place. She held back the urge to grieve, then looked back at Officer Williams. "Ruby doesn't have any family to speak of. Who do I contact to make arrangements for her?"

He gave Zanique the points of contact so she could claim Ruby's body and make the necessary provisions.

...

This harsh winter remained in Ashland until the end of December. The leaves were gone from the trees, and the blue skies had turned to gray. Snow kept falling and falling. And yet, Mother Earth's voice remained, singing to those who had ears to hear in a voice that seemed to hold all secrets for those that might listen. Her ancient voice came as a cold vibration pulsating through the air, bringing a stronger chill with every word.

The veil was thin in Lithia Park, and during the four days after Ruby's death, visitors to the park spoke of experiencing something that somehow gently blew away their troubles in life and the boredom of a complicated, overly critical, self-centered society that was filled with too much noise. In those few days, Mother Earth offered a pause to Her guests in Lithia Park, people that had previously been rushing anxiously through the world. Some were lucky when they took the time to sit and observe the park, for they saw the trailing lights and shadows that usually remain invisible to the naked eye. They noticed the energy that exists in the park and seems to bend and distort the illusion of reality and opens doorways in the aether that allow spirits to walk between worlds.

People in the park reported flashes of light and shimmers of white luminous forms. They said ghostly figures were walking the paths and trails in the park before dissolving into thin air. Some said they'd seen the ghost of a woman with cherry-chocolate hair holding hands with a handsome, well-dressed man, and there was a wolf by her side.

Could it be true?

Other people said that when it was quiet in the park and the general public wasn't paying attention, the paths that lace the park together have traces of the footprints of this ghostly couple, clear evidence of the woman, the man, and the dog walking side by side.

Proof?

Guests of the park began to claim that out of the silence and thin air walked the ghosts of three souls, not anything scary, they hastened to say, but when they saw them, these witnesses felt a sense of comfort, a sense of love. "The ghosts politely smile, and the dog wags his tail, all very friendly," said one witness in a brief article in the *Ashland Daily Tiding*. Others reported seeing a woman who slid between the trees or disappeared behind the bushes and shrubs. "She seems to be waiting for a particular person to happen by," they reported on social media. But most citizens of Ashland still just saw an empty park. They didn't notice the glimmering shadows or the footprints. However, some of those who didn't see the ghosts reported hearing someone calling out from the empty spaces of the park. "I heard it clearly," a witness wrote, "and it's a woman's voice calling to someone. The voice said, *Obadiah*."

Perhaps those with eyes to see had only glimpses and those with ears to hear got the faint voice of a woman and a man and a wolf-pedigree dog. Those encounters seemed to have no rational explanation in our ordinary language.

...

Zanique had fallen into the traps of her mind. She was snared in perplexity. When she was making her way to the hospital's morgue, her mind tried to approach everything rationally. She was afraid to agitate the river of her emotions too much, afraid she'd be swept away by the strong current. *This world isn't a very agreeable place to live in anymore,* she told herself.

Her life had become disagreeable. She wanted to move away from this town filled with painful memories and draw up someplace new where life was simpler. She had come to the point of realizing that life would no longer have any joy in it, no matter what heights of prosperity or adventure she might achieve.

There was no escape. Pain was stealing away every part of her life, leaving her empty. *This must have been the state of mind Ruby was in when she became,* she told herself. *When life seems lost, so unappealing that one wants to paint graveyards and headstones. Perhaps, in the end, Ruby decided to strip away the world of pain, loneliness, financial worries... all the things that made her life awful. She longed for and painted a world of graciousness... a world with Obadiah in it.*

When she reached the hospital, her feet felt heavy, the floor felt hard, and it hurt her feet as she walked. She had never been to a morgue before. The mere thought of it scared her. Thinking Ruby would be there, cold and lifeless, brought her face to face with absolute dread. If she hadn't loved Ruby, there would be no way she could do this, but she was determined to take care of Ruby the best she could.

How can it be that I was reaching my highest happiness only a few nights ago, and now pain and suffering have fastened themselves to me so quickly? Are joy and sorrow two energies that are joined together?

Her thoughts were meandering, searching for coherent reason in the world without Ruby, looking for a simple explanation as to why this day had come. The antiseptic smell of the hospital made her want to retch.

Ruby, what have you done to me? Ruby, what have you done?

After a short ride in the elevator, she found the office she was looking for. As she reached for the doorknob, the door unexpectedly opened.

"Thank you for coming down, Mr. and Mrs. Birk," said a voice. "We'll take good care of your daughter and have her body sent back for you." The morgue attendant was speaking to the couple who brushed past Zanique.

Zanique stepped back and froze for a second. "Mr. and Mrs. Birk?" she said aloud. "Ruby's parents?"

"Yes, that's right," said Ida Birk.

"Wow, are you fucking kidding me?" Zanique looked at them. "Your daughter needed you for years and years, but you wouldn't give her the time of day. You threw her away like trash. She was raped at the school you shipped her off to. She told you about it, she needed your help, but what did you do? What did you do?"

Jeffrey and Ida Birk were speechless. All they could do was stare at the stranger.

"I'll tell you what you did," Zanique went on. "You blamed her. You refused to help her! You rejected her! And now you come out here from Christianville, U.S.A., to do what? To show how much you care about Ruby? Oh, hell no! Get the fuck out of here! Go back to where you came from, go back to your other daughter and your son, you know, the ones you chose over Ruby. Ruby doesn't need anything from you now. She's dead!"

"Young lady," Jeffrey Birk began, "we don't appreciate your language, especially—"

Zanique cut him off. "No, asshole, you don't get to do that with me. You don't get to come in here like some loving father and demand respect." She looked as if through Ruby's eyes at the morgue attendant, who was pulling out his cell phone to call security. "I'd put that phone away if you know what's good for you," she told him. "I'm a woman that has suddenly, very suddenly, lost her best friend and I'm not feeling very stable right now... I might do something I can't come back from."

The attendant stopped dialing and put the phone back in his pocket. "I'm just trying to do my job."

Zanique ignored him and refocused on Ruby's parents. "You didn't *suddenly* lose a daughter. You chose to lose her years ago."

"I'm sorry for you because your best friend has passed away," Ida said sharply loudly, "but you are only a friend. We are her parents!"

"You wanna get loud? I can get loud, too. BITCH!" Zanique closed the gap between them. "Here's what's going to happen." She was close enough that Ida could feel her breath. "And this isn't a request, I'm taking care of Ruby's remains. She is going to be buried here in Ashland, in a place she lived in and loved for many years. You can get the idea of taking her back to wherever the hell it is you people come from out of your head right now. Ruby stays here!" Zanique's fast hand movements caused Ida to jerk away in fear of being hit. "We'll have a small funeral for Ruby with the people that knew her, that loved her." She then gave them the finger. "And if you don't piss me off any further, I'll allow you to come to the service." She looked from Ida to Jeffrey. "Any complaints? Any arguments?"

But Jeffrey wasn't looking at Zanique. He seemed to be looking at the wall behind her as he answered her. "I... uh... uh, I think—"

"Shut up! You don't get to think. Just say yes and then leave." She pointed down the hall toward the elevators.

Jeffrey turned away, looking like something had just startled him, but Ida was too scared to move. He had to take one of her arms and pull on her to get her started.

As they began walking toward the elevators, Zanique took a deep breath, held it, then exhaled slowly. "Ahh, that felt good," she muttered. "I needed to vent." She turned around to address the morgue attendant and was surprised to see Dutch standing near the door. "Oh, shit! How long have you been standing there?"

He smiled. "Since about the time you got loud."

"Why didn't you stop me? I was about to lose control."

"Nah, they needed that. Ruby told me about them, and to be honest, I don't like them, either." He scratched his head. "At first, I had no idea who they were and couldn't figure out why you were yelling at them. But when I heard you say they *chose to lose* their daughter years ago, I got it. A nice touch, I might add."

Zanique took another calming breath. "I assume you've heard about Ruby. I was going to come to the gallery after I finished here and tell you about it."

"Yeah. My sister was in the park when they found Ruby and Yukon."

"I was at the vet before this. Yukon is being cremated tomorrow, then I'm going to have his ashes put in Ruby's casket."

Dutch looked at the floor. Suddenly he was feeling the effects of Ruby's death again. He desperately wanted to stay in control. He barely heard Zanique's question.

"Why are you here, Dutch?"

"I... uh, well, she'd told me that she didn't have any contact with her family, so, I thought I'd come... and take care of her."

Zanique heard him sniffle. He still wasn't looking at her. "That's so nice of you," she said. "I've got plenty of money, so let me handle it, but I sure would like your help with all the arrangements. Would that be okay with you?"

He nodded. "Yeah, that sounds good and all... but I'm not good at arrangements, either." He paused for a catch in his throat to subside. "My sister, Nora, she would be a big help. She loved Ruby and Yukon very much, and it would do her good. A way for her to process this by helping."

Zanique felt the rush of sorrow radiating from Dutch. "Sure. Your sister... the three of us will give Ruby a good funeral." She didn't know what to do next. She wasn't the kind to embrace or offer affection to people she didn't know very well. "I guess we all need to process what happened. To tell the truth, it hasn't sunk in yet. I've been keeping myself so busy taking care of stuff that I haven't stopped to really understand that Ruby's dead."

The morgue assistant escaped by slipping back into his office. He quietly closed the door.

"Excuse me for a moment," Zanique said to Dutch. "I'll be right back." She walked to the door and banged on it until the assistant opened it.

"Can I help you?"

"*Can you help me?* Are you trying to get on my bad side?"

The attendant took a step back from this dangerous woman. "No. I'm sorry. What did I do?"

"You know why I'm here and you walked away... oh, never mind. Listen, Ruby Birk will be sent to the Mountain View Funeral Home. Here's the information." She handed him a business card. "If her parents come back after I leave and if they try to have Ruby sent back to Nebraska, you will politely tell them all the arrangements have been taken care of." She looked him up and down. "You really don't want me to come back here, do you?"

"No, no I don't. Besides, I don't think her parents will be back, anyway."

"Why not?"

"Well, you were pretty scary. But I don't think you would have intimidated them too much, 'cuz you're kind of small. But when that big guy out there showed up, the guy with the scars on his face, well, that pretty much scared the shit out of Mr. Birk. I doubt they'll be back."

She looked out the door's narrow window at Dutch, who was still standing in the hallway. She hadn't noticed the scars until now, and his size... he looked like he'd been through a war. "Oh, yeah, right," she turned back to the attendant. "Good point." She opened the door. "We aren't bad people," she said. "It's just we both loved Ruby so much. This has been really hard."

"I understand."

Zanique closed the door behind her, took another deep breath in and let it out slowly, trying to reduce her heart rate. The sight of Ruby's parents had provoked her into expressing her hidden violence. But it was now, thankfully, subsiding. She collected herself and looked at Dutch. "Well, it's over. That was the last of it. Ruby's funeral will be in four days."

"No," he said, "it's not over." He stepped forward and walked with Zanique to the elevator. "It'll never be over for me."

She watched him curiously in the elevator as it went up. They crossed the lobby together and headed for the parking lot.

"I never really got say to good-bye to Ruby," Dutch told Zanique as they approached the Hummer. "She came to see me the other night and told me she was leaving, but I didn't believe her. I had no idea she was talking about *this*." He held out his hand, "Thank you for what you're doing for Ruby. Please come by the gallery tomorrow so Nora and I can help you with the arrangements."

She stood motionless, still looking at him, unable to smile. She suddenly recognized how jealous she was of Dutch. He and Ruby had loved, they had made love, they had shared more intimate moments than Zanique had ever shared with Ruby. Jealousy combined with grief, and she felt another impulse to be angry. But she controlled it. "What do you mean by you didn't believe her and now this?"

"I'm not sure." He shook his head. "I've questioned it over and over in my mind... did Ruby do this on purpose?"

His words puzzled her. "Because of all that's happened I'm in danger of losing my mind. Suicide? Is that what you're saying?"

"Forget it," he said. "I'm also in danger of losing my mind. I'm not thinking clearly. Forget I said anything."

Zanique finally took his hand and shook it. "For whatever reason," she told him, "Ruby was in Lithia Park last night and she got caught in a freak weather event. Nothing more to it than that. I think it's important that we hold her memory in our hearts without doubts, or criticisms."

"Yeah. She got stuck in a freak weather event. You're right. It's not healthy to think too much about... about this."

"It's especially hard for us," she said, "because we both loved her so much. And I know how much she loved you. She told me. And because she loved both of us, we can work together and give her a wonderful send-off." She released his hand. "We can say good-bye to her and Yukon at the funeral."

"Thank you, Zanique. I'm sorry I said anything. I'm going to go back to the gallery now and talk to Nora."

They went their separate ways under a clear sky on a day in a city that was still in the grip of a freakish, cold weather event.

Chapter 20

*T*he mysterious world where hope rests is not orbiting a distant shining star. It is within reach if we seek out the sacred space and find what lies about us as an atmosphere unseen yet near. The veil of ordinary, material life often hides our earthly eyes from the splendors of which we are capable. But sometimes when the veil is thin, and the mortal stress is willed away, we might be carried away by the rushing mighty wind of inspiration. In such an atmosphere, an everyday person can be offered a magical experience like Ruby's.

It was from that mysterious other world that the owl came flying out of the veil and across the sky. In the misty light of the winter sun, it descended, circling once, twice, then a third time before it came to rest high in the crown of a ponderosa pine. Unrivaled in its blessedness, the owl's otherworldly constitution allows this ancient spirit guide to communicate with the trembling human soul. Thanks to Mother Earth's own magic, the owl may steal across our shifting boundaries and breathe the hope of a brighter world into our mundane one. Because this messenger can fly from the earth octave, past the lunar, and further up into the spiritual octave, it is a gift to those in need. It flies from the heavenly realm down to the sacred lands of our Mother Earth as wisdom, as love, as pure spirit.

Today, it is sitting high in a tree looking down at the graveside service.

...

Lying on the soft upholstery of her casket, Ruby looked like she was at peace. Her cherry chocolate hair was fanned out over the pillow, and the makeup on her face was as Ruby had always worn it: powder-pale cheeks, deep crimson lips, and striking black eyes. Zanique had insisted that Ruby look just like she did when she was alive and strongly warned the mortician not to put colorful makeup on her. Now, as people began to gather at the grave, Zanique bent down and kissed her friend. The kiss was her way of saying goodbye. She believed that Ruby could in some way see her and that she'd smiled at her after the kiss.

The muffled conversations around Ruby's casket sometimes sounded like the resonant humming of bees, but when the talk became gloomy, it sounded more like the distant chugging of old machinery struggling to perform its work. Then there would be moments of pause, but then conversations would begin again with sibilant whispers and, at the end, choirs of weeping.

Dutch paid little attention to the people at the grave. His mind was wandering through strange visions he could not keep out of his head. Images crept in and out of his mind, as if pulled by some magical filament. He thought somehow of Ruby's soul, and then wondered where it might be right now. He looked up when he heard the cry of the owl and he saw it high in the tree. It looked like the owl that had flown alongside Ruby the last time he'd seen her. That was when she'd told him good-bye and left his house, walking with the wind at her back into the dark of night. Into the unknown. The bird up there, he thought, must be some lonely flying creature faced with a long journey, a journey with no place for it to rest. He imagined its hoot was a melancholy cry for the loss of Ruby. The owl's cry confirmed that she was dead.

Ruby is dead. This is what today is all about. Bowing his head, he continued to imagine that the owl had some connection to Ruby. Or was its appearance here above her grave just a coincidence? He shivered—it was damn cold today, though not as cold as the night Ruby and Yukon had frozen to death. Graveyards, he thought, were always cold.

He and Nora had helped Zanique get the funeral properly arranged, getting the wreaths, flowers, and so on. But he had refused to participate in the funeral.

He left the eulogy and the public speaking to Zanique, not out of selfishness, but out of grief. He was unable to be a part of the funeral because he hadn't yet accepted Ruby's death. Yes, he told himself, he was in denial. Zanique and Nora understood and let him help in the ways that were comfortable.

He could hear someone singing. It might be a custom to have someone sing at a funeral, but the singing irritated him. He recognized the song, "Angel," by Sarah McLachlan, and when the singer ended, the melody still ran through his head. He could not put it out of his mind. The lyrics reached in and found a home in his mind.

He straightened himself up and looked at the midnight satin and silver brush casket. It was surreal to see Ruby lying there as if asleep, her hair spread across the pillow, her eyes closed, her hands folded above her heart. It just couldn't be true! He wished he could wake up from this nightmare. He closed his eyes so he couldn't see the casket, but then his thoughts began replaying the first time Ruby had walked into his gallery and how she made him feel. And then... there was the scene when they made love the first time, and he remembered how she'd made him feel that night, too. The mundane reality of this funeral was taking him to some dim, unearthly place. Occasionally the song would come back into his mind and strike an unexpected musical blow. *Why?*

he asked himself. Why had he met Ruby? Why had he fallen in love with her? Was there some greater purpose in this love, or was all the energy he'd put into their relationship just a waste of time? He stood beside the grave, silent, examining his own being and finding his existence, now an existence of dim desires and his sad, shadowy imagination.

When he opened his eyes again and looked for the singer, he discovered he'd been listening to Zanique. Her flute-like soprano had fallen gently upon the ears of Dutch and the other attendees. He stared at her in bewilderment. When they'd been working on the details of the funeral, she had never mentioned that she was going to sing. He almost smiled as he told himself it was marvelous how well she had managed to perform the song when he knew that this day tortured her emotions, too.

"Oh my God," said Ida Birk, "you have a beautiful voice." After much debate, she and her husband had decided to attend the funeral. But until this minute, they had stayed away from Zanique.

"Thank you," Zanique replied.

Dutch detected in her polite response a hidden expression of anger—the still-uncontrolled, majestic anger she kept hidden.

Zanique smiled at Dutch and Nora and two people she assumed were Dutch's parents standing with them. Then she spotted Mrs. Bimby, standing in her heavy coat and staring in disbelief at Ruby's casket. Nearby were several people from the art community who had known Ruby only causally but showed up anyway to give their condolences. Her eyes then fell on a man that Zanique knew had to be Turner, Ruby's ex-husband, with some girl who looked completely out of place standing next to him.

Odessa and Jimmy were off to the side, standing with Mrs. Brost from the Jameson Mansion. Odessa and Jimmy had come at her request. They were her family, and today she needed her family around her.

An older, gray-haired man stepped up to Zanique and whispered in her ear. Her eyes went wide, but she nodded and introduced him to the mourners.

"Thank you all for coming on this cold day," she said to the small group, "I had prepared something to say, but I think singing was enough for me... and to be honest, I don't think I can hold it together long enough to get through what I prepared. However, in my stead, this is Bernard Griffith, and he'd like to speak the eulogy." She stepped back as the stranger stepped forward and began to speak.

"Our friends here died in the cold in Lithia Park," he began. "This artist and her loyal Yukon at her feet. Ruby once told me that she struggled to be an artist. She didn't decide to become an artist. She was called upon to be an artist, and faced the same struggles as would a priest called to serve the Church.

"All of us here might have a calling to do something, but if so, what of this calling? If we are called upon, should we act? Did the Divine whisper in Ruby's ear and call her outside on that cold and dreadful night? I've heard people talking here at this gathering, asking others if Ruby did this on purpose. Did she go out that night knowing what would happen... in other words, did she take her own life?

"If you knew Ruby at all, you know that's not what she did. Ruby might have harmed herself, but she would have never harmed Yukon. She would've given him to Zanique, knowing fully well that she would care for him as Ruby would have. If Ruby were depressed, she might have done a thing like that. But Ruby wasn't depressed anymore. She had found love, and she was going out to meet the man she loved in the park. That is why she was there. *Love*. It's love that motivates us. It's love that saves, it's love that gets us into trouble. It's love that makes us do things we wouldn't normally do. And at last, it's the power of love that can travel beyond time and reach into our soul."

Dutch blinked his eyes. He didn't know this man, Ruby might have mentioned his name once, but why was he here, speaking at her funeral? Was this Bernard Griffith from a part of her life that she hadn't felt comfortable sharing with him? But more importantly, this odd, older man was talking as if he had heard what was going on in Dutch's mind.

This stranger was answering his unspoken questions. Dutch had wondered if Ruby had gone out on purpose. The last time he saw her, she was talking crazy. It was possible that she'd taken her own life. But now he had an answer, and it was true: Ruby would never have harmed Yukon. Griffith was saying the things that he urgently needed to hear, and he was thankful.

"It's a mystery, for sure, the last days of Ruby's life here," Griffith way saying. "She was talking about a man, a husband, from another time, right here in Ashland, but back in 1912."

"Husband?" Ruby's mother gasped.

"Shush," Nora said.

Griffith ignored the interruption. "Some of you here doubted her story. You believed that she was fantasizing. Or losing her mind. I mean, how could it be that she had a husband from another time? How is it possible that there are pictures of her from 1912, when she obviously couldn't have been there at that time?"

Ruby's friends were moved from grief to interest in Griffith's words. This unknown older man seemed to have known Ruby better than anyone else standing around the gravesite. Zanique looked confused, but remained quiet in order to hear what he had to say.

"It's simple," he said as if answering their questions. "It's... magic." He moved to center himself in front of the casket. "First, you must think with an artist's mind. Artists deal with creativity. They think of possibilities, they think of abstract and alternate realities all the time. They have the perfect mind for magic."

It was cold there in the cemetery, but the people were captivated by this man who was speaking not about death, but about love, life, and magic.

"Magic, you see, reaches us on a fundamental level. It's part of our primitive existence. For most of us—the common people, the uninitiated—magic happens when we're not expecting it. It's those crazy moments when we have those experiences in life that are beyond words, outside our language. They surpass explanation. I believe that in the end, Ruby began to understand that magic is very similar to art. For you see, magic uses the principles of energy, time, creativity, charm, form, harmony, balance, and process.

The same elements that give artists the freedom and flexibility to explore their world also let them venture into the alternate and inner realities from which they paint us a picture.

"It's 2018, not 1912. This is when we live. But what if time were nothing like we think? What if pure energy is not confined to time and we are all part of a wonderful cosmic flow of energy?" He paused again to give his listeners time to think about his questions.

"Ruby understood that magic, just like art, is open to interpretation, and that is one of the beautiful things about it. It doesn't jump out and declare, 'This is technology, and this is a detailed schematic of how this energy works.' Instead, magic requires you to have an open, inquiring mind. It's important to enter into it openly and see where it takes you. Ruby's mind had the freedom to explore magic, and she assigned her own meaning to her experiences. She told me that being an artist was an intensely personal process that enriched her."

"Magic!" Jeffrey Birk exclaimed across the distance between him and Bernard Griffith. "You, sir, you dare speak of magic at my daughter's funeral! We are Christ-following, church-attending people, and this is blasphemy. I will not stand for it. I say you must politely dismiss yourself so that we may conduct a proper eulogy complete with the words of God, Jesus about redemption."

"I understand where you are coming from, Mr. Birk," Griffith replied. "Understanding an abstraction like magic doesn't come naturally to everyone. Magic is an energy that makes some people scratch their heads and say, 'That is evil,' or 'that is unholy.' What people don't realize is that magic originated with the gods. The Old Testament is laced with magic, starting with the mystical priest Melchizedek. So, Mr. and Mrs. Birk, you can rest easy. I'm not preaching, or trying to sell you anything. What I'm offering you, and everyone here, is an understanding of Ruby that will hopefully ease some pain in the hearts that loved her. So if I may continue?"

Everyone was staring at the Birks with expressions of annoyance on their faces.

Jeffrey nodded and motioned for Griffith to continue.

Griffith nodded. "As I was saying, magic can make people uneasy because they don't automatically know how it works. Real magic doesn't contain recognizable science, so it would appear that there is nothing to mentally grasp or hold on to. This can be very confusing, even threatening, to those who are not used to assigning their own meaning to what they see before them." He shifted his stance and touched the casket. "You all see that Ruby's here, that she's dead, that she and Yukon are no more. But I argue that Ruby went out that night under the protection of magic. She left us, that is true, but she left us for another time. I say she went back to 1912. Perhaps she couldn't take her 21st-century body with her. Perhaps the abstract is so far beyond us that we can't comprehend the actual truth of what happened in Lithia Park."

Could it be? Dutch asked himself. *No, she's dead, that's her lifeless body in the casket. There's no way she went back to Obadiah. This guy's out of his mind.*

Zanique, too, had had enough of Griffith's eulogy. Ruby didn't go back to 1912. She and Yukon hadn't returned to the past because her body was right here in 2018, dead, and her body in that casket was proof. Ruby had some visions with her necklace, Zanique told herself, but those were just episodes. She started to approach Griffith and politely thank him and get him to leave. But before she could take a step, he started talking again.

"Often in magic, a person needs a tool to help them achieve their goal. Ruby had a powerful tool, a tool that allowed her to not only see the past, but to join it." He reached into his pocket and produced an ankh. "She had a key like this one." He held it up, and Zanique's jaw dropped. She felt her neck. Yes, she was still wearing the ankh Ruby had given her.

"Yes," Griffith was saying, "Ruby had a necklace that was a gift from Mother Earth, the ankh with an enchantment written on it. Words of magic from the Goddess Herself."

"Goddess? Magic? Enchantments?" Jeffrey Birk stepped forward. "I've heard all I'm willing to stand for! This is the work of the Devil! Ruby was into some strange things out here." He stomped his foot, then walked away with Ida in tow.

"I told you when she left school she would fall into the hands of evil," Ida said to her husband, but loud enough for everyone to hear. Trying to keep up with Jeffrey's long stride, the portly woman held her nose in the air and squinted her eyes as she walked past Zanique.

"Great," Zanique said under her breath.

"Son," Dutch's father whispered in his son's ear, "I don't care for Ruby's parents, but I have to agree. This funeral is strange. What the hell is that man talking about?"

"Not now, Dad."

"Was Ruby married, for Christ sakes?"

"I'll explain later." Dutch moved to the other side of Nora, away from his father.

"Well," his mother said, "I for one can't afford to leave because I'm curious." Then she added, "You know, there's something strange at work here, but in a lovely way. That man speaking... there's something fantastic about him."

Roger made his way back around to Dutch's ear. "I assume you slept with Ruby. Didn't she make wife noises in the bedroom?"

"What?"

"Oh, come on, boy! You know a woman makes noises in the bedroom, but they're different when they're married. They're quieter. Less rambunctious. That would've told you right there that Ruby was married. Where is her husband, anyway?"

"Back in 1912!" his wife barked in his ear. "Haven't you been listening? Now be quiet. The man is trying to talk."

Zanique had already noticed that Dutch and his family were getting restless. She thought that she should go and see what the matter was. She was also hoping that Nora, or Dutch, would help her steer this funeral back on track. Bernard Griffith had taken this in a whole new direction, one Zanique was uncomfortable with.

"Is everything all right?" she whispered to Dutch.

"Uh, well, my parents are getting edgy," he whispered back.

"I know. Me, too. When Bernard showed up, he told me that he had answers to Ruby's death that we all would want to hear. I had no idea he would go off on this tangent."

"Who the hell is that guy?" Dutch asked. "Did Ruby know him? How did she know him? Did she know him very well?"

"No. Ruby and I just met him once. It was at dinner the night Ruby and I spent together—"

"Spent together?"

"Um, uh, I meant that Bernard was at my Christmas party."

"So he met her once and after one conversation, now he's talking like he knew her for years." Dutch frowned, "The thing is, some of what he's saying makes complete sense."

"Yeah, I thought that, too, but I don't think her funeral is where he should be sharing... all this."

Dutch felt a strong pat on his back. Roger had just given him an affectionate slap. "Now, son, this girl's a keeper. She's beautiful!"

"Dad, please—"

"You don't want your son with the likes of me." Zanique quickly interrupted the whispered conversation. "If you thought Ruby was bad news, you haven't seen anything yet."

At this point, Bernard Griffith realized that he had lost his audience and signaled to Zanique to step forward. But before she moved, she looked at Dutch and said, sotto voce, "I knew I should've had Ruby cremated with Yukon and climbed Mount Shasta and buried them both up there all by myself. This funeral has turned out to be a mess."

Dutch merely shook his head.

Back in front of everyone, Zanique noticed that most eyes were glazed over in perplexity and most jaws had gone slack. "Well," she said brightly, "that's it, folks. It's cold, so we're going to cut this short. Thank you all for coming." Then she turned and whispered to her friend. "Great, Ruby, just great. I'm sorry. I really wanted to give you a special send-off."

Griffith approached her. "Please don't worry about the funeral. What I had to say was mainly for you and Dutch to hear. The others, well, they *heard* something, but they won't remember what I said. All they'll remember is that nice things were said here. They'll have a good memory."

Zanique squinted at him, "What are you talking about, Bernard? You are a strange fuck, you know that? I can't believe you came here and said all that shit. You don't even know Ruby, but you talked like you've known her for years."

"I have known her and Obadiah for years. They are my best friends."

Zanique froze. "Say again?"

He held up his ankh again, "I know them from 1912." He now had Zanique's full attention. "Yes. Ruby wanted me to come here and help you and Dutch to understand what has happened. She feared the two of you would be left with too many unanswered questions."

"Well, I sure haven't had all of my questions answered."

"It's simple," he said. "She went home. She is with Obadiah."

Zanique's eyes narrowed. "You know what? It's too soon for me to hear this shit. I'm not even sure what you're saying. But I know I don't want to hear it."

He shrugged. "That's your choice. I'm going to go, then." He patted her on the shoulder. "In time you will come to understand."

She watched him walk between the headstones until he disappeared. That was when Nora walked up. "Zanique," she said, "you did a wonderful job on the funeral. Ruby and Yukon would've been proud."

"I doubt that after Mr. Nut Job's speech." She pointed to where Bernard Griffith had gone.

"Who? Mr. Griffith? I thought he was very good. His eulogy was perfect for them. You couldn't have asked for anyone better."

Dutch came forward now. "Well... that was different."

"Right?" Zanique said.

"Don't listen to him," Dutch's mother said. "My son has never taken funerals very well. He has a soft heart. I think the service was beautiful. And Mr. Griffith? Captivating, truly captivating."

"Captivating?" Roger jumped in. "Who talks like that? I've never found anyone *captivating*... what the hell does that mean, anyway?"

Dutch winked at Zanique. "I'd better get them out of the cold," he said. "It was good to see you again. Stop by the gallery sometime, Nora and I would like to see you again." She nodded, and with that Dutch and Nora were carefully leading their parents to their car.

Zanique next went over to where Jimmy and Odessa were standing. "Thank you so much for coming," she said, hugging them both. "I really needed you guys here! Losing Ruby has been the hardest thing I've ever been through."

"We know, Honey," Odessa said. "And what a fine funeral you put on for her. And that man... I loved his eulogy. What a special tribute he gave her."

"Didn't you think he said some strange things?"

"No, not at all. I can't seem to remember exactly what he said, but his words were perfect for the moment."

"Yes," Jimmy said. "Wow. From Bernard's words, I gather that Ruby was one hell of a woman!"

Zanique scratched her head. "Yes, Ruby was a special person. I'm glad you liked it all."

"Why don't you come home and be with us tonight?" Odessa asked. "Jimmy can fix you a nice breakfast in the morning. I think it'll do you some good."

"That'd be great! I don't want to be by myself tonight. And some pancakes in the morning would go a long way toward making me feel better."

Zanique was the last person to leave as the cemetery workers lowered Ruby's casket and began to fill the grave. A few snow flurries came down, and then the wind kicked up, swirling the snow and playing tricks on Zanique's eyes. She thought she could see Ruby standing right there, but then the wind blew in her eyes and she couldn't see anything but the snow. Next, the snow began sticking to her eyelashes and blowing down her neck. It brought with it the sound of Christmas bells ringing, and then—coincidentally or not—carolers began singing from the nearby Most Pure Heart of Mary Catholic Church. Zanique looked back toward the church. She was getting goosebumps. The cheerful voices of the carolers bothered her.

She cried out:

Ruby

Ruby Birk

Ruby Birk Jameson

...

The owl took flight. A symbol of wisdom for Mother Earth, wisdom neither good nor bad, it soared from the graveyard to high above Lithia Park's sacred landscape. Its flight was a testament to Ruby's dynamic relationship with our Mother Earth.

Chapter 21

$\mathscr{T}$he night blessed Dutch with sleep and dreams as he huddled into his quilt. Another dream about Ruby. A casual dream, a lovely dream that gave him the illusion that Ruby had moved in some months ago and was living with him in his home. They were happy together. In his dream, she was there, sleeping next to him. Right where he wanted her to be. He could feel the warmth of her skin against his, could smell her perfume, a simple, exotic scent of jasmine smoothed over by sandalwood. Having her next to him was pure delight. She was so close to him that he was able to stretch and kiss her bare shoulder. It was a soft kiss, a heavenly kiss. Life was comfortable here, he was satisfied to his core.

"Dutch...."

"Yes?"

A long pause hung over them.

"Have you ever thought of what might have been if...."

"If what?"

"If I had stayed with you?"

He kissed her again. "If you had stayed? You're here with me now, I don't remember you ever leaving." In his dream, he believed that they had a continuing relationship, one with no interruptions. In this dream, she was alive, and her death was a long way in the future.

A sigh flowed out of her, and with a muffled voice she said, "I did love you, I really did. I'm sorry that I hurt you when I left. I'm sorry that I broke your heart."

"What are you talking about, Ruby?" He touched her arm, allowing his hand to linger for a moment. "We are together, you haven't left, and you didn't break my heart."

"Oh, Dutch, I want you to remember that I did love you. Remember that I want you to be happy. Please... move on, go out, live your life. Love will come to you again, one day, I know it will."

In his confusion, the room grew quiet again, and the silence swallowed up even the smallest sound. She faded away, and now he was alone in his bed, alone in his dream. Soon the warmth of the morning sun crept silently into the bedroom, ominous and dreadfully quiet, yet tugging him awake. His dream was swallowed up by the yellow vortex of sunlight.

He wanted to continue sleeping. He kept hoping Ruby would still be here with him, but the brazen daylight ripped the fabric of his vision, heaved him out of his wonderful dream, carelessly pushing him one way and his dream another.

Outside, it was early morning. Another new day had come around. From his position in bed, Dutch could see out the window and up into the blue sky. His sudden loneliness disturbed him, and he sat up, letting the quilt fall away. Next to him was nothing but a vacant space where she had been sleeping in his dream. As he imagined Ruby's face gazing at him from the other side of his dream, his heart pounded. He struggled to catch his breath. If he could only see her again, kiss her for real.

It was a normal, humdrum morning, time to get up and go through the routine of getting ready for the day and then going to work. His house was warm, his bed was comfortable, and the sun shone through his window just as it had for years during the winter season, but he felt cold inside, and his bed was so empty that it wasn't comfortable anymore. Nothing felt normal because she was missing. And as he looked at the vacant side of his bed, if he used his imagination, he could almost make out where her head had been lying, indenting the pillow. He knew it was only his imagination and wishful thinking.

It was a year since her funeral. A year! He'd been certain that by now he'd have gotten over her, or at least his feelings of grief would have subsided a little. But the year had brought little in the way of relief.

Her death was as prominent in his mind as it had been a year before. A small part of him was glad she was free from the woes that come with living. She was free. But he wasn't. He was stuck here in a life that knew no love, he was stuck in the secular world while she was in a heavenly place. She had left him behind, left him with no soul. He was empty. Oh, how he envied her in death, even as he had envied her in life.

While she was alive, Ruby had dared to imagine the world not moving in a linear progression as everyone else sees it, but rather in phases that could be traveled. Her art was the trigger that elevated her above the ordinary and into the extraordinary, and it was through her art that she had been free to explore the esoteric realities. Thoughts of her were haunting him not because she was ghostly, but because she, when alive, had been convinced enough of her time travel, of her reality in the early 20th century, that she had forced Dutch to keep examining his own time, his own reality.

He could barely breathe. Sitting there on his lonely bed, he wished he could see her again, could touch her, just once more. If only time travel were possible, if only he could go back in time, return to her, and say something different, be able to change the past with his love for her. If only he could return and stoke the fires of love that had burned between them. If given the opportunity, he was certain that with his love he could persuade her to stay with him. Then she wouldn't have gone out that night because she would have been with him in the warmth of his house, safe in the comfort of his bed.

If only... He gave a sigh of surrender. It was only a wish, a hopeful but impossible thought. It was asking too much of life to rewind itself and take him back to her. He recalled every kiss she had given him all the way up to that last kiss... and how that last kiss had meant goodbye. In his heart was a deep place where the words of love echoed down the dark canyons of his emotions. And it was down in the emotional canyon where relief from heartache was beyond his reach. A large part of him was still stuck down there, unable to rise above its walls.

But he knew that words of love did echo down there, and he cherished the recollection of her voice. He wished he could hear her say those endearments just one more time.

He shook his head and pushed himself to his feet, feeling the floor under him, rubbing his eyes, and wishing now he hadn't woken up. He was wishing he had died last night in his sleep. He had no zest for life anymore, no motivation to make the day a good day. He paused at the window and looked at the sun up there in the empty sky and thought that the sun looked all alone.

At least the Moon has stars to keep her company, he thought.

He moved slowly to his dresser, pulled out his clothes for the day, then found his wristwatch and grabbed his wallet. As he went through the morning routine of washing and getting dressed, his mind wondered why she had to go away. As he put on his clothes, he thought about where the soul might go after the body dies. No tears fell now, he'd gotten used enough to waking up alone to cease crying about it two months ago, but the lack of crying didn't signify that grief was through with him. What, if anything, could end this misery?

This winter had been completely different from the winter he had known with Ruby. This winter was mild, warm, enjoyable. If his world hadn't been taken from him last year, he would've appreciated it. He moved without vigor, picking up his keys and some pocket change from the bowl where he kept things of that nature, then trudged out the door to his Land Rover. During the year he had taken steps to move on, tried to learn how to live without her. He concentrated on the gallery, on art and helping local artists get their work on display. But since Ruby had died, nearly everyone agreed that ol' Dutch was no longer the guy they'd always known. True, there was pain, but almost every other emotion or feeling had turned into numbness. The "learning how to live without her" wasn't going too well.

Last spring, Nora had thought it would be therapeutic to bring all of Ruby's paintings down and dedicate a section of Kaleidoscope to her work. The new memorial gallery now displayed her paintings and drawings of headstones, graveyards, some portraits of Obadiah, and the Lithia Park-themed canvasses, and of course that one—the painting of her in Paris dated 1912.

On the counter across from the display and near the main computer sat an offer for one of Ruby's paintings. It pissed him off. Society hadn't appreciated her when she was alive, and now... now he thought about how odd society is. It seemed as though society did what it could to break an artist. That made it a challenge for artists to earn a good living, at least while they were alive. Ruby had had trouble selling her artwork when she was alive, but since her death, and even though the sign plainly read *This section is for display only, these pieces are not for sale,* people still asked to purchase her work, and many wanted to pay a handsome amount, especially after the strange rumors of her talent for time travel and news of her death in the park got out. The Paris piece in particular, which was now being dubbed *The 1912 Piece,* had garnered some obscenely lavish offers.

Why do we refuse to give artists money when they are alive and struggling? he wondered. And why are people so morbid as to see the value of their work go up so dramatically when the artist dies? The poor artist. Society may flatter them with admiration or wound them with reproach when they're alive, but in death, society glorifies them. Dutch wanted to kick this bad mood he was in, but it wouldn't budge.

He paused in front of *The 1912 Piece* and saw Yukon and Ruby, Ruby smiling and happy. With him. He trembled as he said the man's name under his breath. "Obadiah. She's not with him, she's dead! You went to her funeral," he reminded himself, "you saw her buried." But he couldn't help it, he was jealous of Obadiah. *The 1912 Piece* troubled him. "She's not with him," he said again. "No matter what Bernard claimed. Dead is dead!"

Now, he began to imagine her looking down from unimagined heavenly landscapes, and sending him messages in his dreams across the shifting boundary. Like this morning. In his dreams with her, he was a better man. Those dreams with her were things to look forward to, and sometimes the dreams would breathe hope into the air around him and offer him a brighter world. But not today. Today he missed her enough to say that his suffering might even have grown worse.

"Did you get the offer I laid on the counter?" Nora asked, breaking his reverie.

"Yeah, I saw it," he grunted, "None of Ruby's work is for sale, no matter how much anybody offers. People should stop asking!"

"Easy there, li'l brother. The people that come in here, you know the customers, they're looking for what you're selling. You can't fault them for asking about her work. They aren't really trying to offend you."

He nodded. "Okay, you're right. Maybe I should take this display down and store it at my house. It's too distracting, anyway."

"You will not do that!" Nora said. "I enjoy seeing all of these pieces here. Dutch, they belong here."

"I suppose." His voice broke, he looked sideways and began to tremble, "When... Nora, when will I get over her?"

She put her arms around him. "I don't know. Ruby was special and special takes an awful long time to get over."

"You're right about that," he admitted. "It's been a year! I just thought this pain would ease a little, but it's as intense as it was the day you came in here and told me they'd found her. And every day since has felt like a funeral. Every day I feel her loss."

"I wish I could make it better for you," she said, "but this is one of those things you have to go through yourself. No matter how painful it is, this is your life experience, and you have to experience it."

Trying to hide the pain, he looked out the window. "I feel like half a man without her... like half of me is buried with her in that grave down the street."

"If it makes it any better for you, I miss her every day too. And Yukon, I miss him so much." She rubbed her hands. "I know you feel like you're all alone, but I'm here, little brother, and I'll always help you get through."

He smiled at her and gave her a return hug. "Yes, and speaking of special, Yukon... now, he was a special dog." He tightened the hug and then released her. "Thanks, sis. I don't know what I'd do without you. You are so good to me."

"Gee. Maybe we should talk about a raise in pay since you are appreciating me so much." She laughed, trying to lift the mood.

Dutch gave a weak laugh. "Well, I suppose I should do some work. I've got some inventory to post online." He turned away. "I'll be in my office for the rest of the day."

He sat at his desk and turned on his computer, waited for it to go through its normal startup, which felt like it took an unusually long time. Just as he was starting to type, Nora came in, interrupting him again.

"This came for you... hand delivery."

"I don't want another offer for Ruby's work!"

"Still grouchy, I see." She shoved an opened envelope in front of him. "You'll want to read this."

He looked up at her. "What is it? Who's it from?"

"Just open it and read it!"

He opened it and pulled out a decorated invitation.

YOU AND A GUEST ARE FORMALLY INVITED TO
A HOLIDAY DINNER AND CELEBRATION

OF

Ruby Birk Jameson's

ARTWORK

HOSTED BY

H. Brost

SUNDAY DECEMBER 23RD 2018 AT 6:00 P.M.
AT THE JAMESON MANSION

ONLY A FEW GUESTS ARE INVITED.
PLEASE RSVP BY REGISTERING ONLINE:
RUBYBIRKJAMENSONARTCOLLECTION.COM

KIND REGARDS

H. Brost

Nora smiled. "I knew you'd want to read that right away."

Dutch tossed the invitation across his desk and looked up at Nora. "Ruby Birk Jameson Art Collection? Strange."

"Are you going to RSVP?"

"No, I don't think so. I have her work here, I don't need to see any more."

Nora slapped his desk so hard the sound made him jerk and look up at her.

"Good. I have your attention." She stood up tall and looked down at her younger brother. "You and I are going, and I won't take no for an answer. This is an event concerning Ruby and Yukon, and it's at the mansion celebrating her work and the holiday season. You're not going to ruin it with self-pity!" She picked up the invitation, "I'm going to make our reservations right now. You just sit there and don't say a word. Do not protest in any way."

"But how can she have artwork there at the mansion? I mean, I knew her, and she kept everything at her apartment, and now we have all of her work here on display... right?"

"Dutch, you told me about her connection to the mansion, and Bernard told us all about her time travel, but what if, well, even you said there were other paintings at the mansion. What if...."

"Nope, no way. If it's true, then she went back to Obadiah, and if she painted more works in the past, then that means he'll be in her paintings and... and I don't know if I could handle seeing them together."

"Be strong, little brother. You can handle it, and we are going, end of story." Nora marched off to her computer, leaving Dutch sitting there, puzzled.

He squinted at his monitor, trying to focus on the task at hand, listing and selling art—but not hers!—online. After eleven minutes and twenty-two seconds, he heard the bell above the door. Nora usually handled the customers, but he wanted an excuse to get up and move around, so he went out to the floor.

An attractive, middle-aged woman with big brown eyes, smooth, deeply tanned skin, and full, glossy lips was standing in front of Ruby's display and studying the pieces.

"May I help you?" Dutch asked.

The woman didn't answer straight away, but coolly walked closer to one of the paintings. After a minute, she turned and looked at him. "I'm not sure if you can help me."

"Oh?"

She tilted her head. "Something strange is at play here. I doubt you would understand."

What could he say? "I suppose I wouldn't understand. All I was asking was if you would like me to show you artwork that is for sale. These pieces are not for sale, only for display." He pointed at the sign.

"I'm not here to purchase anything." She reached into her purse and pulled out an envelope. "I got this invitation to a holiday party here in Ashland. Then I started doing some research online and discovered that you have some of Ruby's work on display here. So, I decided that since I was in town I'd stop in and have a look at her other work."

Dutch saw that the invitation in her hand was identical to the one Nora had shown him just moments ago. "My name is Dutch," he said in a friendlier voice, "and if you have any questions... well, enjoy Ruby's exhibit."

As she turned back to one of the paintings and then moved to the next one, Dutch detected a restlessness, a moodiness about her. She paused at *The 1912 Piece*. He thought she was unusually tall. And proud. Her expression was a little hard, and her eyes shone large and somber. She looked at him again, then back at a drawing, then she moved to a painting of a cemetery.

"She did incredible work," the woman said. "I love the technique and the mixture of pigments she used." She worked her way around the display. "It seems to me that since the beginning of time women have created essential and impressive works of art, yet never quite got any acknowledgement for it."

"I've always thought that, too."

"I believe you. That is rare, especially in a man."

Dutch blinked, not knowing how to respond.

The woman continued. "I like the display. Each piece is exquisite. But something's not right. It appears to me that you have two separate artists here, but they have the same name."

"No," Dutch felt a catch in his throat, "same artist."

"Oh, Dutch, I don't think so. You are seriously mistaken." She turned to face him. "My great grandmother was Ruby Birk Jameson. It's not possible that she painted this cemetery." She pointed to the year, 2017, under Ruby's signature. "My great grandmother died long before this was painted. Besides, I have some of her work at my home back in Chicago. I know her work."

Dutch's face drained of all color and he felt dizzy. "Is that so?" He looked around the room. "Nora, umm, could you come over here, please."

"What is it? Are you okay? You look like you've seen a ghost."

It was quiet now, no one knowing what to say next. Nora was at a loss—she hadn't heard the woman tell Dutch who she was—but she knew by the look on her brother's face that something wasn't good. She approached the visitor and held out one hand. "I'm Nora, Dutch's sister, perhaps I could be of some assistance?"

"Hello, Nora, my name is Danu Birk Winston, my maiden name is Jameson." They shook hands. "Ruby was my great grandmother."

"Oh. Oh!" Nora stepped back, then stepped forward again. "Well... welcome, these are all Ruby's pieces." She gestured toward the exhibit. "I think Dutch did a fine job of displaying her work, don't you?"

"But this can't all be her work," Danu repeated.

"I can assure you it is."

"Wait," Dutch jumped in, "wait, wait! I don't understand. How can you be Ruby's great-granddaughter?"

Danu locked eyes with him. It was obvious that they were both confused and searching the other for answers. "There must be two Ruby Birk Jamesons. I'm looking at these pieces of art," she made a gesture that took in the whole wall, "they don't differ in style from this one... *The 1912 Piece*. But what stands out to me is the obvious. The dates differ by over a hundred years, and most were recently painted. During the past decade. How could that be?"

Dutch's eyes came to rest on one of Ruby's paintings. The cemetery, the same one Danu had been looking at. The cemetery was empty, no human visitors, just the lonely headstones. He imagined the corpses under the ground and suddenly began wondering if their lives had meant something while they were alive, or if those people's lives mean anything to anyone in death? Did life have meaning? The way Ruby had painted the graveyard, her color choices and the texture of the graves gave the impression that life came there to die. It was the end for those buried there. The headstones made him lose his breath. Not too far from the Kaleidoscope was a graveyard with a headstone that read Ruby Birk. His eyes stung when he broke himself away from the painting and looked at Danu again.

"Indeed," he said, "how can that be... when Ruby died she was childless?" He couldn't deny it: other than the color of her skin, Danu looked just like Ruby. Nora saw it too.

Danu went back to studying the paintings, walking slowly around the display as if her feet were now weighted down with lead shoes. She would look from a painting to Dutch, then back to another painting, then over to Nora. "I don't know what to say."

"There's nothing you need to say," Nora said, "It's confusing to see your great-grandmother's work displayed here. And the dates. It's confusing to us as well. But your great-grandmother was a special woman."

"Do you think you actually knew my great grandmother?"

"I'm not sure anymore. All I know is that Dutch and I knew Ruby Birk. And she was a special woman."

Dutch stood still, watching the woman as she went back and forth along the display trying to mentally process the significance of the dates. Midmorning had passed: a shadow crept up the far brick wall, but the sun was some distance from noon and the growing sunlight shone on Danu. It was perplexing to watch this woman, yet it was also an exquisite moment when her smallest movements seemed familiar to him, marked by an evident distinction. Danu Birk Winston's movements were an admirable combination of recognizable grace and voice, Dutch saw as she moved, spoke, and gestured. This woman not only had some resemblance to Ruby, but her body language was spot on.

"... and this." Danu handed Nora the invitation that was identical to the one the gallery had received.

Nora pulled out their invitation. "We have one, too."

"I knew my great grandmother lived here in Ashland," Danu said, "and I was told that her mansion was now kind of a museum or historical landmark. I was told she was an artist. As I said, I have some of her work in my home. But are you honestly trying to tell me that she was alive here? A year ago? I don't believe it, and even if I did, I don't understand how that's possible."

Dutch could hardly speak. "P-per-perhaps, it will be at this 'Holiday Dinner' that our host will clear up this matter. I'm sure there must be a simple answer to all of the questions we have." He turned away from Danu. The sight of her was making his heart break even more. "You are welcome to admire Ruby's work for as long as you like, but if you'll please excuse me, I have some work to do in the back room."

Dutch's words, his whole manner, came across as odd to Danu. He smiled at her and then at Nora, hugging her again as if to ground himself, then walked on unsteady feet back to his office.

It was obvious to Nora that her brother was hurting and needed to escape, for she, too, saw the resemblance to Ruby. "Danu, please excuse my brother, but he was very close to Ruby and her death has been very hard on him."

"Yes, about her death... when did she die?"

"We buried her a year ago."

"Well then, see right there... the Ruby you all know can't be my great grandmother. My great grandmother died when I was seven, that's over forty years ago. Not the same person." Then she stopped at the 1912 painting again. "As I have said, I think you have two artists with the same name. This piece here, that's my great grandmother sitting there with my great grandfather."

"That is interesting, for sure," Nora replied. "All the work you see here is in fact by the same Ruby Birk. There are rumors, and Ruby confessed to my brother that she traveled back in time on occasion. We were all surprised when we saw this painting. There was some doubt about its authenticity. But we had experts examine it. It's the real deal, the paint and canvas have been dated to the early 20th century, and the real 'proof,' if you will, is in the photograph fixed to the back of this painting. The photograph is authentic and was the reference for the painting. The Ruby that painted this was the Ruby we all knew and loved. She lived not far from here and died in Lithia Park a year ago." She lifted the painting and pulled away the photograph, which she handed to Danu.

"Incredible!" Danu cried. "This is so strange! First, I get this peculiar invitation, and now to make matters even more weird, you and Dutch claim to have known her. Do you think it's possible that she could travel back and forth in time?"

Nora shrugged. "I have had my doubts. After all, it's not logical, but, then, if I sit and think about it long enough, I can convince myself that it's true. We loved Ruby. We don't want to doubt what she claimed, what she believed happened to her."

By the unusual operations of a counterintuitive, mysterious law of nature where the strange attracts and holds on to the ordinary, Danu drew a soulful connection. This was a paradoxical experience, yet a moment that seemed to reign supreme. She couldn't describe the sensation, but there was an air of familiarity here in the Kaleidoscope. Nora radiated a warmth that one generally receives from family. And she could sense how deep the grief ran in Dutch. She felt it, she understood it. She rubbed her forehead, feeling overcome by this irregular law of the recognizable mixing with the anomalous.

Without speaking, she reached into her memories for a source that would maintain some sense of reality, memories of her great grandmother. Danu had been told stories about her great grandmother while she was growing up. It was hearsay, but folks described Ruby as endlessly interesting, a somewhat abnormal woman with progressive ideas regarding equality for women and people of color. People said it was because her son had brown skin. In her time, she was considered strong-willed, and the men of her time claimed that she was a product of the new sophisticated century, a quote, modern woman, unquote. Some women regarded her as a Jezebel, evidently having had a child from a man other than her husband. Some even spoke of magic and went as far as to call Ruby a witch. Danu's great grandparents were spoken of in whispers, with relatives saying they were mystics who had abilities to predict future events, able to sidestep financial disaster in 1929 when the Great Depression happened, able to heal people with unknown medicines. Collectively, the stories always made Danu wonder who the 'other brown-skinned man' was that was her real great grandfather. No one knew, and because of the stories of infidelity and magic, Danu generally held a low opinion of her great grandparents.

"My great grandmother is a mystery, for sure, especially with all of this talk of her being alive a year ago and dying childless, yet being the same person that gave birth to my grandfather. It has me vexed to the point of headache. Who on earth could believe such a story?" Danu's features stiffened with a sensation that was a mix of resentment and thoughtful sentiment. "What, if anything, about my great grandmother can I trust to be true?" Strong feelings made her eyes dilate, raised her blood pressure. Yet, conversely, there was also gladness in her, though a gladness not without an element of alarm. Within the gladness was the treasured feeling of a chance at discovery, a bit of self-discovery, possibly learning where one comes from, touching one's origins.

"The Ruby that I knew was loving," Nora said softly, "but could be intense about things, and her intensity would cause her to withdraw and isolate herself. I think within her isolation she knew things the rest of us don't often even dream about. She saw life, everyday things... reality differently."

"Loving?"

"Well, she loved my brother, and I think she loved me, too, in a sisterly kind of way. And my brother fell very hard for her. Like I said, she was special." She pointed at his closed office door, "It's obvious that he gave her his heart. And if she were here now, I know she would give you, her great-granddaughter, all of the love she could. Unconditionally."

"She would love me?"

"I'm sure of it. She was just that kind of person."

Danu looked at the office door and thought for a moment. "I'm afraid that I didn't stop to consider Dutch's feelings carefully. I hope that I didn't cause him too much pain."

"He'll be all right in time."

"I appreciate you taking the time to visit with me. I think I'll go now, I'm staying at the Ashland Springs Hotel. I suppose I'll see you and Dutch at the Holiday Dinner."

"Yes, we'll be there. I'll look forward to visiting with you again." Nora touched Danu's arm and then walked her to the door. "You are always welcome to come and look at Ruby's display."

"Thank you. You are so kind." She started to walk out, but paused at the door. "Please tell Dutch that

I'm sorry our conversation upset him. You are good people. I don't want to bring any disruption into your lives."

"I'll tell him, but don't you worry. You haven't brought us anything that would be considered negative."

Danu turned and walked out the door, then walked further away from the gallery and toward the plaza, the main entrance of Lithia Park, where she stopped and stood watching the city's Christmas tree being decorated by civil workers. A group of young carolers led by their schoolteacher began singing "Oh Christmas Tree." Danu observed and listened... or at least that's what she appeared to be doing. In actuality, she was hardly listening to the song. Her inner eyes were back at the exhibition, specifically looking at *The 1912 Piece.*

She spoke to herself. "Could it be true, Ruby traveled through time? Could it be?"

Chapter 22

Zanique pulled the talisman (the ankh) out of an inner pocket of her coat and laid it around her neck. Today was the one-year anniversary of Ruby's memorial service, but she couldn't believe it had already been a whole year. She was disappointed to discover she hadn't lost any of the heartache or grief she felt for her friend.

The elegance of the feminine intellect is infinite, the subtleties of the male understanding also limitless, and Zanique possessed both, for as an intersexual she had capacity and complexity beyond most people. So complex was she that she could play hide-and-seek with her emotions. Yet even in the most complex development of humanity, within Zanique there was more often than not an underlying simplicity. And it was precisely this abiding simplicity and inner goodness that prompted her to go and visit her friend's grave today. Simple, raw emotion... grief and all that it symbolized had brought her to do this difficult thing on this difficult day.

She took her time walking through the cemetery. Standing there at the foot of Ruby's grave and validating her death gave her a bittersweet awareness. So far, Zanique had regarded her one-time lover from a positive point of view rather than from a negative one. It was her choice, and she had thought long and hard about it, coming to the conclusion that she should choose to be more optimistic about their inconceivable lovemaking. She now believed their act of love had made her a better person.

Standing there alone and wrapped in her coat... wrapped in her insecurity... she spoke aloud to Ruby as if she were alive and could hear her.

"Well, girlfriend, it's been a year since I laid eyes on you. It's been a long year, and to tell you the truth, I just can't seem to get over you. I feel so connected to you. It's like you're alive and I'll see you any day now walking through the park." Her face began to burn with anger. "That damn park! It was the death of you." She hung her head and stood still. "I look for you every day there. I watch the park thinking I'll see you sitting on the bench working on a drawing." She took in a deep breath. "I miss you, Ruby. Oh God, how I miss you!"

She fell to the earth, down on the winter's grass and held her head between her hands, waiting for the dam holding her tears back to burst. For a while she sat there at Ruby's grave and listened to the silence of the cemetery. Here was a fit place for a performance of grief, a calling-out of the pain under a cloudless day where the sun could witness her concert of sobbing. She was rooting out of her heart all thoughts of any other lover, focusing only on Ruby, to whom she had given herself wholly and without compromise on that one night. To this day, their act of love filled her heart with a love that had now turned into sorrow.

Zanique's intention to come here with her grief was unquestionably a right and pure one. Most times, she chose to camouflage her emotions in fantastic garments of artificial happiness. She had always hoped that her outward appearance clothed in bright colors hid her true emotions from the world.

In her memory surged swelling words, fiery thoughts, hasty emotions that flowed through her heroically as if chasing after the fabled pot of gold hidden at the end of that lovely rainbow called romance. Romance she would have nothing to do with anymore. She was sure romance was the enemy, and she took up arms against it, refusing it lodging and entertainment, for she had sternly buried all of her romance with Ruby a year ago. The year had passed now, but each day brought more and more sadness, and each night was filled with silence and the despairing yearning to hear Ruby's voice again.

"You went away," she said aloud to the grave, "and you left me here with only memories of you. I know you didn't hurt me on purpose, you're not that sort." She felt that talking to a dead person was weird, but she also hoped that on a deeper level maybe, just maybe, Ruby could hear her. She smiled as she went on. "I'll never forget what we shared that night of my Christmas party. You looked in my eyes and said you loved me and at that moment I loved you, too... more than I had ever loved anyone else. And now I'm here without you. It's hard, you know? I miss my friend, I miss our times together. I know I have to get over you. But not today. Someday, but not today. I love you, Ruby." She stood up, wiped her eyes, and brushed the grass off her pants.

Now she was satisfied. She knew that romance was buried there with Ruby. And then, to avoid all provocation for further grief or broken-heartedness, she knew it was time to leave Ruby's grave. She walked away from the fantasies of what might have been, and, trying hard to think of something else, set herself on the path to Lithia Park.

When she arrived at the main entrance of the park, where she stopped to watch the city's Christmas tree being decorated, a group of young carolers were singing "O Christmas tree." The carol brought Zanique back to the present; she had almost forgotten it was the holiday season again. The Christmas tree and the children's singing lifted her grief for a moment. It was a lovely moment.

When the children then began to sing "Joy to the World," the lyrics seemed to make a harsh wind blow around inside her, bringing with it a shadow. It was the juxtaposition of the theological verse and her childhood memories that made her shiver. As the children finished their song to the applause of others in the plaza, she noted the chilly, distressed feelings she still associated with Christmastime as an orphaned child.

Suddenly her heart was racing and she couldn't catch her breath, then pain spread across her chest. The sky above, the pavement below her, the buildings in the plaza all began vibrating. She could feel her balance fluctuating. The city seemed to be shifting and blurry. She gripped at her chest and felt the ankh under her fingers.

A heart attack?

Now she had the sense of slipping away from this world, falling away into the unknown. Depression, heartache, and sadness were fading, becoming unimportant. She was clutching life, believing it was all over, convinced she was experiencing death. She gave in to it and fell to the ground. Darkness fell over her. And yet, she could still hear things around her. She decided that though her body must be dying, her consciousness was still alive.

She lay there in Lithia Park for what seemed to be a very long time, hearing the goings on around her.

Her eyes were open, but she saw nothing. She was afraid, paralyzed, claustrophobic inside her own body. She had the impression that she was being drawn down into some dark region. Pulling up all the will power she could find in herself, she resisted falling further into the unknown. Along with the cold and darkness, she realized, she was facing sadness and loneliness, feelings that were vivid and recognizable and absolute. For a moment, Zanique lost control of herself, and all her emotions of severe grief, shamed loathing, and disconnection struck like battering fists on the door of her reason.

She was beginning to understand just how often she had felt this deep sadness and emptiness in her life. When she looked back on her life, she saw fear with its ugly head standing in front of her, and it stood there even stronger when she looked ahead. So many negative emotions had recently weighed her down with such a heavy weight of sentiment that she considered this to be the cause of her death today.

All went silent.

Did her internal clock stop measuring time?

Time was now what it was intended to be. Not something moving forward, but a period of peace, a period to rest. There was healing for Zanique in this time.

And a light appeared. A very pure, very perfect, angelic light brighter than sunlight dawned from deep within the park, and within this light, she could see the figure of a woman standing with open arms. The woman stood there, seeming to be the soul of Lithia Park and offering an expression of aloofness from all things ugly, a reflection of tenderness, a profound calm, exposing a far-off freedom from any sadness. Then Zanique believed she could hear the wonderful sound of the park's murmuring.

"Zanique," it called.

It was as if the woman she saw was Nature herself and was capable of taking the whole of Lithia Park into her loving arms, or perhaps of holding the entire planet as gently as a mother holds her sleeping child. In this moment of glory, the grandeur departed and was replaced by something better than glory: peace, love, and pervading promise of lasting things beyond.

Oh, how Zanique wanted to get up and walk toward this beautiful woman, but she was unable to speak or move. She could only gaze. She felt warm, safe, and loved in a way she had never felt before. In an odd way, she also felt a very new receptiveness, a critical receiving of her entire world—the superficial world but, more importantly, her inner reality—and a fresh set of values with which to reassess her life.

Suddenly, as if released from some imprisoning spell, Zanique felt free to move. She could see clearly. She got up and went to the woman and fell into her embrace.

"Have I died and gone to heaven?"

No, child, you are here between moments of time. This is a gift for you.

The woman lifted Zanique, held her. She smelled like sweet sandalwood blended with rose and jasmine, and Zanique knew this was a divine moment, something that seemed like death yet was a rebirth of sorts. A moment absent of consciousness that might interfere, criticize, or negate, a true, simple moment without complicated personal judgment. It was a true moment of love. Then the divine woman released Zanique and stepped aside to reveal Ruby standing under a dazzle of sunshine.

"Ruby! Is that you?"

Zanique went toward Ruby as Ruby ran to her. It was a moment that Zanique knew in her soul was a gift from what Ruby had often spoken so highly of when she was alive: The Spirit of the Park. They embraced. The feeling of having Ruby in her arms was thrilling.

As Zanique peeked around Ruby's shoulder, what she saw made her gasp. It was nothing important, only a simple carriage coming along the road through the park. The driver smiled and waved at her. The foam from his horse's bit bespattered the pedestrian traffic, pedestrians wearing clothes from a century ago. The carriage came on and passed her, and she noticed the golden sunlight on the hills, hills whose summer greenness had been dimmed by winter just moments ago. She saw the outline of the sun through the silvery clouds. The valley in which lay the park was filled by an enchanted ochre mist, and the grass at her feet had a tawny overtone. The shadows under the spruces and elms were golden. The strangeness of this spectacle awed Zanique, still held in the overpowering embrace of her dear friend who had died a year ago.

She tried to keep herself composed, tried to prevent breaking whatever enchantment she was under. She felt the heat of summer air heavy on her skin.

"I know you don't understand," she heard Ruby saying. "And I'd rather not get into the details. I only wanted to reach out to you and try to ease your grief." Ruby held her at arm's length. "First of all, I'm fine, I'm happy here, and, second, you and I have worked a miracle!"

What could Zanique say? She was silent. She meant to say a whole lot, she meant to ask many questions, but she remained silent. She asked no questions. She was too intoxicated by the experience. She knew she was in the early 20th century with Ruby. This experience was unraveling the way she saw the world. It polished the lens of her perception, dropped her into a deeper sense of existence.

"My poor Zanique," Ruby said suddenly in the clear, incisive voice she had always had, "you've lost your zest for life, haven't you. I want to see you interested again. Genuinely, contagiously, interested in life again."

Zanique learned that she could speak now. "Life feels very different for me now that you're gone. Ruby, I'm lost without you. It's like you took some part of me when you died, and now I'm just a fragment of who I used to be."

"Oh, no, you mustn't say that. I haven't taken any part of you. You gave yourself to me and I gave myself to you and during that one night a remarkable thing happened."

"What happened?"

"Love happened!"

Zanique shook her head. "What good is love when the person that loves you isn't available, is... um... dead?"

"We had love with results...."

Ruby's words began to echo, and Zanique began to feel dizzy. Then a desperate and quiet aching settled over her. Standing with Ruby, she felt small, childlike. She had a sudden memory of her young girlhood, the whole intensity and sordidness, the rejection, the fear all came back to her.

One of the mysteries of being human, Zanique thought, is that we are in a constant state of change, and change equals transformation, whether it be mental, physical, or spiritual. Transformation had begun when she was born. She was different from everyone else, and it was her difference that created transformation throughout her life. Her life's journey as an intersexual person was nothing less than a struggle because her biology didn't fit neatly into society's traditional classifications of sex or gender. All of those years, she struggled to accept who she was, what she was (a boy or a girl?). She struggled to hide her difference from the world. She struggled to fit in. She grew from a vulnerable scared child into a confident person living on the edge of society, stealing from the criminally wealthy to help the needy. She was the Deep Net Hunter, an outcast turned outlaw. Today, in this moment, with the help of some hidden goddess overlooking Lithia Park, transformation continued to reshape her lens of perception. The events in her life might have changed from time to time, but her soul had crossed life-changing thresholds and shaped her into the person she had become.

Only minutes ago, she had thought she was dying, but now—lo and behold—instead of dying, she was looking at Ruby. And now, listening to Ruby cracked her whole life open. She felt uplifted, and her perspective grew into the knowing that every moment of her life, every second of her transformation, had brought her to this moment. Ruby wasn't altogether right; Zanique did understand a little. Even further, she was keenly aware of her soul expanding, her emotions being soothed.

She studied Ruby, her face, her hair, her white and beautiful profile. She smiled contentedly. Then she frowned, though only a little. "Ruby, you didn't choose me... you chose Obadiah over me."

"I'm sorry, Zanique. It's not that I don't care for you," Ruby drew her closer and kissed her, "but you have to understand that Obadiah and I belong together. We are in love. Soulmates. But I carry a part of you with me everywhere I go. You gave me such a wonderful gift."

Zanique pulled herself back, trying to control her stability so she wouldn't fall down. She was feeling light headed. "A gift?"

"Yes. You and I connected in the most special way. That's how you are able to come here and see me now. We are connected."

"I have always felt connected to you, girl."

And before another word could be spoken, Yukon came charging and jumped high with excitement, wedging himself between them.

"Yukon!" Zanique kneeled on the ground, hugging and kissing him. "I have missed you so much!" She looked up at Ruby "Oh, My. God. I have missed the two of you so much it breaks my heart." She buried her face in Yukon's fur and wept.

After a second or another year, she looked up. "Something's happening." An unexpected lassitude crept over her, a dreadful weight dragged against her heart. She could hardly move. It was as if an immense burden were pulling her down and away. The ambient temperature dropped suddenly, and the colors of summer began to oscillate. Ruby and Yukon began to fade. They were untouchable now. Zanique's eyes rolled back, and she had the overwhelming sensation of falling.

Falling. Falling.

...

Danu was watching the carolers until she saw a woman fall to the ground. She and a city worker ran to Zanique.

"Did you see what happened to her?" the man asked.

"I don't know," Danu said. "I was listening to the carolers over there, and then I saw her fall. She didn't scream. She didn't make a fuss. She just went limp."

"I'm calling for an ambulance." The man pulled his mobile phone out of his pocket and began pushing keys.

Danu thought the woman's necklace might be choking her, so she reached around and unhooked it.

Once the necklace was off and away from Zanique, she suddenly woke up. "Ruby!" she yelled.

"It's okay," Danu said. "I'm not sure you should get up yet."

Zanique looked around in bewilderment. "Where am I?"

"You're in Lithia Park, in Ashland—"

"What year is it?"

"It's 2018."

Looking deflated, Zanique sank back to the ground. Ruby, Yukon, the horse and carriage… they all were gone. She looked up at the strange woman. "What happened?"

Danu squatted down in an attempt to help her sit up. "You just fell down. I took off your necklace, and you instantly came out of it." She handed the ankh back to Zanique.

Zanique looked at it, then tucked it into her pocket. Then, "Get your hands off of me! I can get my own ass up off the ground."

"I was only trying to help."

"If I wanted your help, I would've asked for it. Now stand aside." She jumped to her feet and straightened herself, then began walking away.

Danu watched her closely while trying not to appear to stare. This slight, but muscular woman had obviously been embarrassed by her collapse in a public park. Danu looked back down and saw that some of the contents of the strange woman's purse had spilled out. Among them was an envelope. "Excuse me," she called, "but before you go, some things have fallen out of your purse." As she extended her hand holding the envelope, she recognized it. It was another invitation to the holiday party. The same one she'd received, that the owners of the art gallery had received.

Zanique took the envelope and put it back in her purse. "Thank you." Then she looked down at the ground. "I'm sorry. I feel a bit humiliated, and that put me in a bad mood. Thank you for helping me." Apology spoken, she walked down the sidewalk away from Lithia Park, leaving Danu wanting to know more.

Chapter 23

The day of the celebration of Ruby was a particularly felicitous one for a gala. There had been a heavy snowfall two days before, but the snow had melted, and today's pale gray sky had by two o'clock given way to the most delicate blue. This afternoon, Ashland was a display of vivid color and fresh and fragrant air. By six o'clock when the guests were scheduled to arrive, the Jameson Mansion was lit from top to bottom with holiday lights. Nothing ostentatious, of course, just enough to give off a flare of festivity.

A few food preparers and servers had been hired for the evening and by midday were engaged in the kitchen and dining areas. The dining table was a-glitter with silver and gold, a beautiful dinner service, and decorated crystal. Holiday candles were lit and placed throughout the mansion. It was a small event compared to the entertaining that Ruby and Obadiah had done when they lived here, but no one could argue that this little engagement was less than elegant, with the food prepared by Stavros Mori, a well-known chef, and music played live by the famous pianist Kashika Jaccard-Bradoc. Usually the mansion sat quiet and unnoticed on Nutley Street, but tonight it looked inviting and charmingly decorated.

Dutch walked slowly up the front steps. Nora had already pushed the doorbell, which pealed long and melodiously. As he waited, he shifted from one foot to the other. The evening was cool, yet he was nervous and sweating. He looked down at what he was wearing and wondered if his apparel was fitting for such an occasion. He had on, not his usual faded jeans with a hole in the knee, but a newer, fresher version of the jeans, plus a dress shirt, a tie, and his best jacket. The jacket was at least fifteen years old, but it fit, and he told himself it was still fashionable... classic, in fact.

"Look at this place," he suddenly said. "I don't think I'm dressed properly, we should go. I'll bet everyone else will be in formal attire."

Nora smiled at him. "Oh, stop! You look fine. We are going to enjoy this."

Timidity wasn't a characteristic Dutch ever saw in himself, but then, this night was all about Ruby, and anything having to do with her made him feel clumsy and uncomfortable. He turned around and looked back across the front yard's holiday decorations. The colorful lights that adorned natural pines enriched the evening's darkness.

Helma Brost opened the front door. "Good evening Nora, Dutch. The air is nice, isn't it? I think the inversion has lifted and the winter air is so fresh."

"Yes," Dutch said. "It is agreeable. Better than it was this time last year."

Helma motioned to them to follow her to the sitting room. The timeless tune "Morning Mood" was playing in the background. It was a song Dutch found particularly soothing, and the melody seemed to come from everywhere and nowhere particular, weaving itself around them as they walked into the room. He wondered if he had ever heard this music before, maybe with Ruby, once, somewhere. He couldn't remember what they had ever listened to together.

"You are the first to arrive," Helma said, "Please have a seat while I finish up a few things in the dining room. There are hors d'oeuvres." She pointed to a silver tray on a fine serving table.

Nora sat on a sofa with feet shaped like lions' paws and dating from the later 19th century. For an antique, it was quite comfortable, and she sat with an anticipatory look on her face.

Dutch wasn't as composed as his sister. He stood stiffly in the middle of the room. "Tell me, Helma, how did you happen to know how to contact me, my address... how did you come to invite me here?" Nora shot him a look of disapproval. "I saw you at Ruby's funeral," he added, "but we never spoke. I've been in this house before, that was well over a year ago, I was here for an auction. I didn't buy anything, though. Is that where you got my name and address?"

"No, sir," the estate manager replied. "I was instructed to contact you as I was all of the guests tonight." As she was about to elaborate, the doorbell rang and she moved toward the door. "I'll talk to you more about it later if you like, but I should go and answer that."

"Dutch!" Nora said as Helma left the room. "Don't be rude."

"I'm not trying to be rude, but I would like to know why this woman contacted me, that's all." He looked around the room. "The music is a nice touch."

"Yes, it is. Very lovely."

"It sounds live... do you think there's a pianist here?"

"Most certainly, though I'm not sure where. I didn't see a piano when we came in."

At this point, Helma led Zanique into the room. "Please have a seat in here. I believe you know Dutch and Nora."

When Dutch noticed the well-worn black FjällRäven adventure pants and hiking boots that Zanique was wearing, he felt a bit more at ease about his own casual attire.

Zanique looked surprised to see them. "Of course," she said, "Yes, I know them." She turned to the gallery owners. "It's good to see you again. I haven't seen the two of you since..." her voice fell off "... a year ago."

Dutch shook her hand. "It's funny. Ashland isn't a big city, yet we can lose track of our friends within the span of a year."

Nora rose to her feet and hugged Zanique. "Gosh, it's good to see you. We had no idea that you would be here."

The doorbell rang again. "Please excuse me," Helma said. When she returned this time, she had Danu in tow. "Everyone, this is Danu Birk Winston. Danu, this is Dutch. And his lovely sister, Nora."

Danu smiled at them as Dutch shook her hand. "Yes, we've already met."

"And this is—"

Zanique looked more closely at Danu. "It's you... the woman in the park!"

"Yes, that was me."

"How odd it is that you were there in the park and came to me when... " she cleared her throat, "... and now you are part of this celebration for Ruby."

"Wait," said Danu, "you knew Ruby Birk Jameson, too?"

"I did." Zanique looked at Dutch and Nora. "We all knew her. How did you know her? Are you a fellow artist? Some long-lost friend?"

"Ruby was...."

"Why don't we all go into the dining room," Helma interjected smoothly. "The first course is about to be served."

As they followed her to the dining room, Dutch spotted a portrait of Obadiah hanging on the wall in the grand gallery. He pushed down the jealousy that began creeping through him and he looked down the hall at the front door. He wanted to turn and go to it, but his legs wouldn't obey his mind. Instead, he loosened his tie and ran a finger around his collar and said, sotto voce, "This is ridiculous! This place, Obadiah, and Ruby! How did I get talked into coming here?"

The mansion was large, every public room decorated for the holidays. They could still hear the piano, and now they could also hear the ticking of a grandfather clock. Dutch forced himself to ease up. "Chill out," he told himself as he focused on the music. It was beautiful, it was romantic. Romantic! He finally felt the charm of the mansion and told himself if Ruby was to be believed, this was her house, the house she shared with Obadiah. This was the reminder of their love, their romance, that he was sensing.

He turned to his sister, and she whispered, "You'll be okay, I'm here for you."

Zanique's mind was racing from thought to thought, her heart was beating much too fast, and her breath felt tight like the surge of unbearable grief in her breast. This was nothing like the episode in the park, but it was still concerning to her. She began talking to herself. "Ruby's house. Ruby's house. Ruby and Obadiah lived here. They were happy. I can feel the energy of their love in this house." After her vision in the park, she wasn't sure what was real and what she was imagining. What she felt was a most curious consciousness of herself, an intensity in her awareness of her sexual identity. What part of her, she wondered, felt most connected to Ruby, the male in her or the female in her? Her mind was still overrun with her inner quarrel. Had Ruby rejected only part of her? And if so, which part? Or had Ruby rejected all of her? Nothing was clear. She was a complete muddle. All she understood right now was that this had been Ruby's house and Ruby had chosen to die in order to go back and be with Obadiah. More than that, she wasn't sure.

As the guests gathered in the dining room, they immediately saw Ruby's paintings displayed nicely on easels. Zanique took in a deep breath. The paintings were unbelievable. She raised her eyes to look more closely at each painting. Dutch was watching her and saw how dilated her eyes were, how filled with some strange and involuntary emotion that looked like fear. When Zanique looked away from the paintings, she saw Dutch, but saw only him smiling at her with warm respect. She moistened her dry lips and whispered to him, "I'm not exactly comfortable here."

"Yeah. Me neither." And the jealous sickness that had almost filled him drained away. They shared an uneasiness about this affair. He leaned closer to Zanique. "There was a time that Ruby confessed to me," he whispered back, "that she was afraid time had stood still, and she was imprisoned forever in winter. Coming here tonight, I get the impression she found a way to escape the winter. She is now free. I'm rather surprised to see these spring and summery pieces of hers. There she is, looking so alive and happy."

"Yes, it is odd," Zanique replied. "But I have come to realize that Ruby didn't die. She returned and lived a full life. These pictures are a testament to that."

"I'm not convinced of that," he said, "but every picture here shows her vibrant and alive over a hundred years ago." He looked away, then back at Zanique. "How can you be so sure?"

"Be sure?" She asked the question in a sincere voice. "The one infallible way of knowing anything is to know it without knowing the process behind it, yet knowing it on a deeper level with experience and intuition."

It was in her voice, her confidence, that he understood she knew more than she was telling him. But further than that, she was attracting his attention, puzzling him. It was in her walk, in the sway of her hips, in her voice, her gestures, her words, and in the blackness of her abundant hair braided low upon the nape of her neck that she impressed him. And this impression, stronger than the impression of beauty because it was subtle, yet provocative, caught and held his attention.

"Intuition?" he repeated. "Since I'm a man I doubt I have a good intuition. I'm here and I just want to understand. Do you think," he added, "a man can acquire intuition? Or does he have to be born with it?"

As Zanique walked beside him she felt the slight contact of his shoulder and found suddenly she was rejoicing in the masculine quality of his presence, in his strength, in the vibrant tones of his voice and the ardent vitality with which he moved.

"I think intuition's another name for wisdom," she replied as Helma made an announcement.

"Please find your seat and make yourselves comfortable," Helma said. "As you can see, we have several paintings on display. I thought I knew every piece of artwork on the estate. For years I inventoried this place and accounted for everything. But about two months ago, I received a correspondence from the Jameson Trust that instructed me to go out to the studio where Ruby did her work. There in a large closet where she stored her paintings were these fine pieces. The correspondence requested that I contact each of you and invite you here for dinner and to enjoy Ruby's work."

Zanique, who hadn't taken her seat yet, walked slowly among the paintings and stopped at one. Reading the title card, she saw it was The Gift. It showed Ruby sitting here in the very room gazing out the window to the back yard where picturesque rays of sunshine came through. The sun showered light over Ruby and the baby she held in her arms. It was one of the most beautiful images on canvas Zanique thought she had ever seen.

"At the time," Helma continued, "the correspondence seemed very vague. But now, in retrospect, I can see that it was entirely pertinent. When I read it the first time, it seemed like something out of a dream. A dream with residue." She leaned toward one of the paintings. "The correspondence was a letter from Ruby addressed to me! I was thinking, of course, that this was from Ruby Jameson from the past. But that Ruby couldn't have known I would be here." By now, everyone was staring at her. "I never really believed that a person could travel through time. My world has always and consistently moved forward. In other words, I have always believed that time only moves one way." She looked at Zanique. "However, once I began to read the letter, I realized that the Ruby who had written that letter was indeed Ruby Birk, the woman who came here with you a year ago" She paused. "Well, what can I say? I needed some time to mentally process that letter." She stopped and smiled with embarrassment. She could see the skeptical faces around her.

Dutch sat up straighter. "I'll be damned! It is a strange thing, our Ruby and her time travel. She's dead. We all know that. With the exception of Danu here, we all went to her funeral. We saw her in her casket. But now I see these 'new' paintings and I see that she lived a full life all the way into old age." His face twisted with his perplexity. "Such a very odd thing. Is this a dream? And if so, who is giving me this dream? How was this dream conceived? This almost feels cruel to the point of madness sometimes."

"Our view," Zanique said, looking at Dutch, "is from the narrow perspective of time as we know it. What we've been taught about life and death. We never expect the landscape of our reality to ever change. To us, the reality of the world remains the same forever, we never question it. But for Ruby? It didn't. She dared to ask the question 'what if?' Perhaps we stall out on the plateau of human monotony and tediousness." The episode she'd had in the park, the perception she'd had, was paramount in her mind now. "What if we are so focused on what we see—or think we really see—that we don't open our minds for what could be? And now, like Helma said, we see that Ruby traveled back in time. Over a century, we see the truth in front of us now. In her work. And because we are faced with the truth, the ground on which we stand seems less stable. We are forced to admit that the ground is now capable of change. I look at these paintings and I see Ruby—happy, in love, living life to its fullest, even raising a family. Yes, Dutch, it seems like a dream, but I, for one, believe that Ruby was able to go back in time and build a new life."

Danu's gown of pale rose velvet and demure lace was cut on the conservative and proper lines and was highlighted by the jewels she wore around her neck and wrist. Her manner was intellectual, and so no one heard her sigh as she gazed at the paintings these people said were by her great grandmother. She had a skeptical eye, she always tried to keep herself from leaping to conclusions. What she was hearing made her feel very cautious in allowing herself to believe it.

She was a gentle skeptic, one who had built her life on reason and logic. But now, she was faced with time travel. An impossible, unreasonable idea. Logic, she thought, is the great conformist, the great sensibility. It is the judge of intellect. If logic were mankind's only characteristic, then our progress would never have had the energy to advance. But fortunately, she told herself, when faced with unbelievable circumstances, we turn to the enemy of logic: instinct. She believed herself to be open-minded to the mysterious powers and forces of the universe. And she realized that in regard to her family, especially her great grandparents, she had always been closed minded.

But not tonight. Tonight, she found herself opening up to all possibilities, and for the first time she opened her heart to the possibility of love for these people.

Dutch was still pondering Zanique's words as the servers brought out the first course, smoky butternut squash soup. When he took the first spoonful of the creamy soup, he discovered it had a kick to it from chipotle chilies. He savored it for a moment, then returned his attention to the paintings. He noticed something this time. He recalled when Ruby had told him about Obadiah, and how he was going to take her places. Well, right there in front of him he saw the evidence. He could hear her ghostly voice saying, 'Obadiah is going to take me to Florence, Paris, and Prague and walk with me on the beaches of the Mediterranean Sea. He told me he would take me to the Gates of Gibraltar.' Trying to wrap his mind around this, he shook his head. There was a painting of each location.

He continued to eat the soup, still studying the details of the paintings. First was a delightful painting of the Ponte Vecchio over the Arno River, done with watercolors rather than her usual oil. An experiment? Next came an oil, the Charles Bridge in Prague. The two bridges were different, the Ponte Vecchio in watercolors under the morning sun and the Charles in oil at sunset. He was sure something about the bridges was symbolic, but he couldn't quite figure it out.

And then there was an oil of Ruby, Obadiah, Yukon, and a baby at the newly-built Eiffel Tower. There were other oils of coastal cities on the Mediterranean, places like Naxos, Greece. Dubrovnik, Croatia, on the Adriatic Sea. Haifa, Israel. And she had painted Gibraltar from the north, facing south, allowing the viewer to see Morocco. He thought it was brilliant. He laughed to himself, and thought, *She didn't paint any graves or cemeteries.*

Helma tapped her wineglass to get her guests' attention. "If I may," she said, "I'd like to read you the letter Ruby wrote. It's to all of you."

Dear friends and family,

I asked Helma to reach out to each of you, as I considered you the people I loved. I wanted to offer you some time in our home, an evening to share a meal and view my work. Autobiographical work really. I also asked Helma to reach out to any living relatives or descendants and invite a representative from my family.

It's 1936 as I put this pen to paper, and twenty-six years since I suddenly left your world. I came back to Obadiah in 1910, a full decade after the Nineteenth Century had come to an end, and regarding the turn of the century as an "event," the global populace, including me, appreciated the positive changes our world was going through. The dawning of the

Twentieth Century was filled with optimism and joy. When Obadiah brought me home to the Jameson mansion, Halley's Comet was in the night sky. It was up there, bright as a nighttime sun, as if to announce our reunion.

At the moment I left your time, I didn't know I was pregnant. When I left Lithia Park, somehow my pregnancy was allowed to travel with me. A true blessing. My baby was born January 23rd, 1910. We named him Attis, and as you can tell from my work, he's a special boy. I'm so very proud of him and where he comes from. I won't give out the secret of how I conceived him, yet I believe that one of you will recognize him....

Everyone except Zanique looked at Dutch. She was still staring at The Gift, studying the depiction of Ruby and the baby in bright sunlight. She looked more closely at the baby... and saw her own eyes staring back at her. The color of his skin, the curl of his hair, the slight slant of his eyes... she recognized him. There was no mistaking it—he was her child. Beyond what she saw, she also felt that the little boy was indeed her baby. That one night they had shared and made love had created a baby.

And, as Zanique had seen in deeper visions, all life is evolution. The transformation of consciousness belongs to something greater than us. She now saw that every moment of her life had led to this moment. She also saw in this moment of revelation that she was capable of creating life. Her night with Ruby flashed back before her, and in a sudden swiftness of memory that predicted the juxtaposition of the life of this baby boy with the death of her friend, she understood that both her illusions and her disenchantment were necessary to the building of the structure of her soul. Every stitch of pain she had suffered was but the rending of the veil between her flesh and her spirit.

She felt both the joy and the pain of grief. Her overflowing emotions, in fact, made her shift in her chair. "Holy shit!" she muttered.

Everyone turned to look at her.

"I'm sorry," she said, "it's just that I can't imagine Ruby as a mother."

But Danu's eyes went back to Dutch. "So you are my true great grandfather?"

Dutch's jaw fell open. He didn't know what to say.

Quiet footsteps came down the hall as the servers brought in the main course of roast turkey, prime rib with au jus sauce, creamy mashed potatoes, dressing, and cranberries. Dutch thought about using the arrival of the food as a way to avoid asking or answering personal questions, but then he thought better of it and attempted to speak.

Zanique beat him to the punch. "Great grandfather? What the hell is she talking about?"

"Danu is Ruby's great-granddaughter," Nora told her.

Dutch finally got his chance. "It's not that I don't want to be the father of that child," he ventured, "but I... I don't think Attis is mine." He tried taking a bite of prime rib. "We, umm. Well... we...." He turned several shades of red, "we used protection. Ruby insisted on it." He looked at Danu but was unable to speak.

Zanique also looked at Danu, then back at the painting. "Holy shit!"

"What is it?" Danu asked.

Zanique shook her head as if trying to shake something out. "I just can't believe what I'm hearing and seeing. I thought I knew Ruby very well. But tonight it seems like I didn't know her at all." She didn't think anyone knew her anatomical secret, but she was nevertheless having trouble containing her outbursts. Danu and I are related, she is my great-granddaughter... how fucked up is that!

Helma, now thoroughly confused, thought quickly. "May I continue reading Ruby's letter?"

"Yes, please," said Danu. The others nodded.

The paintings that Helma has hung for your viewing pleasure were begun in 1910, when I painted Halley's Comet from our back porch late one night when my belly was swollen with Attis and Obadiah was sleeping. In those days people were not used to seeing things in the sky, so when Halley came around, people made a fuss about it. Some had parties, and some shrank back in fear that it predicted the end of the world. I saw it as heavenly beauty and enjoyed painting it. I especially enjoyed painting the stretched-out tail. I also rejoiced in knowing that Attis would see it again in 1986. At times, I find it entertaining to know what the future will bring and what certain outcomes will be. I can always reassure my son that everything will be okay because Obadiah and I can navigate around troublesome times.

Then, in 1912, when my baby was two years old, Obadiah kept his promise and gave us a journey around the world, and the world became my subject. What a privilege I felt in traveling and painting. Obadiah bought a rather expensive camera in New York before we boarded our liner. He fancies photography. I have attached to each of these paintings a photo (on the back of the canvas).

We arrived in Cherbourg, Normandy, by way of the RMS Caronia on April 10, 1912, only a few days before the Titanic made port there. I had a nagging desire to warn any, if not all, of the passengers aboard the Titanic what their fate would be, but the rules of time travel are to not change what will come to pass. So we reluctantly left Cherbourg for Paris.

In Paris, I was able to immerse myself in la vie bohème. We had a fantastic time there! It was a young century and Paris was unquestionably the place to be, the center of the Creative Universe. And women, for the first time ever, were granted access to fine art schools and galleries. It was grand to witness women from around the world recognizing this change and embracing the opportunity. The neon light had been invented a couple years prior to our arrival, and by the time we came the colorful nighttime signage made the experience even more special. The specialness of our trip was further marked by a beautiful solar eclipse on April 17th.

Of course, I went to 2142 Boulevard Raspail, where Picasso was living at this time. He was experimenting with his famous modern style, and I was able to see him at work and discuss technique and style with him. However, he was quite an eccentric fellow and didn't seem to have much time or interest to spend with me.

As you can see from my paintings, Obadiah took me to many countries in Europe and around the Mediterranean. Our trip was wonderful. The Mediterranean countries were especially enjoyable, as every small village was full of welcoming people and wonderful food.

We spent almost two years traveling, going from country to country, and my husband was very patient with me, waiting while I painted every chance I got. In February of 1914, we were back in Normandy and boarded *the RMS* Lusitania *back to New York and eventually went by train back to Ashland. Unfortunate, but of course we knew that the world would be at war within months that same year.*

As Helma paused for a sip of water, the dinner guests all avoided looking at each other. After another sip, she returned to Ruby's letter.

Time travel is odd, as you can imagine. The things I read about in history and never really considered... but now I was able to see history unfolding before me, and I was a part of that unfolding, and what's more, making life all the richer for me. One afternoon shortly after we returned to Ashland, Attis and I were going to the Star Theater for a Novelty Photoplay when an older man approached us. He told me he was a veteran of the Civil War. Then he reached down and picked up Attis and hugged him. "This is why I fought in that ugly war," he told me. "So a child of color or children that were mulatto could be free to enjoy the things our society has to offer."

Can you imagine? In 1914 I met a Civil War veteran, and he rejoiced in holding my son. I thanked him for his service, and then we parted. I was so impressed by him that I smiled the whole day.

"That really is incredible," Danu said. Helma nodded and continued reading.

In 2018, I felt that Art, Romance, Poetry, and Literature were utterly vanishing from our world, defeated by the stupendous technology and science of the Twenty-first Century. I believe it's possible in your time that aesthetic creation will no longer gratify the sense of taste for human genius. Rather, technology and science are what will fulfill the conditions of creativity. Having lived in both the past and the future, I see that, though technology is far from undervalued as I write, by your time it's eventually grown to eclipse the creative arts, pushing them aside and forgetting them for more "practical" pursuits. I'm so happy I chose to be here in the Twentieth because I see my art being appreciated, and I appreciate the simpler life. I'm sure you ask yourself if I miss the convenience of the Twenty-first, and my answer is no, not at all. True, life is slower here, but to me it is more meaningful.

As Helma read, she kept glancing at her guests. She saw they all had odd expressions on their faces and were pushing their food around on their plates, apparently too surprised by Ruby's words to eat. The letter wasn't Ruby's apology for leaving, but, instead, affirmed that she was where she belonged. Along with the paintings, the letter gave them a testament to her happy life. It seemed to offer vague explanations about time travel, but there was nothing solid, nothing to grasp with what they knew of reality.

Zanique looked up at the ceiling as if she could see beyond it and was suddenly filled with a calm ecstasy, almost a rapture of understanding. It wasn't faith she was feeling. It was something much deeper, something much more tender, much more profound. It was almost enough, she thought, to know that Attis was her son. Evidently, Ruby hadn't known she was pregnant when she chose to travel back in time, and Attis had been just an innocent passenger who must have struggled to understand how he came to be.

Zanique leaned back in her chair and regarded Danu, seated to her right, with loving consideration. Danu was a part of her, too, a great-granddaughter, an idea she found almost impossible to accept. But she also felt comforted in some odd way. She was touched by this peculiar atmosphere of the room, by unsaid words. She rubbed her forehead. Everything seemed to become remote, there were shadows of new memories, voices whispering from the past. She took a deep breath to ground herself.

She didn't feel obligated to explain to Danu that she had fathered Attis. As far as she, Zanique, was concerned, this was one fucked-up family tree, and she didn't want to be the one walking around breaking branches. After all, how could she explain the conception of Attis? Well, maybe she could point out his similarities to her, then pull her pants down and wave her cock around. Knowing she would never do such a thing, she laughed out loud at the thought.

While waiting for dessert and still hearing the piano, she went to the paintings again, then looked up once more and gave thanks to the divine. Her instinct told her that the Spirit of Lithia Park, the ankh, and Obadiah had made all of this possible. She was thankful that her friend Ruby was—had been? was going to have? was able to have?—a happy and satisfying life. She also gave thanks for Attis. She could see that he was special. If anyone deserved to be happy, Zanique told herself, it was Ruby and her baby. She enjoyed looking at the paintings that showed Ruby aging but never losing her allure, even as an older woman.

Then she felt a hand on her shoulder. "Zanique," Helma said, "would you follow me? There is something I'd like to show you."

Surprised, Zanique followed her down the hall. When Helma stopped and held the door for her, she entered a dimly lit room where a single lamp shone on another painting.

Helma then closed the door behind her so no one could intrude. "Ruby wanted me to show you this piece in private," she said. "It's titled 'The Results Of Love.'"

Sitting on an easel was a canvas of Ruby in Lithia Park with baby Attis. In almost ghostly shadows around the main image was Attis in different stages of life: the toddler, the rambunctious boy, the athletic teenager, the young man, the professional adult.

Zanique choked up. She had to look away.

"This painting is a gift for you," Helma murmured. "Ruby wanted you to have this."

"For me? It's beautiful... he's beautiful. Thank you."

"I'll have it delivered to you, so you won't have to carry it out to your vehicle and the others won't ask questions." Helma put her arm around her. "I don't understand how it's possible that Attis is your child, but after the strange things that have happened lately, well, I don't question what is possible anymore."

"Wait—you knew?"

"Yes, Ruby told me in her letter to me personally, but like I said, she didn't give me any details. To tell you the truth, I didn't believe it until I saw you standing next to The Gift. That's when I saw the resemblance in his face to yours. And now having you standing here next to this one, well, there is no mistake, that beautiful child does have your face."

Zanique sucked in her breath. "Yes, he does."

"A beautiful child that resembles the better parts of you and Ruby."

Zanique inclined her head toward her and smiled. "You are very thoughtful, and I appreciate you. Thank you for keeping this private."

"No worries. We should return now. Dessert will be served soon, and the others will be wondering where you are. The less questions, the better."

Back in the dining room, the other guests were

complimenting the servers. "The dinner was excellent," Nora was saying. "Both hearty and quite elegant."

...

After dessert and applause for both the chef and pianist, Helma resumed her role as M.C. "Ruby instructed me to open the floor and invite you to study her paintings more closely and choose one you would like to have. Once you have made your choice, I'll tag it, and have it delivered to your home. Please enjoy this time and celebrate the Ruby we all knew and loved."

Zanique got up and moved through the paintings, not choosing one, but rather walking among them as if she were almost a part of each one. She allowed her eyes to capture the images, memorize them. Love had lived here in this house and she felt lucky enough to touch the remnants of that love.

Danu, too, was walking around the paintings. She bumped into Zanique. "You know," she said, "when I look at these paintings, I see my family and feel at home. This one of Great-Grandma Ruby with Attis fills my heart. Having a baby seems to complete a person. Do you have any children?"

Zanique eyed Danu guardedly. "There is nothing, I'm told, so settling for a woman as having babies. I understand they are very satisfying. Never had any myself, though," she confided, "I'm not a maternal woman. Of course, that is very unnatural of me, but I'm a most unusual woman. I prefer adventure to domestic life. But in a world so hell-bent on being natural and dull, it's very satisfying for me to be unnatural."

Danu's smile was a little forced. "I understand that it's the adventurous women who make history. Moreover, they have a hypnotic effect on the natural."

Zanique considered Attis and understood that he was from her, but she further understood that Danu was speaking of motherhood in general, the act of giving birth and raising a child, so she was being truthful in that sense. "I suspect you're correct." She smiled. "I have hypnotized natural men into falling in love with me. Some even gentlemen, but like I said, I never wanted to be domesticated. I can't think of anything worse than being house-broken."

Hearing this, Danu leaned in closer. "I don't blame them, men must find you rather exciting, I mean, look at you, you are so pretty. I'm a mother. To me, it's one of the most rewarding undertakings. I enjoyed watching my children grow from infancy to cute toddlers. I even more or less enjoyed the angst of the teenage years. Then they became parents, too. I have been proud of my children every step of the way. However, I'm jealous of people like you. Somewhere within me is a person that wanted to be adventurous, wanted to see the world. Climb mountains and so on.

Zanique shook her head as she realized that her great-granddaughter was actually older than she was. It was mind-boggling, but she kept her act up. "How sweet of you." A cool wind of pride momentarily blew over the fiery evolution of her life as she recalled some of the fantastic places she had climbed, trekked, and camped. She thought of how much she appreciated nature and remote places as opposed to places of population. Then she thought about family. She'd never had one. "To be honest, Danu, I envy you a bit, too. Having a family, loving your children... well, that is priceless. There are times, especially as of late, when I find myself alone and wondering if I should have done things differently in my life. Don't get me wrong, I don't have regrets. But I do wish I had a family to grow old with."

"Well," Danu replied, "we can envy one another without resentment because we both have lived lives we thought to be the best life we could live."

"Indeed," Zanique agreed. "I'm so glad I had the opportunity to meet you, Danu. Ruby was very special to me, and to know that, as strange as it seems to me, I met her great-granddaughter has made this evening one I will never forget." She turned, went back to the table, and gathered up her things.

Dutch didn't know how long he had been standing there, but his next awareness was that people were moving and talking around him. The painting in front of him had captured his attention to the point of complete distraction. It was set back from the others, as if it didn't quite belong to the collection. It was a self-portrait of Ruby walking through Lithia Park with an owl flying beside her. A delicate crescent moon hung in the purple night sky. She was wearing a simple white linen shift dress and her feet were bare. Her cherry-chocolate hair was tied back in a long ponytail, and the ankh around her neck shone in the light. She looked just like she had in his dream a few nights ago. He sucked in some air, and with the inhalation felt again the pain of his heartache. It was familiar, too familiar. Ruby had titled the painting "The Night Eagle."

He turned to his sister. "Nora, this is the owl I told you about the last time I saw Ruby," he said. "Look how she painted the eyes of the owl, they're so transcendent. And look, there's something about that necklace... strange, but so realistic... the details of it..." His words trailed off. He felt awkward in front of Ruby and the owl.

Looking at the owl, Nora felt a chill that ran the length of her spine. "It must've been a very strange night, the last time you saw Ruby," she said after a minute. "If this huge bird was there with her, and the way you said she was acting... well, I just can't imagine... This painting, as with all of her work... it appears that she had gained some skill and technique when she returned to her time."

"I agree." He lowered his voice so only Nora could hear him. "You know, looking at all these paintings, I'm reminded of when I saw Ruby for the very first time. The contrast between her dreamy eyes and the intensity of her manner was as great as the contrast between the first impression formed by a glance of her pale face and old-fashioned dress and the second, when I realized that here was someone well worth looking at, well worth studying. Well worth meditating on. Perhaps she wasn't beautiful, I'm not quite sure that she was beautiful, but she was surely lovely, with the loveliness which brings life to any room she entered. I wish I could've offered her what she was looking for. Then she wouldn't have left me."

Nora touched his chest. "She was a little white moth who drifted to another sphere, Dutch. You couldn't have offered her anything more. She left because she wanted so much that our world, this time on earth, would have gone bankrupt had it attempted to satisfy her."

"Very poetic," he said. "I suppose you're right, but I just wish she'd chosen me."

"I know. But she didn't. You have to move on at some point."

Here they were interrupted by Zanique, who was saying, "I'm sorry, but it's time for me to go. It was good seeing you all again. Danu, have a safe trip home, and I hope I can see you again some time." And then she quietly slipped out the door.

In less than half an hour after Zanique left, the party came to a close. After bidding Helma a good evening and happy holidays, Dutch and Nora walked out with Danu, who still seemed a bit dazed, but also pleasantly surprised by the night.

"Please stop by the gallery before you leave town," Nora told her. "We'd love to see you before you go." Dutch nodded in agreement.

"I'll try, but my plane leaves tomorrow. I promised my family I'd be home for Christmas."

"Oh, I almost forgot—tomorrow is Christmas Eve isn't it. Well, then, have a safe trip home, and if you come back to Ashland, please look us up."

"I think I'll come back in the summer. I'd like to see some of the plays, you know, the Shakespeare Festival."

"That would be great!" Nora took her hand. "And good luck getting Festival tickets. You might want to start shopping for tickets early."

After shaking hands with both of them, Danu said, "It was great meeting you and Dutch. Here's my business card, let's stay in touch. That's my email address at the bottom." Then she gave them both a hug, got into her rental car, and drove off.

Chapter 24

Zanique was acutely aware of everything around her and fixed her eyes on the road as she drove to the Black Sheep Pub. Her mind was empty. She kept it so sternly and deliberately controlled so that the sudden, sharp trembling that ran over her wouldn't get out of control. She drove down Windburn Way on the edge of Lithia Park. The park was (or had been) important to Ruby, and so every time Zanique came near it, she felt close to Ruby. She was filled with astonishment regarding Attis, Ruby, and Danu. Before she met Ruby, she reflected, her life had been simple. She had lived on the surface of earthly life, and the surface had possibly deceived her into thinking she was satisfied. It had never occurred to her to question if she had the best from life that it could offer, even though, in moments of doubt, she sometimes wondered why it was that there could be no end under the sun to a woman's pursuit of satisfaction. When she looked back now over the years of her life, what she saw was a life full of exploits, but not much love. She also felt cheated out of raising Attis with Ruby. Her mind was so a-whirl with such thoughts that she had decided she needed something to calm her nerves. The pub was her destination and her answer, at least for now.

Her wheels scraped the curb as she turned hard and found a parking place in the lot. The pub was moderately busy, but she wasn't surprised to see that there were very few women there. There were several open seats at the bar; after all, it was Sunday and the Sunday before Christmas. She chose a seat near the corner of the bar and ordered a peach martini with raspberry vodka.

Her cocktail stood tall in the glass, but just sat there as her heart strained and her mind continued to jump from thought to thought. She felt as if she had aged in the few hours she had spent at the mansion. She closed her eyes and began concentrating on the voices and hard tones of the men around her. When she tried to focus on some comforting rational thought, however, she found only a vacancy of scattered considerations. What would a rational thought mean to her now? What thought would be of any help to her now?

Keeping her eyes closed, she lost herself and all her emotions for a moment until she finally forced herself to drink her fancy cocktail, still wondering if she had in some way invited this crazy chaos into her life.

Unbeknownst to her, Dutch had also headed for the Black Sheep Pub. He found a parking place further away than he liked. On the way, he'd decided the idea of walking in on Zanique at a pub might be a good idea, but now, strolling up to the door, he felt like a damned fool. What would he say to her without sounding like an idiot? He took a deep breath, opened the door, and went in. He could see her at the far end of the bar. She hadn't noticed his entrance, of course, because she appeared to be staring at her drink.

Actually, Zanique was watching her reflection in the mirror behind the bar. At a back table sat a group of men that had noticed her and were obviously making comments about her. She winced as the hatred of their belligerent remarks struck her. She just wanted to be left alone, but one of the men, the most obnoxious of the group, came over and took a seat two bar stools down from her.

"Lemme buy you a drink," he said.

"No. I'm fine, thank you."

"Oh, come on, baby! It's the time of year for giving, and I feel like giving you a drink."

At this, Zanique got the bartender's attention. "What's your name?" she asked him.

"Ed."

"Okay, Big Ed. You heard me decline this man's offer to buy me a drink, right?"

"Yeah. So?"

"I want you to be aware of it, because this dumbass and his friends have been making unwanted remarks about me, and if I have to handle this on my own, you won't like it."

"Whatever." Ed had zero interest in the potential situation. "It's just an offer to buy you a drink. Take the drink and lighten up."

The man who'd made the offer smiled. "Yeah, don't be foolish, it's only a drink. I was getting ready to leave, but then you walked in, and I thought I should stay and buy a drink and see where the night might take us."

Dutch, out of earshot, could see that Zanique had a man talking to her. He hoped he, himself, wasn't intruding on her. What if this guy's her date? What if I walk up on her and she gets angry? He knew what her temper was like, so he became very cautious.

"Wow, you just don't get it," Zanique was telling her unwanted admirer. "Leave me alone! I don't want a drink from you, I don't want anything from you." She looked back at Ed. "I'll just leave," she informed him, "and you will lose a customer, a valuable customer. I know a lot of people in this town, and I'll tell them you did nothing about this guy."

"Why?" the admirer asked. "What's wrong with me?" The man got up and moved over one bar stool closer to her, pulling his beer along with him. "You don't know what you're saying, Girly. I'm just being friendly." Then he leaned in so Ed couldn't hear him. "And if you leave, don't you know that I'll follow you until I find you?"

Dutch saw the man moving closer to her. He was closer to the door than he was to Zanique and was wondering if he should turn around and leave before he made a fool of himself, but just then he saw something in her face that made him walk toward her.

Zanique's face seemed to have turned purple. Her eyes were blazing. "I think you're drunk," she shot back at the admirer, "and I think you're obnoxious, too, and if you have any thoughts of us having sex, I can tell you right now this bar doesn't have enough booze in it for me to sleep with you!"

Her admirer just kept smiling. "Ahh, Sweetie, I'm the man that would make your dreams come true."

Dutch was now close enough to hear the conversation. He didn't like what he was hearing. "Hey, Zanique," he said as he reached the bar, "what's up?"

Zanique's eyes widened when she looked up and saw Dutch. He thought she must have felt his casual affection, with its implications of familiarity, for she winked at him. "I'm glad you're here," she said.

"I was on my home when I saw your yellow beast out there," he replied in his folksiest voice, "and I thought I'd buy you a drink."

The admirer stood up. "She doesn't want anyone to buy her drinks tonight," he growled. "I've offered, and she keeps turning me down." His voice was too loud. "You woulda thought I asked her to go somewhere and fuck." He laughed, and his friends across the room chimed in with laughter, too. "She's a bitch, I tell ya."

"Bitch?" Zanique's voice was also too loud.

Dutch's face turned red and his hands went into fists. Seeing this, Zanique reached over and put her hand over his fists. "Thanks for the thought, Dutch, but I've got this. Promise me, no matter what happens, you'll just sit here, but please don't follow me."

Wondering what the hell was going to happen, Dutch gave a reluctant nod.

She tapped the bar. "Hey, Big Ed, I'd like another peach martini and a shot of Fireball Whiskey."

"You got it."

"Oh, and Big Ed...."

"Yes?"

"I warned you." She turned to her heckler. "Okay, you win, you can buy me one drink, but first let's go outside to my vehicle, I'd like to take you up on your offer. If you can make my dreams come true, who knows, maybe this is the beginning of my fantasy romance. Come on, let's go. I like to fuck and I'm good at it."

The man's face brightened up and he looked over at his friends. "See this, boys? She's come to her senses. I can't wait to see if this little lady will moan for me."

Zanique looked almost like a wee shadow next to the big man she was walking out the door with. "Oh," she said, taking his hand, "I guarantee there will be some moaning all right."

Ed looked at Dutch. "What just happened?"

Dutch looked over his shoulder at the door. "I'm not sure." He considered his promise to her, but asked Ed, anyway. "Should I go out there?"

"I've got an idea," Ed said. He lifted a security monitor from behind the bar. "We can watch her from here, I have cameras out there."

So Dutch and Ed watched as Zanique and her admirer came into view. They saw an accusatory finger from Zanique in his face and could see her yelling. They couldn't make out the words, but it was obvious that she was shouting. As they watched, wild rage took over and she slapped the man across the face. He shook his head, made a fist with one hand and raised the other hand in a threatening gesture. When she saw his hand rise, she gave him a dark, hostile smile. She ducked his swing at her. He tried to reset himself for another swing, but then all hell broke loose as she tore into him.

Zanique almost looked as if she were dancing, the way she bounced in and around the man, striking him with skilled but painful attacks. It happened so fast it looked like someone had thrown gas onto a fire and the blaze flared up and out. Zanique's fury was unleashed. The man looked like he was trying to fight off a swarm of wasps. All at once, his friends jumped up and rushed out the door to help him. Dutch and the bartender took off after them. Other patrons of the bar crowded up to the windows to watch the bare-knuckle brawl. The moment Dutch got outside, he saw that everyone else had stopped.

Zanique's blows were so fast that people had trouble seeing them, though the sounds of contact left no doubt that the man was being hit repeatedly. Her fists landed on him so savagely that he couldn't defend himself. When she stopped for a moment, yelling at him, he cupped both hands around his bloody nose.

"You're a fucking dog," she was yelling. "And no dog fucks with this bitch without consequences!" This was accompanied by uproarious laughter from the bystanders.

Dutch took in a deep breath when he saw Zanique reach down and grab the man's genitals. The man's arms came down, and then he stood very still. Both eyes, his nose, and his lips were bleeding. All of the men standing around the fight gave out groans, knowing that their friend was now in a world of hurt from the force that Zanique's hand was applying. They also knew that he must certainly be regretting coming on to this wild woman.

She was yelling again. "I told you I didn't want anything from you, I warned everyone this would happen. But, no, you had to go and call me a bitch. I hate that fucking word! You don't know me, you know nothing about me, yet you think you can judge me? I'll bet you're sorry now. Say it!"

"Yes, yes. I'm sorry. Anything. Just please let go."

Not letting go of his balls, Zanique looked at Ed. "Are you gonna call the cops?"

"Why?"

"If you're gonna call the cops, then I'm gonna crush this man's nuts. I figure if I'm going to jail for assault, then I'm going to assault this man seriously."

Ed retreated a step. "I see no need to call the police." He looked around. "If everyone here is cool with that?"

Everyone, including the man in pain, was cool with it. Zanique slowly released her grip. "Well," she said, shaking her hand to relax it, "I've quite enjoyed myself. Now, you piece of shit, you go back in there and pay for my drink and then get the hell out of my way."

Dutch finally walked closer to her. "Goddamn," he said, "you're a wild woman."

"You have no idea." She laughed all the way back to the bar, where her martini was waiting for her.

"Are you okay?" Dutch asked, matching her step for step. "Did he hurt you in any way?"

"Nope, I'm fine. All the blood and pain are his."

When Ed (back behind the bar) came over to her, he was laughing. "You're damn small, but you fight like a tiger. I like that. Where on earth did you learn to fight like that?"

"I grew up on the streets of St. Louis, the bad side of the city. I had to learn to fight in order to survive. It was a rough neighborhood. We had to fight for everything there, sometimes two and three fights a day. It was just a way of life back then, but I never forgot. I learned to meet bullies head-on. If you give in to a bully, they will eventually take everything from you."

Ed nodded. "Well, it was a pleasure to watch you put that man in his place. If we ever need a new bouncer, I'll look you up."

She shook her head. "Ed, you're a dick, you could've prevented all of this... I just wished you would have said something to him earlier so I wouldn't have had to do that."

"Yeah, I'm sorry about that. I didn't think he meant any harm. I should've tossed him out. My bad!" He reached over the bar and patted her on the shoulder. "You sure taught him a lesson, though!" He laughed and went back to his other customers.

Zanique turned her attention back to Dutch. "So why are you here?"

"I was driving by on my way to take Nora home and saw your Hummer parked out there." He pointed in the direction of her truck. "After I dropped her off, I thought I would buy you a drink and maybe chat for a bit."

"Well, now you see that I'm not such a good person. I'm really not good at all. I hate being violent. I hate it in spite of the fact that I'm good at it." She smiled, but it was a sad and strangely vulnerable smile.

"I can see that a reasonable woman like yourself is justified in committing an act of violence when provoked."

"Don't have any illusions concerning me," she said, taking a sip of her cocktail. "It's hard to reconcile instinct with reason."

Dutch was a realist, and so he accepted the inevitable, even without quite understanding it. "I'm sorry that guy was bothering you, anyway. I wish I'd gotten here sooner."

"Why? Do you think it would've made a difference?"

"Well, if you weren't alone, he wouldn't have seen you as a target."

Zanique cleared her throat. "Dutch, you're sweet. But I'm always alone, I'm used to being alone, and if you knew me, really knew me, you'd know that I have to protect myself all of the time."

Ed came back. "What are you drinking, Buddy?" he said to Dutch.

"Oh, I'll have a hot chocolate."

"Do you know where you are?" Ed looked around. "A hot chocolate? You're standing at a bar! Where people drink alcohol. Do you want me to fix it with some peppermint schnapps?"

"Nope. Just the hot chocolate. Oh, and no whipped cream. I'll take it straight."

"Hilarious!" Both men began laughing. "Whatever you say, man."

"My girlfriend always drank hot chocolate," Dutch explained. "She died a year ago, and tonight we had a remembrance for her. So I'm drinking in honor of her."

Ed looked at Dutch and his laughter died. "Dude. I'm sorry, that's rough."

Dutch nodded and looked at Zanique. "I'm afraid I'm speaking in quite detestable self-pity, but tonight made me a little sentimental."

She looked back at him, speechless. Her impression of him had been that he was a rugged, scar-faced man. Men like him didn't carry sentimental feelings. But, really, he wasn't as unimaginative, or insensitive, as she had thought. He understood more than she had suspected. Her eyes welled up. "That's why I'm here, too," she said in a softer voice. "I was drinking to Ruby. Not to honor her, but in hopes I'd get numb enough to sleep tonight. I've been told that liquor helps the heart to forget, but whoever fed me that line of shit lied. I was also told it'll relax the mind, but the more I drink, the more I feel like crying."

"Then don't drink the hard stuff." He looked around. "Besides, I'd worry about you driving home if you got drunk."

Dutch heard the sound of someone walking up behind him. He turned. It was the man that Zanique had taken outside.

"I've paid for your drink," he said, "and I'm leaving now. Ma'am, I just wanted to offer you a sincere apology for earlier. I was drunk, but that's no excuse. If I see you in here again, I hope we can be decent to one another."

Her face was flushed now, but she regarded him without wavering. "Yes," she said clearly. "I presume you'll be more respectful, not only to me, but to any other woman you come across."

"Of course." With that said, and his eyes, nose and lip now turning black and blue, he turned and left the bar. Both Dutch and Zanique noticed that his friends were much more discreet now, their voices very low.

Ed brought Dutch the hot chocolate, and Dutch took the mug and whisked the dark brown liquid with a spoon. Then he paused. "Will you join me?"

Zanique picked up her martini, and Ed picked up his glass of ice water. They both raised their glasses.

"To Ruby," Dutch said. "I miss her every day."

They brought their drinks together in a toast, and Zanique repeated his words then brought her glass to her lips. Then she set the martini down and picked up the shot of whiskey and tossed it down. She was no fool, Dutch saw. She didn't pretend to possess decorum or gentility. She was who she was.

Her complexion was dark, Dutch noted, and her eyes were also dark, and although she was small, her erect posture was somewhat intimidating. Her face was eloquent and feminine. She had a kind of exquisite attractiveness along with her high energy. Dutch could tell she was uncompromising in temperament. In his few times alone with her, he had felt they were in competition for Ruby's attention. He chuckled as he considered how much sympathy and human emotion he could feel for her now that Ruby was gone.

"So," he asked, not thinking what his question might imply, "how close were you and Ruby, anyway? I mean, your friendship seemed to go beyond that of normal friendship."

Zanique was usually more guarded and out of loyalty to Ruby would have indignantly repelled his curiosity. But now, feeling the effects of her drinks, she let her guard down. "Yes, we were more than just friends. We confided in each other more than sisters do. We shared love and life more than any two people ought to have shared."

As Dutch looked at her, his eyes seemed to have a hypnotic effect on this woman who considered herself unloved and loveless.

Her eyes moistened again. "I enjoy talking to you, Dutch. You make me feel as though I'm liked." She sort of smiled. "Not many people know me well enough to like me. Don't get me wrong—a good many

have thought they loved me in one way or another...
but I'd rather be liked."

"I do like you," he said. "You're someone that is
likeable, but you're also unpredictable. Volatile in
some regard. Being with you," he added, "is a bit like
sitting on a pile of dynamite with the fuse hissing and
burning closer and closer."

Her sincerity fled, and she leaned back on her
bar stool, laughing. "Oh, I can't dispute that. At least
I'm not dull and normal! I couldn't live if I were just
normal."

Dutch finished his mug of hot chocolate and set it
on the bar. "Don't change a thing about you, Zanique.
You could be normal if you wanted to, but I bet you'd
lose the valuable person you already are. You're a
good person."

"Ahh, I have you fooled. I told you I'm not a good
person. You should believe that."

"So what? You got into a fight tonight. You brought
a large man to his knees. That doesn't make you a bad
person."

She sighed. "I am capable of taking care of myself,
and, true, that doesn't make me a bad person. What
makes me a bad person is, well, I'm selfish. I've lived a
life for me and only me. It wasn't until I met Ruby that
I began to think differently."

As Dutch considered what she was saying, his
intuition contradicted her words. He trusted his

intuition and smiled at her. "Oh, I see now, yes, indeed, you're a bad person, you have me completely convinced." His sarcasm fell into another chuckle. "If being a little selfish makes you a bad person, then...."

"Then you think I have a poor self-image?"

"I'm just saying that how you see yourself isn't the way I see you."

The stress she was feeling faded away under his gaze, and her smile seemed to be less the result of a conscious decision than her sincere reaction, which came from the curve of his mouth and chin as he looked at her. In this conversation, she was letting her guard down enough for him to peek in at her soul.

"That sounds like something Ruby would have said," she replied.

He now recognized that she appeared to stand apart by some divine election of nature. The hint of emotion in her words produced in him an agreeable feeling of security, and for the first time tonight he came so close to her that he almost touched her.

"Ruby liked you," he said. "Trusted you, felt safe with you. I feel the same way about you."

She thought of Ruby and recalled how Ruby had told her that she loved her—love, a feeling of like, trust, and safety. How could this man who hardly knew her feel the same way Ruby had felt? She wanted to believe him, but her default was not to trust anyone. She looked away. She adjusted her attitude, pulled her guard back up and around her like armor. "You're charming," she said, "but I highly doubt you feel the same way Ruby did. Perhaps you should stick to facts you know something about."

Whether she was outspokenly offended or unaffectedly amused, he could not tell, but she had turned away from him. He paused, then simply added, "I suppose you're right."

He got up from his bar stool and laid out some cash for Ed. "Well, Zanique, I've enjoyed chatting with you, but it's getting late and I should get home. Stop by the gallery sometime. Please don't let another year go by before we speak again."

"Why don't you stay? It's not that late."

"To be honest, I needed a distraction from thinking so much about Ruby. Like you, I need to get her off of my mind so I can sleep tonight. Being here with you, talking about her is nice, but I think I should go."

"That's a pity," she returned, still not looking at him. Her voice struck him as strangely hollow. "Go if you must."

"I'm very tired," he admitted, "but hopefully I'll see you again." It grew quiet between them again, and he waited in vain for some response that might describe what she had not yet thought out clearly in her own dazed mind.

Then, at last, she spoke almost in a whisper. "Could I have your home address? I don't like dropping in at the gallery. I feel like that's your place of work, and I'm uncomfortable making a social call there."

Her request gave him a sudden shock of gladness. "Yes, of course." He pulled out his smartphone and texted his address to her. "I hope you make use of it. You and I have been wounded by the same loss, and I think our conversations could be... well... therapeutic." He turned to leave but then asked, "Do you need me to drive you home or call you an Uber? I don't want you to drive if you're tipsy."

"No, Dutch, I'm good. Thanks. Have a good night."

As he left the pub and started up the sidewalk, he waved through the window and walked across the parking lot.

She was happy, perfectly happy, she told herself, as she called on Ed.

"What can I get you?" he asked.

"Another peach martini and a shot."

Ed didn't move, but instead braced his hands against the bar. "Where did your boyfriend go?"

"My boyfriend?" She looked confused. "Oh, you mean Dutch. He's not my boyfriend. He was Ruby's boyfriend, you know, the girl we told you that died?"

"Yeah, I heard him talking about his girl dying," Ed replied, "but I've worked a bar for many years, I know when two people are into each other." He leaned slightly closer to her and clasped his large white hands together. "Listen, I feel like you and I are friends now after all we've been through tonight." He laughed. "As a friend, I would skip the drinks here and make my way to him."

She raised her empty glass, a reminder of her last request. "He's a good man. He doesn't need someone like me screwing up his life."

"I say he's a lucky chap to even have a chance with you," the bartender said. "And I say further that you're lucky he's expressed an interest in you. So while the luck is about you, I say take a gamble and see what happens. I know people, and you're right: he's a good person, a man ready to fight for you, protect you. Don't let him slip away."

Having no other answer than a smile, she gave Ed a nod, paid him a handsome tip, gathered her things and went out to her Hummer.

Chapter 25

Loneliness can break a man down and take him into dark waters. With every step he took toward his truck, Dutch felt empty, hollow, and lonely. The dinner party, spending a bit of time with Zanique, and the argument in the pub had all been great distractions, but distractions or not, he was still hurting from the loss of Ruby.

The night seemed exceptionally quiet as he crossed the parking lot. The sidewalks were empty, and the stores had all closed hours ago. His Land Rover sat at the far end of the parking lot. When he reached it, he thought he heard singing... a ghostly voice that carried down the street and seemed to have originated from the main entrance of Lithia Park. He stopped for a minute, almost unable to move, then looked around. As he pulled his keys out of his pocket and reached over to unlock the door, the singing got louder. Now it was filling the air.

Singing consists of frequencies of sound waves that can create a new dimension in a man's reality. For Dutch, hearing this singing produced something new and renewed his feelings. The singing recharged his emotions. The voice was like nothing he had ever heard before. His hand stopped just short of the lock and froze. He was captivated by the sound of a voice singing in an unknown language.

Then silence came.

He looked over toward the park. It appeared to be empty. *Nothing there,* he thought, unknowingly holding his breath. *Nothing, you fool!* And then, as if the singing voice had summoned him, perhaps cast a spell over him, instead of unlocking his truck, he turned and began walking toward the snowy park. The voice had gravity to it. It drew him into the park, where he had the impression that someone was watching him, maybe following him.

Someone's behind me. In my footsteps.

Another step, another echo.

For a moment, all of the park's trees were suspended in motion. Leaf, bush, dry lawn, remaining snow... everything had ceased to move. All of the park's energy, every independent vibration halted. Everything seemed to be focused on Dutch. Was the whole park staring at him? His energy flashed and then intertwined with the park's. Now he had the sensation that the world outside the park was slipping away.

The veil between realities is soft in Lithia Park. It's thin, and as Dutch stepped through the boundary, he came into a sense of relaxation, of being gently released from the cares of his daily life. Suddenly the stress he had been feeling melted away, leaving him to enjoy the feeling of being lighter.

Then he heard a voice say his name. Curious, he walked deeper into the park, he felt as if some part of his mind were dramatizing the haunting stories he had always heard about the park but had never believed. Was the park really haunted? He looked around. No ghosts. So far.

Then the sound came.

It was an enigmatic sound filled with words that he heard, but from no source he could see. Sound, different from the singing he had heard minutes earlier, but still nothing more than vibrations at different frequencies. *No*, he thought, *this sound is more.* It had love connected to it, it was warm, it touched him all the way down to his bones. This sound was beyond any ordinary noise. It had sacred properties, for the mathematical relationship that underlines the vibration and frequency is of divine origin. The words weren't anything created by a human mind. They were celestial. They had a calculated energy that he thought must derive from the beautiful nature of the universe. He imagined he was hearing a fractal relationship between the divine and mortal. But he knew it's impossible to hear a fractal. He was hearing magic.

As a child interacts with the world directly, Dutch was open, free, a conduit directly connected to Lithia Park. His senses were blooming and thrusting themselves toward the words he was hearing. He listened to the words and thought he recognized a voice, and part of him—most of him—wanted that voice to belong to Ruby. Bewildered, he kept walking and listening to the sanctified sound that was composed of waves apparently tuned specifically to his own spectrum.

This way, Dutch.

Walking through the park, hearing the voice and the words... he felt serene. He didn't want this moment to end. He had a hunger to be here. He savored the comfort of this moment that was more than terrestrial. The sound, the park, this experience... they were all elevating him in ways he didn't understand, and yet he felt delighted to his core.

He was still walking, looking, listening, but still not finding the source of the voice as it pulled him further, deeper into Lithia Park.

Except for the rising moon, everything was dark, but he walked into that darkness without hesitation. Then, in the distance, in the negative spaces between the trees, he saw an orb of light gliding among the trees, filling the spaces between them with its light.

It changed colors as it drifted through the park, first bright white, then brilliant light blue, next emerald green, finally crimson as it stopped and hovered before him. The orb was slightly bigger than his fist, and agile, too, for now it began darting in one direction, then another. Amused, Dutch decided it must be playing with him and smiled as this orb of light was dancing in the air. It reminded him of how Yukon had jumped and danced when he wanted to play. The playful light circled a tree, then came closer to him. Then it began zipping up and down, back and forth as if it wanted him to interact—*play?* Dutch wondered—with it.

Something was tingling inside him, tickling his inner spaces. The only way he could describe it even to himself was that something was in the space between his being and his soul. Still about three feet away from him, the orb kept bouncing around and changing colors, and now he realized that in addition to its bright light he could see a new, softer, white light. Then he was surprised to see that this new white light was coming from him. It was bleeding out through his pores. It must, he thought (when he could think at all), be the bottled-up energy that had been tickling his spaces and was now being released. He began squinting at the orb that seemed to be communicating with him with light. Dutch's vibration, his own light, was now completely in tune with the light of this sacred park. Before this moment, he hadn't often thought about words, sounds, light, or even touch as energy. Now he had to stop walking. Watching the orb, he began to realize that sound, light, touch, words, and even thoughts were divine blessings. Divine gifts.

Divine energy.

This mysterious energy that was flowing from Lithia Park, flowing through and around Dutch, probably couldn't be explained. But now he knew it existed. He knew he was experiencing something extraordinary. He began to wonder if this energy was the foundation of everything. It was possibly what fueled life, thoughts, emotions.

But what, really, was this energy? Divine Intelligence?

He was certain that every thought, every action, every negative or positive concept in the world arose from this unknown energy. Standing there in the snow, playing with the ball of light, he understood this energy to be a true force.

Something was now glistening on the ground beneath the light of the orb. He knelt down and picked it up. He held it and stared at it. It was an ankh, the breath-of-life talisman, shiny as if newly made. But by what hand? Dutch's own hand trembled as he held that ankh. He felt the energy around him building, getting stronger.

It felt like love all around him.

Still holding the ankh, he said aloud, "This entire experience is beautiful." The moonlight filtered through the city and fell into the park. The air was fragmented with the scents of sandalwood smoke and forest flowers. Light flickering from the orb began bathing Dutch's body in its celestial energy. And then, as if someone had flipped a switch, the park went dark and quiet again. It was black, silent, empty.

Nature had taken Dutch on a journey. It was his time to travel to another time, perhaps back to the past, or maybe into the future. Whatever lay in store for him, Lithia Park's goddess had him now.

...

Zanique walked across the parking lot, still not sure what she was doing. Ed had convinced her that she should pursue Dutch, and in her heart she wanted to. But was she going too far? Was it, she asked herself, his bewildering charm she felt? With a shiver, she realized that she might have stumbled irretrievably into a declaration of love for this man. What a fool she had been. After all, where was her painfully acquired caution about love? Her varied experiences with many men had only taught her not to trust.

As she approached her Hummer, she saw Dutch's Defender still sitting in the parking lot, and just beyond it there was Dutch walking into the park. She decided to follow him, though before entering the park, she told herself emphatically that she would allow her feelings to go only as far as friendship. And yet her mind betrayed her as she found herself entertaining thoughts—to like a man and not make love to him, was that not the reality of her dream? Wasn't it her purer desire to take him inside her and love him? If so, was it beyond her? Still in the distant region of the happier impossibilities? After all, Dutch wasn't aware of her physical uniqueness. Relationships beyond hers with Ruby held few allurements for her. The respect she felt for a relationship with any man was equaled only by the disgust which she regarded as a personal condition, and a shudder ran through her now as she imagined herself tied to—belonging to—a man. She was clearly aware that she had been, and would be, looked upon with worldly eyes as a desirable catch, as fair game for a number of men; and it did not occur to her that Dutch himself might not want her and would remain hopelessly beyond her reach. The thing that troubled her most as she followed Dutch was her recognition of her own impetuous emotions. So impulsive, that her shield was withdrawing, releasing the possibility that passion might plunge her headlong into the abyss of a relationship.

Her mind was busy, so busy that she hardly noticed the park was empty. Even though Dutch was far ahead of her, she didn't race to catch him. She figured she knew exactly where he was going. To Ruby's park bench. She walked along the path, noticing that the air she was breathing was cool, refreshing. With each breath she felt a sense of detachment come over her. She felt within a source of energy, a sense of renewal and peace.

Now, as she walked rapidly through the park, her thoughts were so filled with Dutch and the possibility of happiness that she started to feel she might be awakening (uneasily) from a dream. The next moment the air began swimming before her. She felt her blood rush in a torrent from her heart, for she began to hear a voice, the voice of the Goddess.

She stopped walking, only listening and looking around. She could still see Dutch in the distance, and now she could see a glowing ball that was dancing around him. A quiet voice within her said, *Go to him.*

She smiled and stepped forward on the path. Dutch was her focus. As she drew closer, she could see that he was starting to glow. He was radiant. She felt a vague stir as she watched him get brighter.

Then he vanished.

Everything in Lithia Park stopped. It was quiet, and dark, and that darkness became what seemed to her a physical shelter for the rage she felt. She ran to the spot where Dutch had been standing and felt the emotional chaos he'd left behind. She neither knew what to believe nor what she was suffering; her power to will and her power to think were suspended.

She was conscious only of a curious deadness of sensation somewhere inside her panic. Her mind began telling her at that moment that she was an utter failure, thoughts that forced upon her the anguish of readjustment, the feverish determination to figure out what to do next. As she breathlessly paced back and forth along the path, she began to feel that she was groping for some way back in time, back to Dutch before he vanished.

Why did the Goddess tell her to go to him if She was going to take him away?

Zanique felt like a stranger within her own skin. The arms, legs, body, and eyes... they all belonged to her, and yet felt like she was occupying another body. It was as if her body had betrayed her, made a fool of her, allowed her to merely glimpse happiness. She was ashamed of her vulnerability

She forced herself to stop moving, to stand still on the dark path. She resisted an impulse to curse the Goddess and shake her fists at Her. But she was accustomed to action, to do something, no matter what happened. Now it was difficult for her to stand and listen until she heard the sweet voice of reason above the storm of her passion, until she heard the Goddess speaking from beyond her senses. This was an urgent need she felt, as if there was an intelligent purpose to her future. A way to stop Dutch from being taken from her.

LITHIA PARK

Zanique, profess your want, declare your need, reach for him... you have the key.

Zanique's mind was in a haze. Yes, she heard the Goddess, was she worthy of a blessing? She shook her head. No. She was certain that disappointment was waiting for her. When it came to matters of the heart, nothing good ever happened to her.

In the next instant she remembered with a throb of exhilaration that she did have the key. It was the ankh, the breath of life. She pulled it out of her pocket and held it in both hands. "Dutch," she whispered, "don't leave me. I need you! First Ruby left me, and now you. Come back to me! I don't want to be left here alone."

By her own act she had called out, she was declaring her need to the universe. Then, as if she were between a dream and waking, with a peculiar deepening of her emotions the essence of her soul came suddenly into contact with Dutch's. She felt the energy that is life itself flowing through her body. At this instant, by that divine miracle of renewal, she began to feel new again. She could live again, not her old cynical life, but a life that was larger and more capable.

She trembled with a frequency that made the world around her shift. Dutch was coming back to her, and in this ecstasy of recovered dreams where wishes come true, she felt her soul to be of one substance, not only with the Goddess, but with the stars and the greater Universe. For the love she had formerly recoiled from now overflowed within her heart until she felt that she had touched the boundaries of the Universe.

Wherever, whenever Dutch had been just seconds ago, he had heard the calls of Zanique and the Goddess. Zanique was asking him to return to her. The Goddess was giving him a choice. She gave him the freedom to continue on his own way. Or he could return to Zanique.

As a bouncing light that came close to Zanique, Dutch came playfully, first circling her, then taking his human form as a visible, tangible answer to her call. He shook his head and walked on a few steps. Then he turned and came back to her, "Your voice came to me like a spirit," he told her. He smiled. "I had no idea you were here. I thought you were still back at the bar. When I heard your voice, well, I could see you here. And so I willed myself to return."

"Where did you go?"

"I went looking for happiness," he replied simply. "I suppose I thought my happiness was in another time... well, I'm not sure... but I think I went ahead in time about six or seven years."

"What did you see?"

"It's funny... I saw you living with me and we were happy."

She laughed softly. "I like that."

At first glance, he noticed a change in her, and for a minute he was lost in her, all other consciousness swept away by his pure delight in the mere physical fact of her presence. For the instant that they stood facing each other on that dark path, he felt that not only had she changed, but that life had changed, too. It would be different from now on.

"I was so afraid you left me," she murmured, "and I was going be alone again." Although she wanted to be tough and not show any weakness, something wasn't allowing for any acting tonight.

Even her voice, he thought, had altered. It was fuller, deeper, more exquisitely vibrant, as if some wonderful experience had enriched it. "When I had the opportunity to go," he said, running an uneasy hand through his hair, "I guess I was being selfish. I just wanted to escape my reality. I never thought you and I had a chance." He rubbed his forehead. "I figured you loved Ruby and I loved Ruby, and we both loved her so much, we didn't have room to feel anything toward each other."

For a moment she looked away. When she turned toward him again, she spoke with one of those impulsive gestures he had always found charming and so characteristic.

"Shall I tell you a secret?" she asked.

He bent his head. "Tell me all your secrets if you like."

"Well, I'll only share this one with you right now. I'm not good at relationships. Never have been. But ever since Ruby left us, I've felt something special about you. Something that makes me... makes me want to try to do better."

"I want to try, too. I want to live like I just saw us. Six or so years from now. I want to know what life like that feels like." He sounded impatient. "I want to go through everything with you. Turn every page. Experience all that can be experienced with you."

They started to walk back toward the parking lot arm in arm. "Will you come with me back to my house?" he asked. "I want to spend the night with you."

For a moment she couldn't answer. Then she turned to face him. As they passed under a street lamp, he was hoping for a smile from her, but all he could see was her blank face. "You know," she said without a smile, "when I was following you into the park, I was hoping you would ask me that. But now..."

"But now what?"

"The reality is that I have a deep secret. A secret that might impact the way you see me at this moment."

He stopped walking and took her face in his hands and gently kissed her. Then he breathed his words on her skin, "No, it's not a secret any longer. I've been to the future. I saw us together. I know exactly who you are. You are more than a woman, and from what I witnessed, you and I had no problems."

They began walking toward the parking lot.

"Yes, I'll come home with you." *Is life an evolution into the consciousness of the Goddess?* She wondered through vague instinct. *Is it possible that there is such a thing as fate? Is life built upon my mistakes as much as my aspirations? And is every pang I've suffered nothing but the lifting of the veil between my flesh and my spirit? My whole life experience, either tragic death or the vitality of love... it's all been necessary to the building of my soul.*

...

Lithia Park.

There has always been sacred ground in this park. No matter how many seasons have flowed over the rim of time, the ground here has always been blessed, lying quietly in itself and waiting for those chosen to come and join the light, to gain insight and understand the light's significance. The sacred land has always been here. It has always served as a doorway to the spirit world, always been a symbol, always been a sanctuary.

Mother Earth has held Lithia Park in Her loving arms. She has blessed this place that spins out of time, where God's image is a tree, where sacred music plays. Here Nature has shed Her pine needles in the golden days of autumn upon the park benches where artists have sat, artists who were often unaware of Her true magic. She has set the grasses and flowers of spring into the ground as a natural temple of subjects to be painted. Here Her vines creep up old, forgotten, chain-link fences to hide the park's ancient entrances. Here, the winter's cold on the day of the solstice has kept people away until Nature invites a single person. Here Mother Earth holds all the living creatures hibernating in the park as gently as a nurse holds a sleeping child. Here, Nature summoned Dutch and Zanique. She has blessed them with love, peace, and a sacred promise that time is not something that confines but rather is something that is always growing.

The End

Dedication

*T*his book is dedicated to Lithia Park, to the people who groom its grounds, to the people who visit and respect it, and to the spirits who glisten in hidden places. It is a symbol of beauty in an ugly world.

This book is also dedicated to the artists, writers, sculptors and those of the creative mind. I know how unrewarding it is to be a working artisan struggling with creating something while the people of the so-called real world spin around you. We are not the nine-to-fivers. Most of the time we feel out of place in this real world while trying to create. To the artist, I wish you all the best on your journey to create something special and I praise your conviction to finishing the work others tried to convince you to leave behind.

Acknowledgments

$\mathcal{A}$ joyous thank you goes out to my editor Barbara Ardinger, Ph.D. We had fun with this project and her input was, as always, unique and invaluable. Of course, I would like to thank my team - Patrick Dunphy, for his careful eye while proofreading and his attention to detail. His suggestions were extremely helpful. Sherry Wachter, my book designer. Her artful approach to my work was also instrumental for making a great read. Sherry did an outstanding job in creating the cover art for this book. She reached into the story and created a cover that truly represents this book. Much thanks to my significant other Kathy, for her continued support and encouragement. And what would my life be without the spiritual guidance of Cheri Levenson? May the Great Spirit and Mother Earth bless you with a long life. We need one of Heaven's angels to be with us as long as possible.

I would also like to thank Lithia Park for being the inspiration for this book. Your sacred grounds and gardens have had a wonderful effect on me. I remember the first day I discovered Butler-Perozzi Fountain. Was it my imagination, or a serendipitous event? Whatever it was, I was able to peek back into history, and in that moment, I was touched by something beyond our five senses. All it took was a walk on your paths and I felt the magic and peace within me being restored. Your ghosts greeted me, your secrets opened up to me, and your beauty took my breath away. Thank you. Thank you.

Other books by Ra Lynn LoneWalker

The Personification of Love
On The Other Side Of The Golden Gate
The Giggling Boy
Cinnamon Kisses

About the Author

Ra Lynn LoneWalker is an eclectic mix of European and Shoshone from The Wind River Reservation in Wyoming. "I'm a storyteller," he explains when asked how he decided to become an author. "I listen to the ancestors, the elders, and the living spirits of nature to help tell my stories. I have white skin, a red soul, and an open mind. It's in this juxtaposition of cultures where the fundamental ideas for my writing are based. Beyond my cultural makeup, my work trickles down from the serendipitous experiences that life seems to consistently bring me. The experiences are gifts that should be shared. The Great Sprit has requested it of me, so it must be."

LoneWalker currently lives in Reno, Nevada. If you would like to learn more about his writing, please visit www.Ralynnlonewalker.com

www.ingramcontent.com/pod-product-compliance
Lightning Source LLC
Chambersburg PA
CBHW032258020726
47495CB00001B/151